GAME of
PATIENCE

ALSO BY SUSANNE ALLEYN

A Far Better Rest

GAME of PATIENCE

Susanne Alleyn

THOMAS DUNNE BOOKS
ST. MARTIN'S MINOTAUR
NEW YORK

THOMAS DUNNE BOOKS.
An imprint of St. Martin's Press.

www.minotaurbooks.com

Library of Congress Cataloging-in-Publication Data

Alleyn, Susanne, 1963–
   Game of patience / Susanne Alleyn.—1st ed.
       p.   cm.
   ISBN 0-312-34363-9
   EAN 978-0-312-34363-7
   1. Private investigators—France—Paris—Fiction.   2. Paris (France)—
History—1789–1799—Fiction.   3. Young women—Crimes
against—Fiction.   4. Extortion—Fiction.   I. Title.

PS3551.L4484G36   2006
813'.54—dc22

                                                        2005049773

10   9   8   7   6   5   4   3   2

To Berenice and Walt McDayter,

with love and thanks always

ACKNOWLEDGMENTS

For their unflagging friendship, affection, interest, encouragement, and most of all, endurance as this novel slowly evolved, a gigantic thank-you, as always, to Johanna and also to Erika, Kristi, Benjamin, and the Hudson Writers' Roundtable, particularly Dan, Sean, Ned, and Carol. Equal thanks must go to Peter Wolverton and Don Congdon, my two sternest and best critics.

I also owe a debt of gratitude to Professors Laura Mason, Michael Sibalis, and Clive Emsley for their kind and invaluable assistance with details of eighteenth-century French law and policing. *Merci à tous.*

FOREWORD

The Republican Calendar, used officially in France from 1793 to 1809, consisted of twelve months with three ten-day weeks, called *décades*, in each; *décadi*, "tenth day," was the Republican Sunday and day off. Five additional festival days (six in leap years) completed the calendar. The Republican year began on September 22 of the Gregorian calendar and was dated from September 22, 1792.

The title *commissaire* is usually translated into English as "commissioner," though this may lead to puzzlement among readers for whom a police commissioner is the chief of a large city's police force. As an eighteenth-century Parisian *commissaire* was a local official, roughly equivalent to a precinct commander or lieutenant, I have chosen to stay with the French term.

The perplexing French word *hôtel* can mean a hostelry, a large public building (*hôtel de ville*, city hall), or a private town house or mansion (*hôtel particulier*). To dispel any confusion, I have used the French form, with the circumflex over the *o*, whenever referring to a mansion or municipal hall, and the unaccented English word when referring to public accommodations.

———————

Much of the tangle of medieval streets in the heart of Paris disappeared during Haussmann's extensive rebuilding of the city in the 1860s. Many other streets have had their names, or the spelling of their names, changed over the course of the past two centuries. To make matters even more confusing, many street names still in use today were temporarily changed or altered during the most radical phase of the Revolution to eliminate references to royalty, aristocracy, or Christianity. All streets and street names mentioned in this novel, however, existed in the 1790s.

GAME of
PATIENCE

1

9 Brumaire, Year V of the Republic
(October 30, 1796)

Aristide did not often set foot in the Place de Grève. It was an ill-omened place, the Golgotha of Paris, the site of uncounted butcheries across five centuries, and he loathed public executions.

He shivered and cast a fleeting glance toward the guillotine, waiting high above the heads of the crowd as the sharp breeze of a Parisian October whipped lank dark hair into his eyes. Perhaps, he brooded, not for the first time, he was oversensitive for a man who worked for the police. Police officials, his friend and employer Brasseur among them, did their duty and washed their hands of the affair, leaving the rest to the Criminal Tribunal and the public prosecutor. But the police and the law courts, he thought, in their determined efforts to maintain order in a city still unsettled after seven years of revolutionary upheaval, could sometimes be wrong.

He elbowed his way onward, through the clamorous crowd of errand boys in smocks, domestics in shabby cast-off finery, and craftsmen in work aprons who slouched about, playing truant from their trades for half an hour's free entertainment. The muddy square between the city hall and the Seine swarmed with spectators, pushing, joking. Here and there a spruce bourgeois or stylish *incroyable*, flaunting the exaggerated fashions of the season, blossomed like a hothouse flower amid the weeds. Though Aristide wore no tricolor sash, the mark of a police inspector or commissaire, they made way for him, reluctantly parting ranks before the austere black suit that instantly placed him among such traditional dignitaries as police, civil servants, or magistrates.

He shouldered his way through the spectators until he could push no farther against the eager, humming barricade of bodies. He could see well enough; he stood half a head taller than most of his neighbors. The guillotine loomed above him against the leaden sky like a doorway to nowhere. Two men, silently overseen by a third in a fashionable black frock coat and tall hat, hovered about it, brisk and impassive, tightening ropes, testing moving parts, greasing grooves and hinges. Aristide offered a silent prayer of thanks that at least the guillotine was far swifter and gentler than the punishment meted out to murderers and bandits in the decades before the Revolution.

The crowd stirred and muttered, growing bored with idling. A few fights broke out. Rough-voiced street peddlers sold rolls, oranges, vinegar-water, hot chocolate, and cheap brandy.

A pair of mounted gendarmes appeared at the edge of the square. Behind them creaked the executioner's cart and the murmur grew into an uproar. Those who often attended such free public entertainment self-importantly pointed out the approaching actors: there the attending priest in civilian costume; there the old executioner, come out of retirement for the day, Old Sanson who had topped the king, and Danton, and Robespierre, and so many others, in those disagreeable years 1793 and 1794; there his assistants. Young Sanson, the new master executioner, they told one another, was already waiting on the scaffold: a good-looking, well-made young fellow, wasn't he?

In the cart a splash of crimson, a smock the color of blood. The central performers of the show stood between executioner and priest. One of the three condemned men had fainted and was lying nearly out of sight in the bottom of the cart.

A shout pierced the crowd's babble.

"I am guilty!"

The man in the crimson smock leaned forward across the cart's rail, straining at his guard's tight grip on his bound arms.

"I am guilty, citizens! But Lesurques is innocent!"

"That's Courriol," said someone in the crowd, "one of the bandits. . . ."

Aristide swallowed and squeezed his hands together behind his back as a chill crept from the pit of his stomach to the center of his chest. When even a confessed killer insisted upon his comrade's innocence . . .

The second man stood erect in the cart, his pale, youthful face betraying neither fear nor hope. His fair hair was cropped short for the blade, but unlike his companion, he wore no red shirt, the emblem of a condemned murderer; waistcoat, culotte, shirt cut open at the neck—all were spotless white.

Absence of the usual formalities betrayed some belated sympathy on the public prosecutor's part. What must it be like, Aristide wondered, to live in doubt, to have to ask yourself for the rest of your life whether, in the performance of your duty, you had condemned an innocent man?

"Lesurques is innocent!" Courriol repeated. His crimson smock fluttered in the wind. "I am guilty!"

The cart creaked to a stop before the scaffold. Above, Young Sanson waited silently, hands at his sides, ignoring the wind's bite.

A raindrop stung Aristide's cheek. Mathieu had died on just such a day as this, he recalled, a bleak autumn morning with a cold, leaden sky and spattering rain. Three years ago . . . the last day of October 1793. Perhaps under the same steel blade. He closed his eyes for an instant at the touch of another cold drop.

The assistant executioners lowered the cart's tailboard and lugged the unconscious man up the narrow steps. Carefully impassive, they strapped him to the plank and slid it forward beneath the blade. The wooden collar clapped down over his neck. Young Sanson stepped to the machine's right-hand upright and tugged at a lever.

Aristide blinked. Did anyone ever see the blade in the midst of its fall? Yet there it hung, at rest at the bottom of the uprights, smeared with glistening red, and blood was weeping between the boards of the scaffold onto the sawdust below.

"I am guilty! Lesurques is innocent!" shouted Courriol as hands reached for him and swung him down from the cart. He struggled a moment, twisting about to shout once again to the crowd as the execution-ers marched him toward the waiting plank. "Lesurques is innocent!"

Aristide watched, motionless. Here, at least, simple justice had taken its course. *But God help us all,* he thought, *if the criminal court has condemned a blameless man.*

"Lesurques is—"

The crowd grew silent as Lesurques climbed the steps. Upon reaching the platform, he paused.

"I am innocent of this crime. May God forgive my judges as I have forgiven them."

For the third time, the great blade scraped and thudded home.

Aristide thrust his way past the gawkers and paused at the edge of the square, gasping for breath. At last he found an upturned skiff on the riverside and dropped down on it, elbows on knees, staring into the murky shallows of the Seine. Had the police he worked for, so determined to keep the peace, instead been so horribly wrong?

He clasped cold hands before him, shivering suddenly, not from the chill river breeze alone. Men made mistakes; it was the natural way of things. Impossible that you would never make a mistake, accuse wrongly, perhaps unwittingly destroy a life . . .

He sat brooding a while longer, watching the stray raindrops ripple across the river as it slid silently past. *Forget this,* he told himself at last. *You can do nothing about it. Even if you could somehow learn the truth, and clear his name, he will still be beyond help. There is nothing you can do.* He sighed, pushed himself to his feet, and turned his steps westward along the quay, letting the walk and the chill breeze calm him.

Like a great ship, the Île de la Cité parted the river, the cathedral at one end of the island and the Law Courts at the other. As Aristide passed along the shore of the Right Bank, the brooding medieval tow-ers of the Conciergerie, the ancient prison attached to the courts, caught and held his gaze. All his misgivings returned in a rush.

What if I, too, in my time, have sent innocent men to that place, and even to the executioner?

2

Aristide dreamed of the execution for a second night, heard the shouts, the thud of the blade, and woke sweating and trembling at dawn, as his small mantel clock chimed seven. Grateful for the common, raucous noise of morning, carts and peddlers in the street below, he stared at the fine web of cracks in the plaster ceiling above his bed alcove as the twilight slowly brightened. Swiftly he thought back through the murders he and Brasseur had solved during the ten years past—or had thought they had solved. Could anyone ever be so completely sure he was right? The evidence had borne them out—but still . . .

Someone pounded on the door, jerking him back to the present. He struggled out of bed and pulled on his culotte and stockings as the pounding continued.

"Ravel, for heaven's sake, wake up!"

It was Brasseur's voice. Aristide unbolted the door to the landing to find his friend's fist poised for another hammer-blow as his landlady hovered behind him with a breakfast tray.

"I didn't want to let him upstairs, citizen," she protested, "not at this hour."

Brasseur scowled at her and she hastily pushed aside a few books and broken quills on Aristide's writing-desk, set down the tray, and scuttled away. Brasseur's broad shoulders and bayonet-scarred face had led more than one timid witness into wondering if he were being questioned by a brigand rather than a district police chief.

"Ravel, I need you. I have a double murder on my hands."

"*Double* murder?"

"And this on top of the hotel murder a month ago," Brasseur added, stepping inside and shutting the door. Aristide poured cold water into the basin on the washstand and splashed it on his face as Brasseur continued. "This one looks like a crime of passion, Didier said. No robbery evident."

"Didier's there, is he?" Aristide said.

"Well, I had to send somebody." Brasseur glanced about the crowded room, at the litter of books and dirty coffee cups left on top of shelves, a wrinkled cravat hanging about a candlestick on the desk, coat tossed carelessly over a chair. "Doesn't your landlady keep things tidy for you?"

Aristide shrugged. "She'd love to." He wolfed down a few mouthfuls of breakfast, sour, gritty bread with a spoonful of lard scraped across it. So again there was no butter to be had. "If Clotilde had her way, she'd tidy this place up so well I'd never find what I need."

"Are you ready, then? I've a cab waiting. It's not far." Brasseur headed for the stairs as Aristide gulped down a cup of milky coffee—at least half of it roasted chicory, he thought with a grimace—and struggled into his coat.

Only a single black-clad inspector on guard at the front door of the house indicated anything amiss on Rue du Hasard. The building was a modest five-story apartment house, lacking a carriage gate and central courtyard, built, Aristide guessed, within the past thirty years. Inside the ground-floor passage that led to a small backyard and common privy, a stone staircase spiraled upward at their left, opposite the door to the porter's lodging. A few stucco moldings ornamented the walls and ceilings in the now outmoded rococo style.

Inspector Didier approached them, his expression grim.

"Commissaire Brasseur—second floor, if you please. They sent word you were coming." Didier caught sight of Aristide and they exchanged frigid glances. "Him, too."

Aristide gave him a cool nod and followed Brasseur into the foyer and up the two flights of stairs. Two guardsmen passed them, a draped stretcher between them. "The other'll be down in a moment, Commissaire," one of them told Brasseur as they edged past him along the narrow staircase.

"Wait a moment!" Brasseur said as they continued. "Who told you to take away the bodies?"

The man jerked his head at Didier, who had trailed them. "The inspector here."

"For God's sake!" Aristide said, turning on Didier. "What do you think you're doing?"

Didier reddened. "I'm doing my job!"

"Surely Brasseur's told you never to move the corpse? Of all the—"

"Enough, Ravel," Brasseur grunted. "Obviously the damage has been done. You men, you bring that up again and wait with the body here on the landing. Damn it, Didier, leave a murder scene intact until I've seen it—and that includes the corpse. You ought to know better."

"Sorry, Commissaire," Didier muttered. He darted a venomous glance at Aristide. "Dr. Prunelle was done inspecting them. I did take notes."

A fat lot of good they'll be, Aristide thought. He turned his back on Didier and climbed to the next landing. The inspector sullenly pointed the way through a door hanging ajar. Aristide glanced at the lock and latch. They were intact, the wood of the door unsplintered.

"It's the man's apartment," Didier said. "Him on the litter. Louis Saint-Ange. Age thirty-eight, according to his papers; property owner, lived on his rents."

Aristide noticed the smell as soon as he stepped past the door, the acrid scent of powder smoke in a closed chamber. Then he caught a glimpse of the girl on the stretcher as they drew a sheet over her face, and the memories that for three decades he had tried to forget came flooding back, sharp as daggers. He halted in the foyer, gazing at the scene.

It was the apartment of a comfortable bachelor, a man of fashion and taste. Two chairs, back and seats upholstered in rich crimson brocade, lay on their sides, as did a table that had once held a gilt clock. Candelabrum, inkwell, paper, sand shaker, blotter, and quills had been swept from the mahogany writing-desk. Ink lay across the rose-colored carpet and the scattered writing paper in a broad black splash like spilled blood.

Half a dozen colored engravings hung on the walls, daintily salacious scenes of plump, blushing, scantily clad maidens squirming in the clutches of smirking young Adonises. Three of the framed engravings hung crookedly; a fourth lay on the floor at the base of the wall, its glass shattered. Books and a pair of small bronze sculptures lay tumbled from overturned side tables.

The smell—yes, the smell of stale, burned powder was exactly the same as he remembered, the same caustic tang in the air assailing his senses. *She* had lain dead, too, so small in her thin chemise, sprawled across the floor, the other nearby. And a huge shadowed figure had loomed above them, shaking hand still clutching the pistol, a colossal ogre to his nine-year-old eyes staring terrified in the smoky twilight.

"Ravel?" said Brasseur, behind him. He drew a quick breath.

It's not she, he told himself, *it's not she*. It's not she, and he is not here, standing trembling above their still-warm corpses; here is only death, and silence, and the dispassionate aftermath. These are strangers here, and someone, some other stranger, has murdered them, and you are here to discover who did this.

"Ravel?"

"I'm all right." He stepped forward into the salon.

"Bullet wounds on both of them," said Dr. Prunelle, the police surgeon, catching sight of Brasseur as he pulled his coat on. "Undoubtedly mortal. Judging from the rigor mortis they died late yesterday afternoon."

"Between four o'clock yesterday and seven o'clock this morning," said Didier, "according to the servant. He was out for the night and found them when he came back."

"I repeat," Prunelle said severely, "judging from the degree of rigor mortis that has set in, they were killed yesterday afternoon or evening. Eight o'clock at the latest."

Aristide paused beside the dead girl on the stretcher and drew back the sheet. Her mouth hung a little open in a sweet childlike face. Someone had closed her eyes and death had smoothed her features, had dissolved the astonishment or terror that must have distorted them at the moment of her sudden, violent death. His mother's face had borne the same blank expression.

"Damn it," he whispered, and with an effort thrust aside the memory, thankful the girl looked nothing like his mother. She was young, little more than twenty, slight and fair-haired, and her gown and fashionable short jacket with long cashmere scarf were of good cloth and well made. Blood had oozed and spread in a broad red-brown stain across the front of the jacket and the bodice of her gauzy white day dress.

"Any papers?"

Didier shook his head. "No. No identity card."

"No wedding ring, either." Her hands were soft and well kept.

"All she had was a watch and fifteen sous in her pocket. No other money, no notes at all. And not even a latchkey on her."

"She wouldn't have a key," Aristide said, fingering the fine muslin of her gown. "For heaven's sake, look at her hands and her clothes." Fashionable girls called their revealing gowns "Grecian," in accordance with the new fad for all things classical, but in late autumn the thin draperies were unfortunately more suited to the sunny hills of Attica than to damp and chilly Paris. "She has plenty of money, or her family does, even if she has none on her. A girl like this doesn't need a key to her own house; that's what servants are for." Ignoring Didier's resentful glare, he moved around her to gaze at her in the light from the tall window.

"She was crying . . . tears have dried on her cheek."

"Begging the murderer to spare her?" said Brasseur.

"But he killed her anyway. . . ."

"It looks as if this Saint-Ange was the murderer's primary victim, though. It was his apartment, after all. The girl may just have been in the way."

Aristide nodded. Though he had supposed Brasseur stolid and unimaginative when he had first begun to work with him, he had soon realized his friend's patience and tenacity were the ideal foils for his own nervy, febrile imagination.

"Each victim was shot with a single bullet," said Dr. Prunelle. "The one that killed the girl went horizontally, straight through her corset; she must have died quickly."

"No powder burns on the cloth," Brasseur said, peering at the girl's bodice. "Well—we can't do much about her until we know who she is."

"The servant says he's never seen her," ventured Didier, "or rather, he claims women often visited Saint-Ange, but she's not one he's seen here before."

"What sort of women?"

Didier grunted. "He brought home plenty of women of a certain sort, whores or just good-time girls, living almost next door to the Palais-Égalité like this." The pleasure garden of the Palais-Égalité, just a few steps from Rue du Hasard, was renowned not only for its dozens of fashionable shops, cafés, restaurants, gambling-parlors, and theaters, but also for its brothels.

"And manifestly this young woman is *not* of that sort," Aristide said. "So where does that leave you?"

"Where were the bodies when you found them?" Brasseur asked, forestalling Didier's reply.

Didier pointed. "The girl was about here, near the middle of the room, lying on the carpet; Saint-Ange was over there, on the floor behind the sofa. It pretty well concealed him."

Aristide crossed the room to the sofa and gazed at the floor, frowning. He could see no bloodstains on the parquet or on the edge of the burgundy and rose carpet.

"The man was killed instantly?" he asked the surgeon. "Not much blood?"

"No, no blood. Bullet straight to the brain, and lodged there. It's not often you see such a neat job of it," Prunelle added. "Usually, with a musket ball or similar projectile, the bullet exits the cranium—"

"Blood and brains all over the place," muttered Brasseur, grimacing.

"—but this seems to have been quite a small bullet from a small firearm. Probably the same gun that killed the young woman."

"Perhaps a pocket pistol," said Brasseur. "Could have been double-barreled, one shot for each."

"Like this," Aristide said, twitching aside his frock coat to reveal the tiny pistol, smaller than the length of his hand, that he kept tucked in his belt to ward off footpads.

"Saint-Ange had a pistol," Didier said, marching to a low cabinet lacquered in the Chinese style, on top of which the dead man and woman's personal possessions had been laid out. "It's here, with his effects."

"Where'd you find it?" Brasseur demanded. "In its case? In his hand?"

"Almost under the sofa. Might have fallen from his hand when he was shot."

Aristide lifted the pistol. It was large and heavy, a gold-inlaid pattern ornamenting the grip. He sniffed at the muzzle, scenting the familiar tang of scorched powder, and handed it to Brasseur. "Doctor, this has been fired. Could it have inflicted the wound that killed him?"

"Certainly not. A ball from that, at close range, would have made a nasty mess of his head."

"He was shot at close range?"

"Go see for yourself. Shot right through the forehead, an inch or two away at most."

"Dueling pistol, I'd guess," Brasseur said with a closer look at it. "Expensive, too. A housebreaker wouldn't have overlooked it, nor those trinkets, either," he added, with a nod toward a side table where a gold snuffbox sat on a silver tray between two silver candelabra. "The servant will know, but at a glance I'd guess nothing is missing."

"Saint-Ange had money on him," said Didier, returning to the cabinet. "No robbery here. And over there, in the cabinet in the bottom of the buffet, we found a case with a matching pistol in it. Looks as if the pistols were his, all right."

Aristide glanced at the marble-topped buffet. A single half-empty wineglass stood on it, surrounded by a few deep crimson splotches, a fine film of dust floating on its ruby surface. "Was the cabinet door open or shut when you found it?"

"Open, I think."

"Then why is it shut now?"

"I suppose one of my men shut it after we searched it."

"Death of the devil!" Brasseur exclaimed. "When will you block-heads learn to leave things as they were? Don't you understand how much you can learn, sometimes, from something as trifling as that? Or do you do your best to make a mess of the scene?"

Aristide pointedly ignored Didier and strode out to the landing to turn back the sheet covering the dead man's face. The neat round bullet wound in the center of the corpse's forehead marred the man's sharp good looks. Though the skin was scorched and blackened from the explosion of the gunpowder, the wound had scarcely bled.

"Brasseur," Aristide said suddenly, "look at this." He brushed aside a few strands of the man's long, sandy hair. "This mark on his temple. What do you make of it?"

"Looks like a slight scrape or a scratch," Brasseur said, joining him and laboriously kneeling. "Scarcely bled, though. Doctor?"

"I was wondering if you would find that," said Prunelle smugly. "I barely did myself. And there's a hint of bruising. Feel the wound; the cranium is thin at that spot, and something cracked the bone like a porcelain coffee cup."

Aristide prodded lightly at the dead man's temple. Beneath his fingertip, the bone gave way.

"Something struck this man hard, shortly before he died," continued the police surgeon. "Dead bodies don't bruise or bleed. The blow itself might have killed him, after ten or twenty minutes, if the bullet hadn't finished him off first."

"It's likely," Aristide agreed, running his fingers carefully through the dead man's hair in case the wound extended farther beyond the hairline.

"What do you think struck him?" Brasseur said, turning to the surgeon. "Fire iron?"

Dr. Prunelle inspected the irons by the fireplace and turned the poker over in his hands, frowning, before replacing it. "No, I'd say the weapon was round. These squared edges would have left a mark."

"Prunelle," Aristide said sharply. His searching fingers had found a sticky spot on the back of the corpse's head. "There's another wound here."

He rose as the police surgeon knelt beside the body, and returned to the salon, glancing around him. "There," he said, beckoning Brasseur over, just as Dr. Prunelle coughed.

"There *is* a contused wound, on the back of the skull. . . ."

"A wound that could have been caused by falling against some heavy object?" Aristide pointed to the buffet and to the small smudge of brownish red, inconspicuous among the dried wine stains, at the beveled corner of the pink marble. "I'd guess that's blood. The murderer hits him, he staggers, falls backward, strikes his head on the edge—shaking the buffet enough to slop some wine from the glass—and goes down."

"Why do it?" Brasseur demanded to no one in particular. "That is, why knock him unconscious with a killing blow, and then burn his brains?"

"Who knows?" Aristide absently gnawed at his thumbnail. An abominable habit, he reminded himself. "He came in," he began at last. "Or she . . . but we'll say 'he' for simplicity's sake, and this looks more like a man's crime . . . the murderer was admitted, probably by Saint-Ange himself—" He paused, staring about the salon, thinking. Abruptly he strode to the wall on which the engravings hung, gazing at the empty space where one picture had crashed to the floor. The wall was covered with an expensive paper in an ornate pattern of Grecian columns and dark green acanthus leaves, in the new fashion that had begun to supplant the carved and painted rococo paneling or boiseries of the past century.

"What's that you're looking at?" Brasseur said after a moment.

"A bullet hole. From Saint-Ange's gun, I expect. Here." He brushed his fingertips across a hole partially disguised by the pattern of the wallpaper. Bending, he picked up the fallen engraving in its frame and held it against the wall. "You see? A tear and a hole in the print, where the glass was shattered." He rehung the print on its peg. "See here, it's plain: Saint-Ange recognized his murderer and defended himself as best he could, pushing furniture in the murderer's way. He was trying to get to his own pistols, there in the buffet. They might have struggled. Saint-Ange at last got hold of a pistol and fired at his attacker—but he missed, and the bullet hit the wall."

"Missed?" said Brasseur. "Of course; no blood at that side of the room."

"In the struggle, the murderer either fired at Saint-Ange and missed—we should look for bullet holes in the opposite wall—or else he didn't want to waste his shot in the chance of shooting wide. So instead, after Saint-Ange fired—these dueling pistols are only single-shot—he pursued him, and swung his own pistol at Saint-Ange's head—so"—clutching an imaginary pistol, Aristide swung his arm in a wide arc—"*Crack*—and Saint-Ange loses his balance and stumbles backward, and hits his head on the buffet, and falls to the floor, stunned, where the murderer shoots him."

Brasseur snapped his fingers. "That's it—a gun barrel, or the grip. Round, solid."

The surgeon stirred. "The skin is severely scorched about the bullet wound. The gun was held against his head, or no more than a finger's breadth away, when fired."

Kneeling behind the sofa, Aristide closed his hand once more around the imaginary pistol and lowered it slowly to the spot where the dead man had lain. "Saint-Ange is unconscious . . . now the murderer has ample time to reload if he needs to, and aim, and bring it down, close to his head, so, before squeezing the trigger . . ." He jerked his hand up with a sigh. Something was not right with the little drama he had fashioned.

"That wound . . . it's too perfect."

"Perfect?" the surgeon echoed him.

"You've come here in search of an enemy, with murder in your heart," Aristide said, "and you're frantic to get it over with, cover your traces, and flee before someone finds you. You're probably shaking with rage, or fear, or at least agitation and fatigue from the struggle."

"That's reasonable."

"Of course, you want to kill your intended victim, who is lying helpless before you. But do you squeeze off a shot at his heart or head and run for it . . . or do you take the time to aim your pistol, probably while your hand is trembling, so precisely and symmetrically at his forehead?" He gnawed at his thumbnail again for a moment, frowning. "This precise, deliberate killing means something. It has to."

"Revenge?" said Brasseur.

"Possibly. Something to do with the girl, even?"

"Could be . . . though it looks as if the girl was simply killed to silence a witness."

"Wouldn't she have run for it as soon as the murderer came in and the fun began?"

Brasseur shrugged. "Women just freeze sometimes when they panic. She might have cowered there, too frightened to move. And then the killer shot her."

"Revenge for an injury . . . punishment for a crime . . ." Aristide returned to the corpse on its stretcher and gazed at it a moment longer, reflecting. "Yes . . . Saint-Ange must have been the one he wanted to kill. Look at the wound, Brasseur, right in the center of his forehead like the mark of Cain. Branded like a felon. Our murderer wanted this man dead for some private, profound reason—not merely dead, but executed."

3

Aristide turned away at last from the dead man. "Didier, have you found the murderer's pistol?"

"No. Must have taken it with him."

"You say Saint-Ange's manservant discovered the bodies?"

Didier jerked his head toward a door in the salon. "He's in the dressing room. He'd gone out on errands for his master at about four o'clock yesterday and was gone all night. When he returned, he found what you see."

"Did no one else see or hear anything?"

"We're inquiring now. Half the house is untenanted. The rent's high in this quarter."

"And there are plenty of empty mansions for the wealthy to buy cheap," added Brasseur, "if you do have the money to live in style. Who'd want to live in a flat when you can have some duke's fancy town house? Well, go on," he told Didier.

"The apartment below is vacant, so no one seems to have heard the struggle or the shots."

"But the servant's absence, combined with Prunelle's opinion, gives us the time it happened, within an hour or two," Aristide said. "Unless you suspect the servant?"

Didier shrugged. "Not likely. What motive are you thinking he'd have?"

"I agree," Aristide said, ignoring Didier's deliberate insolence. "Unless there was something between him and the girl, but that does seem improbable."

At a nod from Brasseur, the waiting guardsmen carried the two bodies down the stairs. Aristide knelt on the carpet, gazing about him.

"Brasseur."

He held up a fragment of paper between his forefinger and thumb. It was a tiny triangular scrap, cream colored with a black band and narrow black stripe edging the two shorter sides, and frayed on the third edge. He rose and dropped it into Brasseur's outstretched palm. "What do you think?"

"Looks like a piece torn off an assignat," Brasseur said instantly. He pulled a folded banknote from his pocket, glancing from one to the other. "Look there: you can see the printing in the corner, p-u-n, where it says 'The law punishes the counterfeiter with death.'"

"You said Saint-Ange had money on him, Didier? Was it in his pocket?"

Didier nodded. Aristide surveyed the effects laid out on the lacquered cabinet: pocketbook, handkerchief, the girl's reticule, a few copper coins and prerevolutionary silver écus, a thick bundle of assignats in various denominations. "Why not try leaving things as they were, instead of insisting upon your precious inventory?" he added, shuffling rapidly through the notes. Didier glowered.

"Procedure—"

"Quite a lot here," Aristide said, ignoring him. "Several hundred thousand livres' worth."

"A few louis' worth in gold, I expect," Brasseur grunted, "what with the value of paper money these days. I swear, the stuff's fit only to wipe your arse."

"Ah, here, I think." Aristide held up a worn, crumpled five-livre note. One corner was missing and the words at the frayed edge matched the scrap of paper he had found.

"It's only a guess, but I'd venture that this note, and probably others, changed hands recently, if a piece of it was lying on the carpet. He thrusts a handful of notes into a pocket, a frayed corner tears off and falls. When had the room last been swept?"

"The manservant will know," said Didier. "Did you wish to question him now, Commissaire?" He went out and returned with a short, dark man of about forty-five.

"So," Brasseur said, consulting Didier's notes, "you are Barthélemy Thibault, domestic servant, in service with Saint-Ange for two years?" The man nodded. "And you left this house at about four o'clock yesterday to attend to some errands."

"That's right, Citizen Commissaire. I had to complain to the caterer who delivers his meals that the midday roast was overdone."

"You returned this morning? Isn't that a long time to be absent?"

"It was Sunday—I mean *décadi*—" He paused, reddening. "I'm sorry, citizen, I still have trouble with this republican calendar, even after three years . . ."

"Don't we all?" said Brasseur, shrugging. "Go on."

Aristide permitted himself a slight smile. The new official calendar had been created in 1793 to divorce the French Republic from such outdated, superstitious relics of the old order as the Christian reckoning and its numerous religious festivals and saints' days. In his experience, the new months and the ten-day week drove most people to distraction; it was still necessary to include the Christian date, with a discreet "old style" beside it, on all the newspapers.

"Well," Thibault continued, "it was *décadi*, like I said, and he'd given me the evening off, once I was done with the message, so I visited the cabaret for a spell, and had a few glasses with some friends. Then I ran into a girlfriend of mine, you see, and I spent the night at her lodgings. Saint-Ange never rose before nine, so as long as I got back before eight, in time to build up the fire and heat his water and brew his coffee, I was all right."

"Well, go on."

"I got back about seven this morning, I think, or a little after." He rubbed his eyes and grimaced. "Seems already like a year ago. I came up the staircase and tried unlocking the door very quietly, so as not to wake him, but it wasn't locked."

"It looks as if Saint-Ange let the murderer in himself," Aristide said. "The door wasn't broken in."

"So I went in on tiptoe," Thibault continued, "thinking he'd just forgot to lock the door. And first thing I saw was the furniture all every which way, and then the poor young lady. I touched her cheek and she was cold. And then I went farther and saw *him* and I knew right away from that hole in his head that he was dead, and I ran down to send for help. Couldn't have been longer than ten minutes about it."

Aristide stepped forward. "Thibault, I want you to tell us your honest opinion, no matter what it may be. What did you think of Saint-Ange?"

"Well, he was always decent to me." Thibault scratched his head. "Not a difficult man to work for, like some."

"Do you know the source of his income?"

"Said he owned land in the country that he rented to farmers. Bought up cheap when they sold off the church property for the government. Said he'd once owned a sugar plantation in Saint-Domingue, though he lost that when the Negroes revolted."

"Did he?" Aristide glanced about him. "This apartment is furnished more luxuriously, I'd hazard, than a man could afford whose sole income was a few rents. Last year's inflation would have ruined him."

"I wouldn't know about that."

"Kept his affairs to himself? All right then," Aristide continued, "tell me about his friends who called on him. You claim you've never seen the young lady before?"

"Yes. I mean, no, I've never seen *her* before."

"But you've seen other women here."

"Oh, yes, a fair stream of them. His present lady friend was here yesterday. I know her; she's been visiting him for weeks. They went out to the Palais-Égalité for luncheon, then came back here and spent the rest of the afternoon in his bedchamber," he added, with a smirk. "Well, he was a young man, and good-looking, and with enough money in his pocket to have a good time; and living right by the Palais-Égalité, after all! You can't blame him, can you?"

"To each his own taste, I suppose. Did you see this woman leave? Did they seem on good terms?"

"Yes, she left about four o'clock. There wasn't nothing wrong between them—they couldn't keep their hands off each other. That was a little before Citizen Saint-Ange told me to take the message to the caterer."

"Were all his visitors courtesans?"

"He had other visitors now and then. A different sort. Some gentlemen, and other women; what they used to call—before the Revolution—'ladies of quality.' Well dressed; and most of them shy. They'd come wearing veils or deep hoods to their cloaks. Like they didn't want to be recognized."

"Do you know what business they had with Saint-Ange?"

"No, he sent me off on errands when they called, or gave me ten sous and told me to go have a glass in the gardens. And when he gave me ten sous for a glass of red that cost two or three, I was glad enough to get it and keep my mouth shut."

"Just one last question, Thibault. When was this salon swept last?"

"Day before yesterday," Thibault said promptly. "A woman comes in every day to do the heavy cleaning, except for *décadi*. She'll be back today, or she would be if . . ."

Brasseur snapped his notebook shut. "Thanks. You can go with one of the inspectors now, and give him your statement." He turned to the window and stared out to the street as Thibault left the room.

"I tend to wonder," he said, still gazing out the window at the silent, shuttered house opposite, "when I hear of a prosperous fellow with no particular means of income, who's visited by all sorts of women. And who keeps a loaded pistol in his cabinet. Dangerous thing to do, that, but useful if you're on the lookout for trouble."

"What does it all smell like to you?" said Aristide.

"A pander, I expect. A high-class one; a flesh peddler living off loose women."

Aristide shook his head. "Perhaps. But Thibault said many of his visitors, not just the one who died with him, were timid, respectably dressed ladies. And this girl had no money on her at all, except for a few sous, which happen to be about the price of a cab fare home, wherever in Paris home is. And Didier found a sizable bundle of notes on Saint-Ange. The stink is fouler than pandering, I imagine."

Brasseur smacked his fist into his palm.

"Extortion!"

"I think I begin to mislike the late Louis Saint-Ange. And perhaps to believe whoever murdered him did the world a service." Aristide wheeled about, staring down once again at the spot where the dead girl had fallen. "One of his victims must have grown desperate and rid himself—or herself—of a most rapacious parasite. I wouldn't expend too much effort in trying to learn who the killer was. But that poor girl had to die, too. . . ."

"She must have been one of his victims," Brasseur said. "You thought she'd been crying. . . ."

"Yes. Pleading with him, perhaps. Probably she was trying to keep secret some childish indiscretion from a father or a fiancé."

"We'll know more when she's identified," said Brasseur. "A nicely dressed young lady like that, she's sure to have someone wondering where she is, parents or at least servants." He turned to Didier. "Inspector, station a man here in the building, in the porter's room. And try not to let the news of Saint-Ange's death spread too far. Keep that porter quiet; keep him flat-out drunk if you have to. Anyone who comes to call on Saint-Ange is to be held for questioning."

"Whom were you thinking of catching?" Aristide said.

"If we're right about Saint-Ange, another of his victims will probably come by with a payment soon, or at least one of his friends. Didier, I'm to be sent for as soon as you bag someone."

"Yes, Commissaire."

"And mind you treat them properly," Aristide added. "The Terror's over. Innocent witnesses give information more willingly if they're not frightened half to death."

"I don't take orders from you," said Didier, coloring. "You're not even an inspector."

"You will if I say you do," Brasseur snapped. "Ravel works for me and gets paid by me, same as you; he may not have an official title, but he's an agent of the police, understood?"

"Yes, Commissaire," Didier said, adding under his breath: "Never thought I'd be taking orders from a damned spy."

Aristide ignored him. *Spy* or *talebearer* were the first epithets that sprang to most people's minds when they learned he worked for the police, but not openly as an inspector, peace officer, or commissaire. Some aspects of policing had not changed since the collapse of the old regime; the vast majority of "police agents" had always been spies and eavesdroppers, loathed by all including their employers, forever ready, for a small stipend, to repeat indiscreet talk or report observations and rumors.

Aristide held the common police spy in as much contempt as did anyone else, preferring to devote himself to investigation rather than informing. The difference that preserved his self-respect, he thought, was that when he went undercover, it was to obtain evidence about crimes committed, for the sake of justice; while informers usually gathered loose talk and innuendo, hints of crime and sedition that had not yet occurred, for the benefit of suspicious authority.

He strode out to the landing, glad to be away from the room in which the faint smell of gunpowder still hung. "Which of the apartments are tenanted?" he asked Didier over his shoulder. "Have you questioned them all?"

"The people two floors above heard some scuffling yesterday evening," Didier muttered, "but they didn't think anything of it. They're too far above, and you can't hear much in a stone house like this. The wife might have heard shots; but she admitted she got so used to shots in the street in 'ninety-two and 'ninety-three that she scarce thought anything of it, except to close the shutters and be grateful she was indoors. She's a pretty stupid sort of female. They also think they could have heard someone running up and down the staircase. The family just above was out at the theater all evening, every damned one of them, including the servants, and they don't know anything. Most people in the quarter were out for the day, since it was *décadi* and fine weather for a change."

Aristide nodded and they continued down the stairs to the porter's lodging by the street door. The porter sat slouched at a table, a brandy bottle beside him.

"Out in the hallway, if you please, Citizen Grangier," Brasseur said. Eyes darting toward Brasseur's tricolor sash, the porter shambled out to the foyer. The two men carrying the girl's shrouded body stepped forward. With a swift movement, Brasseur jerked away the sheet.

"Know her?"

The porter recoiled and shook his head.

"Sure? Take a good look."

"I—I don't know who she is. I didn't do it. I swear to God, I didn't do it—"

"No one is suggesting you did," Brasseur said patiently. He gestured the man back into his lodging, muttering "Well?" to Aristide as he followed Grangier inside.

"No," said Aristide. "That's not a man with murder on his conscience."

"I agree." Brasseur sat on the nearest bench and gestured Aristide and Dautry, his secretary, to stools.

"But I saw who did, citizen," the porter said eagerly. "It must have been him that did it. I saw him on the staircase. First I heard footsteps going up the stairs. Very fast, they were. I didn't see him then—I'd just woken from my afternoon nap—"

"Isn't that part of your job, to watch who goes in and out, and to direct callers toward the right apartment?"

"Well, yes, but them as knows the house just come in. And if you need to know which floor somebody lives on, you can look at the names outside."

Aristide nodded. Since 1793, the law had required the names of all tenants to be inscribed on the outside of the house by the entrance.

"So you heard someone running up the stairs," he said. "What time was this?"

"About six o'clock. Almost time to light the lamp in the foyer. I get up, and put my head out the door in case he needs anything, but he's gone already. So I sit myself down again and have a dram of brandy and a bit of sausage I've been saving for my supper, and then a bit later I hear the footsteps again, coming down fast. It's all stone and plaster in the stairway, you know, and the sound echoes. So I put my head out again and I just catch sight of him as he races out the door to the street."

"Did you see his face?"

"No, just his back. He had on a dark coat and top boots. And long hair."

"Like mine?" Aristide said, pushing his own long hair away from his face.

"Not so dark, citizen, and his was gathered back. Like I said, I didn't get much of a glimpse of him. But when he came back—"

"He came *back*?" Brasseur exclaimed.

"Yes, he came back, it might have been twenty minutes, a half hour later. That time I got a better look at him. He came running in again like all the devils of Hell were behind him, and I saw his face for a moment then as he passed me. A young fellow, very pale and scared looking."

"Scared looking?" Aristide said, glancing over at the secretary, who was furiously scribbling notes. "Are you getting all this, Dautry? Go on, Grangier; he was frightened of something?"

"Well, no, not frightened, but upset. Like I said, he was white as a sheet."

"A young man? How old?"

Grangier nodded, eyeing the brandy bottle. "Young. Closer to a boy than a man. Twenty-five, maybe. And thin."

"Please describe him as well as you can. His hair was dark brown, you say, but not as dark as mine? What about his eyes?"

"Didn't see. It was getting dark, and he went by too fast."

"How tall was he?"

"A little under medium height, I'd guess. Maybe a couple of fingers shorter than I am. He went by too fast—"

"I understand. Tell me more about his clothing."

"Like I said, top boots and a dark coat."

"What color? What about his culotte and waistcoat?"

The porter reached for the brandy bottle but Brasseur slid it smoothly away from him.

"This won't improve your memory, Grangier. Try to remember."

"Blue," said Grangier after a moment. "Maybe. It was getting dark in the hall. His coat was dark blue. Or it might have been dark green. His breeches were black. Didn't see his waistcoat; he had his coat buttoned."

"Did he wear a hat?"

"I saw dark hair and a ribbon, but . . . no, wait . . ." He screwed up his face, trying to summon the memory. Aristide waited silently, tapping his fingers on the tabletop. "He wasn't wearing his hat when I saw him run out," Grangier said at last. "Must have been carrying it under his arm. But he wore it when he came back. A round one, low-crowned, with a wide brim. Dark. That's why I couldn't see his face so well, because the brim threw a shadow on his face."

Brasseur added a few more notes in his own notebook. "Good. Let's go through your statement again. At about six o'clock in the evening, you heard someone running up the stairs, but didn't see him. Then, a little while later—How long? Ten minutes? Twenty minutes?"

"Maybe ten minutes."

"Ten minutes later, you heard footsteps running down the stairs, and you saw a young man rushing out the street door, but only from the back. Twenty or thirty minutes later, he returned, and you saw his face briefly as he ran past you and up the stairs." Grangier nodded.

"Did you see him leave again?"

Grangier opened his mouth, considered a moment, and frowned. "No, come to think of it, I didn't. I'd gone back in here for another dram of eau-de-vie. I don't meddle with the tenants' business."

"In other words," Aristide said dryly, "you don't trouble yourself keeping watch on the house unless you're asked?"

"Well, I've a bad knee, rheumatism, and I don't fancy climbing the stairs unless I have to."

"So you don't know when he left."

"No. He must have come back down, though, mustn't he? There's no other staircase. But if he was running and making a racket I'd have heard him, what with the echo. He must have walked down, quiet. I wouldn't notice that if the door was closed."

"Which, of course, it was, while you were having your second, or third, glass of brandy."

"Yes, citizen."

Brasseur sighed. "All right, then. You saw a young man of about twenty-five, dark-haired, wearing a dark blue or green coat, and black culotte, top boots, and a dark-colored round hat with a wide brim. He was pale and seemed upset, and took the stairs running. And you've not seen him since he ran up the staircase for the second time."

"No."

"You'll take an oath to all this you've told me?" The porter nodded. "Very well, you'll be summoned to the justice of the peace shortly to give an official statement." He pushed the brandy bottle back to Grangier, who took it with immense relief.

4

The autumn dusk was closing in by the time they were done interrogating possible witnesses, and Brasseur had sealed the apartment. Few people had been about, owing to the fine weather and the day of rest, *décadi*, which in the republican calendar now occurred only every ten days instead of every seven, and none had provided them with anything as useful as the porter's information.

"A young man," Aristide said to Brasseur as they strolled back to the commissariat through the swarming streets of the Butte-des-Moulins section, past peddlers, sightseers, hack drivers awaiting fares, and a few early prostitutes. "That could mean nearly anyone. A victim of Saint-Ange's extortion, or the friend or relative of a victim. Brother, lover, perhaps a husband."

"The bastard," muttered Brasseur. "Well, we'll see what the mousetrap brings in." He glanced at his watch. "Nothing for you to do now, until we know more, and I have to write my report. Care to join me for supper afterward? Marie's stewing a hare."

"What is it you want?"

Brasseur grinned. "Why should I want anything?"

"You always want something of me when you offer to give me dinner."

"Well then, I want you to lend me a hand with that hotel murder from last month."

"Man robbed and stabbed in his bed, probably by the whore he came in with?" Aristide shook his head. "Not interested."

"The whore he came in with, who was wearing men's clothing. A bit unusual, don't you think?"

"Certainly, but I'm still not interested."

"Ravel—"

"You know me better than that. I'm glad to accept what you pay me for providing information or evidence; but only because I find the inter-actions that lead to one human being killing another eternally fascinat-ing. What do I care about a lecher who went looking for an anonymous whore and found a thief and a killer instead? I want justice for that girl, who died merely because she was in somebody's way."

Brasseur turned to a coffee seller on the street and tossed her a sou. "You take care, Ravel," he continued, turning back to him, a battered pewter cup in one hand. "You lose all sense of proportion if you let an affair like this bedevil you."

"I'm not—"

"I've seen it happen before. It's happened to me, once or twice. Don't let it—and her—possess you. I warn you."

"Never you mind about me," Aristide said. He searched his pock-ets for coins as the coffee seller hopefully thrust a second small cup to-ward him.

"Saints, woman, what do you put in this, mud?" Brasseur exclaimed with a grimace. "Did you go to the Place de Grève yesterday?" he con-tinued, more softly, to Aristide, as he sipped gingerly at the coffee.

"It was just as abominable as I'd expected."

"How did Lesurques behave?"

"Like a man resigned to what he hadn't deserved, I thought . . . but what do I know?" Aristide drank his own tepid coffee in a few swallows and handed the cup back to the peddler. "There's the essence of it; what *do* I know? I would dearly like to believe as confidently as the judges and jury did, that he was guilty as sin, but I can't . . . and then I begin to wonder how many other innocent people the police—you and

I included—may have mistakenly delivered over to the courts, and perhaps even to the scaffold."

Brasseur nodded. "I know; that's the hell of our work. But all you can do, every day, is to learn the truth as best you can. You can't go on brooding about something you had nothing to do with and can't fix, or you'll go mad. Forget it, and move on; find the killer who murdered that man and girl instead."

They parted outside the commissariat on Rue Traversine. Aristide stood a moment in the street, pulling his collar more snugly about him in the autumn chill as wagons and fiacres rattled past toward the busy artery of Rue Honoré and impatient pedestrians elbowed by him. Despite Brasseur's words, he could not banish the scene at the Place de Grève from his memory. At last he set off toward the Île de la Cité. To learn whether or not the law had made a terrible error, he mused, who better to ask than one who had seen more than his share of men condemned to die?

Many of the windows were dark by the time he arrived at the Palais de Justice. He bypassed the Grand Stair to the public halls and instead went straight to the far right-hand corner of the May Courtyard and the door in a small lower courtyard below ground level that led directly to the Conciergerie.

"Where can I find Citizen Sanson?" he asked the surprised turnkey who answered the bell.

"Sanson?" the man echoed him. "You mean the executioner? Not here. He doesn't come here unless they're fetching somebody away to be topped. But you might find him, or find word of him, at the public prosecutor's office. Up in the Caesar Tower." He jerked a thumb upward and behind him, toward the three conical towers, remnants of the Conciergerie's origins as a medieval fortress, that edged the quayside. "Here, you're a police agent, aren't you? I've seen you before. You can cut through with me instead of going around the long way to the quay."

Aristide followed the man, glancing silently from side to side as they tramped through the dim corridors. A few gaunt and bedraggled women watched him without interest from open cell doors and from piles of dirty straw. His guide was cheerful for a jailer, and eager to point out spots of interest along their route.

"I expect you know this is the women's side? There, down the passage, that's the cell the queen was in. Two months she was in that nasty damp place! Not that I hold with royalty, but it was cruel, it was. Next door, that's where Robespierre spent his last hours. And just beyond it," the turnkey continued, pointing, "that's the old prison chapel. 'Course they don't hold Mass in it any more. They use it as a common room sometimes. The Brissotin deputies, the twenty-two who were all topped together, they had their last dinner there, you know. Come to think of it, it was almost three years ago exactly, when they were topped. All Hallows' Eve what was. Very sad it was, all those fine young gentlemen."

Mathieu . . .

Aristide stepped forward, peering down the corridor at the gloomy chapel. "May I see it for a moment?"

The turnkey nodded. "Please yourself."

He trod lightly down the short passage. The pale silhouette of a vanished crucifix gleamed faintly on the bare, smoke-grimed plaster and a few chairs and benches stood about amid scattered straw. It seemed suddenly like yesterday, an hour ago, a moment. Here in this dim, chill room they had dined and exchanged their last farewells, and sung "La Marseillaise," and toasted the Republic that had condemned them.

Of course, the scene would not have been as sublime as popular legend already had it. Some of them, he imagined, remembering Mathieu's sardonic descriptions of his comrades in public life, must have been foul-mouthed in their bitterness, or insufferably self-righteous in their political martyrdom.

See that fellow? That's Buzot . . . yes, the one who's always hanging about Minister Roland's wife. But all they do is gawk sentimentally at each other . . . I'd be surprised if Buzot actually knew how to do it, he's such a sanctimonious prig. . . .

But they were all dead now, whatever their faults or merits, and Mathieu with them. No false sublimity for Mathieu at the final moment, but jest after black jest until they climbed the scaffold's steps one by one, anything that might serve to keep the lurking terror of death at bay.

Aristide searched the shadows as if he might find something of Mathieu, a phantom of his wicked smile, lingering there yet. He shut his eyes to the gloom and tried to remember him in happier days, the prankish boy he had known in Bordeaux, or the eager young man, glowing with revolutionary ardor—anything but his last glimpse of him, waiting in the rain before the guillotine.

By force of childhood habit he hurriedly made the sign of the cross, for the sake of all the souls who had passed through that cold stone chamber. *"Requiescat in pace."*

"This way," said the turnkey, beckoning him on. "Just up those stairs." He unlocked a heavy iron-bound door that led to a spiral staircase. "Someone above can show you the way."

Aristide thanked him and climbed the stairs to the landing. Approaching the nearest clerk, he explained his errand.

"Sanson?" echoed the clerk. "No, he's not here. But Desmorets, his chief assistant, is." He pointed to a middle-aged man, just emerging from the inner office.

Young Sanson, it seemed, often spent some time after an execution in a wineshop near the Châtelet, the medieval castle in the center of the city that now housed jails, morgue, and police courts. The assistants, Desmorets added, generally gathered to drink together in a cabaret in the faubourg Denis, their own neighborhood, but Sanson, he was a bit standoffish and didn't mix much with them. "His father, he was just the same," he concluded. "We lodge at his house, most of us, and serve at his table, but he doesn't care to be seen with us, beyond the work, that is."

The work, Aristide repeated to himself. An innocuous euphemism for a repugnant vocation. Though he had spoken with the elder executioner and his assistants before, in the course of his own work, he found he still harbored a trace of uneasy distaste toward men who put their fellow beings to death for pay.

"Do you—do you enjoy your trade?"

Desmorets glanced at him, passive reproach in his gaze. "I'm used to it. Doesn't mean I enjoy it. And the son of an executioner has precious little choice in the matter. Take up your father's trade or go hungry. No one else will employ you."

"Forgive me. I spoke without thinking."

"No offense taken, citizen. It's not as bad as it was before the Revolution. Used to be some folk were afraid to touch us, for fear they'd be contaminated. But during the Terror, all of a sudden it seemed we were the keystones of society. That's what some of them called Old Sanson: 'Keystone of the Terror.' He didn't care for it, but it was better than being called butcher, and scum, and worse."

Aristide nodded. He had crossed paths with the elder Sanson in 1793, and he could imagine how that dignified and taciturn public official might have reacted to the crude adulation of tipsy sans-culottes.

He found the wineshop soon enough, on a narrow side street winding off in the shadow of the Châtelet's towers. After a moment's search among the crowded, noisy tables of card players, he recognized his quarry, seated alone at a small dimly lit table in a corner, staring at his empty bottle.

"May I?" he inquired, and slid into a chair opposite the younger Sanson, quickly taking stock of him. The new executioner of Paris was a robust, classically handsome young man of no more than thirty, who would not have seemed out of place strutting in an army officers' mess or riding amid the wealthy and fashionable in the parkland of the Bois de Boulogne. "What are you having?"

Sanson glanced at him, expressionless.

"Are you sure you want to sit with me, citizen?"

"Yes."

"Do you know who I am?"

"Yes."

"Then you have the advantage of me."

"My name is Ravel."

Sanson shrugged. "Stay, if you must."

Aristide ordered a half bottle of red wine from a barmaid and then returned to the table and his companion. "Citizen Sanson," he said without wasting words in idle talk, "do you believe Lesurques was guilty?"

Sanson raised his head and glowered at him.

"What should it matter what *I* think? It can't be undone. Let the dead rest in peace."

"I ask you because I, too, am a servant of the law."

Sanson glanced at him again, with vague interest. "Are you—"

"No," Aristide said hastily, "I'm not one of your . . . colleagues . . . but I do serve justice. I assist one of the section commissaires, a friend of mine."

"Informer?" Sanson inquired with a contemptuous twist of his lips.

"Certainly not. An investigator."

"Well?"

"I had nothing to do with the case, though I've followed it. But I do believe that every servant of the law must take some of the burden upon himself for such a terrible error, if an error was made. If Lesurques was innocent as he claimed."

Sanson was silent for a few minutes, drinking down the last of his wine and staring at the play of the candlelight on the empty glass. "My father has probably presided over more executions than any man in history," he said. "For forty years he's watched felons expire on the wheel, or at the end of a rope, and he saw plenty of the innocent die as well, in 'ninety-three and 'ninety-four. He's seen enough to know how a man with a clear conscience dies. When it was over, this time, he said to me: 'We've executed an innocent man.'"

"And you, you believe that as well?"

Sanson nodded. "Lesurques didn't look like a felon; he looked like one of the poor sods sent to the guillotine for no good reason during the Terror. Stunned, resigned, scared maybe; but not cocky like some cold-blooded ruffian, or whining and blubbering like a worm who knows he deserves what he's about to get."

"Thank you," said Aristide. "Though I wish you'd been able to say you believed he was guilty."

"What the devil can you do about it now?"

"Nothing at all. But I hope to do my best to ensure that such a thing never happens again."

The wine arrived and Aristide poured out a glass for Sanson. He splashed a token swallow into his own glass, preferring the stimulation of coffee to the intoxication of alcohol, and paused for an instant, wondering whether or not he ought to toast his companion.

"I'll save you the trouble of scrambling for a tactful toast," said Sanson. "To the health of the ladies who are dearest to our hearts. That's a safe one, don't you think?"

Aristide nodded and repeated "To the ladies," though in truth there was no one dear to his heart.

"You married?" inquired Sanson.

"No."

"I am. Three months ago. Gave up my mistress and my dissolute bachelor ways, and let my mother find me a respectable girl who'd overlook our profession for the sake of our fortune." He fell silent again, glowering into the garnet depths of his glass.

It was a cruel twist of fate, Aristide mused, that had condemned the fine young man before him to a distasteful trade and the life of an exile in his own land.

"Why should the police give a damn how an affair turns out, once it's tied up and handed over to the public prosecutor?" Sanson suddenly demanded. "Why do *you* care?"

"Isn't it just as much the duty of the police to free the innocent, as to bring the guilty to justice?"

"I don't imagine many think of it that way. Usually it's nothing more than 'Do your duty, and leave the issue to Heaven.'"

"But you believe as I do," Aristide said, concealing his surprise that the public executioner should quote a classic dramatist like Corneille. But then again, he thought, performing a distasteful duty ought not to prevent a man from being a scholar or a gentleman.

"I have to, or I'd run mad. I have to believe the law doesn't make mistakes. Most of the time." Sanson poured himself another glass and drained it. Aristide sipped at his own wine, shaking his head when Sanson made a move to refill his glass. "Of course, there are times, too, when the law doesn't give a damn who gets caught beneath its wheels. What were *you* doing during the Terror, citizen police spy?"

"Nothing connected with the Revolutionary Tribunal, if that's what you're thinking," Aristide said mildly, refusing to be goaded by his companion's acrimony. "I told you, I'm no informer."

"Plenty deny it now, who were proud of it three years ago."

"I was never a talebearer," he repeated, "for the public prosecutor's office or the Committee of Security or anyone else." That was not entirely the truth, though he had preferred to call himself an "agent" of Danton in 1793, when the ill-conceived war against Prussia and Austria had proved disastrous for France and many people had whispered of foreign plots to undermine the Revolution. Rumors and hysteria, most of the whispers, while distrust and uncertainty had been at their height; but he and Brasseur could testify that not all of them had been groundless. . . .

"I've no cause to have loved Robespierre's government," he added. "My dearest friend—"

He abruptly realized it was likely that the man before him had been present himself at Mathieu's death. They exchanged level stares.

"Forgive my poor manners," Sanson said at last. "I don't like myself on execution days, and after I've been drinking to forget them, I like myself even less." He pushed back his chair. "I thank you for the wine. Good evening. I won't embarrass you by offering you my hand to shake."

"But I offer you mine," Aristide said, rising.

Sanson gazed for a moment at Aristide's outstretched hand. At last he pressed it, muttered a good-bye, and strode away.

5

12 Brumaire (November 2)

Nothing new yet on the Rue du Hasard affair?" Aristide inquired as he wandered into Brasseur's office.

"Nothing as of this morning," Brasseur grumbled without looking up from the reports and letters strewn across his desk. "You needn't have come in."

"Ah, well, what better have I to do?" Aristide tossed his hat on a bench. Hands clasped behind him, he looked over the dossiers in their cardboard folders, crammed onto the rows of shelves that covered one whitewashed wall of the small chamber. Most of them were the tawdry, humdrum records of petty thieves and confidence tricksters, crooked merchants, registered prostitutes; but a few evoked memories of shared chases and challenges. He turned to Brasseur, about to murmur, *Do you remember the Martin affair?* when he thought instead, *Did we really get the right man there?* He sighed, thinking back to a few occasions when a murderer had gone to the scaffold although they had never found indisputable proof of his guilt.

A junior inspector thrust his head into the office and Brasseur glanced up impatiently. "Commissaire, Inspector Didier sent me over. They're holding a woman who went up to Saint-Ange's apartment half an hour ago."

"Well, well," said Brasseur, brightening, "seems I spoke too soon. What's she look like? A whore?"

"Nicely dressed, young, looks scared to death. Should they bring her over here?"

"Good God, no," Aristide said, retrieving his hat. "She's probably harmless. Let's keep it discreet." Brasseur grunted and gestured him out.

"She's in the porter's room," Didier announced with a sullen glance at Aristide. "The commissaire did say we were to hold visitors for questioning."

Aristide brushed past him, Brasseur's secretary following. Within, a petite, veiled woman perched on the edge of a rickety chair like a terrified bird.

"Out, if you please," Aristide told the inspector who waited beside her. "Good day, citizeness," he continued when the man had left them and he had shut the door in Didier's face. "My name is Ravel; I represent Commissaire Brasseur of the Section de la Butte-des-Moulins, and this is his secretary, citizen Dautry."

"Am I under arrest?" the woman quavered. "I haven't done anything . . ."

Aristide sighed. "Did the inspector give you that impression? I apologize. I merely need answers to a few questions. Your name?"

"Marie-Sidonie Beaumontel, née Chambly," she whispered. She pushed an identity card toward him bearing an address in the prosperous faubourg Honoré and quickly looked away, shivering. "Please—I don't know what I can tell you. I . . . I was merely visiting a friend."

"The friend you were visiting was Louis Saint-Ange?" Aristide said. She nodded. "I must inform you that citizen Saint-Ange is dead."

"Dead!" she gasped. "But I—I don't understand."

"Saint-Ange was murdered two days ago."

She sat frozen in her seat for a moment before hiding her face in her hands. Aristide let her sob for a few minutes, drumming his fingers on the table before him, and silently handed her a handkerchief when her own grew sodden. At length she calmed and lifted away her veil. Beneath it she was ashen, with dark smudges beneath her eyes, her face powder blotched and streaked with tears.

"Was Saint-Ange extorting money from you?"

She went even paler beneath the remains of her powder.

"Was he?" Aristide repeated. "We need to know."

"Please—if my husband hears a breath of this, my life won't be worth a sou."

"You can trust our discretion."

"You—you don't think *I* murdered him?" She clutched at his arm. "I swear—"

"Citeness . . . please, tell me the truth."

She swallowed but said nothing. Aristide sighed and gestured to Dautry to cease writing. "Very well. Perhaps the commissaire couldn't, in good conscience, do this; but I can." He took Dautry's notes and dropped them in the fire, but not before he had made a mental note of her address.

"You're right," she said after a moment of silence. "He was demanding money from me. He—he knew I had a lover . . . I don't know how he knew . . . I'm married to a man seventeen years my senior. He treats me well enough, but he's horribly suspicious; he sees infidelity in every word I exchange with another man. Until eight months ago I'd never given him reason to be jealous."

"But you've fallen in love?"

"Yes—with a younger man, who is kind and sympathetic. I was lonely, and I broke my marriage vows . . . I—I kept his letters. I was a fool. I ought to have thrown them on the fire after I'd read them. But I couldn't."

Aristide nodded. "And Saint-Ange got hold of these letters?"

"I don't know how. I knew him slightly, but he'd never been a guest at my house. One day I received a message, telling me to meet him at a certain café, and it enclosed one of Fernand's—one of my lover's letters. I went to their hiding place—beneath the lining of my jewelry case—and the letters were gone. I don't know how he could have taken them. Not even my maid knows where I kept them."

"What sort of woman is your maid?"

Madame Beaumontel frowned, puzzled. "Victoire? She's an ordinary sort of woman, not terribly clever perhaps, though I've no complaints about her work."

"Is she young and pretty?"

"No, not especially; she's older than I, about forty."

"I ask because usually it's a lady's maid who unwittingly allows men of this sort to do their work. Before you found the letters were missing, was Victoire behaving in an unusual manner? Was she more animated, perhaps?"

"I think—yes, she was. She was looking pleased with herself."

Aristide nodded. "Then you may count on it she'd found a lover. Plain, unmarried women of that age are usually susceptible. Tell me, how long did she behave in this fashion? Not long?"

Madame Beaumontel frowned. "I was so distressed I scarcely noticed her behavior . . . but yes, she suddenly became preoccupied . . . and then ill-natured and morose." She drew a quick breath. "Oh, no—do you mean *Saint-Ange* was the man?"

"I expect so. As I said, a woman of that age is an easy target for a seducer. He probably flirted with her on her afternoons off, made love to her; she secretly let him inside the house, and one night, while she was asleep, he crept into your boudoir and searched for anything incriminating."

"But how could he have known that—that I had a secret to protect?"

"Well," Aristide said, "young, pretty wife, middle-aged husband . . . there's usually a lover somewhere. And I'm sure Saint-Ange was a practiced observer of human nature, since he evidently depended on extortion for his livelihood. Did you think you were the only one paying him to keep a secret?"

She stared at him, speechless. "Gossip must have been his food and drink," he continued. "If you say you'd known him—"

"We had met a few times, at the theater, and at the homes of friends."

"Then he would have had his suspicions. He needed only the proof. No doubt he knew all the places where women think their secrets will be safe. He stole your letters and promptly deserted Victoire, having no further use for her."

"Oh, the beast," she whispered. "Poor stupid Victoire."

"So he demanded money in exchange for the letters?"

"Yes. He asked for far more than I had. My husband is wealthy—he owns two foundries and they make cannon for the army—but he rarely gives me money. Saint-Ange wanted fifty louis in gold. I told him I would bring him what I could. Today . . . today was the fourth time I'd come. I thought I should never be free of him." She broke off, eyes pleading. "Have you found the letters?"

Aristide shook his head. "Not yet. If the police find them, I assure you the commissaire or I will take great pleasure in handing them back to you ourselves."

"And now we can guess why the dead girl was there," said Dautry after Madame Beaumontel had left them, discreetly veiled once more.

"Well, he couldn't have secured such a comfortable income from a few rents." Aristide grimaced. "Go on back to headquarters. I'll come by shortly, after I lambaste Didier for overstepping his authority."

"He won't take kindly to you telling him off."

"I really don't care. When will that man remember it's no longer 1793?"

Aristide returned to the commissariat and elbowed his way to Brasseur's office through the midmorning crush of inspectors, clerks, complainants, and the inevitable half-dozen men and women of all sorts and conditions who were presumably spies with information to sell, waiting furtively or patiently on benches in the outer chamber. He found Brasseur looking much more pleased with himself than before.

"Here's another stroke of luck. The girl from Rue du Hasard's been identified." He waved a creased form at Aristide. "Just as you suggested; she's no cheap slut. Her father visited the morgue at the Basse-Geôle yesterday and identified her; her name is Célie Montereau."

"Montereau?" Aristide echoed him. "Wasn't there a member of the National Convention named Montereau, an ex-aristocrat, quite wealthy . . ."

"The same. Honoré-Charles-Éléonor Montereau, formerly the

Comte de Soyecourt. We're to question him this afternoon, after a visit to the morgue to see what they have to say there. In Montereau's mansion in the faubourg Germain if you please. You'll have to show me how to mind my manners in a house like that."

"My uncle was a lawyer, not a duke," Aristide said absently as he followed Brasseur through the clamor of the antechamber. Brasseur grunted.

It was market day outside the Châtelet and their hired fiacre rolled slowly through the disorderly cluster of farm carts and stalls, where leather-throated vendors hawked their wares. Cabbages, turnips, onions, and apples lay stacked in careful pyramids beside cheeses, sausages, and jumbled heaps of old clothes and shoes, the tattered castoffs of the prosperous. Amid the bustle, the beggars shuffled or crouched in corners, mutely stretching out grimy hands.

The fiacre left the marketplace behind and approached the looming walls of the Châtelet to halt in a gloomy, vaulted passage of sooty masonry that provided a public way through the center of the old fortress. To their left, a small door led to the Basse-Geôle de la Seine, the morgue where unidentified corpses and victims of violent death were sent. Leaving Dautry, who refused to accompany them inside, behind in the cab, Brasseur exchanged a few words with the dour clerk on duty. They passed through a grille that the clerk unlocked for them, and the faint odor of spoiled meat drifted to their nostrils as they descended a short staircase.

The stagnant smell was far stronger in the chill, lamplit cellar below, hanging like fog over the half-dozen shrouded figures lying on their stone tables. A second clerk, a pop-eyed man with a long, mournful face like a bloodhound, straightened as they approached, tugged a sheet back over a corpse, and plunged his hands into a basin of dirty water.

"Morning, Bouille," said Brasseur. "Do you have anything more for us about the Rue du Hasard murders?"

"Here's my report," said the concierge with a quick swallow from his pocket flask. Aristide glanced over Brasseur's shoulder. Deceased, female, had been identified by her father as Marie-Célie-Josèphe-Élisabeth Montereau, age twenty-two years and five months, in good health and well-nourished, bearing no scars or highly individual features. Examination of the corpse had revealed a wound consistent with a single shot to the heart from a small firearm, as stated in the police surgeon's report. Deceased had worn one chemise of good linen, one gown of white muslin bearing no marks or repairs (other than such damage caused by the shot that had killed deceased), one rose-pink carmagnole jacket of lightweight wool showing little wear (other than the aforementioned damage), one pair red leather shoes without high heels and showing little wear, one pair thread stockings showing little wear, one scarf of pink cashmere. . . .

Brasseur glanced quickly over the second sheet, the report on Louis Saint-Ange, rolled the papers into a tube, and tapped it against his lips. "Nothing much new here."

"Might I see the girl?" Aristide said.

Bouille shuffled to one of the draped forms and folded back the sheet. Aristide gazed at the pallid, pretty young face, calm and inscrutable in death, and raised a hand to brush away a stray thread that had fallen across her cheek.

Bouille glanced at his notes. "Do you want to see the other one? We're done with them, and the identification's in order. The relatives can claim them whenever they like."

"Who formally identified Saint-Ange?" Brasseur asked. "His servant?"

"Hmmm . . . Barthélemy Thibault, domestic official, identified him; and the girl's father, citizen Montereau, confirmed it."

"Montereau!"

Bouille nodded. "We showed him the second corpse, just as a matter of form, and Montereau recognized him. Seemed very surprised. Claimed he was a relation."

"Well, well." Brasseur wrote a few lines in his notebook. "Nothing else?"

"Sorry. Be sure to tell the relatives they can claim the bodies," Bouille reminded them as they retreated. "Daude's done with the inventory of the clothing and effects. He's very efficient that way."

Very efficient, Aristide thought as they climbed the steps out of the corpse-stink.

6

After a quarter hour at the Basse-Geôle, neither Aristide nor Brasseur felt inclined toward more luncheon than a roll and a stiff two-sou glass of cheap brandy, commonly known as eau-de-vie or "water of life," from a street hawker. They continued to the faubourg Germain and, telling the cabman to wait, alighted from their fiacre in a spacious, cobbled courtyard. A groom hurried forward to lead the horse to a marble watering-trough.

The manservant who led them inside wore no aristocratic livery, but the republican austerity of 1793 and 1794 seemed to have made little other impression on the ex–Comte de Soyecourt's manner of living. A chilly, elegant marble foyer led upstairs to a series of richly furnished antechambers and salons, hung with satin curtains and decorated with delicate carved and painted paneling, where silent servants were hanging black draperies over windows, mirrors, chandeliers, and clocks. Montereau rose from a writing-desk to meet them as they entered the library.

"Citizen Commissaire? They told me at—at the Basse-Geôle that someone would call. Coffee for the citizens, Michel," he added to the lackey.

Aristide took stock of Montereau as Brasseur introduced himself and Dautry pulled out his notebook. The dead girl's father was thickset and dark, lines of grief marking what would have been in better times a good-natured, though harassed, countenance beneath an untidy powdered wig.

"This is all so terribly sudden," he said, hastily thrusting away a handkerchief. "To be occupying myself with offers for her hand one day, and then to order her coffin the next; but this . . . she was in excellent health, I never suspected . . ."

He absently scratched his head, pushing his wig askew, and rubbed his eyes. An amiable untidiness seemed to be the essence of Montereau's temperament, Aristide thought. Though his black silk frock coat was finely tailored, its cut was some years out of fashion and it hung on his sturdy shoulders as if he had been wearing a peasant's smock.

Aristide seated himself on the nearest chair. Brasseur gingerly lowered his large frame onto a graceful Louis XV sofa and perched on the edge. Across the ceiling above them, simpering cherubs surrounded a pair of nude pagan gods who reclined among rosy clouds. Brasseur glanced upward, blushed, and tried to look as if he saw such suggestive opulence every day.

"They told me my daughter had been murdered," Montereau said. "Who—who could have done such a thing?"

"We hope to find that out, citizen Montereau," Brasseur told him, "but it looks as if she was just the victim of bad luck, in the wrong place at the wrong time. When was the last time you saw your daughter?"

"*Décadi*, in the morning. The day she disappeared. We—we breakfasted together as we usually did. Then I went to the Tuileries to meet—pardon me, the National Palace—to meet some friends; I joined them for dinner at Méot's, and didn't return home until nearly eleven o'clock that evening."

Aristide nodded. Méot was a fashionable and expensive *restaurateur* near the Palais-Égalité and Montereau's presence there could be easily verified.

"Célie wasn't here when I returned. Her maid told me she had gone out on an errand."

"What sort of errand?" said Aristide.

"I don't know. Pierrette didn't know. Célie left at about five o'clock, after she'd dined, and said she would be gone only an hour or two. She said she was only going on an errand. . . ."

"Did your daughter often go out alone?" Brasseur inquired.

"Usually she took Pierrette with her—her maid—but now and then she insisted she could go alone. She could . . . she could take care of herself, she claimed, and after all she was twenty-two. She was so delicate and gentle, but though she didn't look it she had a mind of her own." A maid arrived with the coffee tray and Aristide accepted a cup, balancing it in his hands as Montereau continued. "There was no danger in going out alone, she said, not in going abroad in a respectable neighborhood in full daylight."

The coffee was strong and bitter. Out of the corner of his eye Aristide saw Brasseur, who preferred his coffee well sugared, grimacing at the peculiar tastes of the well-to-do.

"Citizen, they told us you identified the body of Louis Saint-Ange."

"He is—was—a distant cousin of my first wife's. I couldn't believe my eyes when I recognized him. Why was my daughter's body found in his lodgings? What has he to do with this? We've not seen him for years . . . since 'eighty-nine. He emigrated to Saint-Domingue. Of course, we were not close; his reputation was a trifle unsavory."

"Well," Brasseur said, "it seems that Saint-Ange might have had some kind of hold over your daughter."

"Hold?"

"He might have possessed some secret of hers that she wouldn't have wanted spread about. He seems to have made a living from extortion."

"Extortion?" Montereau echoed him. "That scarcely surprises me, from what I remember of him, but what possible hold could he have had over Célie?"

"No doubt it was something quite trivial," Aristide said. "Can you think of any other reason why Citizeness Montereau should have been calling upon Saint-Ange?"

Montereau slowly shook his head. "None. She would never—I would have sworn an oath that she would never have gone alone and called on a young man, even a distant relative. She would never have risked her reputation in such a fashion. Dear God—what secret would she have feared to reveal to me?"

Brasseur set his cup and saucer aside on a pearl-inlaid table and began to scribble his own notes in addition to the transcript Dautry was meticulously recording. "No chance there might have been a . . . a clandestine affair of the heart—maybe with somebody unsuitable?"

"Citizen! My daughter was not that sort of woman!" Montereau exclaimed. "If I'd ever supposed otherwise, I'd—I'd—" He stopped abruptly and clamped his lips shut. "I was about to say," he continued, more calmly, after a pause to collect himself, "that I would have killed the man who dared to take advantage of her. But those would seem to be injudicious words at such an occasion . . ." His voice trailed off and he blew his nose loudly.

"Who lives here with you, citizen, beside the domestics?" Brasseur inquired, glancing up from his notebook.

"Only my children—" Montereau checked himself and drew a deep breath. "Only my son and I, now. . . ."

An image flashed across Aristide's mind, that of an aristocratic, quick-tempered youth disposing of an enemy as he might shoot a marauding wolf, and then killing his own sister for the sake of outraged family honor. "We shall have to question your son."

"Théodore?" said Montereau, bewildered. "My son is barely six years old."

Relieved, Aristide raised an inquisitive eyebrow. Many years lay between a daughter of twenty-two and a son of six.

"It might be useful to talk to him," Brasseur said. "Children notice things, you know."

Yes, Aristide thought, children often had a way of noticing things that should better have remained hidden. He swiftly fixed his gaze on a tall, royal blue porcelain vase with gilt handles, which probably had cost more than Brasseur earned in a year.

"Dear me," Montereau added, "sometimes I don't see her for days at a time: my late wife's old great-aunt, Madame de—pardon me, Citizeness Laroque, lives here. She's nearly a cripple and rarely leaves her rooms."

Brasseur scribbled another note. "And the old lady, too, then, if she's, er, got her wits about her. Did she know Saint-Ange?"

"No, I'm sure she never did; Saint-Ange was related to my first wife, and madame to my second."

"Were she and Célie at all close?" said Aristide.

"Close?" echoed Montereau. "Well, she's ninety-four; I doubt they shared a great deal in common. But Célie was fond of her, to be sure. She often visited her."

"Then perhaps the citizeness can help us," Aristide said, "if only by allowing us to understand your daughter better. Women, of whatever age, share secrets with each other more readily than they share them with men, especially fathers."

"Very well, if you wish." Montereau rang the bell again.

"You go," Brasseur muttered to Aristide. "I'll see to the servants. I'm sure you can manage an old dowager better than I can."

A lackey led Aristide through corridors and up stairways to a distant wing of the house. A curtseying maidservant gestured him inside to a cozy, shabby parlor that smelled of lavender and, more perceptibly, of cats, and shyly announced him as "Monsieur Ravel." A tiny, wrinkled, black-clad woman, wisps of white hair escaping from beneath her old-fashioned frilled bonnet, peered up at him from the white cat in her lap as he approached her wheeled chair and bowed.

"And who might you be?"

Despite her age, her voice was strong, and the eyes she turned to him were bright and lively. Calling this aristocratic old lady "citizeness" would only vex her, Aristide decided, or at best confuse her.

"I am an agent of the police, madame."

"The police!" she exclaimed, clutching reflexively at the cat's thick fur. The cat, disturbed, turned drowsy blue eyes toward him. Madame de Laroque clucked and took a scrap from a half-eaten plate of roast quail and peas beside her. "No kin of mine has ever been entangled with the police," she declared, feeding the cat. "Of course, there was that unpleasantness with poor Marsillac," she added, waving a vague hand toward a portrait on the wall, "but he suffered for his indiscretions in the end . . . well! What is it you want from me?"

"My business here regards your great-grand-niece, madame," Aristide said.

"Poor Célie," sighed Madame de Laroque, continuing to feed the cat bits of quail. "Poor child. And after our family withstood this horrid revolution with nothing more than a few inconveniences . . . and I'm told so many people did lose someone close to them . . . after all that, to have some monster kill poor little Célie . . . it *must* have been a madman. No one could have deliberately murdered her, no one who knew her." She paused and peered at him. "Are you wearing mourning for the king, too?"

Aristide found himself speechless for an instant before realizing she had mistaken his black suit for mourning costume. He could scarcely remember a time when he had not worn the same austere black; he had worn mourning for his mother and father, as he was told to, when he was nine years old, and somehow had never abandoned it.

"Police officials customarily wear black suits, madame."

"A police official," she mused. "The royal lieutenants of police are commonly *noblesse de robe*, I believe, like the magistrates, buying their titles; not *real* nobility. But most of them are of good family, if not quite genuine aristocracy. Are you a gentleman?"

"I hope so, madame."

Somehow, Aristide thought, the Revolution seemed to have passed Madame de Laroque by without making very much impression upon her. How could one tell such a woman, anchored in the prerevolutionary past, that there was no more royal lieutenant of police in Paris, no more "nobility of the robe" in France, no more nobility at all?

"I shall give you the benefit of the doubt. You may sit down."

Aristide took the armchair she pointed out to him, after evicting an enormous, sleepy black-and-white cat. "Please, if you would, tell me about Célie."

"I don't know what I can tell you. A young thing of twenty isn't likely to seek advice from an old relic like me. The world has changed so much, you know, since I was a girl. The Grand Monarch himself was still alive in those days, think of that!" She paused, sighing and shaking her head. "To think I could live to see the day when the rabble would actually spill the king's blood. If the Grand Monarch had been alive . . ." She stroked the white cat's head and it arched its neck, purring. "I call *him* the Sun King, just as a little joke, because he's so regal. Isn't he beautiful?"

"He's very handsome," Aristide agreed. The black-and-white cat leaped onto his lap and he absently scratched its chin. "Madame, what did you and Célie talk about when she visited you? Did she confide in you?"

"Look, Mouchette likes you. What did we talk about? Oh . . . whatever crossed our minds. My grand-niece—her mother—died four years ago, and I imagine Célie brought me the little quandaries she'd otherwise have taken to her mother. Just small matters of friends and etiquette and so on. Once or twice she said her father had mentioned offers of marriage. She was already in love, of course, and prospective marriage does put a damper on one's young love affairs."

"In love?" Aristide echoed her.

Madame de Laroque uttered a sound he interpreted as a refined and ladylike snort. "She was keeping it a secret from her father, I suppose, but it was plain as the nose on your face. Five or six months she came here all smiles and misty-eyed. You can't hide that when you're a chit of twenty. Are you married, young man?"

Aristide shook his head. "No, madame."

"How well do *you* know women?"

"Not well, I fear."

The old lady snorted again. "I see. Well, I say Célie was in love, no matter what her father may know, or not know. But I'd guess something soured the affair in the end. She wasn't at all happy the last half-dozen times I saw her."

"No?"

"Worried, under some strain. I expect her sweetheart had discarded her, though how any man could reject a girl as pretty and tenderhearted as Célie, I'll never know. But men are often like that. They grow bored with simple goodness and want a woman who is dangerous, a challenge. My great-nephew Marsillac was precisely that sort." She glanced at the portrait on the wall. Aristide followed her gaze. An elegant young man of about thirty, impeccably curled and powdered in the style of 1780, sat gazing coolly out from the painting. "He had a bad reputation, I fear," the old lady continued, "though he was always courteous and thoughtful to me. But then, he was my heir," she added dryly, and fell silent.

"He is dead?" Aristide said, hoping to start her talking again.

"Killed in a duel, after debauching one too many women. It was a highly unpleasant scandal. Dear, dear . . . poor Marsillac . . . ah, well, it was years ago. What else do you wish to ask me, monsieur?"

"Did Célie ever ask you for money?"

"Money?" said Madame de Laroque sharply. "Yes, in fact she did, not long ago. Said it was terribly urgent. I hadn't much, but I did have a valuable necklace that I gave her. It ought to have gone to Célie's mother, but poor Marie-Josèphe died young, too, so it would have gone to Célie in any case when I died." She shook her head. "We seem to have had more than our share of misfortune in this family of late. First Marsillac, then Josèphe, now poor Célie. And I am convinced it was the doctor who killed Josèphe; she was expecting, and had a miscarriage, and bled to death. And that butcher thought cupping her and bleeding her was the best remedy! Poor Josèphe had had a strong, healthy child just two years before, that scamp Théodore, so I don't see why she should have died of the next one. And she was only thirty-eight. I don't suppose you could arrest that doctor and have him up for murder?"

"No, I fear not, madame, not after so much time has passed."

Madame de Laroque sighed. "Pity. Give me a good trained midwife any day, not these charlatans who spout their Latin. *They've* never had a baby, have they? Let them stick to setting bones and lancing boils."

Aristide disengaged the cat from his lap and rose, brushing away stray hairs. "I apologize once again for this intrusion—"

"No intrusion, young man. You've diverted me for a quarter of an hour. Perhaps," she added with the air of a queen granting favors, "you will visit me again soon, and tell me what you've learned."

"Of course, madame."

"Célie's to be buried tomorrow, Honoré tells me. I daresay you may join the procession if you're able to. Ten o'clock."

"If I'm not otherwise engaged." He avoided funerals when he could; they reminded him far too much of matters he would rather have forgotten.

"Of course," added the old lady, "you would spend your time more profitably in finding the wretch who killed her. Anyone who could have hurt a dear girl like that—you wouldn't understand, I suppose, unless you'd known her. Merry and generous and kind-hearted, always, until this silly trouble with a sweetheart. . . . You ought to have seen her with the child, young Théodore. Most girls wouldn't bother themselves about a baby brother who was sixteen years younger; they're far more interested in balls, and new gowns, and dancing and weddings. But as soon as the boy came back from his wet nurse, Célie adored him, and dandled and cosseted him as if he was a new lapdog, and Josèphe let her do as she liked. Sometimes I think she was generous to a fault—it's a mercy he hasn't become a spoiled little monster. But he's an agreeable child, thank Providence, in spite of her indulging him. Have you met the lad yet?"

Aristide shook his head. "Not yet."

"Talk to him if you can; small boys always know things. I expect you to find this brute who killed Célie, do you hear me? And send him to the scaffold as he deserves. I hear they've done away with hanging, and with breaking on the wheel?"

"Yes, madame." He kept his voice steady, indifferent. "Several years ago."

"And now every criminal is allowed to be beheaded, like a gentleman?"

"Yes."

"That's far too good for them," she said with a snap of her mouth like an old, ill-tempered tortoise, and rang the bell for her maid.

7

"I hope your visit didn't distress madame overmuch?" Montereau inquired when Aristide returned, still brushing away white hairs from his waistcoat, to the study where Brasseur and the ex-count awaited him.

"Not at all. Citizen, with your permission, I think we ought to search your daughter's rooms."

Montereau rose and led the way. As they approached the broad, curving staircase, a small, fair-haired boy raced down it and skidded to a stop before them.

"Are you the police?" he demanded.

"My son, Théodore," Montereau said. He let his hand linger for a moment on the boy's disheveled head before stepping aside and murmuring, "I've not yet told him what has happened; all he knows is that Célie is missing."

"Yes, we're the police," said Brasseur, kindly. "I am Commissaire Brasseur and these are Citizens Ravel and Dautry."

"I want to be a gendarme or a soldier and ride on a horse," the boy announced. "They have swords, and mustaches, and splendid uniforms. Not like those," he added, staring from Brasseur to Aristide. The funereal ensemble worn by police officials—black coat, hat, waistcoat, culotte, stockings, and shoes, relieved only by a discreet white cravat—

had remained unchanged throughout the Revolution save for the addition of a tricolor sash or cockade.

"Théodore, that's not polite," his father said.

Aristide summoned a slight smile. "Let him be, citizen. . . . It's the mounted gendarmes who draw all the attention, it's true, while the police go about looking like undertakers." Though he privately thought the austere costume suited him, a little self-deprecation often served to put nervous witnesses at ease.

"But do you know what, young Théodore?" said Brasseur. "Those gendarmes in their fancy uniforms are just for show; it's the commissaires who do all the real work, and catch the criminals and send them to justice." He patted the boy's cheek and moved on toward the staircase.

The boy tagged along behind them as they entered the rooms Célie Montereau had occupied. The bedchamber and boudoir were airy and feminine in white and pale spring green. The painted panels of the boiseries lining the walls complemented the figured bed curtains and the rich emerald velvet window curtains and brocade upholstery of the footstools, chairs, and love seat.

Aristide glanced over the small stack of books on a side table. *The Castle of Néville, or, The Orphan Heiress*, read one pair of tooled leather spines. *Works of the Abbé Delille.* The breathless tale of *Caroline, or, The Vicissitudes of Fortune*, filled another three small volumes. Shaking his head at youthful female taste, he shook the books one by one as Brasseur and Dautry advanced gingerly toward the wardrobe and chest of drawers. Aristide did not expect to find anything there, although sometimes girls, like his sister Thérèse, might hide secrets among their underlinen.

Nothing fell from the books but a milliner's bill and a few pressed and faded flowers. He turned to the dressing table, thinking of Madame Beaumontel and her jewelry box. He reached for the lid to Célie's, found it locked as he expected, and turned to Montereau.

"May I?"

Montereau nodded. Aristide took a ring of false keys from his pocket and forced the simple lock. He could have as easily opened it with a hairpin, he thought, eyeing a small porcelain jar of them on the dressing table; why did women assume their darkest secrets would be safe in such fragile coffers?

No secret letters, no compromising notes lay inside. He lifted out a colorful bead necklace, judged it to be glass, and replaced it. A pair of tarnished silver earrings, a cameo on a black velvet ribbon, a cloisonné brooch, and a few hair ornaments studded with glass gems completed the inventory.

"Did your daughter have much jewelry?" he asked Montereau, after prodding the lining to be sure Célie had hidden nothing beneath the sky-blue silk.

"A few valuable pieces. A diamond brooch that was a gift from her godmother, and I'd given her a pair of pearl bracelets for her sixteenth birthday. She also wore some of my late wife's jewelry now and then, on special occasions, when we entertained."

"I see no pearl bracelets or diamond brooches here." Aristide stepped aside so that Montereau could peer into the jewelry box.

"Bless me—what has become of it all?"

"I saw her take away some things," piped a voice. Aristide turned to the boy, startled.

"She was going out of the house and she had a little packet wrapped up in a handkerchief and she dropped it and a ring fell out." Théodore stepped up to the dressing table and solemnly eyed the near-empty jewelry box. "It's not here, and it's—it had a green stone in it. Célie said it was our mamma's."

"What did your sister tell you she was doing with the ring?" Aristide asked him.

"She didn't say anything. She just took the ring and told me not to tell anybody that I saw her going out."

"When was this, Théodore?"

The boy shifted from one foot to another, pulling at his lower lip. "I don't know. This summer."

"That's very helpful. Thank you."

Théodore grinned. A handsome boy, with traces of Célie's delicate features, Aristide mused, though he favored his stocky father not at all.

"But what does this mean?" Montereau demanded after sending Théodore back to the nursery. "Why would Célie have disposed of her jewels? To give to Saint-Ange? Why would anyone coerce Célie?" He sat heavily on the nearest footstool and pushed his wig more askew than ever. "I know nothing that could be held against my daughter. She is . . . she was a lovely girl. She was modest and virtuous and a man couldn't have wished for a dearer child."

"You're sure she had no—forgive me—no entanglements with any young men?" Aristide asked him, wondering if Montereau had been as observant as had Madame de Laroque.

"Certainly not. She scarcely looked at young men. I'd spoken of marriage to her, of course, but only to mention a few suitable young gentlemen who had approached me regarding her hand. She only said she was not yet eager to marry, and I respected her wishes. She never gave me any reason to think she had already given her heart to another."

"Nevertheless, it seems Saint-Ange had some sort of hold over her."

"I cannot think what," said Montereau, shaking his head.

"We'll know more when they're done searching his apartment," Brasseur said. "We'll be as discreet as possible. Meanwhile," he added, glancing at his notes, "perhaps you could call your daughter's maid, and give me the addresses of her friends. We'll need to question them."

Pierrette arrived in answer to the summons. Pierrette was most distressed. Her mistress had been such a sweet young lady, so pretty and gentle. It must have been some horrible bandit who had killed her, for no one would want to kill a lovely young creature like Ma'm'selle who didn't have an enemy in the world.

At length Brasseur broke through the torrent of words and inquired about the last time she had seen Célie.

Why, it was just as she had told the master. At quarter to five Ma'm'selle Célie had said she was going out. No, she hadn't said where, just on an errand. Yes, her mistress often went out by herself, but usually she visited friends, very respectable friends; there was no harm in that, was there?

Aristide agreed there was no harm in that. Pierrette turned a pert, wide-eyed face to his and continued, a faint blush creeping along her cheeks. She'd supposed Ma'm'selle had visited a friend who'd invited her to the theater. Most of Ma'm'selle's friends were married ladies who kept boxes at the theater or the opera house, and after the performance they would ordinarily send her home in their carriages. Ma'm'selle didn't often care to be burdened with a chaperon unless it was Pierrette herself. Poor Ma'm'selle had grown very independent, though she was sweet as ever, since her poor mother had died; perhaps she'd risked her reputation just the tiniest bit, but surely no one could imagine any wickedness of her. Ma'm'selle Célie had been dreadfully ill some years back, though she'd recovered well enough, and perhaps surviving an illness like that made you fearless of anything that might come.

"Go on, please," Aristide told her, attempting to ignore her gaze. He had no idea why some women seemed to find him appealing; he had never flattered himself that he was a pretty fellow, lean and somber as he was, though he might admit he was not altogether ill-favored.

She hadn't been there herself when Ma'm'selle Célie had been so ill, she'd only been engaged two years ago, but she'd heard all about it. Abed for months, she was, the poor thing, and it must have been something catching, for her mother had forbidden any of the servants to do for her; Madame had cared for her all by herself and brought her all her meals. . . .

With difficulty, Brasseur returned to the subject of Célie's friends. Who was her closest friend?

That would be Citizeness Villemain, who lived on Rue du Bac, not far away. They had been friends since they were little girls, before the Revolution. A very well-bred married lady. And there was another lady, a Citizeness Clément, that Ma'm'selle Célie was very friendly with, though the citizeness didn't often call at the house. A lady from a family of quality before the Revolution, Ma'm'selle Célie had said, but with no fortune. She thought Citizeness Clément lived in a boardinghouse near the Luxembourg Palace; the coachman would know, for Ma'm'selle Célie had sometimes visited her friend's lodgings.

With some relief, Brasseur concluded the interview and sent Pierrette on her way with a five-sou piece in her pocket. The other servants could say only that their mistress had been the sweetest and kindest of young ladies. Avoiding Montereau's persistent questions, Brasseur thanked him for his assistance, assured him he would inform him as soon as they learned anything, and departed the house.

"Rue du Bac, I think," Brasseur said as they returned to their fiacre. "This friend of hers might know something."

"I'd rather go back first to the Basse-Geôle," said Aristide.

"Good God, what for?"

"Just a hunch."

Brasseur shrugged and told the driver to return to the Châtelet. "What's this to do with Saint-Ange's murder?" he inquired as the fiacre jolted out of the courtyard.

"Nothing much, I fear; but I like to have my questions answered. I have my suspicions about Célie Montereau's secret."

"You think she wasn't as innocent as her father would believe?"

"That's usually the secret young girls want to keep from their parents. And that long illness of hers—no severe illness is contagious for months on end, is it?"

Brasseur frowned, but Aristide said nothing else until they had arrived at the cellar beneath the Châtelet again. "Bouille," Aristide said to the concierge as they stood over Célie's shrouded body, "when you take inventory and examine a corpse, do you look for anything other than to confirm the police-surgeon's opinion as to the cause of death?"

"What do you mean?"

"Well . . . I wondered if you, or a doctor, had ascertained whether or not this young woman was a virgin."

"You're not asking him to . . ." Brasseur demanded, outraged. "God in Heaven!"

"We think she was in Saint-Ange's apartment because he was extorting money from her," Aristide said, unruffled by his companion's indignation. "But what sort of frightful secret could a well-bred girl like Célie Montereau have to hide, except for something that would, if revealed, ruin her reputation? I know it's a matter of some delicacy . . . but I'd like to see my suspicions confirmed."

"That's not part of the usual examination, no," Bouille mumbled. He turned his dolorous gaze to Brasseur, who scowled and swiftly nodded. Aristide turned away as Bouille lifted the sheet and bent over the young woman's corpse.

"You're right," said Bouille, a moment later.

"Not a virgin?"

"No."

"Could you tell if, perhaps, she had given birth to a child?" Aristide said.

Bouille frowned and took a swallow from his pocket flask. "Well, I'm no doctor, though I've studied a few medical books, and I shouldn't like to voice any slanderous accusations without proof . . . but working here I've seen a great many corpses, and just between you and me I would say it's very likely indeed. Not recently, though."

"Ha," said Brasseur, as Aristide nodded. "More than enough for extortion. Though I don't know how far I'd trust that drunk's opinion," he muttered to Aristide, out of Bouille's hearing.

A career spent examining and stripping an incessant stream of corpses in various stages of putrescence, Aristide thought, might drive any man to drink.

"Best not say anything to her father about it, if we see him again," Brasseur cautioned him as they left the cellar. "He doesn't need a second nasty shock." Aristide nodded again without speaking.

So that fragile young creature, who scarcely looked at young men, had not been as chaste as she seemed.

To whom, he wondered, would the extortioner have threatened to reveal Célie Montereau's shame? Father, sweetheart . . . the world?

They returned to the Left Bank and Rue du Bac to call on Hélène Villemain, who received them in her elegant teal blue parlor, a silent footman in attendance.

"I don't know what I can tell you," she said, pouring them tiny cups of hot chocolate. "I'm shocked and grieved at Célie's death, of course."

Aristide had planned to be more circumspect, but decided the calm young woman before him, eyes swollen but otherwise composed, could endure plain speaking. "Did you know it's likely someone was extorting payment from Célie?"

Hélène abruptly set down the chocolate-pot. "Gracious, no. Whatever can have brought you to that conclusion? Do you have proof?"

"We think so."

"I did warn her she sometimes behaved a little too independently for a young unmarried woman." She shook her head and abstractedly patted at a few dark curls that had escaped from beneath the pins and ribbons keeping her fashionable Grecian coiffure in place. "But surely no one would have found it worth his while to force money from her for a few minor indiscretions."

"Not minor; there's indication that . . . that she had had a lover once."

Hélène said nothing for a moment, absentmindedly stirring her chocolate. "That explains it, then. That explains quite a lot I never dared ask her about." She abruptly dismissed the hovering servant, then turned back to Aristide and Brasseur. "You won't let her father know about our conversation, will you, unless it's absolutely necessary?" Aristide glanced at Brasseur and silently shook his head.

"Well then; Célie and I were at the same convent, but I was two years older. When I left Sainte-Cécile's, Célie was exactly the sort of person you expect an aristocratic, convent-educated girl to be: well-mannered, accomplished, religious, shy, and completely ignorant of the . . . the essential facts of human existence. She came home the following year—late in 'eighty-nine, when she was fifteen—and she was just the same. But then I was taken to England for three months, and during that time Célie changed somehow, became more assertive, more self-confident. Now that I think back, I realize the difference was that between a shy, inexperienced girl and a married woman. Or a girl who is no longer so inexperienced."

"So young," Aristide said. "Do you believe at that age it was a genuine love affair, or that some rake seduced her?"

"Oh, I'd suspect the latter, wouldn't you? Célie adored reading silly novels when she was at Sainte-Cécile's. We hid them from the nuns, you know," she added with a melancholy smile. "If she'd truly fallen in love, he would have been the sort of virtuous young prig who would write tearful poems about her and wait for marriage. Like the hero of a novel. But one thing more I think you should know," she continued, her brow puckering with the effort of recollection. "It all fits with what you tell me. Some time after I returned from England, Célie fell ill and was confined to her bed for several months, and they let no one come near her."

Aristide nodded. "She was pregnant."

"Yes, I think she must have been."

"And her mother knew?"

"Of course. Célie must have hidden herself away, with her mother's connivance, as soon as she could no longer conceal her condition simply by loosening her bodice."

"But what became of Célie's child?"

"Who knows?" said Hélène with a sigh. "It may have been stillborn, or died soon after birth. If not, I expect Madame Montereau handed it over to some petty bourgeois family or hard-up country squire who was to adopt it. I doubt Célie's father ever knew anything of it; I recall he was away in Russia, something to do with the Foreign Ministry, for most of Célie's 'illness.' Come to think of it, she and her mother went to the country for a month for her health, or so they said, and she was completely recovered by the time he arrived home."

"Now *that's* a secret you don't want to see exposed," said Brasseur. "You don't imagine *he* found out about it, and—"

"And murdered his own daughter for the sake of the family honor?" Aristide said. "No, unless I'm sadly mistaken, he's not the man to do that. And he said he was at Méot's, which can be confirmed easily enough. But Saint-Ange must have learned of the existence of this bastard child. A rumor of a youthful indiscretion might be laughed off, but living proof of an indiscretion is not so easily hidden."

"Poor Célie," murmured Hélène.

"Did you ever have any idea who this lover—or seducer—might have been?"

"None at all. I told you she had grown more self-confident in her manner. But at the same time, she grew cool toward young men. She must have resolved never to make the same mistake again."

"It would surprise you to know, then, that she was secretly in love?"

She stared at Aristide for an instant. "Yes, it would. Who?"

"We were hoping you could tell us. Do you know anyone to whom she might have been attracted? Someone like 'the hero of a novel,' as you said?"

"No. That is . . . I know of one young man, the son of a banker, who might be the sentimental sort. Célie knew him; we often met him at the theater. Feydeau de la Beyré. I believe he lives somewhere near the Place Vendôme, by the Boulevard."

"Probably a comfortable bachelor apartment, if he's a wealthy young sprig of a banking family," said Aristide as Brasseur scribbled down the name.

"But if he and Célie were in love, I don't see why she would have preserved such secrecy. I doubt her father would have objected to him as a son-in-law. He is rich, of respectable though not noble family, and I've never heard anything against him." She rose. "Please, call on me if I can be of any more assistance. And, Commissaire—find whoever did this."

8

Montereau's coachman had provided Brasseur with an address for Célie's other friend, Citizeness Clément, who lived in a cheap boardinghouse near the Sorbonne. While Brasseur returned to the Right Bank and his reports, Aristide turned his own steps toward the Latin Quarter.

"I keep a respectable house here," the landlady repeated for the third time, over her shoulder, as she led Aristide to the fifth-floor attic and sourly scratched on the door. "If one of my lodgers is mixed up in something illegal, I'm sure I know nothing about it, nor do any of the other lodgers. They're quiet, respectable folk. I'll thank you not to let it be known that somebody from the police has been asking questions in *my* establishment. Citizeness Clément! A person is here to see you!"

Aristide assured her his visit was no imputation on her character and shouldered aside her assertions of law-abiding propriety as the door opened a crack, revealing a pale, unsmiling young woman. "Are you Citizeness Rosalie Clément?" he said. "I represent the police of the Butte-des-Moulins section."

"What do you want?" she demanded, eyeing him. "And what are you doing here on the Left Bank? Don't you inspectors stay inside your own sections?"

"I'm not an inspector, citizeness; merely an unofficial agent of the police. I'm trying to learn all I can about Célie Montereau."

"Why on earth should the police be inquiring about Célie?"

"Do you not know? Has no one told you, sent a message?"

She shook her head. "About what?"

"Citizeness Montereau . . . is dead."

"Dead!"

"You didn't know?"

"Dear God, no. I suppose no one thought to tell me. I—" She bowed her head for a moment as she fumbled for a handkerchief. "I . . . I didn't move in the same circles as Célie's other acquaintances."

"Were you close?"

"We were good friends," she continued, more calmly, "though perhaps not as intimate as she and her school friend were."

The landlady nodded. "Citizeness Montereau called quite often. She arrived in her own carriage," she added. "The other lodgers were most impressed."

"Perhaps you can help me," Aristide said to Rosalie. "May I come inside?"

"Certainly not," Rosalie said with a glance at the landlady. "Citizeness Deluc wouldn't approve at all." He heard a subtle undertone of laughter in her voice, despite the tears she tried to blink away, as she continued. She was more attractive than he had thought at first glance, and her dark eyes were intelligent. "But I'm sure she wouldn't mind if we had a decorous conversation in the parlor."

She led the way downstairs to an unheated salon, where heavy, faded velvet curtains seemed to shut away the last traces of the feeble autumn daylight. The Maison Deluc had been someone's fine town house fifty years ago, but the opulence of the paneled rococo salon was now threadbare in many places. Empty ovals above the windows and the pair of dingy white double doors spoke of overdoor paintings sold one by one, and the paint was flaking from the fingers and noses of the cherubs lurking in the moldings.

A small puff of dust rose from the upholstery as Rosalie sat down on a well-worn sofa. "Now. How can I help you? Would you care for some coffee? I can ask the cook for some, if you'd like."

"Thank you, no," Aristide told her, imagining what sort of coffee was probably served at that down-at-heel boardinghouse. He looked about him at the threadbare room, thinking how the shabby young woman opposite him seemed to belong there, with her unmistakable air of proud, faded gentility. "How did you and Célie meet, citizeness?"

"In the gardens of the Luxembourg; we met there frequently, walking, and eventually became friends." She leaned forward, hands clasped tightly in her lap. "What happened? I've not seen her for several days. Did she fall ill? Was it an accident?"

"She was murdered."

There was no way to soften the brutal word, no matter how he might try.

"Murdered . . ."

"Though she seems not to have been the intended victim; they found her in the lodgings of a man she scarcely knew, his own body nearby. No one we've questioned thus far has had any motive to harm her."

"Of course they wouldn't," Rosalie said promptly. "It's ridiculous."

"Citizeness, did Célie ever talk to you about a love affair?"

Rosalie clasped her hands and gazed at the moth-eaten carpet at her feet, her brow puckered. Her eyes glistened in the faint light from the window and she quickly wiped away a stray tear that slid down her cheek. "Yes," she said at length. "She did. She confided in me now and then. I was married once, you see, and I suppose she looked to me for advice, as someone older, with more experience, who wasn't *too* drearily elderly."

"Her friend Citizeness Villemain is married, and a little older than she. Wouldn't Célie have confided in her?"

Rosalie shook her head. "Perhaps not. All those people—the ex-aristocrats, the ones who still have money and influence—they all know each other. If she'd told her friend anything, it might have reached her father, in time; while nothing she told me would have gone farther than this house."

"Go on."

"Well . . . she told me, after swearing me to silence, that a certain young man had been secretly courting her, and had asked her to marry him."

"What did she tell you about him?"

"Oh, the usual things girls say about their sweethearts: how handsome he was, and what a gentleman he was, and so on. I didn't believe all of it, of course. But she did say he had been active in 'ninety-two and 'ninety-three, with the Brissotins. Evidently he was always talking about them, and their lofty principles, and their great love of their country; that they were incompetent statesmen didn't seem to matter. Of course Célie also thought all the Brissotins were terribly tragic," she added. "There's nothing like being decapitated for your ideals, to ensure that your memory will be cherished in the hearts of sentimental young women."

"She might have imagined otherwise," Aristide remarked, "if she'd known them."

"You knew them?" Rosalie inquired, surprised.

"A few. They were human beings, like the rest of us; no better, no worse. Better orators, perhaps. And they did die well." He fought away the stark memory of blood and rain in the Place de la Révolution. "Please . . . I didn't mean to interrupt you."

"There's not much more to tell you. I believe he was arrested after the second of June, when so many of the Brissotins and their hangers-on were arrested; but he managed to escape, and spent the next year in hiding, until Robespierre's fall. Then all at once he was in favor with Tallien and Fréron and that lot, and his fortunes began to improve."

"Do you know why?"

"No, Célie never said what he was or did. Only that she was sure he had a fine future ahead of him."

"Did she tell you the name of this young man?"

"She spoke of 'Philippe,'" Rosalie said promptly. "I don't think she ever mentioned his surname. I'm sorry."

"It's something," Aristide said. He could think of nothing else to ask her. She rose to show him to the door.

"Citizen? You might do me one favor, if you can: learn when she's to be buried."

"Tomorrow, they told me."

She glanced down with a brief, bitter laugh at her shabby white gown. "Oh, damn, I'll have to borrow something to wear . . . I don't even have a black gown. . . ."

Abruptly she dropped into the nearest chair and hid her face in her hands, shoulders trembling. Aristide paused a moment, wondering if he should send for a servant, but at last decided she would be better alone with her grief, and let himself out.

13 Brumaire (November 3)

Aristide prowled about his room the next morning, half-dressed, with the nagging sense that he had overlooked something. Taking up the nearest book, a volume of English plays, he settled in the shabby, comfortable armchair by the hearth but soon found he could not attend properly to Congreve's witticisms. At last he extracted an old pack of cards from beneath a litter of newspapers and letters from his sister, flung himself down at his writing-desk, and, pushing aside his breakfast tray, began to lay them out. A round or two of patience, he had found, concentrated his thoughts and occupied his restless hands.

Philippe.

How many hundreds of young men named Philippe lived in Paris?

A hanger-on of the Brissotins: that was something. Mathieu might even have known him . . . had Mathieu ever spoken of an earnest, sentimental youth named Philippe?

The columns of cards before him stretched across the desktop. Impossible that the pattern would work itself out. Impatiently he pushed them together, shuffled them, and began again.

Philippe. If only he had a surname, matters would be so much simpler.

And what was it pricking his memory? Something Brasseur had said. . . .

His landlady interrupted his musings by rapping on the door and entering without awaiting his answer. "Message for you," she said with an arch smile. "Let me clear away that crockery. Is there anything you need?"

"More coffee, if you please." He waved absently at his breakfast tray and an odd cup atop the bookshelf and unfolded the note she handed him. It was from Brasseur, asking him to come at once to Rue Traversine.

He finished dressing, gulped down the coffee Clotilde brought him, and hurried down Rue de la Loi to the commissariat. Brasseur greeted him with a broad grin and gestured to a dusty, padlocked metal box on his desk.

"Can you guess what I've got here?"

"Judging from how smug you look, I'd guess . . . is it Saint-Ange's hoard?"

"Right you are. Or at least that's what I expect. They found it under a floorboard in his bedchamber last night. Why don't you and Dautry be my witnesses." He struggled with the lock for a moment, trying several of his picklocks, until at last it gave way.

Half a dozen neat packets of letters and papers, secured with string, lay within, beside three thick bundles of high-denomination assignats and a small leather bag. Brasseur upended the bag and whistled as dozens of gold louis spilled out.

"Looks like squeezing the wealthy is a profitable business. You'd get thousands in paper for this—I haven't seen this much gold since 'ninety-one."

Aristide glanced over the packets of letters and riffled through one without untying it. "None of them addressed to Célie Montereau. It wasn't compromising letters, then. What hold did he have over her, do you suppose?" A name caught his eye and he took up another bundle, reading the address on the first letter: *To Citizeness Beaumontel, care of Citizeness Delvert, florist, Rue du Faubourg Honoré near Rue d'Aguesseau.*

"Brasseur, I promised this woman I'd return her letters, if we found them."

"They're needed as evidence," Brasseur said.

"You've got the others. Proof enough that Saint-Ange was in a dirty line of work."

"What if this Beaumontel woman had something to do with the murders? You can't just go handing her back the evidence."

"Honestly, she seemed scared to death, but I doubt very much that she had a hand in the murders. Even though Saint-Ange was making her life hell, I can't see her shooting him, or even persuading anyone else to do it for her. That timid sort of woman is the perfect victim; she'd never dare take the offensive. And you wouldn't be able to make her testify at anyone's trial—that would reveal her little amour, and she's far too frightened of her husband to ever admit anything. She'd willingly risk prison first."

Brasseur grunted and extracted six letters from the packet before handing it back to Aristide. "We'll keep back a few of them, then, just in case. You can always give them to her later." Aristide nodded, thrust the packet in his coat, and went outside.

"You!" Sidonie Beaumontel gasped, stopping short in the glover's doorway. "How did you find me?"

"You gave me your address, if you remember," said Aristide. "I simply followed you here when I saw you leave the house. I have something of yours that you'll be glad to get back." He reached into his coat but she thrust her hands in front of her, palms outward, her glance darting anxiously from side to side.

"Stop! Not here. Someone might see me." She hurried out to the busy Rue du Faubourg Honoré, Aristide following a few paces behind. Three streets farther on, she paused and turned. He passed the letters to her and she swiftly crammed them into her reticule. "How can I thank you?"

"My pleasure, citizeness. I suggest you burn those as soon as you can."

She nodded. "I won't be such a fool a second time."

"Good day, citizeness." He tipped his hat and turned, pausing as she spoke again.

"Citizen—have they found who—who did it?"

"The murders? Not yet."

"Do you . . . have you any idea . . . ?"

Her cheeks were flushed and her hands moved in nervous birdlike little jerks. *She knows something,* Aristide thought. *And she did have reason to wish him dead. . . .*

"We're looking for a man in his twenties, with long, dark hair, slender." He watched her, unsurprised by her tiny gasp as he repeated the description of the stranger. "Do you know such a man? Have you seen him at Saint-Ange's apartment?"

"No . . ."

"Are you sure?"

"Yes." She glanced at him, clutching at her reticule. "I'm sorry," she said abruptly. "I wish I could help you."

Aristide wondered suddenly if the dark-haired young man could have been her illicit lover. Frederic—no, Fernand, that was the name; though she had been careful not to mention his surname. Fernand, in penning letters to his mistress, had taken care to sign them only "Your friend" or simply "F." Here, perhaps, in fearing for her safety should her husband learn of their affair, was a man with cause to murder Saint-Ange. . . .

"Citizeness," he said, "I must speak with your friend."

"My friend?"

"You know who I mean. The man whose Christian name is Fernand." She paled and shrank back. "Must you?"

"It's essential. I need his name and address." She hesitated and he continued, merciless. "I don't like forcing you to this, but we have to pursue every angle. The police still have six of his letters to you. Once we've investigated your friend and cleared him of suspicion, we'll return them to you, but not before."

"But—you don't think *he*—he looks nothing like the man you described—"

"Can you sleep easily, knowing that an innocent young woman may have died in order to conceal your love affair? Wouldn't you rather know he had nothing to do with it?"

She swallowed and nodded. "All right. Fernand Lafontaine, number twelve, Chaussée d'Antin. But you'll find him at the Ministry of Justice; he's one of the chief clerks. Please, I beg you—give me back those letters as soon as you're able; and whatever you do, just don't let my husband know of any of this. . . ."

She scurried away. Aristide gazed after her, frowning.

What is it she's not saying?

He pondered Sidonie Beaumontel's behavior as he strolled back eastward along Rue Honoré, dodging smart carriages on their way outside the city to the parklands of Monceau or the Bois de Boulogne. Was she simply fearful that, having had a powerful motive herself to be rid of Saint-Ange, she might be suspected of his murder?

Or had she seen something once, or someone, during a previous visit to Saint-Ange's apartment? Something or someone she had noticed without meaning to, something that had meant nothing at the time?

A quarter hour's brisk walk took him to the Place Vendôme and the Ministry of Justice. After showing his police card to several undersecretaries and officials, he at last came face to face with Lafontaine in a sumptuously gilded and mirrored office, a relic of the old regime.

"I don't believe I'll have to inconvenience you for long," Aristide said, eyeing him. Sidonie Beaumontel's lover was somewhere between thirty-five and forty, lean, tall, and red-haired. It was remotely conceivable, Aristide thought, that Lafontaine might still be the murderer of Saint-Ange and Célie Montereau, but it was impossible that he should be the slight, dark young man whom the porter had seen on the stairs. "Where were you on the afternoon and evening of the tenth of this month, three days ago?"

"This past *décadi*?" Lafontaine echoed him. "I was . . . I was outside Versailles, visiting my sister at her country cottage. What's this about?"

"Your sister can vouch for your whereabouts?"

"Of course. So can her husband, and their cook. You say you're an agent of the police? What on earth do you want with me?"

"Louis Saint-Ange," Aristide said, watching him closely. Lafontaine merely gazed at him, puzzled.

"Who is Louis Saint-Ange?"

Either Lafontaine was an exceptional actor worthy of the Comédie-Française, Aristide thought, or else Sidonie had kept her predicament from him. "I expect Citizeness Beaumontel will tell you shortly," he said. "If you'll give me your sister's name and address, we'll no longer trouble you."

Lafontaine's brief statement in his pocket, Aristide left the ministry, thinking hard. All the likely trails that led from Saint-Ange seemed to be petering out to nothing. Perhaps they had been deceived in thinking that Saint-Ange had been the murderer's target, and Célie Montereau merely an unlucky bystander.

The girl had been concealing a damning secret, a secret that might have inspired murderous rage in one who felt betrayed in love or honor. Might the truth, he wondered, be the other way round?

9

Brasseur," Aristide said the following morning, after a peace officer had been dispatched to interview Lafontaine's sister and brother-in-law, "I'd like to see Saint-Ange's apartment again, and ask his servant some questions. I think we're following a false scent here."

"If you want," grunted Brasseur, fetching the key from a drawer, "but why do you say that?"

"Our 'leads' seem to lead nowhere. I think you'll find that Lafontaine was speaking the truth and has a sound alibi. Have you found any evidence at all that Saint-Ange had a mortal enemy who also had the opportunity to murder him that day?"

Brasseur shrugged. "Several people who wished him in Hell, but . . ."

"Have you interrogated all the people whose letters and papers he was holding hostage? Did any of them seem capable of murder? What about his mistress?"

"I can't say they did," Brasseur admitted. "His mistress is right out of it; she went straight to her own apartment to meet another gentleman friend, and we've got the friend's sworn statement, and her maid's, that she was very much occupied from half past four till the next morning."

"And Saint-Ange's victims?"

"Well, one of the women had already had it out with her husband and they're divorcing; another fellow, a bank clerk who'd embezzled to spend money on a high-class whore, he drowned himself in the river a fortnight ago. Not that that bothered Saint-Ange much, I suppose," he added sourly. "The others were all rich women who'd been indiscreet at one time or another. One of them seemed like the sort who might turn to murder, but she'd been with a whole raft of friends all that day who can swear where she was. The rest, I expect they were just like your Beaumontel woman: born victims, timid, terrified that their husbands should find out. They'd never have told anyone about Saint-Ange, much less shot him themselves."

"So that leaves us with the other alternative, doesn't it?"

They walked the short distance to the Palais-Égalité, collected the manservant Thibault, who had found work in the household of a nearby bachelor, and continued to Rue du Hasard. The porter Grangier, Aristide noticed, was now perched dutifully on a stool in the foyer, though slouched back against the wall and comfortably snoring.

No one interrupted them as they climbed the stairs to Saint-Ange's apartment. Brasseur peeled the official seals from the door and unlocked it.

"We've been pursuing the idea that someone must have come here with the intention of killing Saint-Ange, as he richly deserved," said Aristide as he strode through the foyer and into the salon. "That Saint-Ange was the target, and the first to die, and that Célie Montereau was merely an unlucky bystander. But what if she wasn't?"

"That changes matters," Brasseur agreed. "We know she had something to hide, after all. But how do you prove it?"

"Well, I don't know if anything can be proven yet, but . . . Thibault, I want you to think back. Try to remember exactly what you did and saw when you came in that morning and found the bodies."

Thibault scratched his head and gazed around him. "All right, well, I came up the stairs . . ."

Aristide nodded. "Go out to the landing, please, and do exactly what you did then."

Thibault obediently returned to the landing. After a moment Aristide heard him say "I took out my key, but then I found the door was open, so I came inside. I thought Saint-Ange had forgotten to lock it the night before, since that's part of my job, of course." He tiptoed into the foyer and shut the door behind him. "Then I went along here and into the salon, to light the fire. I'd built a fire the day before, but the weather was fine and he'd said it wasn't necessary to light it. But I knew he'd want a fire when he woke up and took his breakfast. So I came in here," he added, entering the salon, "and there was the young lady, lying right in front of me." He knelt near the center of the carpet. "I touched her to see if there was any help for her, but she was cold as a stone . . . then I saw him, over behind the sofa. I could just see his boot sticking out."

"Célie Montereau was lying right in front of you?" Aristide echoed him. "Show us exactly where she was lying."

"Here," the manservant said, gesturing. Brasseur nodded.

"That's what Didier said, more or less."

"But Didier moved the body, like a fool," said Aristide. "Thibault, would you lie on the carpet in the position in which you found the young lady? It seems ridiculous, I know, but this is important."

Thibault grinned weakly and obeyed. "She was lying on her back, so." He arranged himself, knees slightly bent, arms askew, one hand raised near his head.

"And this is precisely where she was lying, and her position, to the best of your recollection?" Aristide said. "Her head here, and feet there?"

"Yes, citizen."

"Célie was shot first," Aristide said to Brasseur. "She had to have been."

"We ought to have seen it," Brasseur agreed.

"If she'd been a witness to that struggle between Saint-Ange and the attacker, she might have run for it immediately and escaped; or she might have frozen, cowered, tried to hide as best she could. But instead she's right here, nowhere near any piece of furniture large enough to have hidden her or protected her. She was standing when she was shot, and she saw her murderer. Brasseur, be the murderer and come in here from the foyer. You're holding a pistol at your side."

Brasseur retreated and then advanced, holding an imaginary pistol.

Aristide stood in the center of the room, his back to him. "Célie is pleading with Saint-Ange to take pity on her. There is a rap—or pounding—on the door. Thibault is out. Saint-Ange sets his glass of wine down on the buffet, goes to the door himself, and opens it. Célie turns toward the newcomer, as anyone does when someone enters a room." He turned to face Brasseur and raised both hands to his face in a fearful gesture. "Probably she recognizes him, takes a step toward him. Shoot me."

Brasseur raised his arm and crooked his finger. "Bang."

"The pistol is four or five feet away," said Aristide, "impossible to miss, but not close enough to leave powder burns on her gown. She is shot through the heart and dies within seconds." He took one halting step rearward, recoiling from the pretended force of the shot, and collapsed backward to land crumpled on the carpet, knees bent and hands outflung.

"That's it," Thibault exclaimed. "That's how she looked. Right there."

"Then," Aristide said, sitting up, "the murderer kept on—Saint-Ange went for his pistols—we know the rest. But the murderer came for *her*. Perhaps he followed her here. He entered, found Célie, and shot her. Célie was his first target, not Saint-Ange. She wasn't expecting him and she put up no resistance in the bare instant she had."

Brasseur nodded. "So . . . who would want to deliberately kill Célie Montereau, then? This secret sweetheart of hers? Because Saint-Ange had told him the dirt on her? He kills her in anger, a pure crime of passion, and then does away with Saint-Ange for being a bloodsucking swine?"

"Possibly."

"Thibault, are you sure Saint-Ange had no visitors on *décadi* besides his mistress, and that he didn't go out except to take luncheon with her?"

"Positive, citizen."

"What about letters?" Aristide said. "Did Saint-Ange write any letters on the day he died, or during the previous day or two?"

"None," Thibault said promptly. "He didn't give me any to post; besides, he was a careless writer and a hard man with quills, he was, and he was always spattering ink on his desk or having me trim his quills for him or cut him new ones. When I went out on the tenth, the last time I saw him, his writing-desk was still neat as a pin the way I'd left it. He hadn't been doing any writing."

Brasseur exchanged glances with Aristide and sighed. "We'll have to talk to the whole Montereau household again. Perhaps the boy noticed something else. . . ."

Children notice things, you know.

Yes, Aristide thought, children noticed things. Children noticed when things were out of place, when the safe, reassuring routine of life was disrupted by something that was not as it ought to have been, or something missing from its place, or someone who ought not to have been there. He closed his eyes for an instant.

The boy Théodore. In Célie's bedchamber. What was it he had said, and then hesitated, as if he had said too much? Something about Célie's jewelry, her mother's ring—*It's not here, and it's . . .* —and then he had stumbled over his words and added something trivial about the ring.

"Let me speak to the boy alone, first," he said.

It's not here, and it's . . . not in a certain other place, either? A private hiding place, perhaps, a cache more secure than her jewelry case, where all manner of treasures or secrets might be hidden?

A lackey at the Hôtel de Montereau looked Aristide over, dubious, as he climbed from the cab. "Are you a friend of the family?"

"Police. I need to speak with the boy."

"This is a house of mourning. The family is receiving friends—"

"I think Citizen Montereau will receive me," Aristide said, thrusting his police card at the man. "I need only to speak with the boy, not to invade the salon."

Montereau came down to the foyer to meet him, puzzled, but offered no objection to a visit with Théodore after Aristide explained his purpose. "Well, at such a melancholy time . . . the distraction will be good for him, poor child."

Aristide followed a servant girl upstairs to the nursery. The boy scrambled up from his chair as a dyspeptic-looking young man hovered at the rear of the room. "Citizen policeman! Did you catch him? Did you catch the man who hurt Célie?"

"No, I fear not," Aristide said. "Not yet. But perhaps you can help me find him. I hope you are well?"

Théodore clasped his hands behind him and stared at his shoes. "Papa said Célie's in Heaven now. They buried her yesterday. I had to walk with Papa, behind the carriage that took her away."

Aristide recalled another black-clad boy, rigid with misery, hands clutched painfully behind his back, waiting for the funeral procession to set out. It had been a long, long journey to the cemetery on the day they had buried his mother.

But there had been no funeral for his father.

. . . And the remains consumed in fire, and the ashes scattered to the winds . . .

"I know," he said softly. "I know what it's like, following someone's coffin."

"Lots of Célie's friends were there, and Papa's friends. They're here today, too. Citizeness Villemain gave me some macaroons when Papa wasn't looking."

"That was kind of her."

His aunt . . . his aunt had given him some candied ginger that day. Strange that he had nearly forgotten.

"Théodore, do you want to find the person who killed your sister?"

The boy nodded vigorously.

"Then I hope you'll tell me something. The day before yesterday, when you told us you had seen Célie taking away her jewelry, I think you were going to say something else. Were you going to say that Célie had a secret place where she kept her special treasures, and her jewelry wasn't there, either?"

Théodore grimaced and sucked his lower lip between his teeth. "No."

"Come," Aristide said, steering the boy outside into the passage by the stairs and closing the door. "Your tutor can't hear us here. We're all alone. You do know where your sister kept her treasures, don't you?"

Théodore shook his head as a faint blush crept into his cheeks.

"You can tell *me*. Whatever it is you want to keep secret, I promise you I won't tell your father, or anyone."

Théodore remained stubbornly silent. Aristide thought rapidly back to his own boyhood, to the hazy, uneventful years before his world had dissolved in calamity, wondering as he did so of whom the boy reminded him. Perhaps himself, he mused.

"It's natural to be curious, you know. Did you see Célie hide something while you were hiding yourself in a cupboard?"

Théodore stared back at him. "How did you know?"

"Was it a cupboard, then?"

"Behind the curtains."

"I once did the same thing at your age. When my grown-up cousin Amélie came to visit. I was an abominably curious little boy and I hid in the wardrobe because I wanted to see what she looked like without her chemise on."

Théodore stifled a conspiratorial giggle before gazing at him wide-eyed. "You *promise* you won't tell Papa?"

"Certainly. It's none of my business how you educate yourself."

Théodore stared at him, uncomprehending—after all, Aristide told himself, the boy was only six—and he summoned a smile. "I promise I won't tell your papa."

"All right," the boy admitted, "well, I saw it once. The secret hiding place. It's in her writing-desk."

"This is important, Théodore," Aristide said. "I need to see the secret drawer, and whatever is inside it."

"All right," said Théodore after a moment's deliberation. "But there isn't any treasure in it. I looked yesterday, when Papa said she—she'd gone to Heaven and wasn't coming back. It's just some old letters in there."

"Letters?"

"In the stories about bandits, like Cartouche, they always hide gold."

"I need to see these letters. Let's visit Célie's boudoir, shall we?"

His hand in Aristide's, Théodore led him to the dainty green bed-chamber and pointed at the desk that stood between the two tall windows. "There. You pull this out"—he unlocked a drawer and pulled it out of the desk, then reached into the empty space—"and then you feel *up* with your hand and slide up the secret door to get inside. It's behind that little cupboard on top, you see, but you can't get into the secret part from the cupboard. You have to go from the drawer." He withdrew a dusty arm, a packet of folded papers in his fist. "See? Just letters. You can have them."

"You've been more than helpful, Théodore," Aristide said, pocketing them. Compromising documents were best kept out of the reach of inquisitive relatives until one could determine their usefulness. "You needn't tell anyone about these. Let's keep this our secret, shall we? A secret between you, and me, and Célie?"

"I miss Célie," Théodore said abruptly. Two tears trickled down his cheeks and he rubbed them away, sniffling. "I wanted to write something about Célie today, but Citizen Tourneur won't let me. He says it's nothing to do with my lessons. I *hate* him. And he says I'll have to study Latin and ciphering and all kinds of horrid things when I go to school. I'd rather be a soldier than study Latin. Do you know Latin?"

Aristide nodded. "Yes, I studied it, and I wasn't much good at it. But one needs to know Latin if one is going to study law."

"But you're not a lawyer. You're a policeman. Maybe I could be a policeman, like you," Théodore said hopefully.

Aristide found himself smiling. "Well, you wouldn't want to be the sort of policeman I am. I'm more of an errand-boy for my friend the commissaire, and I go about everywhere and ask questions, especially when it might be inconvenient for a police inspector to barge in. But if you want to be a commissaire of police like Citizen Brasseur, you might do well to become a lawyer first. Then the Ministry appoints you to the position, you see."

"Was Citizen Brasseur a lawyer?"

Caught in my own argument, he reflected ruefully. "No, Brasseur was a soldier for a long time. But I think you ought to keep on studying, no matter what. Army officers need a proper education, too, if they're to lead men and ride on fine horses."

Théodore pouted for a moment, shifting from one foot to the other as he considered the alternatives. Amused, Aristide watched him as they walked back to the nursery. The boy did not, after all, so much resemble Célie as he had first supposed, though he had Célie's fair, reddish-blond hair. He could not recall having seen any portraits of the late Madame Montereau, and wondered once again of whom the boy's features reminded him.

"I must go now, but it was a pleasure to meet you again, Théodore."

Théodore shook his hand and bowed solemnly. "Good day, citizen."

A charming boy, Aristide thought as he took his leave, and properly reared. The future of the house of Montereau was in good hands.

"Here," he said, dropping the letters on Brasseur's desk. "Confirmation. The first one's from Saint-Ange, dated ten weeks ago. He asks for a hundred louis for his discretion regarding 'a certain delicate matter.'"

"A hundred louis!"

"He'll take five hundred thousand francs in paper if she has no gold, though."

"Accommodating fellow." Brasseur read it through, squinting in the candlelight—the day had turned rainy and overcast—and muttering to himself. "Not signed."

"No. No signature, no specifics about the delicate matter. He's covering his tracks."

Brasseur turned toward the door to the adjacent tiny office where his secretary worked. "Dautry! Get me a sample of Saint-Ange's handwriting. What about the others?" he continued, to Aristide. "Also demands from our late unlamented friend?"

Aristide shook his head. "Different writing. Two or three dozen cloying love letters, all alike. Listen to this." He crossed to the window and unfolded another letter. "'My dearest love, you have not written to me for five days now. Imagine how I suffer! Take pity on your beloved, and if I cannot see you, at least let me feast my eyes on the words your dear hand has written to me. Tell me all you do, and say once more that you love me, and do not torment me in so heartless a manner. You know how tenderly I love you. You know how you have enslaved me, and how I wish only to remain fettered by those bonds of love. Send me a letter, and a kiss, and I will know you have not forgotten me. I am your slave always. Your Philippe.' Dated two months ago, but others are more recent. The Clément woman told me the young man's name was Philippe."

"Pompous sort of ass, isn't he?" said Brasseur.

"My cousin Margot would have said as much," Aristide agreed. He handed Brasseur the letter and glanced through the rest. "God, his style is painful. But Margot has an excellent sense of humor. She once had a young admirer who sent her letters like these, and she laughed at every one of them before throwing them on the fire. She said some of the girls she knew, though, the mawkish sort of female who weeps over novels, would be enthralled by such rubbish."

"You think Célie Montereau was that sort of girl?"

"I imagine so. I saw her books: English novels and some repellently sentimental poetry."

"Hmph," said Brasseur with a glance at the small, crowded bookshelf by his desk. For his own pleasure he read, besides the newspapers, only epic poetry and the plays of Corneille, Racine, and a selection of classical Roman authors in translation; dramatic tragedy, he claimed, kept petty human affairs in 1796 in their proper proportion.

"Margot said such girls usually want to be the heroines of novels themselves. They long for romance, peril, and a happy ending with a wedding. Put a good-looking, smooth-tongued, unscrupulous young man in front of them, and they'll be on their backs before you can blink."

Brasseur nodded sagely. "My eldest's like that. It'll be the devil's own job keeping her honest in a year or two. Do you think Célie's young man had already had her?"

"God knows. So the question now becomes, who is he? And did he kill her? Could he have killed her in a fit of jealousy because of the secret Saint-Ange discovered?"

"We've no evidence that he saw any strangers that day, or wrote to anybody," Brasseur grumbled. "If this man learned the dirt, he didn't learn it from Saint-Ange."

Aristide gathered up a handful of the letters and glanced over them again, shaking his head. "Brasseur, if the murderer had confined himself to burning Saint-Ange's brains, I'd say good riddance and hunt no further. But the man who could kill that poor, silly, harmless girl—" He sighed and thrust the letters in a pocket. "I'm going to talk to the Clément woman again."

Rosalie Clément read two of the letters Aristide handed her and paused to shake out her crumpled handkerchief and blow her nose. "Oh, it's too pathetic. Poor Célie."

"Do you think he was sincere in his declarations of love," Aristide said, "or merely playing a part to dazzle her?"

Rosalie read another of the letters. "On the whole, I'd guess he was sincere. Célie might not have been able to tell the difference between sincerity and affectation, but I think I could. For one thing," she added dryly, "a cynical man would have written more gracefully. But the question you ought to ask is: Why was she keeping this whole business so secret?"

"I don't understand," Aristide said, wondering how much else he did not know about young women in love.

"Wealthy and prominent parents want their children to marry advantageously, don't they? It's nothing to do with love. This Philippe must have been someone whom Montereau wouldn't have considered as a son-in-law, and I expect Célie knew quite well that her father wouldn't have approved of him. Of course, it could have been something as simple as lack of fortune. Or it might have been low birth or bad reputation. But I honestly don't think an unscrupulous man, one who was simply pursuing Célie's favors or fortune, could have written these letters, or at any rate written them so badly." She handed them back to him. "I'm sure this man really does believe every word he writes."

Aristide nodded and penciled a few notes. "I think a portrait is beginning to emerge. He's young...he writes like a sixteen-year-old schoolboy."

"Yes. No more than thirty, or twenty-five even."

"Might be found hovering at the edge of government, if he's found favor with the Directors as you mentioned before...He's sincere, earnest, romantic, probably quite attractive to women—"

"In a graceful, girlish sort of way, I expect," interrupted Rosalie, "if I read Célie properly and she was anything like me. When I was fifteen, I used to melt at the sight of a pretty youth with curls and long eyelashes."

"And he's a poor judge of literary merit, I may add."

"You may," she agreed.

"Yet unacceptable to Montereau. Perhaps poor; perhaps lacking in family connections; possibly disreputable. Or there might be some private quarrel between them." He added a few more notes and turned once more to Rosalie. "Do you think—Forgive me for asking so indelicate a question, but you and I are both adults with knowledge of the world . . . do you think this young man might have taken advantage of Célie?"

"Are you suggesting that she . . ." Her voice trailed off as she looked away, staring at the musty curtains. "I see. Well, it happens to the best of us. So she had a secret to conceal."

"Could this man have been her lover—in a carnal sense, I mean?"

"No," she said promptly. "No, certainly not. A man who could write this sort of letter, and mean it, will be just as mawkish as the woman who would swoon over it. He'd never touch her except in the marriage bed. That sort wants to believe that all young women, or at least all the young women whom *he* falls in love with, are blushing virgins."

"And what if such a man had discovered that his idolized, virtuous beauty was not as virtuous as he had believed?"

"I daresay he might do something terribly theatrical, like . . . publicly accusing her of immorality."

"Or murdering her?"

"Yes," she said after an instant's thought. "I think such a man might be capable of that."

10

Aristide snatched a quick, solitary luncheon of bread and cold meat at a nearby eating-house, buffeted by the clamor of the midday crowd of workmen shoveling down pot-au-feu from thick earthenware dishes. Choosing privacy over the warmth of the hearth, he found a place at the end of a long table, where he could avoid chance jabs from his companions' elbows and where the gamy reek of boiled mutton and turnips did not hang quite so heavy above him. He thankfully escaped after half an hour and returned to the Butte-des-Moulins section commissariat, where he found Inspector Caillou reporting to Brasseur.

"Number One, Rue de Caumartin, second floor. E.-A.-P. Feydeau de la Beyré, unmarried with two servants, domiciled there since Vendémiaire of Year Three."

"Feydeau?" said Aristide.

"The fellow that Citizeness Villemain told us about," Brasseur reminded him. "Let's go. That's a fashionable quarter; with any luck, he'll be lounging at home until it's time to go to a dinner party or whatnot. Ravel, are you coming?"

They arrived at Rue de Caumartin at three o'clock with Dautry, two of their own inspectors, and an inspector from the Place-Vendôme section in tow. Number 1, at the corner of the Boulevard, was an elegant new apartment house, sporting a round corner tower ornamented with rococo trophies and a pair of demure neoclassical statues. One inspector stationed himself at the bottom of the staircase as the rest of the party followed the porter up the stairs.

A nervous manservant gestured them into a small parlor. The room reminded Aristide of Saint-Ange's apartment, luxuriously and tastefully furnished, though no salacious engravings hung on the walls. After a moment a weedy, blond young man with a pleasant, rather vacant countenance strolled in, knotting the sash of his dressing gown and blinking.

"Chapellier tells me you're the police. Whatever can you want with *me?*"

"Citizen Feydeau," Brasseur said, "I'm Commissaire Brasseur of the Butte-des-Moulins section, and behind me is Inspector Normand of your own section. Would you mind giving us your full name, date of birth, place of birth, and condition?"

"Not at all," said the young man, still puzzled. "Edmé-Antoine-Philippe Feydeau de la Beyré, born—"

Aristide gestured to the mahogany writing-table in the corner of the parlor. "Why don't you write it all down for him. Otherwise the commissaire's secretary is sure to spell your name incorrectly." Dautry shot him an indignant glance.

"What's all this about?" Feydeau inquired, sitting and lifting the lid from a crystal inkwell.

"It concerns a certain Louis Saint-Ange, of Rue du Hasard—"

"Never heard of him."

"And a young woman of your acquaintance, Citizeness Montereau."

"Montereau?" echoed Feydeau, pausing in his writing. "Oh, yes! Charming little thing. See her at the Comédie sometimes, with her friends."

"We're looking for her murderer."

"Good God! *Murdered?* What's Paris coming to? I supposed all that sort of unpleasantness was over and done with in 'ninety-four." He scrawled a few lines, shook sand on the paper, blew on it, and handed it to Brasseur. "There you are, Commissaire. Though what you need me for . . ." Feydeau's voice trailed away into silence as the import of his words at last penetrated his understanding. "Oh, dear heavens, you don't honestly think *I*—why, I scarcely knew the girl. Ask anyone you like."

"Citizeness Montereau's secret lover may have murdered her," Brasseur said. "One of your forenames is Philippe, like his. Just saying that you scarcely knew her won't do. Where were you on the afternoon and evening of the tenth of Brumaire?"

"The tenth . . ." The young man did a rapid calculation on his fingers, with a feeble titter. "Let me see, that would have been four days ago, Monday the thirty-first of October . . . Monday! Yes, I remember. I spent the evening visiting a friend." He looked up brightly at Brasseur.

"Your friend's name and address, please. He'll confirm your story?"

Feydeau frowned. "Is—is that necessary, Commissaire?"

"Certainly."

"Well then . . ." He leaned forward, lowering his voice. "Might I have a word in private?"

Aristide followed Brasseur and Feydeau into the adjoining chamber, a snug library where gleaming gold-stamped leather spines shone in glass-fronted bookcases.

"You see," Feydeau began, and stopped. "It's a terribly delicate matter."

"You can trust our discretion if it's nothing to do with the murder," Brasseur growled.

"Well then," Feydeau began again, and paused for a second time. "You said the murderer of that poor child might have been her lover. Er . . . I was *not* this secret lover of whom you speak, I assure you." He paused once again, blushed, coughed, and drew a deep breath. "My . . . er . . . tastes . . . don't run in the direction of young girls." Sweeping an arm towards the bookshelves, he smiled sheepishly. "Take a look at my book collection if you doubt me."

"I see," Brasseur said, reddening.

"The paper, Brasseur," Aristide said. "With Feydeau's name."

Brasseur thrust it at him. A glance told him Feydeau's handwriting was nothing like that of the mysterious Philippe. "Forgive this intrusion, citizen. If you would add your friend's name and address to this same sheet of paper, we won't inconvenience you further."

"You—you won't have to talk to my friend, will you?" Feydeau inquired, rapidly blinking. "He's married, you see."

"Only a discreet word in private, I think. Other evidence confirms your story."

"Other evidence?"

"Your handwriting, and the color of your hair."

"Oh," said the young man. "And you're sure word of . . . of my . . . private life . . . won't be made public?"

"Your private activities have been legal since 1791. It's none of our affair."

"Oh," said Feydeau again. "Yes. Very well." He took a quill from a nearby writing-table and added a few lines. "Do keep it to yourself, won't you? What did you mean, the color of my hair? Do you mean the man you want is dark?"

"Yes, we believe so."

"Lucky for me!" Feydeau exclaimed. He scratched his head and scowled fiercely with the effort of thinking. "Don't go, Commissaire. I'm trying to remember . . . yes, by God, it *was* the little Montereau girl. I'm sure of it."

"Would you care to tell us about it?" Brasseur said when Feydeau said nothing more.

"Oh! Yes. Merely something I saw at the opera not too long ago. The girl and her friend, what's her name . . ."

"Citizeness Villemain?"

"Yes, that's the one . . . they were there, you see, with the friend's husband, and during the interval I saw the little Montereau in the corridor, outside the boxes. Most people had gone in again for the final act. She was with a young fellow whom I didn't know, and they were standing close together, behind a column, and he was kissing her hand. Very, *very* tenderly, if you know what I mean."

"And the young man was dark-haired?" said Aristide.

"Didn't I say that? Yes, he had dark hair. Tied back with a ribbon, not hanging in dogs' ears the way some fellows are wearing it."

"How old?"

"Old? Oh ... twenty-five? Twenty-eight? He was terribly good-looking. I couldn't help noticing *that*."

"And when was this?"

Feydeau shrugged. "I don't recall the date. Six or eight weeks ago, more or less."

"Perhaps you remember the opera you were attending?"

"Oh, no, they all sound alike. I don't care much for music, you know, but one must have a box all the same."

"Thank you, citizen," Brasseur said. "Looks as if our errand wasn't wasted after all."

Brasseur and Aristide spent an hour at the commissariat putting the statements, notes, and evidence regarding the murders of Célie Montereau and Louis Saint-Ange in order. At length, as the ormolu clock on the mantelpiece struck seven, Brasseur thrust the entire heap of papers into a cardboard folder, pushed it aside, and fetched a bottle of red wine and two glasses from a cabinet.

"So," said Brasseur, after pouring a second glass for himself, "here we are where we started. Imagine that young idiot murdering anyone. So much for the Villemain woman's guesses."

"We're not back where we started," said Aristide, taking a pack of cards from a drawer. "Feydeau's evidence confirms Grangier's. A young man, handsome, dark-haired. Citizeness Villemain was only incorrect about the individual."

"But how do we find him?"

"Feydeau said he saw him at the Opera House."

Brasseur grinned. "Right. So our young man is prosperous enough to go to the opera, and probably to sit in a box somewhere near to the Villemains', in the first or second circle, which doesn't come cheap. Unless he'd been a guest in somebody else's box?"

"Well, though Feydeau may be an amiable nitwit," Aristide said, swiftly laying down the cards, "the one thing he would have noticed and remembered would be if the young man in question had been shabbily dressed; he'd have remarked upon that. Chances are the young man is at least comfortable. That narrows the field considerably."

Brasseur nodded. "Yes. I suppose another visit to Montereau is in order?"

"I'd recommend it. It's time he knew about Célie's love letters. The man you want may have been under Montereau's nose all the time." Aristide looked over the cards, frowned, and pushed them together into a heap.

"You weren't done," said Brasseur, who was accustomed to his frequent rounds of patience.

"Sometimes you can see, halfway through, that the game can't be won." He shuffled the cards, thrust them back into their drawer, and rose. "I'm going to get some dinner. Care to join me?"

"No, I'd better be off. Didier is on duty tonight and Marie'll make me sleep on the landing if I miss supper again. Good night, then."

15 Brumaire (November 5)

Aristide went alone the next afternoon to the great house on Rue de l'Université, where Montereau received him in his private study, his complexion sickly with grief and fatigue. As Aristide summarized their investigations, Montereau frequently glanced at the portrait of Célie that hung on the opposite wall, black crepe draped about it. Though suspecting that Montereau had scarcely heard what he was saying, Aristide concluded with the description he had assembled from Feydeau's statement and Rosalie Clément's suggestions.

"A young man," he concluded, "between twenty-five and thirty, dark-haired and good-looking, probably well-off, and with an ardent, emotional, romantic temperament. A man who is idealistic and sentimental, at least where love and women are concerned." He handed Montereau one of the letters. Montereau read it through, speechless.

"I know of no one among our present acquaintance who fits your description. No one who could have written this. The young men of our acquaintance are steadier, shall we say; more practical, or mundane, than that. That is to say, I believe young Joubert-Saint-Hilaire once fought a duel over a girl, but everyone knew it began as a drunken brawl in a brothel." He shook his head. "I wish I could help you."

16 Brumaire (November 6)

"A lady's waiting for Citizen Brasseur, in his office," an inspector told Aristide when he arrived at the commissariat late the next morning, shaking away raindrops from his hat. "She wouldn't reveal her errand."

"A lady?" Aristide echoed him, raising an eyebrow.

"And a message. Perhaps you'd make sure he reads it."

Brasseur returned at that moment from resolving a noisy dispute between two street peddlers and impatiently unfolded the letter. "Hmph. Saint-Ange's corpse is still at the Basse-Geôle. . . . 'The remains and effects continue unclaimed although the commissaire has given authorization for the deceased's next of kin to take away the body. . . . In another twenty-four hours it will be necessary to send away the body for burial for reasons of public health. . . .' What the devil do I care about some corpse? I wish those two ghouls wouldn't harass me with this nonsense."

Still clutching the letter in one hand, he strode away to his office. Following him, Aristide discovered a veiled woman in black waiting in an armchair. She rose as they approached, and lifted her veil.

"Citizeness Villemain," Brasseur said. "I didn't expect to see you here."

"Especially so soon after Célie's funeral," Aristide added. "I hope it wasn't too distressing for you. How may we assist you?"

"I think perhaps I can be of some service to you, citizens. The young man you spoke of—the one who may have done this . . . this dreadful thing—I told you I knew of no one except for Citizen Feydeau."

Brasseur shook his head. "We questioned Feydeau. He's not the man."

"It did seem rather improbable. But I've been trying to remember everything I knew about Célie when we were girls. And I did recall one thing: when we were both home from the abbey, just before I was married, we used to sigh over her father's private secretary. He was young, about twenty-one, and remarkably handsome. Being girls of fifteen and seventeen, we adored him."

Aristide thought back to his errand of the day before and recalled a fleeting glimpse of a man in a black wig copying letters at a desk in the library, a man who could not have been described as either young or handsome. "I saw no such man at Montereau's house."

"No, you wouldn't have. Célie's father dismissed him. We learned, much later, that he'd been dismissed because he had been mixed up in a scandal a few years before. He'd killed a man in a duel, and Célie's father doesn't approve of dueling."

"I see," Aristide said. "He must have been still in his teens at the time of the duel, which certainly indicates a passionate temperament. . . . You think this could be a man with whom Célie would have fallen in love?"

Hélène Villemain smiled apologetically. "The age is right. He would be about twenty-eight or twenty-nine now. His surname was Aubry. He was of good family, I recall, but very poor."

"Well, perhaps Montereau can tell me more about this man." Brasseur hastily wrote a note, sealed it, and sent Dautry to find a messenger. "Did he have dark hair?"

Hélène blinked. "How did you know? Dark hair, and great dark eyes. We liked to think he was a poet, because he looked as a poet should have looked. He was *so* handsome; we both imagined ourselves head over heels in love with him." She blushed, ducking her head. "What a ninny I was."

"Not at all," Aristide said with a brief smile. "By the way, I understand you were kind to young Théodore during the funeral procession."

"Did he tell you that? I felt sorry for the poor child. Funerals are such a dreary business."

Hélène left them as Brasseur turned his attention once more to the letter from the Basse-Geôle. "I don't see any reason why Saint-Ange's body shouldn't be released for burial. Do you?"

Aristide dropped into the nearest chair. "Montereau doesn't seem to care. If he chooses to disregard the remote kinship . . ."

The word "kinship" seemed to echo in his mind like the clang of a bell. He scowled, trying to grasp an elusive thought. Something he had just said, something dropped casually in conversation with Hélène and Brasseur. Something about . . . funerals . . . and Saint-Ange. Saint-Ange's dead face flashed before him, cadaverous but undeniably handsome. Something . . . someone . . . who reminded him of Saint-Ange?

A sudden extravagant, impossible idea striking him, he jerked to his feet again and gazed blankly at the vast map of Paris pinned on the whitewashed wall opposite him. The lines and letters swam into a blur. It was preposterous . . . and yet . . .

He snatched up his hat and plunged into the corridor. "Citizeness! Citizeness Villemain, could you spare another hour?"

She turned, surprised. "If you wish."

"I should like you to come with me to confirm—or possibly deny— an implausible observation that's suddenly struck me." He shook the hair away from his face and thrust his hands in the pockets of his coat. "I warn you, it's probably a fool's journey. And it may be distasteful and distressing to you."

"If it will serve to find Célie's murderer—what is it you want me to do?"

"Just come with me, please," he told her, taking her arm. "I won't tell you where we're going, or why, because I'd rather you arrived with no preconceived notions."

Fantastical conjectures whirled through his thoughts as their fiacre jolted through the streets. He was undoubtedly dreaming, he told himself, the result of too much time and commiseration spent on that damnable pair of murders—yet he could not shake off the sense of inevitability hovering about him.

"Where on earth are we going?" Hélène inquired, as the cab slowed at the corner of Rue Denis and he directed the driver to continue to the Châtelet and along the public passage through the center of the fortress. They arrived a moment later at the small door in the passage, dark and close beneath the overcast sky.

"I'm not surprised you've never seen this place," Aristide said as he climbed out of the cab and offered her a helping hand. "This is a lesser-known, and generally avoided, door to the cellars of the Châtelet. The Basse-Geôle de la Seine. Where most victims of accidental or violent death are taken until their bodies are claimed. I'm about to ask you to look at a corpse. Will that distress you?"

"I've seen corpses before."

"At funerals, I expect, neatly laid out in coffins; not week-old corpses stripped of their clothing, waiting until the state can bury them. There is a considerable difference. Have you a scented handkerchief with you?"

Speechless, she drew a handkerchief from her reticule and clutched it as he escorted her through the heavy door. Bouille, the pop-eyed concierge, met them in the murky vestibule, inquired their business, and with a lugubrious sigh unlocked the grille to the lower chamber. The stench rose up to meet them and Aristide fumbled for his own handkerchief as they descended the steps. Pausing now and then to twitch aside a sheet and glance at a tag tied to a wrist, Bouille led them among the silent forms.

"Where do they all come from?" Hélène whispered, shivering. Their footsteps echoed from the stones. "They can't all have been murdered?"

Aristide shook his head. "Most are bodies taken from the river. Suicides or accidental drownings. Bouille says the suicide rate has swelled shockingly over the past couple of years." Life since the Revolution began had grown no easier for the poor, now enduring widespread unemployment, periodic food shortages, and runaway inflation. "Hence the stink," he added. "No one smells like lily of the valley after a few days in the water."

Bouille stopped beside one table, squinted at the tag, and waited stolidly by the shrouded shape. "I had better take a look first," Aristide continued, "in the event it isn't fit for a woman to see."

He nodded and Bouille lifted away the sheet. Louis Saint-Ange's corpse still wore a shirt; no one had claimed even his clothes.

The powder burns and the crust of dried blood around the bullet hole in Saint-Ange's forehead seemed startlingly dark on the pallid, waxy skin. The flesh had settled on the bones, leaving the face gaunt and skull-like; despite the strip of linen that encircled the head and held the dead man's jaws closed, the lips were beginning to sag away from the teeth in the macabre grin of decay.

Aristide studied the dead face for a moment. He had not, after all, imagined the resemblance.

"It's disagreeable," he said, turning away, "but not unduly distressing. Please look at this man for a few moments."

Hélène tiptoed forward and gazed at the corpse. Aristide saw her shiver and swallow.

"Is this the man who was found with Célie?"

"Of whom does he remind you?" he asked her, disregarding her question. "Try to imagine him alive. Death has aged him, but try to see him as a good-looking man of my own age. Think back on all the faces you've seen of late."

She frowned. Aristide watched her. The clammy, pervasive smell of sour flesh and rancid blood was becoming easier to bear.

Abruptly she turned to him, eyes wide in surprise.

"Théodore?"

"Yes," Aristide said. "I thought so, too."

11

B ut what can this *mean*?" said Hélène, after they had retreated to the public passage and she had drawn several deep grateful breaths of fresh air.

"I can think of one explanation immediately," Aristide said, "but it scarcely seems credible."

"*Was* that the man who was found with Célie? I understand he was some sort of distant relative. It might be merely a family resemblance."

Aristide shook his head. "No. Montereau told me Saint-Ange was a relative of his first wife. His second wife was Théodore's mother, so there ought to be no resemblance. Unless it's another sort of family resemblance. . . ."

"If Célie's mother had had a liaison with . . . *no*. I knew her. I simply cannot believe it."

"I did say it scarcely seemed credible."

"But what can this have to do with Célie's murder?"

"I've no idea. It's something we must take into account, though. It may mean nothing; it may mean everything." Aristide turned to her, unsmiling. "I hardly need to ask you to keep this intelligence to yourself."

"But what about—"

"Montereau? What earthly use could there be in afflicting him further, by telling him his son may not be his son? Don't awaken a sleeping cat."

Hélène smiled at the old proverb and nodded. They rode silently through the heavy mist to Rue du Bac.

Aristide returned on foot to the Right Bank, hoping the cool November air would cleanse the clinging fetor of the Basse-Geôle from his clothes. Brasseur was eating his midday dinner at his desk when Aristide returned. "Join me?" Brasseur said. "This caterer is generous with his portions."

Aristide took a deep appreciative sniff of the steam rising from the dish of chicken fricassee and roast potatoes as Brasseur spooned some onto a second plate. "One should eat to live, and not live to eat, according to Molière; but I don't mind if I do."

"So where did you go haring off to with the Villemain woman? The secretaries were most intrigued."

"Ah. Now there's a tale. I took her to the Basse-Geôle."

"Eh?" said Brasseur, pausing with a gravy-soaked morsel of bread halfway to his mouth.

"I wanted to see if she, too, perceived the strong resemblance between the late Louis Saint-Ange and our young friend Théodore Montereau." Aristide poured half a glass of wine for himself, adding: "You might shut your mouth before you catch a few flies."

"But didn't Montereau say—no, curse it, he told us Saint-Ange was related to his *first* wife—saints above, d'you think his wife had been playing in the muck with that young scoundrel, and passed the boy off as Montereau's?"

Aristide shook his head. "Citizeness Villemain couldn't imagine such a thing, and neither can I. In all honesty," he added between mouthfuls, "I'd sooner expect it of Célie, rather than her mother. She must have been just the sort of sentimental, credulous girl that a bounder like Saint-Ange—good God."

They stared at each other over the cooling dish of chicken.

"What became of the child, we asked ourselves. The answer was right before us. The old lady told me that Célie adored the boy, far more than an elder sister might be expected to."

Brasseur smacked his palm down on the tabletop, setting the dishes to rattling. "The Villemain woman said Montereau was away in Russia during Célie's so-called illness. He never knew a thing."

"If her husband was away for a good long time, all Madame Montereau had to do was pin a pillow under her gown for a few months . . . perhaps her maid was in on it, too. You couldn't carry it off now, not with the little wisps women are wearing these days, but you could have done anything under the sort of gowns they were wearing in 'eighty-nine or 'ninety."

"Who's to say Montereau doesn't know everything?" Brasseur suggested. "Say you're a middle-aged nobleman with a nice tidy fortune, and a pretty daughter, but no son. You desperately want an heir, but there's no sign of any more children. Then what should happen but your daughter confesses she's been indiscreet and is in the family way. Mightn't you seize the chance to provide yourself with an heir, and preserve your daughter's reputation, all at the same time?"

Aristide nodded. He meditated a moment, tapping his fork on the table. "Perhaps. It *could* be done in the strictest secrecy. I wonder . . ."

"And if Montereau had a secret to keep, mightn't he have had a motive—no, that's no good. We know where he was that afternoon and evening, dining with three friends at Méot's. I asked Méot myself, and he swore up and down that Montereau had been there for hours on *décadi*."

A puffing messenger boy rapped on the door, shuffled in, and dropped a folded note on Brasseur's desk. "We'll return to this shortly," Brasseur said, and unfolded the note. With a grunt he thrust it at Aristide. "From Montereau."

> *Citizen Commissaire:*
>
> *You ask me about my former secretary. His name was Philippe Aubry and I employed him from February of 1789 to January of 1791. His family was ancient and respected, though penurious.*
>
> *I dismissed him from my service when I learned he had killed a distant kinsman of mine in a duel several years previously,*

when he was only seventeen years old. The unhappy affair, I understand, was conducted in an honorable manner and no prosecution resulted from it (the hapless young man's family, for the sake of his posthumous reputation, chose not to press criminal charges against Aubry). I could not and cannot, however, overlook the fact that Aubry was responsible for the death of one of my relatives, that the affair was most scandalous in all respects, and that dueling is illegal; and that therefore I was sadly deceived in Aubry's character.

I believe he became entangled in politics after leaving my employ, and was attached to the Rolandist party until the unfortunate Jacobin coup of June 2, 1793. I know nothing more of him.

"Philippe Aubry," Aristide repeated.

"You think this is the fellow?"

"Citizeness Clément said he was one of the Brissotins' hangers-on. If he's as sentimental and pompous as his letters, it's likely he agreed with every bloated word that dropped from old Minister Roland's mouth. I think this is Célie's admirer, certainly."

"Well, Philippe Aubry, whoever and wherever you are: Are you a murderer?" Brasseur scrawled a brief letter and shouted for his secretary.

"Dautry, consult our section registers for any trace of this Aubry. If you have no luck, I want copies of this letter sent as soon as possible to the commissaires of the following sections . . ." Rising, he frowned at the map of Paris pinned on the wall. "Tuileries, Place-Vendôme, Champs-Élysées, Unité, Mucius-Scevola, Ouest, Théâtre-Français, Fontaine-de-Grenelle . . . that should do for a start."

"The more genteel sections?" Aristide said, glancing over Brasseur's shoulder. He returned to his chair and leaned back, tapping his fingers on the arm. "Brasseur . . . I think our friend François might be adept at flirting with chambermaids."

Brasseur chuckled. François, they had agreed long ago, was one of the cleverest spies in Paris.

"I think we might send him along to Rue de l'Université to work his way into the Montereau kitchens," Aristide continued, scribbling a brief note and sealing it, "and learn a few trivial facts about the family. The sort of thing any lackey might gossip about over a cup of hot chocolate or a glass of the master's brandy. I do feel an itch to satisfy this abominable curiosity of mine."

He had a reply from François before the day was out. Continuing on foot from the Panthéon, for his cab driver refused to go farther after dusk into the congestion, dirt, and stink of the faubourg Marcel, Aristide followed the tortuous, ill-lit back streets to Rue Geneviève and continued down the hill toward Rue de l'Arbalète, as his friend's note directed him. He paused, hoping he had not lost his way in the tangle of alleys and passageways, just as a sturdy figure shouldered itself through the shabby pedestrians and clapped a hand on his shoulder.

François did have another name, but he was unaccountably reluctant to divulge it. Nor had Aristide ever discovered exactly how old François was. He suspected the young man was little more than twenty, though he possessed the sharp wits and audacity, as well as the powerful build, of a man ten years his senior.

"François. Look here, I have a very discreet job for you—"

"All business, aren't you? Come on, let's have a drink first." He slapped Aristide on the back and led him to a nearby wineshop, all but deserted in the twilight. "What'll you have?"

"Despite your invitation, I suspect I'll be the one to pay for our wine; so you'd better be content with something straight from the cask." Aristide pointed François to the far end of one of the trestle tables, avoiding the handful of roughly dressed men, evidently regulars, who clustered about the meager fire, smoking and playing cards. After ordering a jug of cheap red wine from the scowling counterman who slouched toward them, he glanced dubiously through the smoky gloom at the carter who snored, head cradled on his arms, at the other end of the table.

"*He's* not doing any eavesdropping," François said with a grin. He sidled along the length of the bench, daintily picked a pack of cards from the sleeping man's coat, and returned to Aristide. "I've been polishing my talents since I saw you last."

"At picking pockets?"

"Huh. This fellow wouldn't wake up unless you lit a fire under his rump. No, I meant my talents at card playing. Care for a game?"

"Certainly not," Aristide said, amused. "I imagine you'd have me plucked like a chicken in half an hour."

"So, about this job." François shuffled the cards and fanned them. "I don't suppose it requires card playing? Here, take one."

Aristide chose a card at random. "I fear not."

"Too bad." François took it back, shuffled vigorously, and cut the pack. "That your card? Liberty of worship, otherwise known as the queen of wands?"

"Of course it is. And you've plainly become accomplished at slipping cards into your sleeve." As François took possession of the wine jug, Aristide absently began to lay the cards out on the scarred, wine-stained table. "But I need a pair of eyes, not a cardsharp. What would you say to spending a few days idling in the company of servants in a wealthy household?"

"Pretty girls?" said François, tossing back a glass and pouring himself another.

"A few," Aristide admitted, thinking back to the domestics whom they had questioned at the Hôtel de Montereau. "But for heaven's sake control yourself. How are you to ask questions of everyone if you're in bed over the stable with the kitchen maid?"

"Eh, I see your point. Well, it'll be a sad temptation, but I suppose I can steel myself against it. So what am I asking while I flirt with the girls?"

"The address is the Hôtel de Montereau on Rue de l'Université. Some may still call it the Hôtel de Soyecourt; the master is the ex-Comte de Soyecourt. I want to know some unimportant little facts about the family, facts any chambermaid could tell you if she's inclined to gossip: for example, if a distant relative, a fellow of unsavory reputation named Saint-Ange, was a frequent visitor, oh, six or seven years ago. And whether or not the late lady of the house kept the same lady's maid all during her pregnancy—not the last pregnancy, mind you, not the one that killed her, but when she was pregnant with the boy, Théodore, who is now six years old."

François scribbled a few words on a dirty scrap of paper and nodded. "Lady's maid. Easy. Any chambermaid'll be ready to gossip about the other servants, or why somebody else got sacked. What else?"

"And I want to know where the boy was born."

"Funny questions you have. What's all this leading to?"

"It may be connected to the death of a young woman, the daughter of the house. She was twenty-two years old; whatever foolish errors she may have committed, she didn't deserve to die. Help me find her murderer."

When François had left him, Aristide sat in the wineshop for a half hour more, gazing at the pyramid of oaken casks at the far end of the common room. This grimy tavern, sure to become noisy with local chatter as the evening regulars drifted in, was no place to sit and think, nor yet to spend a leisurely, solitary hour or two. He did not yet want to return to his own lodgings; Clotilde, his landlady, a handsome widow not far past forty, tended to clumsily pursue bachelors. She had taken a special interest in him ever since he had made the mistake, three years before, in a rare impetuous moment, of sharing her bed for a single night. Though he liked her well enough, he knew she would be there as usual in her parlor, like an amiable spider lurking in its web, with a coquettish smile and a bottle and a cozy fire, and he was not in the mood for feminine companionship.

At length he rose, as the shop began to fill with customers, and set off northward over the hill of the Panthéon and toward the Seine. He briefly debated visiting the Café Manoury, in the hope that he might encounter one of a handful of old acquaintances, but at last decided against it in favor of the bright lights, clamor, and restless, anonymous crowds of the Palais-Égalité.

Twenty minutes' walk brought him to Rue Honoré, busy with fashionable diners and theatergoers, and the Palais-Égalité, once the mansion of the dead king's cousin before the Revolution, its enclosed gardens and arcades now the liveliest public ground in Paris. A few whores waiting beneath the trees, bolder than the rest, called out to him as he ambled through the garden, emptier now that many of the cafés had taken in their tables for the winter. He bought a cone of sugared almonds from a girl carrying a tray of sweetmeats and strolled on. Pimps, flower sellers, and sideshow barkers strove for his attention.

The enclosed gardens, once known as the Palais-Royal in the dead-and-gone days of royalty, had grown more riotous than ever since the Terror had ended two years previously. The shopkeepers had already hung their shutters for the night, but the cafés, restaurants, dance halls, theaters, gambling parlors, brothels, and sideshows remained open to serve the vast, pleasure-hungry clientele that had grown rich and come to prominence during the Revolution. Now that most of the old aristocracy had fled or were remaining discreetly unassertive, the speculators and war profiteers had scrambled to take their place and buy their abandoned town houses, flaunting fortunes suddenly made from army contracts, the purchase and resale of confiscated estates and church lands, and other methods that were best not inquired into.

Aristide paused to glance, amused, at the garish bills outside the tiny, disreputable theater where the Wild Man of the Indies pranced about, roared unintelligibly, and abandoned himself to "the mysteries of nature" with a squealing girl twelve times daily (nineteen shows on *décadi*). The Wild Man of the Indies, Brasseur had told him once, was actually a blacksmith from Marseilles, but whom did it hurt to claim otherwise?

Fashionable couples pushed past him along the arcade, wearing garments that would have seemed as bizarre as the Wild Man to the Parisians of a decade ago. He glanced wryly down at his own plain black coat and waistcoat as a slender boy clad in an outlandish striped coat and tall hat sauntered past through the jostling crowds. At thirty-eight he had no desire to ape the outrageous fashions of the spoiled and prodigal eighteen-year-olds who could scarcely remember the old regime. Under the insouciant corruption of the Directory, the governing body that had replaced the National Convention after the Terror's end, the Palais-Égalité swarmed with such fantastic creatures, the voguish youths widely nicknamed *incroyables*, "unbelievables," and their scantily draped, loose-living companions. To them, Aristide thought, 1789 was a lifetime ago, a distant era of history growing faint on the far side of an unthinkably deep chasm. When those young men had been schoolboys, a mere seven years ago, who could have thought that before they were grown a revolution would sweep through France, overturning monarchy, church, and age-old custom, executing a king and queen, exiling nobility, and elevating bourgeois merchants and lawyers to sudden, intoxicating wealth, prestige, and power?

He strolled inside the Café Février and lingered over a demitasse of coffee, savoring the gilt-framed mirrors and crystal chandeliers that shimmered in the candlelight, a haunting reminder of a more refined way of life now seemingly gone forever. A dog-eared news journal abandoned on a table beckoned him. Thirty-three of the agitators involved in the previous month's uprising at the Grenelle military camp had been sentenced to death and shot, while the English occupiers had been driven out of Corsica, thanks to the occupying army in Italy. The war, that ill-conceived war that once had threatened the very existence of the young Republic, was at last turning in France's favor, with the armies led now by such fresh, talented men as General Bonaparte. It was indeed a new era, Aristide reflected, not without a touch of mingled relief and regret; the dazzling, decadent world of the old regime would never return.

He recognized a familiar face as he looked up from the journal. Not far from him, Sanson sat alone, elegant in a well-tailored coat with velvet collar and crisp muslin cravat, a newspaper and a half-empty liqueur glass before him. Their eyes met and they exchanged gazes for a moment before Sanson turned away. Aristide rose.

"Would you care to keep me company?"

"You're the police agent," Sanson said. "Sorry; I've forgotten your name."

"Ravel."

"Of course you won't have forgotten mine." Sanson hesitated and at last took his glass and joined Aristide at his table. "Well, why not. Do you come here often, then?"

"Now and then. I supposed you spent your evenings more often at the tavern on Rue des Lavandières."

Sanson nodded. "I used to live not far from there, when I was still in the National Guard. But sometimes one wants something a bit more civilized."

The waiter arrived with another glass of anisette for Sanson and they sipped their drinks in silence. Aristide covertly observed his companion. *The executioner dresses better than I do*, he thought with a flicker of amusement.

"What do you want this time?" Sanson asked after setting down his empty glass.

"Nothing but a comrade, I assure you."

"You could find more congenial comrades than I."

"I don't choose to."

Sanson absently turned his glass in his fingers. The man had fine hands, Aristide mused, long and well-shaped, the deft, sensitive hands of an artist or a surgeon rather than a hangman.

"Listen," said Sanson, "I don't know why you think you want to befriend me, unless it's some kind of morbid curiosity; but you ought to know that men like me don't have friends."

Aristide stirred. "The Revolution has changed things—"

"It might have changed our status under the law, but it didn't change people's hearts. Some people still shy away from my father and my uncles and me, as if we'd give them the plague. I don't imagine you'd want the son of a hangman working for you, or dining at your table, or marrying your daughter."

"It wouldn't make any difference to me, if he were a decent man."

"I beg your pardon," Sanson said after a moment more of uneasy silence. "I'm being damn rude, and I apologize. I've gone for most of my life expecting people to snub me, so I've grown accustomed to giving back as good as I get. But I, of all people, shouldn't strike at a hand offered me in friendship. Let me buy you a glass."

"Coffee will do. Thanks."

"Like you, I imagined the Revolution would change things, but in the end . . ." Sanson shook his head and beckoned a waiter over to order, then turned back to Aristide. "When I was a boy, I wanted to be a cavalry officer with a fine uniform and a magnificent horse. Then I learned what my father was, and his father before him, and *his* father, five generations back, and I also learned no military academy would have me. But thanks to the Revolution, I realized I did have a chance at some other life. I joined the National Guard, and for the first time in my life people were treating me with real respect." He paused, savoring the memory.

"I made captain after we went on some expeditions in the country, and I thought I might fulfill my dream of being a soldier after all. I enjoyed it, I truly did. The pay wasn't bad and I had my own lodgings—I transferred to a permanent posting in the city later on—and I was living like any other man with some money in his pocket. People treated me as an equal; though you can be sure I didn't go about announcing whose son I was. Thank God Sanson's a common name."

Aristide looked at him, imagining the handsome young officer he had been, proud and self-assured in his smart blue-and-white uniform. "What happened to change your mind?"

"What happened? Last year my father decided to retire; he sat me down and asked me about my plans, because he could hand over his office directly to me, if I wanted it. Was I sure I wanted to be a soldier, and did I think there was a future in it for me. Did I think, if the monarchy ever returned, that I'd be allowed to hold onto the rank I'd gained. He didn't *want* me to become an executioner, God knows, but in his heart he felt I had no other choice, no more than he'd had. 'Accept the position and be guaranteed a good income,' he said. 'The prejudice against us will always exist.' Prejudice might keep me from advancing any farther; it might even, someday, take away my military rank." He sighed.

"Well, the old man is a realist; he's had to be, these forty years. So am I. I resigned my commission and sold my dreams for a mess of pottage; though, unlike Esau, I surrendered to my birthright instead of giving it away. And here I am, no different from my ancestors, no matter how hard I'd tried to escape their legacy. People who once were proud to shake my hand now shy away from me. It's been that way for five hundred years; you can't understand what it's like."

"Can't I?"

Sanson frowned. "You told me you weren't one of us."

"I'm not. But I think I understand as well as you, what it is to be whispered about, and shunned and insulted, merely because we're our fathers' sons. And later to be denied our choice of a place in the world, a place we might otherwise deserve through our own merits, because we're our father's sons."

"Not an executioner," Sanson said at last. "The other way round?"

"Yes," Aristide said, without meeting his eyes, "the other way round. The one thing more contemptible than the hangman." He pushed away his coffee cup. "Now you may tell me, if you like, that I'm not worthy of your friendship, because I'm my father's son."

"I'm sorry."

"I don't want your pity, just as you don't want mine; but I'd like your friendship."

Sanson nodded. "Maybe I'm too thin-skinned about it at times. But if you'd gone all your life with fingers pointing at you . . ."

"I have," Aristide said. "Not all my life, but long enough."

"My father, he even used to use an assumed name sometimes when he went outside our quarter, so no one would know who he was. It was worse then, of course, in the 'sixties when he was young. Finally he decided to brazen it out; he claimed that as an officer of the law courts he deserved a title of nobility as much as any magistrate, and wore a blue brocade coat and a dress sword, like a duke. And then the royal prosecutor told him he shouldn't wear blue in public, because it was the color of nobility and he, of all people, wasn't entitled to it. God in Heaven!"

"What did your father do then?"

"Told the fellow exactly what he could do with his blue, and wore green brocade instead. Listen, do you ride?" he added as Aristide smiled.

"For pleasure? Now and then, when I have the chance to."

"I often hire a good saddle horse and go riding in the Bois, or Monceau, or out to Saint-Denis. You're welcome to join me if you have an afternoon free."

"Thanks," said Aristide. "I'll keep it in mind. If I have an afternoon free."

12

So far I've reports from six different sections, of eighteen people whose name may or may not be Philippe Aubry," said Brasseur, glancing up from his desk as Aristide wandered into his office the following morning. "And I've some interesting news about that hotel murder last month."

"Still not interested in looking at it," Aristide said automatically, "if that's what you're about to bring up. Or have you found the woman?"

"No, Didier hasn't come up with anything, but I've just had a complaint from a hotel keeper on Rue Montpensier who claimed a man and woman came in together last night, asked for a room, and then had words. The woman suggested they have champagne sent up, and the man didn't want to go to the extra expense for a whore. She insisted, and the man refused, and suddenly she calls him a rude name and walks out."

"And the woman was wearing men's clothes?" Aristide said, amused, taking the report Brasseur handed him.

Brasseur nodded. "Exactly. Though the clerk couldn't describe her, worse luck."

"I'd think she would be quite memorable—"

"Oh, yes, the clothes. Breeches and riding boots, striped satin coat, a tall hat. But he was so busy ogling a woman showing off her legs and her arse in a pair of tight breeches, that he scarcely noticed the *woman*. All he could say was that she was fair-haired, pretty, in her twenties. And sounded like a lady. Till she called the fellow a stingy prick."

"A lady?"

"Well-bred. Not like a common streetwalker. But he didn't notice one damned thing else. Not the color of her eyes, shape of her face, nose, nothing. It's not much to work with. I doubt he'd be able to identify her if we put her in front of him—without the men's clothes, that is."

"And if you do find her, and parade her before him in male costume," Aristide said, nodding, "any defense counsel worth his salt can play merry havoc with the case, claiming mistaken identity, that the witness is identifying the clothing and not the woman. And of course he'd be right." He sighed and read through the report.

"Blue striped satin coat," he said, rereading the witness's statement. "Cut high, with long tails. And a tall hat . . . my God, Brasseur, I think I saw her myself!"

"You? When?"

"Last night, at the Palais-Égalité." He searched his memory, recalling a slender, fair-haired figure in the crowd. The face . . . the face was a blur, a hazy recollection of youthful features. He shook his head. "I scarcely paid attention, and she was a good few paces away. Damn! I wasn't close enough to recognize her for a woman; I supposed she was merely one more strutting *incroyable,* some rich army contractor's brat."

"Never mind; perhaps we'll get lucky again. At least no one died last night, and that's something." Brasseur patted the heap of reports on his desk. "Pull up a chair; let's find Philippe Aubry."

"It would have been too much to ask that this Aubry should live in your section," Aristide grumbled twenty minutes later, glancing up from another letter that reported an "Aubry, P." on a section register. "Why can't these commissaires at least write down a full name in their records?"

Brasseur grunted. "Never mind. Toss out the ones you can."

"Aubry, Ph.-L., physician, age forty-seven, Fontaine-de-Grenelle section. I think not. Aubry, Ph.-J.-B., age fourteen, same address, clearly his son. What about you?"

"I've found one who'd be the right age. Aubry, P.-M.-J., *rentier,* age twenty-eight, Cour de Rouen, Théâtre-Français section. Now '*rentier*' covers a lot of possibilities; plenty of people claim they're living on rents from their property if they have an income they don't want anyone to look at too closely."

The clock struck noon. Aristide took up the last letter from the heap at his left. "P. Aubry, son of J.-N. Aubry, age four. I think we can safely eliminate him."

"So what are we left with?" said Brasseur.

"I have three who could fit our description. You?"

"Just the one. So it's four, all told. Tomorrow we'll pay visits to these gentlemen, shall we?"

18 Brumaire (November 8)

Brasseur closed the door on Philippe-Nicolas Aubry, apothecary, of the Section de la Place-Vendôme, who was stout, sandy-haired, pockmarked, and blessed with a wife and howling baby. "Well, damned if I can imagine that silly girl falling for *him*."

"Will that be all, then?" inquired the peace officer from the local commissariat, who had accompanied them. "I've my rounds to make."

They parted company at the street corner. "Hmm," Brasseur said, consulting the list of names, "let's see; the Tuileries section is closest. Fancy a walk?"

Ph.-M. Aubry of Rue Froidmanteau, however, proved to be not Philippe Aubry but Philibert Aubry of the Municipal Guard, a gigantic young man with menacing mustaches. They retreated, with apologies.

"Cour de Rouen?" said Brasseur, glancing at the list.

They flagged down a passing fiacre and jounced across the Seine to the Théâtre-Français section, where the porter at Cour de Rouen informed them that citizen Aubry was not at home.

"Does he often go out?" Aristide inquired pleasantly, settling himself on a bench in the arched public passage through the ground floor of the building to brush the dust from his sleeves.

"Usually he spends *décadi* at home, or taking the air in the gardens. But he hasn't been home so much this past week. Now he does go out in the evening a fair bit, to be sure."

"Does he. To call on friends?"

"I expect so. He goes often to the theater, too. A cordial young gentleman, he is."

"Let me be sure I have the right man," Aristide said, consulting the list of names. "This is one Philibert Aubry, lieutenant in the Municipal Guard?"

The porter shook his head. "No, the young man who lodges upstairs is Philippe Aubry, and he's no soldier. Something to do with the government, though somebody told me he was an aristo before the Revolution."

"Many ex-nobles are active in the government, aren't they?" Aristide said vaguely, rising. "Director Barras, even. Well, evidently we have the wrong address. Come along, Brasseur."

"*Got* him," said Brasseur, with deep satisfaction, as soon as they had turned the corner to the Cour du Commerce. "I think this calls for a modest celebration, and here we are at the back door to Zoppi's. What do you say to a glass of something before we visit the local commissariat?"

"What now?"

"We set a watch on the house, with the commissaire's cooperation, and engage someone to gossip with the servants. Discreetly. It wouldn't do to frighten off the bird before we're ready to trap it."

"I'll do it," Aristide said.

"You?"

"I want to do it. I want to lay hold of this swine, if he's the one, and see him on his way to the Grève. Give me enough to buy some old clothes and I'll start day after tomorrow."

"All right, if you're so eager. Come on, let's have that drink."

————

20 Brumaire (November 10)

Collecting information from strangers was easier than it seemed, if one was a passable actor. Aristide visited a few peddlers in his own quarter who sold secondhand clothing and outfitted himself in a shabby old brown coat and waistcoat that had seen their best days ten years before. A day's worth of razor stubble on his face, and a battered, once-respectable three-cornered hat and a pair of scuffed shoes secured with laces, not buckles, completed his costume of an unemployed domestic servant, alcoholic and down on his luck.

Fearing the porter at Aubry's house would recognize him, he hauled François away for a day from his pursuit of the maidservants on Rue de l'Université. While François passed the time around the corner with the porter, Aristide lounged about in the Cour du Commerce, listening to the rhythmic clack-bang from a nearby printer's shop and gazing at the bills stuck on the walls advertising theatrical performances, fashionable shops, and miracle cures. From time to time, in keeping with his disguise, he assisted well-dressed women across the gutter of black, viscous mud that ran down the center of the street, receiving a few deniers for his service.

By midafternoon when François rejoined him, the narrow street was in shadow and the November breeze had a bite to it. "That was easy," François muttered, leaning nonchalantly against the wall beside him. "The porter's name is Deschamps and he'd talk your ear off if you let him. Misses his family back in Switzerland, and panting for someone to pass the time with. Even stood me to a shot of brandy."

Aristide rubbed icy hands together, wishing he had included a pair of gloves in his disreputable costume. "Well?"

"Philippe Aubry. Second floor front, bachelor with one manservant. Third son of some country baron. Works for none other than Director La Revellière-Lépeaux himself. Calls himself an undersecretary. But a tag like that can mean just about anything."

Aristide raised an eyebrow. The information tallied, more or less, with what Rosalie Clément had told him.

"A spy in high places?"

"Looks like it. The sort who hangs about fashionable salons, eats and drinks plenty of whatever he's offered, and reports everything he hears to the boss."

"Go on," Aristide said.

"He's been in and out of the house, Deschamps says. He came into the foyer while I was having that glass. Deschamps is the accommodating sort . . . you know, 'Is there anything you need, citizen,' 'Let me help you with that parcel, citizen,' always with his hand out for a sou or two. But Aubry hurried up the stairs without more than a 'Good day.' Looked struck with a case of nerves, if you ask me. Walks fast, won't meet people's eyes, paler than he ought to be."

"What about Aubry's manservant?" Aristide inquired. He caught sight of a cocoa seller and ambled over to his handcart, François slouching along behind him.

"Name's Brelot. Deschamps pointed him out to me. Want me to follow him when he goes out?"

"We both will. Try to get him into a tavern if you can. He'll be the one with the goods, if there's anything to tell." He sipped at the cup of hot chocolate the vendor handed him. It was a vile, muddy brew, as he had expected, but he was grateful for the heat of the tin cup in his chilled fingers.

"Got a sou to spare?" François said, eyeing the vendor's charcoal-heated copper vat hungrily. "I haven't had any dinner today—hoy! That's him. Aubry."

Aristide gulped down the last of the chocolate, thrust the cup back at the man, and peered down the street. His first thought was that Rosalie's perception had been extraordinarily acute. The man hurrying past them was a slender young Adonis of classic beauty, his delicate, almost feminine features and clear complexion scarcely marred by the unhealthy pallor that surely was not natural to him. Long eyelashes framed large dark eyes beneath thick, dark, waving hair. Aristide could well believe that such a pretty fellow could have captured a susceptible girl's heart.

Aubry strode toward the gate leading out to Rue des Cordeliers. Despite his comeliness, as Aubry neared him Aristide could tell that he stood scarcely at middle height. Aristide considered himself tolerably good-looking, in an austere sort of way, but he became painfully aware of his own lank, gray-flecked hair and somber mien and for an instant found himself absurdly pleased that he was half a head taller than Aubry.

François was hissing something in his ear. He tore his gaze from Aubry's retreating back. "What's that?"

"I said, d'you want me to go after him? Make sure he doesn't run?"

"He won't, if he hasn't already. The servant's the one I want." He turned about, ready to slink into the Cour de Rouen and watch the house, but instead, to his dismay, found himself face-to-face with Rosalie Clément.

"Citizen Ravel!" she exclaimed. "I thought it was you, though I couldn't quite believe it. Whatever are you doing in those frightful clothes?"

Oh, damn, Aristide said to himself, and promptly seized her arm and led her away toward the Rue des Arcs gate, praying that François would ignore them and continue to wait for Brelot. "Forgive me," he muttered to her as he hurried her beneath the archway to the swarming street beyond, "but you've come by at an inopportune time. I'd rather not be recognized."

She stared at him round-eyed for an instant before comprehending and clapping a hand over her mouth. "Oh, I'm sorry! Have I spoiled everything?"

"No, it's all right. Perhaps you can help me. Does the name Aubry mean anything to you?"

"No, I don't think so." A few strands of dark chestnut hair, escaped from beneath her neat linen bonnet, danced about her face in the damp breeze as she shook her head. "Is that Célie's 'Philippe,' then?"

"It's probable."

"You've found him? Are you going to arrest him?"

"If it's likely he committed the murders, and we can collect enough evidence."

"Citizen," she said abruptly, "will you send word to me when you have him? I want to see him—to see him get everything he deserves for what he did. I want to see him writhe."

He paused for an instant, taken off guard by her naked rancor. She glanced up at him.

"Célie was my friend. Wouldn't you want to see your friend's murderer pay for his crime?"

"We don't yet know that it was he who murdered her," Aristide reminded her.

"Who else *could* it have been?" she snapped. "Don't be obtuse. Only lovers can turn so violently from love to hatred. Who else could possibly have wanted to hurt her?" She glared at him for a moment, looking away as her lower lip trembled. "I want justice for Célie. If I can do anything to help you find this man and make him pay, I'll do it."

"That's generous of you," said Aristide, "but I think we have it well in hand."

"Nevertheless, if there's anything I can do—asking questions, whatever it is you do," she added with a quick sardonic glance at his costume, "and if I can be of help, don't hesitate to ask me. You know where to find me."

She gave him a quick nod and without further words vanished amid the passersby on Rue des Arcs. Aristide gazed after her for a moment, thoughtful, before slouching back into the more tranquil Cour du Commerce. François had disappeared. Guessing that François had spotted Brelot and followed him, and that he need not loiter about in the cold until François had reported his progress with the manservant, he thankfully strolled out to the quay and turned his steps homeward.

13

Anote from François, thrust underneath his door, awaited him the
next morning. *Found Brelot—went to cabaret—getting friendly. Meet
me Cour du Com. 9 o'clock. F.*

That would be nine o'clock in the evening, of course; François
never rose before noon if he could help it. Aristide considered several
ways of passing the day after a quick stop to report his progress to
Brasseur, and at last decided upon a visit to Rosalie Clément.

She was just leaving the boardinghouse after the midday dinner
when he arrived and tipped his hat to her.

"I wished to apologize for my rather abrupt behavior yesterday."

"Why should you apologize? I stupidly intruded."

"There's no harm done, at any rate. Might I walk with you?"

"Come with me if you like," she said indifferently. "I'm going for a
stroll in the gardens."

They crossed Rue Jacques and passed through the gates by the
boarded-up seminary of St. Louis to the public gardens of the Luxembourg Palace. She chose a path beside a long row of graceful
horse-chestnut trees, leafless now in gray late autumn. "Do you walk
here often?" Aristide said, lamely, searching for something to say to
her.

"It's pleasant, and it's nearby. Sometimes I feed the sparrows. My life is not very eventful."

"It must be dull in that boardinghouse," he agreed. "You said you were once married. Widowed?"

"Yes."

"You seem quite young—was he killed in the war?"

"He was guillotined in 1793."

The word *guillotined* sent an icy pang lancing through him and he swallowed hard. "Forgive me—if I've said something I oughtn't, reminded you—"

"Not at all."

"But your husband . . ."

"It was a marriage of convenience only, and he wasn't an agreeable man. I know it sounds completely callous to say it, but there it is. He fully deserved it. I'm afraid I couldn't conjure up any tears when I learned he'd been shortened."

He recognized some of his own nature in her lack of sentimentality, her prickly pride, and her evident distaste for the company of fools. "I didn't quite know what to make of you when I questioned you the other day," he said at last, "but Célie Montereau's maid was right: you come of gentlefolk, don't you? Or even the aristocracy. You have that certain"—he was about to say "chilly," but substituted a more politic word instead—"that certain stoic manner about you."

"What if I do? Blue blood doesn't count for much these days, unless you have money. And though he had the dubious distinction of being embraced by Sainte Guillotine, my late husband was just a wealthy lawyer—whose property was confiscated when they cut his head off, worse luck."

She would be pretty, he realized, with some paint to enhance her dark eyes and soften the sharp angles of her face, and a well-cut, fashionable gown instead of the dowdy India cotton print dress painstakingly altered from the style of three or four years ago.

"I'm sorry."

"That he was guillotined," she inquired, "or that the government took everything?"

"I lost a friend in 'ninety-three—he died with Brissot—"

She laughed. "Oh, no. I'm sure your friend died for his republican principles. My husband, however, died because he'd been caught arranging some affairs for royalist acquaintances who'd emigrated: selling their property and sending gold abroad, of course taking his own fat commission out of it. He imagined he could profit nicely from the Revolution. Well, he discovered otherwise, and they guillotined him as he deserved. *I'm* certainly not sorry about it, except for his lack of foresight in not looking out for his fortune when he fell under suspicion." She nodded and turned away to sit on a bench beside a bed of faded, weather-beaten chrysanthemums. "Good day, citizen."

He recognized a polite but firm dismissal when he encountered it. "I'll send you word when I know anything more about Célie Montereau's death," he told her, and left her alone with the sparrows.

François met him, camouflaged once more in his squalid coat and hat, in the Cour du Commerce after darkness had fallen, and together they waited for Brelot to appear. At last a sturdy, curly-headed young man sauntered out the door, whistling, and François slouched easily along behind him through the murky back streets until he ambled into a tavern near the Place Maubert. Aristide allowed them fifteen minutes to become reacquainted over a glass and then followed them inside.

Brelot and François sat with a half-empty flask between them, laughing uproariously at a joke. The young man's preferred tipple, it seemed, was cheap red Burgundy wine. Aristide joined them, loudly recognizing François as an old and dear friend, and called for another flask of wine. In half an hour the three of them were boasting together as if they had known each other all their lives.

"So how's tricks?" François inquired at last, turning to Aristide. "Your new place better than the last one?"

They had agreed he was to be a down-at-heel manservant, newly engaged by an employer. "Not bad," he said. "He lets me out now and then."

"Heavy work?"

"No worse than anywhere else."

"*My* gentleman," Brelot said, anxious to remain in the conversation, "he's not at all bad to work for. A nice, civil young gentleman with regular habits, bachelor though he is. None of this coming in and out at all hours, and rousting you out of your bed at three in the morning."

"What's he do?" Aristide asked. "Live on his property?"

"No, he's a climber, if you ask me. Hangs about the swells and goes to their parties. But civil, like I said. And the ladies love him, with his looks and all."

"Do they, now," François said with a leer. "A lot of lady visitors?"

"Less than you'd think. Now if it was *me*..." Brelot grinned and poured himself another brimming glass of wine. "If it was me, if I was as pretty as Aubry, you'd see a lot more women about me than he's got."

"Maybe he likes men," Aristide suggested.

"No, he likes women all right. I saw him once in the gardens with a young lady, arm in arm, snug as you please."

"A young lady?"

"Pretty little thing, blond, clothes the latest shout. Gown cut down to there and up to here," he added, elbowing Aristide in the ribs, "if you catch my drift. And my own little friend, she's a dressmaker's assistant, and she tells me the less of a gown you have these days, the more it costs!"

They guffawed, drowning out the clamor in the busy tavern.

"Know who she was?" said François. "An expensive trollop?"

"She didn't look like it. No paint the way the whores wear it. But he was making sheep's eyes; he'd got it bad." Brelot lowered his voice conspiratorially. "But it's none of *my* business. You want to keep your place, you keep your eyes and ears shut. And your mouth, too. Eyes, ears, and mouth," he repeated, laboriously pointing to the features in question, "like I said, I keep 'em shut."

Aristide grinned and poured out more wine for everyone. "Well, what's the use of being in service if you can't amuse yourself with your master's scandals? Gives you something to talk about in the kitchen, or at the cabaret. My own gentleman, he got drunk last week and woke up the whole house with his singing. Enough to make you blush. I had to fetch the porter to help me drag him up the stairs and get him into bed. I ask you!"

"Well, Aubry, he's usually home by midnight, but one night last week he didn't come in till two," said Brelot, not to be outdone. "But he let himself into his rooms with his own key. Must have had to wake the porter to unbolt the street door and let him in the house, but he had the consideration to let a hard-working man get his sleep. That's quality, I can tell you. Consideration for the domestics."

"What was he doing out so late?" Aristide inquired, hiccuping.

"Lord knows."

"Sounds like a bit of a killjoy to me. Not whoring or having a few bottles somewhere?"

"Not him. Though something got him most particularly worked up that afternoon, I can tell you that," Brelot continued, happily disregarding his own self-imposed rule of discretion. "He comes in from a stroll, all smiles and good humor, then twenty minutes later rushes out, without a word, and doesn't return until the small hours. And he looked like death when I brought him his shaving water the next morning, white as a sheet. Must have had a bad evening."

Aristide lurched to his feet, clapping François on the shoulder with a slurred "back in a moment," and stepped with great dignity and care between the tables and out the side door to the mucky alley beyond. He was buttoning his culotte when François joined him, on the same errand.

"'Looked like death'!" François repeated when he had done and they had emerged together from the sewer-stink of the alley. "That sound to you like somebody with something nasty on his conscience?"

"It certainly does. Try to find out if this uncharacteristic behavior of his took place on the tenth of Brumaire."

An additional hour and a third flask of wine drew little else from Brelot. He had passed the stage of drunkeness where men became talkative, and grew boastful and impudent toward the serving maid. At last Aristide suggested that they should all meet at the tavern in two days' time, if they could get the evening from their respective employers, and bade them farewell with many loud and emotional adieux.

———

23 Brumaire (November 13)

"Citizen Ravel," said Rosalie, pausing in the doorway of the boarding-house's unheated and deserted parlor, where a grim, gray maidservant had sent Aristide to wait. "Do you have news already?"

"Nothing I ought to share at present."

"What is it you want, then?"

"To be frank, citizeness, I wanted to spend another hour in your company."

She paused and looked at him as if he had suddenly stripped off all his clothes and capered about the room doing handstands. "Why?"

Why indeed, he said to himself. Perhaps her thirst for justice for Célie spoke to something within him.

"I think I understand," she added a moment later, with a faint smile. "Your vocation has fashioned you into a student of human nature, and I expect you want to put me under your glass. Forgive me, but I'm not interested in becoming one of your specimens, like a two-headed piglet in a jar in somebody's 'cabinet of curiosities.'"

"I trust you'll believe I'd rather pass an hour with you than with a two-headed piglet," Aristide said, remembering a previous affair that had led him to the bizarre collection of scientific oddities at the Veterinary College outside Paris, and the acquaintance of an eccentric and innovative doctor who was rumored to be mad. "I called on you because I find you attractive, or at least you would be if you had some decent clothes and someone to dress your hair; and because your wits are sharp, for that's plain to see after five minutes' conversation with you; and because I find you agreeable, despite your tongue that's as sharp as your wits."

"I ought to tell you now," she said dryly, "that I'm nearly penniless, nearly friendless, and nearly thirty."

"So am I," said Aristide. "Though in truth I'm far nearer forty than thirty. Shall we compare afflictions?"

Slowly she smiled again, with a soft chuckle.

"I thought to stroll in the gardens," he continued, "but there's a chill mist in the air. Would you care to take coffee with me, or a glass of wine?"

She said little until they had arrived at a nearby tavern and taken a table. The common room was ill-lit and close, receding into gloom beneath a low, vaulted stone ceiling, but warm from a generous fire, with a shaggy dog and cat asleep at the hearth.

"To each man his own taste," Rosalie said after Aristide had ordered coffee for them both. He guessed she was not referring to their order. "If you insist on dogging my footsteps, then I suppose I had better give in with a good grace. At least tell me your name."

"Ravel."

"I know that. Haven't you another?"

"Aristide Ravel."

"Aristide?" she echoed him, amused. "Don't tell me you're one of those daft ultrapatriots who renamed themselves after classical republicans. Aristides was a famous lawgiver of Athens, wasn't he?"

"A lawgiver and general," he said as their drink arrived.

"But why not choose a truly mellifluous name like Anaxagoras, for example?" She daintily sipped at her coffee. "No, that's already taken. Poor old Chaumette. All that earnest patriotism, and still he got sent to the chopper. Or what about Cincinnatus—that's a lovely one. And of course there's always Brutus."

Aristide suppressed a smile. "I understand that I was christened Aristide at my mother's request."

"Your mother must have been quite the scholar."

"It's a saint's name," he told her, enjoying the bafflement that for an instant flickered in her face. "Some obscure Greek of antiquity. Did you not know?"

Her shapely mouth twitched into a smile. "You're looking more respectable today than when I interrupted you in the street. Did you learn anything more about this Aubry?"

"I told you, I shouldn't be talking about it at present."

"That's a pity. That was a very convincing costume, you know. Every inch the seedy errand boy. But when you're Aristide Ravel and not some disreputable character skulking in the shadows, do you always look like a crow that's fallen into an inkwell?"

"I confess it," he said, refusing to be baited. The gray tabby cat on the hearth stretched itself to its feet with an inquisitive mew and padded over to them. Rosalie leaned down to stroke it, still glancing quizzically at Aristide.

"Because you appear sober and official in black? Hasn't anyone ever told you that you look just the way people think a police spy ought to look?"

"First of all, I am not a spy—"

"I thought you said you weren't an inspector."

"I'm not. Once I thought I wanted to join the police and work my way up to commissaire; but now you couldn't pay me enough to do Brasseur's work day in and day out, inspecting tradesmen's scales and issuing peddlers' licenses. Sending for the knacker to haul away dead cart horses. Saints preserve me."

"Well, 'police agent,' then, if you insist. Though most people would say that's just a fancy word for a spy. Haven't you anything else to wear?"

"No."

"Seriously?"

"Seriously. Aside from one riding costume, which doesn't get much use here in Paris."

"You must get paid well enough for whatever it is exactly that you do," said Rosalie. "Can't you afford a few other suits of clothes?"

"I have two other suits, one of which is a dress suit, and four waist-coats. They're all black. I find it simplifies matters."

"One would think you were in perpetual mourning for something or other."

He opened his mouth for a sharp retort, but thought better of it and took a hasty swallow of his coffee. She looked at him, tilting an eyebrow almost imperceptibly.

"I think I've brought up a sore subject."

"Forgive me." He summoned a faint smile. "I expect you know, if you've lived for some time in a cheap boardinghouse, that this is the customary dress of any educated man who's down on his luck and can afford no more than one suit of clothes; and I've been a member of *that* fraternity more often than once."

"Well, isn't that exactly the usual sort of man, your unemployed lawyer or scribbler, who isn't above accepting a few livres from the police to keep his eyes and ears open?" She gazed at him solemnly for a moment, then pushed the candle on their table toward him and peered at him, studying him, through the twilit gloom. "I'm teasing you, you know. Don't you ever smile?"

"Now and then."

"I declare you're as solemn as Robespierre. They say *he* never smiled, either."

"They're mistaken. And I smile when I find the occasion appropriate, just as I wear something other than a plain black suit when the occasion is appropriate."

She tilted her head, a little frown puckering her smooth forehead. "You do have a way of completely flattening people. You simply give them that grave stare of yours, and a very, very dry rejoinder, and one feels as if one has committed some unforgivable blunder."

The corners of his mouth twitched and she pounced. "There, you're smiling, Robespierre. Don't worry—I won't tell anyone."

"Please," Aristide said sharply, "please don't call me that."

"Robespierre?" she repeated, puzzled. "Why not?"

"My friend Mathieu used to call me 'Robespierre' sometimes, for the same reason as you did . . . because I don't often smile. He'd known Robespierre, a little, before the rift sprang up between the factions, and he claimed I was quite like him. It made us laugh."

"So why—oh. I see. This Mathieu was your friend who was—who died."

He nodded.

"I'm sorry. I didn't lose anyone I loved to the guillotine, myself. They left me quickly enough of their own volition," she added unexpectedly, her voice hard. Then she reddened, as if she had said too much.

"Another coffee?" he said.

"Thank you, no. I—I should be going."

"Do you think you're the only soul in Paris who's suffered an unhappy love affair?"

"What?"

"Forgive me, but it's not hard to guess why you're bitter, and why you won't trust a man who tells you he finds you attractive."

"You *are* an accomplished student of human nature," she said at last.

"I simply observe, and try to put myself in another's place. If I'd been hurt by someone who meant the world to me, I'd cease trusting others, too."

"Knowing that love has wounded everyone else at one time or another doesn't ease the pain."

"Sometimes telling your sorrows to someone else does."

"It's nothing you've not heard before."

"But it hurt you very much, or you'd not take such pains to pretend it was a trivial matter."

"I was in love," she said rapidly, "I thought no two people could love each other as we did; and one day not long ago he left me, without a word. Without any warning. One day he simply wasn't there. Later he sent me a letter, with no address on it, telling me he loved me, but he could never see me again, and that I shouldn't try to find him. Just like that." She gazed across the table at Aristide, unsmiling, challenging him. "So have you a woeful story of your own to compare?"

"I?"

He remembered his mother lying where she had fallen, his father standing over her weeping.

"No, not of my own."

"It doesn't hurt any less for talking about it to a prying stranger," she said abruptly, and stalked away. Aristide absently stroked the tabby cat as it wound itself about his ankles, and reflected that Rosalie seemed in a great hurry for someone who led a drab and uneventful life.

14

François had agreed to meet him late that afternoon, before going on to join Brelot at his cabaret. Aristide found him nursing a glass in the back of a dim, smoky tavern on Rue Mouffetard.

"So," said François, drinking down the last of his beer and beaming at him through the haze of stale tobacco fumes, "would you like to know how I managed at the Hôtel de Montereau?"

Aristide waved away the approaching barmaid and slid onto a bench opposite him. "Already? You do have a way with maidservants, don't you."

"Well, the younger housemaid, Sophie, the plump blue-eyed one, she's a nice warm armful—"

"I told you to flirt with the maids, not sleep with them!"

François grinned. "Eh, what's the difference? Little slut practically dragged me into the bed. Anyway, she likes to talk inbetweentimes." He drew a few bits of dirty paper from a pocket and signaled the barmaid back. "Two more glasses of beer, love. My friend's paying. So, Montereau has three estates, one in the Limousin, one in Brittany, and one somewhere near Tarbes. The boy Théodore was born in May 1790, while Montereau was in Russia and madame was taking the sea air with her convalescent daughter at the smallest property, the one in Brittany.

Sophie says it's one of those plaster-and-beam manor houses that isn't much more than a country cottage. Rustic simplicity and all that; only two old servants who live there and keep the place going. What the devil d'you want to know all this for?"

"Never mind." Aristide permitted himself a brief smile at the confirmation of his guesses. "What about the lady's maid?"

"Oh, Sophie was fluent on that subject," François said with a chuckle. "Seems madame was ill-tempered during her pregnancy. It does that to some women, I gather. She kept her own maid, but she dismissed not one, but three maids of her daughter's during a space of four months."

"Three? Dear me."

"Dismissed one who'd been with the girl a year with some feeble excuse, hired another, claimed she was unsatisfactory, and sacked her after a month. And the same with the third, who got the sack because madame said she couldn't sew a straight seam. The whole household was shaking in its boots, wondering who'd go next. Then the girl fell ill and madame said a maid wasn't necessary until she recovered."

"What about Madame Montereau's own maid?"

"One of those devoted old gorgons, I understand. Been with her since she was a child and would have fought like a she-wolf to protect her. When the mother died, she became Célie's maid and stayed on till two years ago, when she retired to the country to keep house for her brother."

Aristide nodded. Everything, thus far, confirmed his guesses about Célie Montereau's mysterious illness. "And Saint-Ange?"

"The black-sheep relative?" François said. "Well, he was given to inviting himself to the house more often than he was welcome."

"As a house guest, you mean?"

"Weeks on end, Sophie said. Took all the advantage he could of Montereau's hospitality. But an aristo like Montereau can't just show family the door, even distant cousins; it would cause talk. Oh, Sophie also mentioned," he added with a leer, "that Saint-Ange was a stallion in bed."

"Sleeping with the servants?" Aristide echoed him, raising an eyebrow. "How vulgar of him."

"Well, you can see that Montereau would be a target for a sponger; he's rich, and he has pretty servant girls and a damn fine cook. Anyhow, that was sometime in 'eighty-eight and 'eighty-nine, when everything was in an uproar in Paris. Then suddenly, in the autumn of 'eighty-nine, Saint-Ange announces he's going to buy a sugar plantation and take up farming, and is off on the first boat to Saint-Domingue, and that's the last the family hears of him. What *does* all this rubbish have to do with the price of tea in China?"

"That's none of your affair." Aristide paused, grimacing and waving away the dense smoke that had drifted toward them from a neighbor's pipe. "In fact, I think you ought now to forget everything you've learned. Did you get anything else out of the porter at Aubry's house?"

"Nothing much. Aubry doesn't get many callers. Generally he doesn't entertain much, being a bachelor, and a clean-living lad like Brelot said; he goes out for his fun. Deschamps does remember a street boy coming to the house and asking for Aubry, a fortnight ago, but Aubry had already gone out, all in a great hurry. When Deschamps said he didn't know where Aubry was, the boy cleared out without leaving a message. He remembered it because it was just an hour, or a bit more, after some other messenger boy had left a letter for Aubry."

"A letter? From the post?"

"No, delivered by hand. It was *décadi*, so there was no post that day."

"*Décadi?*" Aristide said sharply. François nodded. "The tenth, then. And Aubry picked up this letter? You mean Aubry received a letter on the tenth, went upstairs and presumably read it, and then rushed out shortly afterward, before the second errand boy arrived?"

"Looks that way," François agreed. "I see what you're getting at— you think he rushed out because of something in the letter."

"Do your best to pump Brelot some more tonight. I want to know exactly what day Aubry ran out in such haste; and if it was also the day that he didn't return until very late. See if you can pin him down to a date. He ought to remember what happened on a *décadi* more readily than he'd remember a regular workday." He reached in a pocket for a crumpled note. "Here's five livres to tide you over. I haven't any coin at the moment," he added when François looked dubiously at the paper. "This will have to do. Although you seem to have enjoyed yourself well enough without running up many expenses; I suppose Sophie fed you, too?"

François winked. "The Montereaus won't miss those chickens. Will you be at the cabaret tonight, then?"

"You can manage by yourself. I need to see Brasseur."

As he expected, Aristide found Brasseur in his office at Rue Traversine, laboriously composing a report.

"Yes," he told him as he settled himself in the armchair, "you were absolutely right about the Montereaus' little secret. François has just told me that the late Madame Montereau had a fiercely devoted maid of her own, but dismissed her daughter's maid and engaged two others in quick succession during her own alleged pregnancy."

"Maid?" Brasseur echoed him, bewildered.

"A lady's personal maid is the person most likely to know her mistress's most intimate secrets ... such as the times of her monthly courses ... or the lack of them ... or their persistence when they ought not to be present. And to know the shape of a woman beneath her chemise."

"Ha."

"But a 'devoted old gorgon,' as François put it, is likely to protect her mistress, and her mistress's secrets, with her last breath. And Théodore happened to be born not in Paris, but at the smallest and most remote of the family holdings. It's obvious, if you think about it. Toward the end of Célie's 'illness,' her mother—allegedly pregnant—whisks her away, well muffled in shawls, to recover in the healthful country air."

"And during the country holiday," said Brasseur, nodding, "madame gives birth to the boy, or so everyone is led to think, with the collusion of the faithful maid. But instead it's the 'convalescing' daughter who produces the kid, in deep secrecy, and they go home with the new heir, and it's all worked out to everyone's satisfaction and everything's covered up nicely . . . until Saint-Ange turns up again. You do think he was the father?"

"It adds up. François reports that he was a frequent, though unpopular, house guest at the Hôtel de Montereau in 1789. Sometime during the summer Saint-Ange seduces Célie, who is straight out of the convent and making sheep's eyes at her father's handsome secretary, who barely notices her. Saint-Ange keeps on amusing himself with Célie right under her father's roof until the poor child discovers she's pregnant . . . September or October, I suppose, if Théodore was born the next May. . . ."

"And as soon as she tells him she thinks she's in trouble," Brasseur said, glancing at the notes in his dossier, "the swine conveniently disappears and makes tracks for Saint-Domingue."

"Yes. Whether or not he ever went to the West Indies is another matter, but you can be sure he wouldn't have shown his face in that house again." Aristide sighed. "Somewhere in Brittany, I've no doubt, lives a rustic midwife, who was once paid very well, six years ago, to attend the lying-in of a young girl whose name she never knew. And somewhere else is a closemouthed old woman guarding a family's secrets. I expect it happens more often than we'd like to think. So," he added, "imagine Saint-Ange threatening to tell the world that Montereau's beloved son and heir is, in fact, his bastard grandson by way of his unmarried daughter."

"How do you suppose Saint-Ange learned of it?"

"All he had to do was look at young Théodore," Aristide began, and stopped in mid-sentence. "*Théodore.* I am a complete fool. The name means 'God's gift.' A welcome gift indeed, to a couple who'd given up hope of more children."

"Ha," said Brasseur again.

"Saint-Ange probably encountered the boy by chance. If you're from a certain level of society, you can take a stroll in the faubourg Germain on a Sunday, or a *décadi*, and you'll meet everyone you ever knew. I expect he's scattered his seed here and there, and could recognize his offspring when it resembled him, as well as count on his fingers. He begins squeezing Célie . . ." Aristide paused, scowling.

"No," he continued, after a moment's reflection, "I'm sure Montereau never knew the truth about Théodore. If Montereau had known the truth, Célie wouldn't have tried so hard to pay Saint-Ange off without her father's knowledge. She'd have gone to Montereau straight away and he'd have confronted Saint-Ange; probably given him a fat purse and told him to get out of France. I expect he could have persuaded a friend in high places to make the fellow's life extremely uncomfortable. And we know he couldn't have killed Saint-Ange."

"I never," said Brasseur. "Until I joined the police," he added, ponderously, "I never dreamed what sort of dirty secrets people want to hide. So what do we do about it?"

"I'd say absolutely nothing. Montereau knows nothing of his wife and daughter's secret . . . and neither do we, not about Théodore. Let it remain a simple matter of a girl led astray and desperately trying to preserve her reputation."

"Well, it's none of my business who inherits Montereau's fortune," Brasseur agreed. "But are you any closer to knowing who killed the girl? Was it Aubry?"

"I believe so."

"What did you get out of the servant?"

Aristide poured himself a splash of wine and swiftly repeated what he had learned about Aubry's letter and his subsequent behavior. "If the dates are right, it might have been something in that letter that set him off like a firework," he concluded. "He could easily have been across the river on Rue du Hasard that evening, committing the murders. And since that day, he's been nervous, distracted, as if something is gnawing at him."

"Excellent," Brasseur muttered, scribbling notes. "Looks like we've got enough here to present a case to a magistrate, once François gets the date out of this Brelot."

"Yes, I think so."

Some quaver or hesitation in Aristide's voice must have betrayed him, for Brasseur gave him a hard stare. "Here, you look like you've a case of nerves yourself. Something disagree with you?"

"It's nothing." Aristide shook his head, thinking, *God grant that we've found the right man.*

————

24 Brumaire (November 14)

While Brasseur visited Montereau to pass along the most recent intelligence about Célie's murder, Aristide returned to Rue des Cordiers and the Maison Deluc. The same middle-aged maidservant showed him into Madame Deluc's frigid salon and sent a scullion running upstairs to fetch Rosalie from her fifth-floor room.

She paused, hand on the door handle, as she saw him. "I thought you would care to know that they'll probably make an arrest within a few days," he told her.

"Is it certain, then?" The color rose in her cheeks and as quickly faded as she eagerly stepped forward. "They're going to arrest this Aubry?"

"I shouldn't mention any names."

"You think I'm likely to run to the man who murdered my friend," she retorted, "and warn him?"

"Without mentioning any names . . . we need to confirm some particulars, but yes, it's likely they'll arrest him. Of course, once they question him, he may offer some perfectly sound explanation for his movements."

She sat on the sofa and gestured Aristide to one of the chairs. "His movements?"

He seated himself and soon found himself, despite his reservations, telling her what they had learned.

"What was in the letter?" Rosalie inquired when he was done.

"I don't know. But I can guess. It seems to have upset him. If indeed he rushed out to commit murder as soon as he'd read it, I'd be willing to guess he'd learned—"

A stout middle-aged woman swept into the parlor, a mousy girl of eighteen behind her, and took a stand at the other end of the sofa with a brisk "Good day, madame."

"Good day, Citizeness Letellier," said Rosalie, frostily, evidently accustomed to her fellow boarder's manner. "Good day, Laure."

"So you have a visitor, do you?" Madame Letellier inquired sweetly. "How unusual."

With scrupulous courtesy that did not quite disguise her vexation, Rosalie introduced Aristide to Madame Letellier and her niece. "But we mustn't disturb you," she added smoothly, before Madame Letellier, with a glance at her diffident and unmarried charge, could proceed to ask Aristide who and what he was. "Citizen Ravel was just about to escort me to the gardens. We'll leave you in privacy."

He played along with her subterfuge and waited, hands clasped behind him, in the chilly parlor while she fetched her jacket and shawl. Madame Letellier plumped herself down on the sofa and eyed him.

"Are you a relative?"

"No, merely an acquaintance. A friend we shared in common died quite suddenly, not long ago." He suspected that the gossip would be all over the boardinghouse by nightfall if he were to mention the word "police." "Doesn't the citizeness receive many callers?"

"Never the one, save the young lady who called sometimes in her own carriage. You'd think there would be a gentleman visitor, of course, but she doesn't show any signs of wanting to remarry, though she's not bad-looking. But I suppose it's her lack of fortune." Madame Letellier sighed wheezily. "Not that Madame Ferré—Madame Clément, I mean—"

"Ferré?"

"Hasn't she told you? She changed her name after her husband was condemned by that horrible tribunal—as I was saying, Madame Clément never behaves without the utmost decorum. We have two young bachelors in this house, students, and several more among the folk who take only their dinners here; and a few of them have flirted with her from time to time. But she won't give them the time of day. Now if they would just pay as much attention to my Laure . . ." She glanced at the girl again, who blushed and gazed miserably at the floor.

"I'm sure someone will soon pay the proper attentions to Citizeness Laure," Aristide said, retreating as he spied Rosalie at the bottom of the staircase.

"Tedious old cow," Rosalie remarked once they were well free of the boardinghouse and on their way to the gardens. "The worst magpie in the house. I hope you didn't tell her you work for the police."

"Not a word."

"That was considerate of you. Now—you were about to suggest Aubry had learned something from that letter. What did you mean? That it had told him . . . about Célie?"

"The affair seems to be connected to that, yes." Aristide paused for a moment at the gates to the gardens and bought a double measure of roasted chestnuts from a man with a handcart, carrying them away in his upturned hat. "But it wasn't Saint-Ange who wrote that letter; his servant swears he hadn't written anything for at least two or three days before he was murdered, and it only takes a day at most for the district post to cross Paris. So who did? And who else knew the truth?"

They strolled farther past the fading flowerbeds, discarding chestnut hulls as they went. "But such a secret as that," said Rosalie. "Célie would never have told anyone. She certainly never told me. Let one rumor get about, true or not, and your reputation is shattered forever. You're only guessing at what this letter said, aren't you?"

They paused at a bench beside the Medici Grotto, the hatful of roast chestnuts upside down between them. She absently peeled another chestnut as she gazed into the murky basin of the fountain, foul with decaying leaves. "Perhaps this letter merely repeated some rumors about her to Aubry," she suggested at last. "Célie could be giddy at times, you know. A spiteful acquaintance might have played on some foolish but perfectly innocent behavior of hers, and let Aubry believe the worst."

"Could Célie have had any enemies?"

"*Everybody* in fashionable society has enemies. No matter who you are, an ugly woman will envy you your beauty, or a poor man will envy you your fortune, or an unhappy woman will envy you your lover, or an ill-tempered shrew will envy you your sweet disposition. Célie was pretty, amiable, and wealthy. Plenty of people, women especially, must have envied her to the point of hatred, and while they'd fall short of murder, they wouldn't have hesitated to sow a few rumors about her."

"But if that's the case, this letter-writer must have known that Philippe Aubry was in love with Célie," Aristide said, reaching into his hat for another chestnut. Rosalie reached for one at the same moment and their fingers brushed. Her hand was warm, despite the autumn chill, but it twitched away at his touch. Carefully, without pulling out a chestnut, she withdrew her hand and huddled into the folds of her shawl.

"And Célie kept their love affair a secret even from her closest friend, Citizeness Villemain," Aristide continued, behaving as if nothing had happened, although her touch had sent a tingle through him. "I think you were the only person she told about it. Perhaps someone among Aubry's friends, rather than Célie's, knew of the affair."

"Revealing disagreeable secrets is the sort of spiteful thing a woman would do if she wanted a young man for herself." Rosalie's voice was steady, remote. "A woman might have seen them together and guessed the rest. If Aubry is as attractive as you say, plenty of women must wish he would look their way."

"It's too cold to sit here," Aristide said, seeing her shiver. He unbuttoned his overcoat. She made a few token protests as he draped it about her, but gratefully pulled it around her shoulders. "Would you care to stroll a bit more? Or shall I walk you home?"

"Our daily platter of roast gristle is served at one. I ought to go back, or that old cat will start to gossip."

He shook the last bits of the chestnut hulls from his hat and donned it, then impulsively offered Rosalie his arm. After an instant's hesitation she slid her arm within his, though he could feel how rigid it was, and together they walked back toward the gates.

Brasseur had received word from François by the time Aristide returned to Rue Traversine. "The final confirmation," Brasseur told him, waving a crumpled letter. "François says he's narrowed the manservant's recollections down to the tenth, as close as can be hoped for. We'll see what Aubry himself has to say."

"Are you bringing him in, then?" Aristide said.

"If the commissaire of his section agrees. Would you care to come along to identify him? You're the only one here who knows him by sight."

Aristide did not, in truth, wish to accompany them on their errand, but he nodded. "If you want."

15

One of the soldiers they had brought with them hammered at the door. Aristide waited at the rear of the group, behind the commissaire of the Théâtre-Français section, a second soldier, Brasseur, and the bewildered porter, fighting to keep his composure as the sound assailed his ears like the nailing of a coffin lid. *Why did I agree to this*, he wondered, rubbing icy hands together in an unsuccessful attempt to warm them.

The door opened. "These citizens," the porter faltered, "they say they have an order to take Citizen Aubry in for questioning."

Astonished, Brelot fell back, protesting that his master was still at breakfast, as the two soldiers pushed their way inside the apartment, Commissaire Dumas and Brasseur behind them. "We want Aubry," said Dumas.

"I am Aubry," the young man said, coming forward, a bowl of breakfast coffee in one hand. He was still in shirtsleeves, his cravat hanging untied about his neck. His clothes were plain but elegant in their simplicity; clearly he disdained the fantastically exaggerated styles the dandies and *incroyables* had adopted. Brasseur glanced at Aristide and he nodded.

"That's he."

Brelot peered at him, recognizing his voice. Abruptly his features took on the mingled fear and contempt that Aristide had grown accustomed to seeing when folk discovered they had spoken too freely before a police spy. *An agent of the police*, he corrected himself.

Aubry's unnatural pallor grew more waxen still. "Why are you here, and what do you want?"

How I detest this part of it, Aristide thought, his own nerves wound tight as a harpsichord string. Dumas stepped forward and threw open his overcoat to reveal the tricolor sash draped across his chest.

"I am Commissaire Dumas of the Section du Théâtre-Français. Are you called Philippe-Marie-Jean Aubry, residing at the Cour de Rouen?"

The formal phrases were reassuring.

"Yes, of course."

"I order you, in the name of the law, to follow me before the justice of the peace. You're summoned for questioning in relation to the murders—"

"Murders!"

"—of Marie-Célie-Josèphe-Élisabeth Montereau and Jean-Louis Saint-Ange on the tenth of Brumaire. Come with us, if you please."

"Come with you where? I've done nothing. I don't know what you're talking about."

"Do you deny that you knew Citizeness Montereau, then?" Dumas inquired, glancing at a secretary who began to scribble notes.

"No—no, of course not. Where are you taking me?"

"To the commissariat of this section, and before the justice of the peace within twenty-four hours," Brasseur said. "He'll decide the rest."

Brasseur's voice sounded suddenly alien, a cold and passionless monotone. No wonder I wouldn't ever want Brasseur's job, Aristide brooded; I am like a squeamish huntsman, who lives for the chase but who can't abide the bloody carnage of the kill.

"Very well," said Aubry, after a moment's hesitation. "Plainly there has been some mistake. I want to clear my name before this nonsense goes any farther."

"That's for the magistrate to decide," Dumas said, impassive.

"Let me dress. Is it cold today?"

"Yes, citizen. Cold and wet."

Aristide eyed the man whom he had sworn, a fortnight before, to find, and clasped icy hands behind his back. *Please, God, let him be the right one; let there be no doubt about him, no doubt at all.* Out of the corner of his eye he caught both their reflections in a tall mirror set in the wall; he looked, he realized, as ashen as the prisoner.

"They detained Philippe Aubry for questioning today," he told Rosalie, once again facing her across the boardinghouse parlor. He could not help but notice that she kept the faded, seat-sprung sofa between them.

"He did it, then."

"All the evidence points that way."

"When will they try him?"

"First he must go before a magistrate in his section, tomorrow, along with the principal witnesses for the police case against him. If the judge thinks our case valid, he'll formally arrest Aubry and send him on to a jury of accusation, which will decide if he should be tried before a full jury at the Criminal Tribunal."

"Such a waste of time," she declared scornfully. "If you say the evidence is against him, why shouldn't he be tried immediately?"

"The process is intended to safeguard the innocent from overzealous public prosecutors," he told her, adding ruefully: "And overzealous police, too."

"It didn't help that poor man whom they guillotined because they thought he was a bandit."

"The Lyons Mail affair was mismanaged," he said, swiftly thrusting aside the memory of Sanson's quiet words: *We've executed an innocent man.* "Lesurques was unlucky; he was arrested almost by chance. But here we have the right man, beyond doubt; a man who knew Célie, wrote her letters. Brasseur obtained some specimens of his handwriting and they match the letters I showed you. And it looks as if he can't account for where he was on the evening of the tenth. Never fear, he'll get what's due him."

"The guillotine, I hope. That's all such a man is fit for . . . a man who could murder someone like Célie . . ." Abruptly she squeezed her eyes shut and bent her head.

"The beast," she burst out a moment later, "the *beast*! She loved him, and he killed her. She never deserved that . . . she was good and kindhearted and happy, and she had everything, she ought to have been happy, and she loved him with all her heart, and he *killed* her. . . ."

Aristide circled about the sofa and cautiously patted her shoulder, wondering if he should ring for a maid. To his relief, though Rosalie went on weeping, she showed no signs of becoming hysterical. At last, hoping she would not cuff him for his audacity, he did the only thing he could think to do, and slipped his arms about her, as he had comforted his sister Thérèse when some cruel slight in their youth had sent her running to her chamber in tears.

She wept into his shoulder for a few moments. At length she gulped back her sobs and turned away from him, her face flushed.

"Are you all right?"

She blew her nose, still blinking away tears. "As well as I ever shall be."

"Should I call one of the maids?"

"What good would they be?" she demanded with a flash of her usual acerbity. "No, I'm all right. You're kind to concern yourself with me." She sank onto the nearest chair and sat gazing at the threadbare carpet.

"I'd forgotten men could be kind now and then," she said at last, dabbing halfheartedly at her eyes with his handkerchief.

What did one say to that, he wondered.

"You were thinking of your own experience, weren't you?" he said at length. "Not this recent love affair of yours; something crueler. Like Célie, you once fell victim to a man who ill-used you, didn't you?"

She nodded, her eyes still fixed on the carpet.

"I doubt it's as shameful a secret as you think," he added. "I've probably heard worse. When you work with the police, after a while nothing shocks you."

"No," she said, after a moment's reflection, "I don't suppose it would be particularly shocking. You've probably heard a dozen like it. I was still practically a child; a certain older man seduced me. He got me with child . . . it was born early, and died, and I caught a fever and nearly died, too. Afterward I entered a convent to escape the gossip. And when the convents were closed I married my late husband, because there was no place else for me to go, and no one else would have me."

"And then?" he said as she paused, guessing there might be more to her story.

"Then . . . then there was Henri, who deserted me. I told you."

"Who was Henri?"

"Henri Longval. He never spoke of his family, but he must have been a nobleman who'd abandoned his title during the Revolution. I'm sure he came of as good a family as I did. He was so handsome, so courteous. I used to tease him and call him my prince. He would laugh at that. . . ."

She smiled, wistful, as if enjoying some private memory. "I first met him—oh, when I'd first come back to Paris in 1791, and my stepfather, who was a beast, made some horrid advances when we were at the Palais-Royal, and I ran away from him and stumbled into Henri. And after my husband was executed in 'ninety-three, I had nothing left but my dowry. Henri lent me money when I needed it, and he found me someplace to live."

"And you became lovers then."

"Yes . . . I loved him so much. He was generous, and kind, and gentlemanly—he had beautiful manners. He was well-read, and he loved music—he played the harpsichord. I was never any good at that. And he . . . oh, I can't describe him without sounding like a sentimental novel."

"But you knew nothing about him?" Aristide said.

"He would never tell me. When we . . . became intimate, and I felt free to ask questions, he would laugh and turn our conversation some other way. It was almost 'ninety-four by then, when everyone was a bit nervous, and I suspected he was a secret royalist, or related to some notorious counterrevolutionary, and simply wanted to keep it quiet and lie low during the Terror."

"But what was his profession? How did he live?"

"He was an artillery officer. Then he went over to the company of mounted soldiers attached to the Tribunal. Six days every week—every *décade*, rather—he was on duty escorting the carts to the guillotine, during the worst of it in 'ninety-three and 'ninety-four, and he hated that—he would describe it, sometimes, and I could tell it broke his heart to see what he saw there. 'I helped to kill them,' he would say. I would try to console him, and tell him over and over again that it wasn't his fault, that someone else would have taken his place, but it never did any good."

"He sounds like a decent man," Aristide said.

"He *was* a decent man. A kind man. Or so I thought, until he discarded me."

Aristide shook his head. "He must have had a reason."

"Of course he had a reason!" she snapped. "Somehow he must have learned about my past. Someone told him what happened to me when I was fifteen, and he decided I wasn't worthy of an ex-aristocrat. And I loved him so—I would have done anything for him." She looked up at him with a brief, harsh laugh. "I still love him. And hate him. It's mad, and I'm a fool to keep on wanting him . . . but he was the kindest man I ever knew, and gentle, and he loved me. I *know* he loved me. But in the end, I wasn't good enough for him."

She drew a long breath and at last rose, dry-eyed. "Men can sleep with a different woman every night and indulge in the most revolting practices—but let an unmarried woman make one mistake, be led astray when she's young and silly and knows nothing of the world, and she's tainted for life and called a harlot! Isn't that why this Aubry murdered Célie? Perhaps she expected him to forgive her because they loved each other. And instead he killed her. Do you wonder that I have little love for your sex?"

He was silent a moment.

"Citizeness . . . Aubry is probably enduring torment from his own conscience, as we speak, worse than any punishment a criminal court could inflict upon him."

"You think so, do you?"

"I . . . I knew a man once who killed his wife and her lover, and then tried to kill himself. He'd loved her and he could no longer live with himself. I don't suppose Aubry can, either."

"Nevertheless," she said, "he is still alive, and Célie is not."

She turned, without another word, and was about to quit the room when Aristide impulsively called after her.

"Where did he live, your artillery officer?"

"What affair is that of yours?"

"Indulge me."

She paused a moment, then shrugged. "Rue St.-Jacques-la-Boucherie, near the Châtelet. Two houses down from the church."

"I should like to help you," Aristide said to her retreating back. "I'd like to see you happy."

She glanced swiftly over her shoulder at him and seemed about to say something, but thought better of it and hurried up the stairs.

A dull, drizzly twilight hung over the city by late afternoon. After leaving the Latin Quarter, Aristide walked down the hill to the river, crossed to the island of the Cité, and visited the barracks behind the Palais de Justice.

"I want to have a word with one of the gendarmes here," he told the captain whom he found lounging alone by the fire in a small officers' messroom, puffing at a pipe. "His name is Henri Longval."

"Longval?" echoed the officer. "No one of that name in this company."

"There must be."

"I assure you, there isn't. No Longval, or Longueville, or anything like it." He pushed himself to his feet and beckoned Aristide into an office. "Look at the current register if you disbelieve me."

Aristide perused the list of names, without much hope.

"Of course," added the captain, as an afterthought, "I've only been assigned here for a bit under a year. Your Longval may have left, or transferred, before I arrived. My orderly may remember him. Frenais!"

Corporal Frenais, when summoned, could not recall anyone named Longval in the company during the past five years. Aristide described Rosalie's lover as best he could from her cursory portrait of him, but Frenais shook his head.

"That might be almost any of them. This company gets its pick of the officers, and the men too, because it's safer duty than the army and they aren't often sent outside the city. Strapping young fellows are thick on the ground here."

Puzzled, Aristide thanked them and departed. He slouched across the Pont-au-Change toward the small riverside fort of the Petit-Châtelet as pedestrians hurried past him, huddling into their coat collars or stretching shawls over their heads to shield themselves from the sting of the cold rain. A few minutes' walk eastward brought him to the church of St. Jacques-la-Boucherie, boarded up and locked, though the freestanding bell tower now seemed to be the center of some peculiar manufactory or foundry, judging from the brick furnaces that had been built about it, and the ladders of raw, unweathered wood that led up into its interior. A weather-stained notice on the church's great doors proclaimed NATIONAL PROPERTY. Above Aristide, the soaring ranks of headless stone saints and angels bore witness to a Revolutionary Section Committee once devoted to guillotining not only the fleshly enemies of the Revolution but its otherworldly foes as well.

The porter two houses down remembered Citizen Longval well. Second floor back, a nice pair of furnished rooms, comfortable for a young bachelor. A good-looking young fellow, always polite as you please, though a bit closemouthed. An ambitious young officer on his way up.

Yes, he remembered the girl, too, Citizeness Clément. She'd taken one of the attics at first, but three months later she'd given it up and moved herself downstairs to Longval's lodgings. A pretty creature, pleasant enough, and head over heels in love with the young man. The fondness was mutual, he'd say. Citizen Longval always treated her with the greatest attention.

No, Longval no longer kept rooms in the house. The girl? Yes, the girl had stayed on a while, though she'd seemed forlorn and unhappy—Longval had paid the rent through the quarter—but when the rent came due again, she'd taken herself off.

"Did either of them ever confide in you?" Aristide inquired.

Oh, no, they kept themselves to themselves. He'd never noticed them becoming overfriendly with the other lodgers. Of course during the Terror folk didn't talk much about themselves; no doubt they had secrets to keep. He wouldn't be at all surprised if young Longval had been an ex-aristo. But he was a fine young gentleman, in his country's service, and surely there was no harm in him. He didn't know why they'd separated. One day Longval had simply left, with a valise, and never returned.

"But he looked wretched," the porter said suddenly. "Like he didn't like it at all, what he was doing."

"But you don't know why?"

"He never confided in me, like I said. Regular oyster of a man."

More baffled than ever, Aristide went home to bed.

16

26 Brumaire (November 16)

The examining magistrate replaced the police reports on the broad, gilt-trimmed table, cleared his throat, and leaned toward the witness, fingers steepled.

"Citizen Montereau: Please state the nature of your relationship to Philippe-Marie-Jean Aubry."

Aristide shifted position to get a better look through the narrow spy hole in an anteroom of Judge Geoffroy's chamber. Beside him, Brasseur stood stolidly, listening, arms folded, as an indifferent clerk sat copying a heap of documents at a desk behind them.

Montereau distractedly patted at his wig, sending powder flying. "I engaged Aubry as my private secretary in February of 1789. He was a younger son of a distinguished family fallen upon hard times. He came well recommended by an acquaintance from Marseilles, a shipowner, and I was pleased with his industry, his scrupulosity, and his intelligence. I trusted his competence and his discretion so far as to take him with me on a minor diplomatic mission to Russia lasting five months. Then, after he had been with me for nearly two years, I learned from a relative that he had once fought a duel and killed a man."

"What relative? Is this person to be trusted?"

"My wife's great-aunt. She knew Aubry personally at the time of the duel. She came to live in my house in January of 1791 and recognized Aubry at once."

"Go on."

"I—I have little more to tell," he faltered. "Only that I immediately dismissed Aubry from my household not only because he had killed a man, but because he was the challenger in the duel and because Marsillac de Saint-Roch, the man he had killed, had been a distant relation of my late wife and her great-aunt."

Of course, Aristide thought, remembering the portrait that hung in old Madame de Laroque's parlor. He strained to listen over the monotonous scratching of the clerk's ill-cut quill behind him.

"Are you accusing Aubry of a previous criminal history?" Geoffroy inquired.

"No. None on record, at least. By all accounts the duel was conducted honorably," Montereau continued, as if reluctant to admit it, "and the matter wasn't brought to the attention of the royal prosecutor, for the sake of Marsillac's reputation and that of his family. Though I must add that Aubry fled Paris, and shortly thereafter left France, as I understand, to avoid any prosecution. Instead of surrendering himself to the king's justice like a gentleman."

"Had you any knowledge of a love affair between Citizen Aubry and your daughter Célie?"

"None whatsoever." He burst out suddenly: "Whether or not he murdered my daughter, and I hope the law will strike him with its fullest severity if he did—I wish to state that Aubry is an unscrupulous wretch and a miserable coward, without the courage to accept the consequences of his actions! He has plenty of nerve with a sword in his hand, to be sure, but evidently he couldn't stomach the idea of facing the public executioner if Marsillac's family had pressed charges of murder—"

Judge Geoffroy raised a hand. "Have the kindness to calm yourself." He took up a letter from the table before him and offered it to Montereau. "Do you recognize this handwriting as that of Philippe-Marie-Jean Aubry?"

"Yes. It's undoubtedly his writing."

"Thank you, citizen. I have no more questions for you at present. You may go. Officer, send in the witness Brelot, if you please."

An usher brought in Aubry's manservant. "Citizen Brelot," said Judge Geoffroy after the preliminary formalities were complete, "kindly describe your employer's actions on the tenth of Brumaire."

"Citizen Aubry stayed in until late morning," said Brelot, glancing about him at the shelves of leather-bound legal tomes, and shifting from foot to foot. "Then he went out, for luncheon and a stroll about the Tuileries, he said. He came back toward the end of the afternoon. He seemed just as usual, in good spirits. He went into his study, and a bit later he came out, looking very upset, and he ran out of the apartment without a word to me."

"When was this?" inquired the judge.

"About five o'clock."

"When did he return?"

"Just before two o'clock in the morning. He let himself in, but it woke me up. Then I heard the clock strike not long after, before I went back to sleep again."

"And lastly, to the best of your knowledge, does Citizen Aubry own a pistol?"

"Yes, a pair of double-barreled pocket pistols with pearl inlay."

"Are these your employer's pistols?" said Geoffroy. Brelot nodded as an usher opened the tooled leather case he held. "Let the record indicate," the magistrate continued, "that Citizen Brelot has identified the pistols, found during the search of Citizen Aubry's lodgings, as items belonging to Citizen Aubry. Brelot, is cleaning your employer's pistols one of your duties?"

"No, citizen. I'm not to touch them, except to polish the case."

"Let the record also indicate that the pistols are clean and do not appear to have been discharged."

Too clean, Aristide mused, squinting through the spy hole for a glimpse of the shining steel barrels. What was to prevent Aubry from returning home, hastily cleaning the murder weapon at night while his servant slept, and replacing it innocently in its case? He stretched for a moment and massaged a crick in his neck; the spy hole that peeped from a shadowed corner of the paneling in the magistrate's chambers had been intended for observers shorter than he.

"Did you notice, when your master left his lodgings so abruptly on the tenth, if one or both of the pistols were missing?"

"No, citizen. Like I said, I'm not to touch them, so I wouldn't have looked."

Geoffroy dismissed Brelot and called for Deschamps, porter at the apartment house belonging to Citizen Hatier in the Cour de Rouen, in which Citizen Aubry resided. Citizen Aubry had received a letter that afternoon, Deschamps declared. He remembered it clearly because no post came on *décadi* and the letter had been delivered by hand, by an errand boy, a street urchin. He didn't know the boy; he might be able to identify him if he saw him again, or he might not.

"Did Aubry read this letter?"

"I don't know if he read it. But I gave it to him when he came in, and he took it upstairs with him. In his pocket."

Geoffroy dismissed him and turned to Commissaire Dumas, who had been hovering in a gloomy corner of the chamber outside the pool of lamplight. "Have you found this letter of which the porter spoke?"

"We found plenty of letters in the citizen's desk," Dumas said. "But nothing dated after the eighth. And nothing that would have been likely to upset the citizen."

"Threw it on the fire, I expect," Aristide whispered to Brasseur. He began to drum his fingers on the nearest stretch of molding on the wall, remembered where he was and that he could be heard, and gnawed at his thumbnail instead. *Dear God, how I detest this part of it.* His stomach felt as if it were tied up in knots.

"Next witness, please," said Geoffroy. Following the usher, young Feydeau strolled in as if he were arriving at a fashionable salon, chin high over the lofty edge of his stylish collar and stock. "Citizen Feydeau, you have given a sworn statement that one day perhaps two months ago you saw the late Célie Montereau with a young man in one of the corridors at the Opera House?"

"Yes, citizen."

"What were they doing?"

"Talking. Great heavens, what else should they be doing?" Feydeau smirked and continued. "I didn't overhear their conversation, but they looked very easy together, and they were clasping hands. And then he lifted her hand to his lips and kissed it."

"Any young man might kiss a young woman's hand."

"Oh, no . . . there's a great deal of difference between the little peck you give a lady's hand when you bid her farewell after a supper party, and the way *he* was holding her hand when he kissed it. A very great deal of difference."

"They seemed affectionate?"

"One glimpse would have told you they were lovers."

At Geoffroy's nod, a gendarme escorted Aubry into the chamber. "Citizen Feydeau," the magistrate continued, "do you recognize this man?"

Feydeau inspected Aubry for a moment. "Yes, I do. That's the fellow who was with the little Montereau girl at the opera, just as I told you."

"You are quite sure this was the man?"

"Oh, yes. I wouldn't forget such a good-looking gentleman."

When Feydeau had gone, Judge Geoffroy turned his attention to Aubry. "So. Philippe-Marie-Jean Aubry, aged twenty-eight, employed in a subordinate secretarial capacity to Director La Revellière-Lépeaux. You stand suspected of having murdered Célie Montereau and Louis Saint-Ange on the tenth of Brumaire last."

"I am innocent," Aubry declared, his voice level. "I know nothing of this."

Aristide could feel the familiar queasiness, that dread mingled with triumph that always accompanied an arrest, swelling in the pit of his stomach. He glanced at Brasseur, silently listening to the evidence, and suppressed the temptation to seize his friend's arm and cry, *Wait— despite everything, I might be wrong—the police and the magistrates have been wrong before—dear God, don't let us send an innocent man to prison and trial, perhaps to his death.*

"Do you deny you knew the late Citizeness Montereau?"

"Of course not. I was once employed in her father's household."

"And you were promptly discharged without a recommendation when Citizen Montereau learned of your past?"

Aubry stiffened. "The duel he'll have told you about was conducted in an honorable fashion, with witnesses. He's trying to call me a murderer. He wants to soil my name with a crime that was no crime!"

"Calm yourself, citizen," said Geoffroy. "Have you forgotten that dueling is, and was, illegal?"

"It was an honorable duel," Aubry repeated, stepping forward to grasp the ornately scalloped edge of the judge's table. "Citizen Judge, Montereau has held a grudge toward me for years—he wants to call me a shoddy adventurer—"

"Citizen, control yourself! Do you deny you cherished tender sentiments toward Célie Montereau?"

Aubry swallowed hard. "When I knew her in 1789 and 1790, she was still almost a child. I treated her with courtesy, as my employer's daughter, but otherwise she meant nothing to me."

"Did you write this letter to Citizeness Montereau?" Geoffroy said, handing it to Aubry. Aubry did not answer.

"Citizen Montereau has already identified your handwriting," said Geoffroy irritably. "His identification can be readily confirmed by comparing the handwriting in these letters to that on papers belonging to Director La Revellière-Lépeaux, which were written and initialed by you. Pray don't waste our time. Perhaps you would like to change your account of your relations with the late citizeness?"

"Yes, damn you," Aubry whispered, his handsome face working with suppressed emotion, "yes, I wrote these letters."

"Perhaps you were intent upon making love to the girl without her father's knowledge, and marrying her for the sake of her undoubtedly ample dowry?"

"That's a damned lie. I loved her. I loved her more than anything on this earth!"

"So you do not now deny you harbored a tender passion for her?"

"No."

"And were your sentiments returned?"

"Yes."

"You were, in fact, lovers?"

"Not in a carnal sense," Aubry said, reddening. "I don't approve of such relations before marriage. I would never ask that of a reputable woman."

"But perhaps you believed the young woman had betrayed your affection with another," said Geoffroy. Aubry made a slight movement.

"No."

"And overcome with rage, you confronted her, and the man you thought to be her lover, and killed them both."

"*No!*"

"The police official who brought you here for questioning has testified that you showed no surprise at being accused of Citizeness Montereau's murder."

"That's a lie! Of course I was surprised—I didn't do it. But I knew she—she was dead. Word travels fast in the circles I move in. Everyone knew about it."

Aristide shifted position and hazarded another glance at Aubry. The young man was livid and trembling, though whether with fear, anger, indignation, or anguish he could not tell.

"I loved Célie! I'd never have hurt her!"

"Even when she had deceived you, or was unfaithful to you?" inquired the judge, silkily.

"I loved her. . . . Oh God, I loved her . . ." Tears began to spill down Aubry's cheeks and he hid his face in his hands, shoulders heaving.

"Calm yourself. Do you deny you went to Rue du Hasard, in the Butte-des-Moulins section, on the evening of the tenth of this month, with the purpose of murdering Célie Montereau and Louis Saint-Ange?"

"Yes. I deny it. I would never have hurt Célie!"

"Can you give an account of your whereabouts on the said evening?"

"I—I went out. For a walk."

"Your servant states that you did not return until two o'clock in the morning. You went out for an evening stroll lasting eight or nine hours?"

"Yes. I—I just walked. Here and there. I went to the Tuileries Gardens for a while."

"Did you see anyone there whom you knew, who can corroborate your story?"

"N-no. I don't think so."

"Have you any proof whatsoever of this long excursion? A bill from a café? A waiter who might remember your face? Can you name any witness who might remember you?"

"I—I don't think so."

"In short, you have no proof that you were elsewhere at the time of the murders," said Geoffroy, turning to his notes. "What was the substance of the letter you received on the tenth of Brumaire?"

"Nothing," Aubry muttered after an infinitesimal pause. "Nothing important."

"Still, I imagine it wasn't a blank sheet of paper?"

"It—it was from a lady. A private matter."

"A lady? Citizeness Montereau?"

"No! A—a courtesan."

"Her name?"

"Émilie. I don't know her surname or anything about her. I swear to you, I never did this! Someone is falsely implicating me—Montereau has hated me for years—or perhaps it's a political matter, someone who wants to injure Citizen La Revellière-Lépeaux by defaming me. . . ."

Judge Geoffroy announced that the accused might retire for a moment to collect himself, and meanwhile called the witness Grangier. An usher returned with the porter from Rue du Hasard, looking hideously uncomfortable in an ancient, moth-eaten worsted coat. He thrust his dilapidated three-cornered hat under his arm and repeated his description of what he had seen in the early evening of the tenth of Brumaire.

"Do you recognize this man?" Geoffroy said when the usher had escorted Aubry into the chamber once more.

Grangier peered at Aubry, squinting and frowning. Aubry stood stiff and motionless, avoiding his scrutiny, his face unreadable.

"No, Citizen Judge," Grangier said at last, "I don't know him."

Aristide straightened and glanced at Brasseur, who met his eyes, scowling. A denial from Grangier was the last thing they had expected.

"Look at him again," said Geoffroy, "and be sure of your testimony. Have you ever seen this man before?"

"No," Grangier said after a moment. "I don't think so."

"Is this not the man you saw running past the door of your lodging on the evening of the tenth?"

The porter stepped closer. At last he grimaced and turned back to the magistrate. "It might have been, Citizen Judge. But I couldn't swear to it."

"Describe again the man you saw on the night of the murders."

"He was young," mumbled Grangier, "and he had long, dark hair and a dark coat and hat, and boots. That's all. Young and dark and thinnish."

"That might describe a great many men," said the judge. "Pray be more precise. How tall was the man you saw? How did he wear his hair?"

"About as tall as me, or a little less," Grangier said promptly. "His hair was tied back with a ribbon—and—and his hat was round, with a low crown."

Aubry started and cast a swift glance at the porter.

"Your portrait could describe this man before you, could it not?" said Geoffroy.

"What I mean to say is," Grangier stammered, "this citizen *might* have been the man. He's about the same height and so on. But I'd had a glass or two of eau-de-vie and it was getting dark, and I couldn't swear to it. I think it was somebody else I saw."

"Citizen Grangier." Geoffroy leaned his elbows on the table before him and pressed his fingertips together. "Will you, or will you not, testify that you saw this man?"

Grangier glanced from the judge to Aubry and back again before reluctantly replying. "No, citizen. He could have been the man, but I couldn't take my oath on it."

Damnation, Aristide said to himself, mentally removing Grangier from the ranks of witnesses for the prosecution to those of the defense. *And what if,* a small persistent voice within him whispered, *what if he is speaking perfect truth, and Aubry is not the man who rushed down those stairs from that scene of death?*

Judge Geoffroy dismissed Grangier and sat for a moment in silence, staring down at the dossier before him.

"Citizen Aubry," he said at last, "I doubt any man here has forgotten a certain recent crime, or the notorious trial and verdict that resulted from it. And each of us holds his own opinion as to whether justice was done, or whether an innocent man was put to death, because of testimony by witnesses who may have been deceived in their identification. For myself, I cannot find it in my conscience to send a man to trial on a capital charge, on the strength of such circumstantial evidence alone. Philippe-Marie-Joseph Aubry, I find insufficient evidence here to hold you on suspicion of murder at this time. You may go."

The gendarmes stepped away from Aubry. He stood motionless for an instant, letting out a long, sighing breath. Aristide turned away from the spy hole and glanced at Brasseur.

"Now what?"

"We go on looking for evidence," said Brasseur with a gloomy shrug. "And we don't let that pretty-faced whelp out of our sights."

Aristide eyed him for a moment, envying his friend's phlegmatic confidence. "What if he *is* just as innocent as he says?" He shook his head, frustrated, and strode from the room.

17

"Aubry," Aristide said, reaching for his sleeve, when the young man had broken away from the handful of well-wishers surrounding him in the corridor outside the magistrate's chambers.

"Who are you? What do you want?"

"I'm the man who tracked you down."

"Haven't you done enough, then?" Aubry said, brushing past him toward the door. "Keep away from me."

Aristide kept pace with him as he flung open the door and hurried down Rue des Arcs. "If you're innocent, tell me the truth and allow me to find the real murderer."

"I've been *telling* the truth."

"No, you haven't. Where were you, really, on the evening of the tenth? You must have been somewhere," Aristide added brutally, "if you weren't on Rue du Hasard, shooting Célie Montereau. If it wasn't you Grangier saw, who was it?"

"How on earth should I know?"

Aristide drew a deep breath and forced himself to pause a moment before replying. "You damned fool, you're not making this any better for yourself. They may have released you today, but that doesn't mean the police won't pick you up again as soon as they can collect more evidence against you. *Somebody* shot those two people. If you weren't the man with the round hat whom the porter saw, then probably the man with the round hat shot them. So if you can think of any other young men who would have a motive to murder Célie, for whatever reason, you had better tell me now."

"A round hat," Aubry said. He gestured Aristide aside into a narrow side street, out of the busy foot traffic. "That man mentioned a low-crowned round hat. I don't *own* a hat like that."

"That's scarcely evidence."

"But it's the truth. I detest the style. Ask my servant. It wasn't I."

"Who might it have been?"

"I haven't the least idea."

"What about this woman, this Émilie?"

"There's nothing to tell," Aubry said uneasily.

Aristide sighed. "For God's sake, is *that* what this is all about? Are you too embarrassed to state where you were on the tenth because you spent the evening at a brothel?"

"No!"

"Aubry, I've studied you," Aristide told him. "I knew what you were before I knew your name. I know you present a certain face to the world, of a man who wants to believe the woman he loves is pure and saintly. I imagine you'd like to believe that of yourself, as well, but in truth . . . perhaps you have baser tastes."

"You don't know what you're talking about," Aubry said, keeping his voice level.

"I don't know or care what sort of revolting amusements you may enjoy in private," Aristide continued relentlessly, "though I can understand you might be reluctant to have them made public. But if faced with a choice of temporary discomfiture or the guillotine, I know which *I* would choose."

"I wasn't at a brothel!" Aubry insisted. "I just went for a walk. The—her letter upset me, and—and I went for a long walk to sort out matters in my head."

"If this prostitute knew your address, then she must know you rather well. Where can we find her?"

Aubry began to pace, hands balled into fists at his side. "She—I don't know anything about her. She's just a girl I picked up one evening. She—wrote me to accuse me of cheating her, that half of the notes I'd given her were counterfeit."

"Were they?"

"I've no idea." He leaned back with a fretful sigh against the nearest wall, arms folded, the great dark eyes wide and troubled. "I didn't do this. I loved Célie and I'd never have hurt her. Why must this have anything to do with me? Couldn't an enemy of this man Saint-Ange have killed him?"

"And then killed Célie because she witnessed the murder?"

"Yes, exactly."

Aristide shook his head. "The evidence suggests otherwise. Do you know where I can find this Émilie? Where did you meet her?"

"At—at the Pont-Neuf. I took her home with me."

"Did your servant see her when you brought her home?"

"No. I'd given Brelot the evening off."

"What about the porter?"

"I—I don't know. I don't think he saw us."

"Why," Aristide said, "were you so upset, when she accused you of cheating her, that you required eight hours of fresh air to sort matters out?"

"Wouldn't you be upset if you were accused of passing bad notes? They guillotine counterfeiters. Or—or she might have been working up to extorting payment from me. Whores do that."

"Good God, Aubry, I'm more astonished at the bachelor who *hasn't*, at one time or another, brought a whore to his apartment. Do you always construct an ox out of an egg?"

"She upset me," Aubry muttered.

"So you still can't say where you were that evening, or produce a witness?"

"I tell you, I just walked about. I was very disturbed. I had a drink of eau-de-vie from an old spirit peddler near the Jacobin Club; an old hag with a cask. Ask her."

"One peddler, a fortnight ago? You're asking a good deal. You realize, don't you, that the moment the police discover any further evidence they can use against you, you'll be back in front of the magistrate again, and the next time he may not be so lenient. You had better offer a stronger alibi than a long, solitary ramble."

"How am I supposed to prove a negative?" Aubry said. "Why should I have provided myself with proof of where I was? Please, for God's sake, believe me. I know it looks bad—"

"I know perfectly well that the evidence, what evidence we have, points toward both your guilt and your innocence," Aristide said. "Listen—nothing terrifies me more than the thought of mistakenly being the cause of a man's death. I *want* to believe you're telling the truth, and that some proof, somewhere, can vindicate you. To be honest, I don't think I like you much; but if you're innocent, you shouldn't be punished for something you didn't do."

Aubry stared across the alley, blinking away the tears glittering in his eyes in the shaft of watery autumn sunshine that lanced across him. "I loved Célie so much," he whispered.

"No doubt you did," Aristide said, more softly. "But thus far, all you have in your favor is that our eyewitness refused to identify you. And I fear, in the end, that that may not be enough to keep you out of prison. If you can't tell me anything else that would prove you were elsewhere when Célie and Saint-Ange were murdered, then I can't help you. You're sure you have no idea who this young man with the round hat could be?"

"None."

"A relative of Célie's? A jilted suitor? An enemy?"

"Célie couldn't possibly have had any enemies."

"She had one," Aristide said.

"You look dreadful," said Rosalie that evening in Madame Deluc's parlor. "What's the matter?"

"Judge Geoffroy interrogated Aubry today. . . ."

"So? Why do you look as if you'd just lost your dearest friend?"

"That's not amusing—"

"Oh, God," she said, coloring. "I'm sorry."

"Never mind."

"You do look ill. Perhaps you ought to get away from Paris. Take a holiday in the country for a few days."

"I can't take a holiday. Not while this affair is still unfinished."

"Unfinished?" she echoed him, startled.

"The porter from Saint-Ange's house wouldn't identify Aubry. Judge Geoffroy let him go."

"*What?*"

"He wouldn't identify him. Or couldn't. He saw a stranger who rushed into the house at the right time, but he wouldn't swear before the judge that Aubry was the man."

She stared at him, wide-eyed, her lips trembling. After a long silence she drew a deep, sighing breath. "We must talk, in privacy. Will you come with me to the Port Salut Tavern?"

At the nearby tavern he followed her to a table for two and threw himself down in the nearest chair as she ordered a glass of red wine from the servant girl. "You prefer coffee, don't you," she added, turning to him. "Or perhaps you want something else. Wine? Eau-de-vie?"

When the servant had gone to fetch their order Rosalie leaned across the table and fixed him with an accusing glare. "Now. *What happened?*"

He described Aubry's interrogation from first to last. Their drink arrived in the midst of his tale and he immediately gulped down half a glassful of brandy, taking perverse pleasure in its fierce burn.

"Dear God," she muttered when he had finished.

He poured himself more brandy and sipped at it, rolling the stinging liquid on his tongue. "I never did like a case based only on circumstantial evidence, no hard proof . . . especially with a capital crime. But since this Lesurques affair . . ." He shook his head, restless. "I think the law made an appalling error there. And I am as fallible as anyone else . . . it's not cut and dried by any means . . . what if Aubry is innocent as well?" He drank down the rest of the glass and leaned back with a long sigh. "I can't help wondering about it. The case against him made perfect sense—but the porter couldn't identify him. I've been so sure; building a theory, following the trail . . . but still there's always the possibility I'm wrong. We can try to dig up more evidence . . . but how could I live with myself if an innocent man, another innocent man, were executed because of my blundering?"

Rosalie knew better than to attempt to console him with a banal platitude. "Are you still sure Aubry committed the murders?" she asked after a long silence.

"No." Aristide rubbed his nose and held out his glass for more brandy.

"You're trembling," she told him.

"The damned porter should have been able to identify him, and he wouldn't. But who else could it have been? *Why* couldn't he say 'This is the man'?"

She splashed a little of the amber liquid into his glass. "Is this porter so important? No one else saw the man? No one at all?"

"Not that we've been able to discover."

Rosalie closed her eyes and leaned her head on her clasped hands for a moment. "But he *is* guilty. He *must* be."

"God!" Aristide exclaimed, his fingers hovering at his lips, too uneasy even to bite his nails. "It's such a hideous, sordid, pitiful little affair. . . ." He clenched his fist, grateful for the faint bracing pain of the ragged fingernails biting into his palm.

"You'll have a nervous attack if you don't watch yourself," Rosalie told him after a long, suffocating silence.

"That starry-eyed young man who believed his sweetheart was a goddess, or a saint," he added, scarcely hearing her, "and that poor, silly, sentimental girl who'd strayed and tried to pretend it never happened—"

"Ravel."

"—and now someday, if we're lucky, some poor wretch will pay on the scaffold for her death. . . ."

Rosalie touched his arm and took the glass from his hand. "You've too much on your shoulders. I tell you, you need some time to clear your mind."

"How can I leave?"

"One day, then. You could go out somewhere on *décadi*. Hire a carriage and drive to the Bois de Boulogne, or along the river, if the weather's good."

"Would you come with me?" he said, to his own surprise. She did not reply for a moment.

"If you wish me to."

He sat silently for a few minutes longer, staring past Rosalie to the mesmerizing flicker and crackle of the flames on the hearth.

"I hate this," he said suddenly. "Sometimes—just sometimes—I wish I could do only what that blockhead Didier does—day after day of safe, dull licenses and patrols and reports, and catching pickpockets and breaking up bread riots and telling people to sweep in front of their shops. He's never held a man's life in his hands. I *hate* this."

Rosalie poured herself a splash of the eau-de-vie, and said nothing.

18

Four days later, when at last the sun prevailed through the ceiling of cloud and promised a *décadi* with mild dry weather and a measure of blue sky, Aristide hired a shabby calèche and collected Rosalie at the Maison Deluc. As he handed her into the open carriage and took his seat beside her, he noticed Madame Letellier's curious moon face peering from between the dusty curtains in the parlor window, and pointedly ignored it.

"Have you learned anything more?" Rosalie asked him as they clattered down Rue Jacques toward the quay.

"I've sent someone to investigate further."

"Investigate what?"

"Aubry offered a very poor alibi to the judge," he told her. "I want to find two people: a brandy seller who was on Rue Honoré on the evening of the tenth, and who sold him a glass of eau-de-vie; and also a whore who plies her trade near the Pont-Neuf, and who spent the night with him at his apartment early in the month; and who may have written the letter he received on the tenth."

"You think *she* was Aubry's mysterious correspondent?"

"That's what Aubry says."

"Do you believe him?"

"I will if we can find her. Either or both of these two women might be able to provide him with an alibi, or deny him one."

Rosalie looked hard at him. "After all this, do you *want* him to be innocent?"

He gazed out across the muddy shore as they turned onto the quay, watching the pale glitter of the sunlight on the water. "You want him to be guilty, don't you?"

"But he did it. Who else would have wanted to murder her?"

"What you want is for Aubry to be guilty," Aristide repeated. "What *I* want is the truth. To *know*, beyond a shadow of a doubt, that he's guilty . . . or that he's innocent. And if he is innocent, I want the proof that will keep him safe."

"You're too scrupulous, I think. Why not simply do your duty, and leave the rest to Providence?"

"And you are too unforgiving."

As he spoke, he remembered his own words to Brasseur not long before: *I want to lay hold of this swine and see him on his way to the Grève.* Perhaps, when it was a matter of murder, he was no more forgiving than was Rosalie.

"Do you blame me?" she said.

They looked at each other in silence. "Let's talk of something else," Aristide said at last.

"Pleasant weather for the time of year, isn't it?"

They held to their tacit understanding until the driver turned the calèche across the bridge that led to the Place de la Concorde, until recently the Place de la Révolution. The weathered, crumbling plaster statue of the goddess Liberty, which for two years had looked down indifferently at a blood-soaked scaffold, stood in the center of the square still. It was only a temporary surrogate for a permanent statue of marble or bronze, but Aristide doubted a more durable Liberty would ever now be erected. He looked away. A course through the vast moated square was the least troublesome route from the Left Bank to the Champs-Élysées and the western barrier, but he wished they could have driven another way.

Cool fingers slid over the back of his hand. He glanced at Rosalie. She was gazing at the statue, avoiding his eyes.

"It reminds you of your friend, doesn't it?" she said.

Mud and blood . . . pools of blood amid the cobbles, dissolving away beneath the drizzle.

"I stood here, watching them die . . . and I didn't have the stomach to stay."

"Not many people of sensibility would."

"I abandoned him."

"He wasn't alone. If it had been I, awaiting my turn under the axe, I think I'd have understood, and forgiven. You oughtn't torment yourself so." She pressed his hand, lightly, and without thinking he turned it over so that their hands were clasped, palm to palm.

They rode on in silence past the market-farms and country villas of the Champs-Élysées, taking quiet pleasure in each other's presence, until they had crossed the customs barrier and entered the woodland. Passing the gardens and dainty miniature château of Bagatelle, at last they reached the banks of the Seine again, where in its serpentine coiling it bent sharply northeast once more, the Île de Puteaux bisecting it. A small inn stood near the ferry to the island.

After a simple luncheon of bread and fresh cheese and cold chicken, they strolled along the grassy riverbank, rustling through the fallen leaves, past fisher boys and floating barges and a few amorous couples ambling arm in arm. They walked without touching, neither quite ready to essay again the unexpected intimacy of their clasped hands.

"Do you think that Aubry—" Rosalie began, and stopped. "No, we said we'd not talk about it. Well then. What task will you turn to when this one is over?"

"Whatever Brasseur asks me to help him with. He had a murder some weeks ago, in a hotel, that's been confounding him. Committed by a woman wearing men's clothes."

"How extraordinary. She's disguised as a man?"

"No, she doesn't try to disguise her sex. She simply wears masculine clothing. You weren't, by any chance, ever a member of any revolutionary women's club, were you?"

"No," she said, surprised. "I went to one women's meeting, once, but I thought it rather a waste of time. What has *that* to do with anything?"

"I wondered if you might have known any women with advanced ideas, women who were demanding equality with men . . . who might have advocated the wearing of male costume, or even worn it themselves."

"Advocated male costume?" Rosalie repeated, with a brief burst of laughter that illuminated her pale features. "Certainly not. Not among those old prunes I saw. A little earnest speechifying was all they were good for. The sight of a woman wearing breeches would have given them apoplexy."

"They didn't demand equality of the sexes?"

"No. Personally, I'd like nothing more than equality with men, and a little justice," she added, "but I don't think we'll see it in our lifetime, no matter what we do." She glanced at him suddenly with a sly smile. "Though a clever female criminal who wears men's clothes is an advancement, of sorts, in equality of the sexes, wouldn't you say?"

"I suppose it is. Certainly the sexes are equal before the criminal court."

"And before the guillotine."

"That, too."

"It's comforting to know we'll be served no differently than men in that one regard at least."

Aristide paused, leaning against a tree, and gazed at her. After a few moments Rosalie returned his gaze, her eyebrows creeping upward, as a few withered leaves drifted to earth between them.

"Whatever can you find so fascinating?"

"I was wondering why it is you patently despise men, yet you don't seem to object to my company."

She drew her shawl closer about her shoulders and huddled into it before replying, as if it were an armor that would protect her from him.

"Most men . . . most men, I've discovered, are selfish, lecherous, hypocritical swine. They think of nothing but themselves: *their* pleasures, *their* honor, *their* glory. Henri was different; he was kind, and generous. Though in the end he abandoned me for the sake of his precious man's honor, just the same. But for a while, he made me happy." A faint blush crept across her cheeks as she continued. "You . . . you remind me of him. You're very like him, in some ways."

"Am I?" he said, surprised.

"You behave like him sometimes. You and he both have a certain stillness within you, a place to which you retreat, where no one can reach you. That collected self-possession of yours . . . he had that, too. The sort of icy calm that men obey, that implies there's steel beneath the surface."

Aristide nearly laughed. "I'm more often a mass of taut nerves than a cool commander of men. Was your artillery officer ever plagued by self-doubt and the terror of committing some disastrous blunder?"

"I would rather see that in a man," she retorted, "than the everlasting conceit and brutishness one usually sees."

He started away from the tree and lightly touched her cheek. "Faith, what was it happened to you that scarred you so?" She shrank back from him. "You didn't mind my touch an hour ago," he reminded her softly. "You weren't seduced as a girl, were you. You were assaulted."

"Let's not mince words. The word is 'raped.'"

"Who could blame you for the violence done you by another?"

"Because it wasn't violence, not really." She crossed her arms in front of her, clutching at the shawl. "Anyone else would say I was seduced, that I'd given myself willingly, and thus it was my own fault. But it was never willing. I never loved him, or even thought I loved him."

Aristide leaned back against the tree, arms folded and head bent, and waited for her to continue.

"I was fifteen. I was straight out of a convent school and shockingly ignorant, though I was about to be married. I still didn't know much about the difference between men and women. I only knew what my mother taught me, that I should rather die than ever allow any man but my husband into my bedchamber.

"We were visiting friends in the country. One of the other guests had the key to my bedroom and let himself in one night. He threatened, if I didn't do as he told me, to tell my mother what we'd done, that I'd invited him in. That would have been far worse than any physical hurt I could imagine. So he had what he wanted, and I supposed that would be the end of it, but he came back the next night, and the next, every night for six weeks. And the beastliest part of it was that he didn't care a sou for me. He held the loftiest contempt for such an insipid, bird-brained little slut, as he called me. It was all just part of a wager."

Aristide stirred. "You might have told your mother, or your host."

"You didn't know my mother. She was one of those stupid, devout, bigoted women who believed every word the priests told them about the sin of Eve, and who were convinced that every carnal sin was entirely the woman's fault. She would have whipped me, and sent me back to the convent to do some wretched penance, and wept to all her horrible scandalmongering friends about how her daughter had been ruined, and then no one would have married me. I was terrified of her, but I thought if I could keep it a secret until I married, I would be all right; and René—the man—he told me about something whores use to counterfeit virginity—he told me to use it on my wedding night, and my husband would never know the difference."

She paused, staring at the tree behind him, where the last dry leaves of autumn drooped from the gray branches. High above them, a sparrow chuckled and twittered.

"But then he died, and as he was dying he decided to unburden himself of his sins. So all of it was exposed, all the women he'd seduced, and the man I was to marry wouldn't have me, because I was soiled goods and I'd been at the center of a public scandal. Nobody else respectable would have had me, either. So I took vows, and I'd be at the abbey still if it hadn't been for the Revolution. Oh, don't mistake me; I grew out of any silly adolescent belief in religion soon enough, but it was peaceful, and safe."

"But your vows were dissolved in 'eighty-nine."

Rosalie nodded. "I left when the abbey was sold off in 1791. And there I was, out in the world again, obliged to find a husband—but I hadn't any dowry," she added, with a sour laugh, "because I'd given everything to the Church. I thought I would never need it again. Of course my mother blamed me for coming back to be a burden on her.

She'd lost half her income, land dues and so on, because the Revolution did away with so much of that, and her new husband spent the rest. He'd only married her for her fortune. So then he decided he'd amuse himself in my bed instead."

"He took advantage of you?" Aristide said sharply.

"I wasn't about to let him. I'd sworn, after René, that no man was ever going to do that to me again." She paused and her mouth hardened, though Aristide saw tears in her eyes. "Fortunately, he drank himself to death not long afterward."

"How did you marry your lawyer?"

"After paying off all the debts, my mother and I went to live with some wealthy relatives, and they had a grown son, and—well, they wanted me out of the way, so they got rid of me by giving me a modest dowry and marrying me off."

Aristide could think of nothing to say that would not have sounded unbearably banal. At last he dared a glance at her. She stood stiff and still, hugging herself in the crisp air.

"So," she added abruptly, her gaze still fixed to the wild long grass at her feet, limp and graying in the autumn chill, "did you find Henri?"

"I'd meant to tell you before, but this matter of Aubry put it out of my mind . . . I visited the barracks at the Palais de Justice a few days ago. They'd never heard of your Henri Longval."

"That's impossible. I saw him in his uniform often enough. You can't tell me he lied to me about that."

"I expect Longval was not his real name."

"I did always like to think he was actually Henri de Longval, count or marquis—or even duke or prince—of something or other. But I imagined he'd simply abandoned his title. It never occurred to me that everything about him might be a lie."

"I'll inquire further, if you wish. Perhaps he had reasons you know nothing of. Perhaps his family called him home. Perhaps it was simply a matter of money, of needing to marry a woman with a rich dowry."

She slowly shook her head. Aristide heard her voice tremble as she spoke. "No. Don't go looking for him. I wish you hadn't. What use would finding him be, except to . . . to provoke a disgusting scene?" Abruptly, no longer able hold back her tears, she turned and hurried away. He followed her, reaching for her elbow.

"Rosalie—"

"For God's sake," she cried, whipping about, "what do you *want* from me?"

"Nothing."

"Everybody wants something!"

"Well then, I want to see you happy! Because I care for you."

"What could you possibly care about? There's no such thing as un-selfish love—I ought to know!"

"Damn it, not all men are self-seeking brutes! I'm not surprised you should detest all men for the misdeeds of a few—but there *are* decent men in this world, and I—I hope I'm one of them."

"I don't want love from you. I don't want another lover, ever again. It always brings you far more misery than it ever makes you happy. Just let me be."

Aristide cautiously edged toward her, as if she were a shy wild thing that might flee if he drew too close, and pressed her hand in his. "Would you allow me to be your friend?"

"I won't be your lover," she insisted.

"I don't *want* a lover."

She said nothing, though she looked sharply at him, the question in her eyes.

"Has it never occurred to you that a man could be just as deeply scarred by life as you have been? That he could go through life alone, by his own choice, never opening his heart, because he never dares trust himself with such intimacy? Because he fears he might be capable of doing a great wrong to the person he most cares about?" He paused, surprised at how much he had confessed to her, and sighed. "Perhaps we're two of a kind. Were you to look into my heart, I suspect you would find that I dread love as much as you do. But there are gentler emotions than love."

He brushed his lips across her fingers and felt her tremble, instinctively stiffening, though she did not pull away from him.

"However cruelly men have used you," he said, "I beg you to believe that at least one cares for you, despite all. . . ."

She squeezed her eyes shut again as tears glinted suddenly in the wan sunshine.

"*He* said he cared for me. I thought it was true."

He did not need to ask whom she meant.

"No," he said, "I'm not your Henri. I don't know who he was or why he abandoned you. And I think that if I kiss you, you'll imagine *his* kiss, *his* touch. So I won't even try. But I hope you'll believe me when I tell you I am your friend."

After he had escorted Rosalie home and dismissed the hired carriage, Aristide stalked through the bustling streets to the Seine, and across the Pont-Neuf toward the Cité. He lingered on the bridge, near the flag-draped recruiting booth below the empty pedestal that had once held the statue of King Henri IV. Brooding, he stared at the moss-green river glittering below him, as behind him the traffic flowed by, endlessly busy, carriages, handcarts, horses, pedestrians, the hordes of Paris.

Ravel, he told himself, *you're a fool; you've come to care far too much for this woman, who carries adversity with her like a burden she can't set down. Why can't you find a measure of happiness with a safe, complacent, prosaic creature like Clotilde?*

The daylight was failing as the inevitable gray clouds gathered once again. He stirred and slouched farther along the raised foot pavement of the bridge, past the peddlers with their trays of sweetmeats and trinkets, and the street singers and prostitutes, and the stalls full of second-hand books.

"Oh, *damn*," he said at last, aloud in the din, "damn, damn," and pushed his way through the crowds toward the Right Bank.

19

A ristide found Brasseur in his office, seething.

"Of all the colossal incompetence!" Brasseur stormed, thrusting a letter at him. "By God, before the Revolution the police had to *answer* to their superiors, and things got done properly! But now nobody tells you anything—every commissaire has his own patch and he can't be bothered with anything outside it—let me get my hands on that fool Dumas—"

"What? Who's Dumas?"

"The commissaire of the Théâtre-Français section! Remember him?"

"What about him?"

"Aubry's vanished!"

"Vanished?" Aristide skimmed the letter.

> *It is my duty to inform you that, as you requested, a watch was put upon the house in the Cour de Rouen in which Citizen Aubry resides, but the person charged with this duty reports that Citizen Aubry left his domicile in the early evening of the 26th of Brumaire and has not yet returned.*

"Four days ago!" Brasseur roared, and stomped across the room. "He's been gone, out of sight, for *four days*, and that idiot didn't think it worth his time to inform me until today!"

"The twenty-sixth," Aristide said. "That's the day Aubry was questioned."

"Damn right it was! And now he's gone—skipped while he had the chance—he's probably in Brussels or Geneva by now!"

"Why would he run?"

"Eh?" Brasseur paused in his angry pacing.

"Our witness failed to identify him. He was in no immediate danger of arrest. I did warn him that he ought to give us a more convincing alibi, but still . . . he had no reason to drop everything and run for it, and make himself look guilty."

Brasseur sighed and threw himself into his chair. "Then where the devil is he?"

"Well . . . we suspect he wasn't telling us everything. Do you suppose he really does know who committed the murders?"

"Christ," Brasseur muttered. "D'you think *he's* dead, too?"

"Perhaps . . . or possibly in hiding from the real killer. I don't think we should dismiss the possibility."

"I need a stiff drink." Brasseur fetched the bottle of brandy he kept locked in the back of a cabinet. "You?"

"Thanks, no." Aristide read the rest of the letter. According to his servant, on the twenty-sixth of Brumaire Aubry had returned from the examining magistrate's chambers, taken a late luncheon alone in his apartment, and then left the apartment without telling the servant where he was going. He had proceeded on foot and had taken no parcels or valises of any kind with him. The police agent assigned to observe Aubry had followed him as far as the Pont-Neuf, where congestion brought about by a carriage accident on the bridge had caused him to lose sight of his quarry, and Aubry had not been seen since.

Brasseur was tossing back his second glass when Dautry thrust his head inside the door.

"Commissaire? A citizen outside seems very agitated, and he says he'll discuss his business only with Ravel—"

"Citizen Ravel?" said a man, shouldering past him. "Is Ravel here?"

"Here," Aristide said, trying to place the man. Tall, red hair, an anxious countenance. "What can I do for you, citizen?"

The man edged closer to him, lowering his voice to a murmur. "Citizeness Beaumontel told me you'd saved her from an embarrassing, perhaps dangerous, predicament."

Of course, Aristide thought, remembering him: Lafontaine, the "friend" of the timid Sidonie Beaumontel, who, he was certain, knew more about the Rue du Hasard murders than she would admit to him. "Yes?"

"And since it was my signature on those letters," Lafontaine continued, "I'd hoped to add my thanks to hers. . . ."

"You're welcome, of course; but it looks as if something more urgent is troubling you?"

"I—can we talk somewhere in private? I'd prefer to shield her reputation. . . ."

Brasseur waved them outside. Aristide gestured Lafontaine out to the street, where the peddlers and carters hurried past them, indifferent. "What's the matter? Why come to me?"

"Sidonie—Citizeness Beaumontel—she's disappeared."

"*She's* disappeared, too?"

"We were to meet the day before yesterday, and she never arrived."

"The husband? You think he learned of your . . . friendship?"

"Her husband was my first thought, too, but he was at a dinner party for hours with a dozen other guests. She'd given the servants the afternoon off and she was to claim a migraine at the last minute, and let Beaumontel go alone to the dinner, which began at three. Then she would slip out of the house and join me at Monceau at a little past three o'clock. We often met there, in the gardens. When she didn't appear, I assumed she hadn't been able to get away. But she sent me no note by way of the florist yesterday morning, no excuses, no apology, nothing. I asked a friend of hers to call on her and learn what might be wrong, but she said they told her Sidonie was not at home to visitors. Today also. No explanation."

"Citizen," Aristide said, "aren't you overreacting? The citizeness may genuinely have fallen ill."

Lafontaine shook his head. "She'd have sent me a message. I—I wouldn't have worried so if it hadn't been for something she told me when we met last, at the Palais-Égalité. She seemed troubled. When I pressed her, she told me she'd just recognized someone. Someone she'd seen outside the house where that swine Saint-Ange was murdered."

"Someone loitering about, you mean?"

"No, you don't understand. When you questioned Sidonie, it was the twelfth of Brumaire, two days after the murders, wasn't it? But what she didn't tell you was that she'd already been there, on the tenth, on the evening of the murders."

Aristide sighed. "So that was it."

"She told me everything. That evening, she'd gone to give Saint-Ange his hush money. Of course she'd made sure the street was nearly empty before she approached. And just as she was about to go inside the house, a young man came rushing out the front door and collided with her. She thought nothing of it, of course, until she continued upstairs—avoiding the porter—to Saint-Ange's apartment. She knocked, received no answer, and at last tried the door. It was unlocked and she went inside, and found the girl, dead, right in front of her. She was still quite warm. Sidonie was so shocked that she could do nothing but tip-toe out of the house. She was too frightened to send for the Watch, even. She was sure no one saw her—naturally she'd taken pains not to be seen. But the man who'd collided with her outside the house might have been the murderer!"

Aristide frowned. "Why did she return to the house on the twelfth, then, if she knew Saint-Ange was dead?"

"She *didn't* know he was dead until you told her yourself. She said she never saw his body, only the girl's."

Aristide nodded, remembering that both Didier and Thibault had said the sofa had all but hidden Saint-Ange's corpse from view.

"So she assumed he was still alive and she came back on the twelfth," Lafontaine continued, "to pay him off, and to learn what she could. And a police inspector detained her and frightened her badly—"

"Didier," Aristide said, disgusted.

"And then you told her Saint-Ange was dead, as well, and she panicked. She feared the police would suspect her of killing him if they knew she'd actually been in the house on the evening of the tenth. She did have good reason for wishing him dead."

"Christ." Aristide beckoned Lafontaine along and set off at a swift stride toward Rue Honoré. "And she told you recently that she'd just seen the man from Rue du Hasard, the man who had collided with her? Did you see him? Did she point him out to you?"

"No. She only said she'd just seen him in the arcades, among the crowd in the Palais-Égalité. A young man—"

Aubry? Or—who?

"And if she saw him and recognized him," Aristide interrupted him, "then he might just as easily have seen her. Oh, damn, *damn.*"

"Where are you going?" Lafontaine panted, hurrying to keep pace with him.

"To the commissariat of her section!"

Though, in theory, the commissariats of Paris were to be open to all citizens every day until ten o'clock at night, most commissaires chose to take *décadi* off from their duties. A visit to the Section du Roule produced only the suggestion, from the bored, glum inspector on duty, that the young wives of middle-aged men often unexpectedly disappeared by their own choice.

"You don't understand," Aristide snapped. "This woman is a witness in a case of murder. She may be in grave danger."

"And what evidence can you offer me," the inspector inquired, "that the lady didn't simply decamp with a paramour?"

"Her paramour is outside in the antechamber, wondering where she can be!"

The inspector sighed. "Look, I'll report it to Commissaire Hubert. Have the man leave a statement with me. I'm sure the commissaire will have someone sent over to ask Beaumontel about his wife."

"When?"

"Tomorrow. There's not much more I can do. Runaway wives aren't really our business unless the husband brings charges of adultery or desertion."

And that would be all the help he would get, Aristide thought as he left Lafontaine behind with the commissaire's secretary. A tight knot of apprehension was growing in his belly.

2 Frimaire (November 22)

A note awaited Aristide at Rue Traversine two days later.

> *Citizen:*
>
> *In accordance with your request to be kept notified of any new intelligence regarding the alleged disappearance of Citizeness Marie-Sidonie Chambly, wife of Citizen Beaumontel, it is my pleasure to inform you that a peace officer yesterday called upon the said Beaumontel. He found the citizen in a state of great agitation. The citizen gave a statement to the peace officer, the essence of which was that his wife had run away with a paramour, but upon being questioned further, could not provide any tangible evidence of her desertion, such as a letter in her handwriting informing him of the fact. The citizeness has been officially registered as a missing person and we are investigating Citizen Beaumontel's movements.*
>
> *Hubert, Commissaire, Section du Roule*

Aristide muttered a curse under his breath and flung the letter into the fire. After a few minutes' debate with himself, he hurried to the

Ministry of Justice, where a junior clerk told him that Lafontaine had stayed home that day by reason of pressing personal business. He went on to the Chaussée d'Antin and found Lafontaine prowling restlessly about his apartment.

"Show me where you waited for Citizeness Beaumontel in the gardens at Monceau."

After a brief, silent journey in a fiacre to the edge of the city, they alighted at the eastern end of the English gardens, now national property, which had once belonged to the royal Orléans family. Lafontaine pointed to the long, curving line of columns just visible through the trees. "There, by the pond. That's where we always met."

"Show me."

They followed a muddy bridle path across the lawn, past leafless thickets drooping sadly beneath the weight of raindrops in the autumn chill. A short distance away the architectural follies built for the late duke's amusement peeped out from amid the fading foliage: an obelisk, a pair of Dutch windmills, a Venetian bridge over the stream that fed the pond, a miniature pyramid, a small Roman arch, a number of lone columns and stone blocks carved in classical style scattered here and there. An artfully crumbling tower, two or three stories high, with a short section of castle wall clinging to it, frowned down upon Aristide. It looked more like a cemetery than a pleasure ground, he thought as they tramped past.

"I waited just here," Lafontaine said as they approached the small, shallow ornamental lake and the broad semicircle of Corinthian columns that embraced one end of it. "I waited two hours."

Aristide surveyed the landscape. Trees and bushes obstructed the view beyond the pond. "She would have been coming from the south, southeast, wouldn't she?"

"Yes, she usually came that way."

Aristide retraced his steps around the pond's edge, turning southward until they stood among the counterfeit ruins. "So she would have entered the gardens there," he said, gazing at a distant gate, "and walked along that path. . . ."

Dwarf trees and thick clumps of lilac bushes flanked the path. The duke's garden would be a fragrant, colorful haven when the trees blossomed, but in the sunless damp of late autumn it was deserted and desolate.

"Is it always this solitary here?" Aristide inquired.

"In winter, yes, aside from a few people out riding. That's why we came here, because we weren't likely to encounter anyone we knew."

"So someone might have followed her here and no one would have noticed."

Lafontaine turned haunted eyes to his. "Dear God, you think . . ."

Aristide pointed to the gate. "You'd better begin over there . . . look among the bushes, in the thickets. Shout if you find any trace of her, or anything out of the ordinary."

He turned back and tramped through the underbrush, glancing from side to side. The shrubs and hedges were running wild. He doubted the gardens had been properly tended since well before the Revolutionary Tribunal had dispatched the Duc d'Orléans, the dead king's cousin, to the guillotine in 1793. The overgrown boxwood hedges, still a deep glossy green amid the fallen leaves, gave off a harsh, acid odor of damp and decay.

He emerged from a clump of wet bushes, shaking droplets from his overcoat, to find himself once again facing the stone garden follies. Sighing, he explored the lawn, finding nothing but a few sundry footprints, nearly obscured by the marks of many horseshoes, several days old and blurred by the last rain. His search took him past the obelisk to the pyramid, where a pair of stiff Egyptian caryatids, supporting a lintel stone, flanked the low entrance to the chamber within. The wooden door stood a trifle ajar. From behind it a faint, rank odor drifted to him on the damp air, the butcher-shop reek he had smelled not long ago at the Basse-Geôle. Seized with a sudden queasy twinge, he stooped and dragged the door open.

Sidonie Beaumontel lay on a bed of mold and rotting leaves with her hands folded on her breast, eyes closed, her muddy white gown arranged decorously about her limbs. But nothing could disguise the blue-black marks of groping, squeezing fingers about her throat.

"Strangled," said the police surgeon, backing out of the pyramid after a cursory examination. "She's been dead a few days."

"How much strength does it require to strangle someone?" Aristide asked him. He did not dare look inside the low stone chamber again.

"A fair amount. Strong hands. But this woman's small, with a delicate frame. Perhaps not so much strength as usual for this one."

"Could a slender man have done it?"

"I expect so, yes. Or even a woman, if she were young and vigorous."

Aristide nodded and moved away from the pyramid and the thing within it. Commissaire Hubert fell in step beside him.

"So your suspicions were founded. You think she went out to meet Lafontaine on the twenty-eighth, and the murderer followed her here and seized his chance when he saw nobody was about?"

"Yes, I expect so. Then he carried her in there so she wouldn't be found by the first matron out exercising her lapdog."

"Lafontaine says they were to meet a little after three. The servants swore the last time any of them saw her was at about quarter to three, when she complained of a headache and dismissed them all for the afternoon. That lets Beaumontel out; he climbed into his carriage at half past two and spent the next five hours at a dinner party. His coachman and a dozen dinner guests can swear to where he was, and then his servants when he arrived home again."

"It wasn't the husband," Aristide said. "Don't waste your time."

"The lover? We have only his word that he waited for her and she didn't arrive. They might have quarreled."

"If that was so, why would he have called my attention to her disappearance?" Aristide shook his head, with a glance at Lafontaine, who sat on a block of stone, head in his hands, shoulders trembling. "Look at him. Commissaire, she's dead because she saw the man who committed the murders on Rue du Hasard. He murdered her to keep her quiet. It's the only reasonable explanation. If only she'd dared to be honest with us!"

Commissaire Hubert sighed. "After the past few years, with everybody looking over his shoulder, would you?"

20

He returned home on foot to Rue d'Amboise, grateful for the touch of fresh air and fine rain on his face, and pushed open the front door.

"Ravel—"

He paused, hand still on the door handle, as Rosalie rose to her feet from a bench in the dim foyer. "Forgive me for intruding."

"How did you get here?"

"I asked for you at the commissariat of the Butte-des-Moulins section. I badgered them until they gave me your address." She met his eyes, then hurriedly looked away again. "Not so long ago, you called on me to apologize for your behavior. I should like to do the same. I behaved childishly on *décadi*. Please forgive me."

"There's little to forgive," Aristide said. He drew a deep breath, trying to banish the stink of putrid flesh with the faint scent of pipe smoke and coffee and frying onions that always lingered on the staircase. Rosalie drew a step nearer.

"Are you quite well? You look pale."

"I had the misfortune to discover a corpse today."

"A corpse . . . ?"

"A witness. A woman who could have identified the man who killed Célie and Saint-Ange."

She stared at him. "Tell me."

Aristide seated himself on the stairs, glad enough to sit down, and repeated the tale Lafontaine had told him. "And then by chance she sees the murderer again," he concluded, "a few days ago, at the Palais-Égalité. But the murderer has recognized her as surely as she's recognized him, and fears she'll betray him . . . so he hangs about and keeps an eye on her, undoubtedly follows her home to the faubourg Honoré, and watches for his opportunity. One day she slips out alone to meet her lover and the murderer follows her to the gardens, to a lonely spot where no one is about, and . . . he strangles her."

"So another innocent person has died in order to conceal this man's guilt," Rosalie whispered. "Oh, God, that poor woman . . . how I will *rejoice* when that man stretches his neck under the blade!"

"You still think it was Aubry, don't you?"

"Yes, I do. Have you examined *his* movements yet? Does he have an alibi for the day this woman disappeared?"

"Aubry's disappeared, too. For all we know, he may be dead as well." Aristide rubbed his eyes. The complexities of investigating a murder whose cast of characters was scattered across Paris had become hopelessly perplexing. In the cumbersome, decentralized system of police jurisdiction that had been the rule since 1790, it was scarcely clear who ought to take charge of an affair that had begun in one section, involving persons who lived in various sections, and a third murder committed in yet another.

"What do you mean, Aubry's disappeared?"

A folded note on the hallway table, addressed in François's familiar scrawl, caught his eye. He tore it open, read it, and glanced at his watch.

"Pardon me, I have to go."

"Are you so eager to be rid of me now, after your persistent pursuit?"

"I don't mean to be rude. I have to meet someone." He thrust the note in front of her.

"Who's this brandy seller?"

"Someone who may be able to give Aubry an alibi for the tenth of Brumaire."

"I don't believe it. What do you mean, he's *disappeared*?"

Aristide paused. "Why don't you come with me now and I'll tell you what I know, and you can hear for yourself whatever it is this peddler has to say. Will that satisfy you?"

They hurried along the Boulevard, heads bent against the chilly breeze as Aristide told her about Aubry's baffling disappearance. François was waiting by the empty pedestal at the center of the Place Vendôme, where once a statue of Louis XIV had stood.

"Are you sure this is the right peddler?" Rosalie demanded after Aristide had hastily introduced them.

"She's the only woman who sells brandy on Rue Honoré," said François. "All the other regulars are men. How do you want to work up to it? She's the sort who'll go deaf and dumb in front of the police."

"Then the police won't ask her any questions." Aristide buttoned his overcoat to the neck, concealing the telltale black suit. "Here," he added, thrusting a few sous into Rosalie's hand, "we're hunting for signs of a friend of ours, who vanished a month ago."

The brandy seller, a weather-beaten woman who looked sixty and who Aristide guessed was probably thirty-five or forty, sat hunched on a disused mounting block, a little cask beside her, near the old Jacobin monastery. Silently pocketing the coins he gave her, she filled a small tin cup from the cask and handed it to him.

"Excellent brandy this," he said, blinking back a few tears after the first burning swallow.

The brandy seller grunted and eyed the pastry shop across the street.

"Do you often come to this spot to sell?"

"Most days."

"I ask because I'm looking for a friend who has unaccountably disappeared," he continued. The woman said nothing. "He was last seen leaving a house just over there," he added, pointing at the house to the right of the pastry shop, "and we wondered if you might have seen him. This was a month ago, so I suppose it's too much to ask."

The woman grunted again.

"He's young," Aristide said, slipping a ten-sou piece into her grimy palm, "and astonishingly good-looking. Dark hair. You'd almost think he was a woman. And he was in some distress, I believe."

The brandy seller bit the coin, slipped it somewhere beneath her layers of ragged shawls, and pondered a moment. "I seen him."

"You have?"

"Least I remember some young gent, wearin' good clothes, with a face like a little girl. Them fine gents, they got their own brandy in cut-glass decanters in their fancy houses, and they don't buy from me, but he did. Last month, I s'pose. All in a pother he was."

"He was upset?" said François. "I feared as much."

"White as a sheet he was, and shaking like a leaf. He had three glasses. Then he looked better and he took himself off."

"I think our friend was last seen in the morning," François said. He took the cup, finished off its contents, and passed it back to the brandy seller along with a double sou.

"Evening," said the woman, shaking her head. "I was pickin' up t'go home. There wasn't nobody much about on foot after lamplighting, but then he comes."

"And did he come out of that house?" Aristide inquired, pointing again at the house next to the pastry shop.

"That? No. Happen he came from over yonder, I think." She jerked a dirty thumb eastward. "He come up the street, lookin' like I don't know what, stumbling like, and all of a sudden he sees me and he says, 'Give me a glass, right away,' and he swallows it down in one gulp, and then another, and then he goes and leans himself against the wall."

"Like this, you mean?" François leaned back nonchalantly against the monastery's doorsill, once entrance to the notorious Jacobin Club, as the breeze whipped at his bushy brown hair.

"T'other way round; he had his back to me. Still in a bad way, he was. He leans his face on his arm, like he's hidin' his eyes. Then after a while he collects himself and he has a third glass, and a little color comes back into his cheeks, and he pays me right enough and goes off."

"And this was around the time of lamplighting?" Rosalie said.

"Aye, just past dark."

Aristide pressed another double sou into her hand and beckoned the others away. "Just past dark two *décades* ago . . . it's dark at half past five now, so on the tenth of Brumaire darkness must have fallen at a few minutes to six. Say Aubry appeared no later than a quarter past six."

"It would take no more than ten minutes or so to walk here from Rue du Hasard," Rosalie said. "He still could have done the murder."

François nodded. "You said the police surgeon swore they were shot before eight o'clock. Maybe Aubry doesn't know that any competent doctor can tell within two or three hours when someone died."

"This alibi of his is no alibi at all," said Rosalie. "And she said he was visibly upset. Like a man who's just murdered the woman he loves, in a fit of passion, and stumbled out of the house in a daze. It's perfectly obvious."

Abruptly François stopped, so absorbed in thought that Aristide was obliged to tug him from the path of a speeding carriage. "I've just thought of something—come on, let's get out of this cold. I could use a bite to eat."

They found a secluded table in a near-deserted eating-house, far from the talkative cluster of friends by the hearth and the man reading aloud from a newspaper about General Bonaparte's victories in Italy. Aristide cupped cold hands around a bowl of steaming lentil soup and turned an inquisitive gaze toward François, who washed a mouthful of soup down with a gulp of beer and proceeded.

"Ravel . . . citizeness . . . what about this? Imagine, first of all, that Grangier's mistaken or confused about his identification. People make mistakes all the time, and you say he's a bit of a drunk."

Rosalie frowned. "Well?"

"Grangier hears footsteps running up the stairs. Ten minutes later a young man rushes down the stairs and out the front door. Then twenty minutes later the young man returns, still in a terrible hurry, and runs upstairs again. Grangier doesn't hear him run down again, so he must have gone down quietly. What if Aubry followed the girl to Saint-Ange's apartment, went upstairs, found them already dead, and raced downstairs to get help and raise the alarm?"

"But he didn't," said Rosalie. "Raise the alarm, that is."

"Then he has second thoughts about it; he fears he'll be accused of murdering them himself, which is right enough. So he races back, to see if anything can be done for them. They're dead, beyond help, and he stumbles downstairs and out to the street."

He glanced from Aristide to Rosalie. Rosalie sat motionless, her untouched glass of red wine before her. "If Grangier was indeed mistaken about who he saw," she said at last, "and he did see Aubry, then why shouldn't Aubry have been the murderer? That's the simplest explanation, after all."

"You're forgetting the round hat," Aristide said between mouthfuls of the thick soup.

"Hat?" Rosalie echoed him.

"Grangier saw a young man wearing a round hat. He may not be sure of Aubry, but he's definite about the hat. And Aubry told me himself that he doesn't wear low-crowned round hats, that he doesn't own any, because he dislikes them."

"Well, of course he'd deny it," she snapped.

"It's the sort of thing his servant can confirm in an instant. So unless he deliberately donned someone else's hat on the spur of the moment to disguise himself, which seems far-fetched, I fear he told the truth there. François, I think you're making it too complex. We have no evidence at all that Célie had *two* passionate admirers. And if it wasn't a jealous lover, who else would have wanted to murder her?" He sighed, scowling, and pushed his empty bowl aside. A pack of dog-eared old playing cards lying on a nearby table caught his eye and he fetched them and began to lay them out one by one.

"In any event," said Rosalie, "if Aubry had really been up there, and found Célie and Saint-Ange dead, but didn't kill them himself, don't you think he'd have told Ravel as much after the magistrate let him go?"

"Not necessarily," said François. "Ravel works for the police, after all. Better to stick to his story that he was never there. If it weren't for that damned hat—"

"Never mind," Aristide said. "We've learned what the brandy seller had to tell. It doesn't clear Aubry, but neither does it condemn him. What about the prostitute, this Émilie?"

Rosalie glanced at him. "Who's Émilie?"

François shook his head, ignoring her. "Sorry. No luck."

"You claimed that all the whores in a quarter know each other," Aristide said. "They certainly do at the Palais-Égalité." He gathered up the cards and laid them out again.

"So they do. And they *don't* know any Émilie who hangs about the Pont-Neuf except for a mulatto girl who was right there and ready to talk." François grinned, took a long swallow of beer, and continued. "Pretty girl, that one. She swore she damned well wasn't writing letters to any gentlemen—she can barely write her own name. Besides, she was home sick with a fever for most of that week. The other girls backed her up; some of them visited her."

"Well, the woman may not be from that quarter after all, in which case we'll have a devil of a time finding her—"

"Or she may not exist."

"If Aubry is lying about this 'Émilie,' then who wrote to him?"

"God knows." François finished his glass of beer. "You won't mind paying for another, will you? Waiter!"

Aristide turned over the seven of hearts from his hand, set it on a six, looked over the tableau for a moment, chose between two eights before him, and swiftly moved a dozen more cards to their respective foundations. "If the person who wrote to Aubry wasn't Émilie the prostitute, then who was he or she, and why is Aubry lying about him? I don't like loose ends. We'd better return to the theory that the letter told him something damning about Célie." He laid the last three liberties and geniuses in place and leaned back in his chair, gazing with mild triumph at the four neat piles of cards. "I prefer to see patterns work out as they should."

"People aren't as predictable or logical as a pack of cards," Rosalie said softly.

"You think not? Nine times out of ten, they are. Perhaps ninety-nine times out of a hundred."

"Well, you were so sure about Aubry, weren't you?" François remarked.

"That, I confess, is worrisome. I would say Aubry, given his past, and suitable provocation, was behaving quite predictably by murdering his sweetheart while in a deranged passion. But it's possible he's the hundredth case."

"And the porter's eyewitness testimony?"

"Oh, he was being completely true to his caste, his age, and his occupation! He won't swear either way to what he saw because, as he admitted readily enough, he'd had a few glasses of eau-de-vie at the time, and can't be sure if he was seeing straight. What's more predictable than that?"

François yawned and watched, chin on fist, as Aristide began to lay out another round of patience. "Ravel," he said suddenly, "we're missing something important here, you know. Do we know exactly what it was that Aubry's mysterious letter told him?"

"If, as you suspect, 'Émilie' is a myth? That Célie had deceived him, of course. What else would send him racing out like that?"

"But that's only a guess, isn't it?"

Aristide slowly nodded.

"Now, a letter *did* exist, because Aubry's porter saw it and handed it to him," François continued, "and Aubry admits getting it, and Brelot told us that soon afterward something upset him; we agree on that much, don't we?"

"Yes, of course."

"What else might it have been about? If it wasn't any nonsense about forged notes, nor yet about Célie's reputation?"

Aristide dropped the cards on the table.

"My God, what was I thinking?" He shot to his feet and paced across the sawdust-strewn floor and back, thrusting empty chairs aside.

"Never take anything on face value, never *assume!*"

He threw himself into the nearest chair. "The letter arrives. Aubry puts it in his pocket, goes upstairs and into his study—and a bit later he runs out, 'looking like death,' as Brelot put it. That's all we know for fact. Everything else is just guesswork. Right?"

"Right," said François. Rosalie nodded, watching Aristide intently.

"So if 'Émilie' *is* a myth," Aristide continued, "what was the letter about, and why did he rush out in such distress and haste? I've assumed all along that this letter-writer told Aubry something damaging about Célie, that Célie had been lying to him, or that she wasn't what she seemed. But we don't *know* that; the letter is undoubtedly ashes, and only Aubry knows the truth, and he's keeping it to himself. What other intelligence could this letter have told him that could have upset him so much?"

"Something about the girl, surely."

"François—do you think—could it have told him *that Célie was already dead?* That *the person who wrote the letter* had shot Célie?"

"The letter arrived at . . . when, about four o'clock?" François objected. "Your police surgeon said they weren't killed before four or so at the earliest."

"Then what if it was a threat, a cruel taunt? Something aimed deliberately at Aubry, a message telling him that the writer was about to harm Célie, the person who meant the most to him in the world?"

They looked at each other, saying nothing. A burning log broke apart in the fireplace with a small hiss and crackle.

"That really doesn't seem very likely," Rosalie said. "Why would anyone do something like that? It's as good as a sworn confession. And why would Aubry have burned the letter?"

"And Aubry," Aristide continued, scarcely hearing her, "for some unknown reason, is shielding this person by saying nothing."

"Someone who knew both Aubry and Célie?" said François.

"A love triangle? A rejected mistress?" Aristide hastily leafed through the notebook he carried in his coat. "We thought another *man*, another unknown admirer of Célie's, wasn't likely—but a female rival?"

"*Not* a fight over Célie, but over Aubry," François mused. "A fellow as pretty as Aubry, he must have had women throwing themselves at him."

Aristide found the notes he had been hunting for. "God, it was right in front of me! I've spoken with her myself. Twice. Hélène Villemain."

"*Who?*" said Rosalie. She turned to him, her eyes huge and dark in the shadows.

"Célie's dear friend . . . who knew Aubry when he was Montereau's secretary, when she and Célie were girls. She admitted herself that they'd both adored him."

"But—oh, no, it *can't* be. You're wrong. You *must* be wrong."

François nodded. "It might be as simple as that. Sheer female jealousy, kept burning for years."

"I wouldn't have said she was the sort . . . but it was she, it was *she* who first directed us toward Aubry," said Aristide. "We would never have heard of him otherwise."

"After getting rid of her rival," François said, frowning, "would she want to risk the life of the man she loved?"

"She might if her affections weren't returned. What revenge could be sweeter than to murder the girl you hate with a jealous passion, and then to see the man who had rejected you—rejected you for *her*—suffer hellishly for the crime?"

"And Aubry is too much of an upstanding little gentleman to tell you the truth and send a woman to her just punishment."

"Because he did rush out to Saint-Ange's apartment, after reading the letter that said 'your darling Célie will soon be lost to you,' and discovered them lying dead, just as you suggested . . . it fits. By God, it fits. He's shielding her, because it's the sort of thing a virtuous ass would do. Brasseur can look into this . . . he'll have to see the commissaire of the Fontaine-de-Grenelle section, in order to question her . . . we'll have to learn if she has an alibi for the tenth of Brumaire."

"What about Grangier and his damned round hat?"

"Grangier was half drunk! Perhaps it *was* Aubry he saw, but his eyes weren't focusing. Perhaps he imagined the hat. Perhaps he fell asleep after seeing a perfectly harmless stranger run downstairs, hours earlier, and dreamed the whole thing. And Hélène Villemain stole in while he was sleeping, and nobody saw her in the house. It's easier than you think."

"Would she have followed Célie to Saint-Ange's?" François said dubiously.

"I suppose she would have followed her anywhere, if she'd had murder in her heart."

"But this is ridiculous!" Rosalie suddenly cried, hammering both fists on the table and rattling the crockery. "Listen to yourselves!"

"Is it?"

"Yes! It's preposterous! You're constructing an elaborate theory on a hopelessly shaky foundation. Why would she murder that Beaumontel woman, if it was a *man* that Citizeness Beaumontel saw in the Palais-Égalité? It's plain: Aubry killed Célie, and then he killed the witness to keep her from fingering him, and then he prudently made himself scarce! What other explanation is there?"

"I wonder," Aristide said softly, "if your private opinion of men has perhaps influenced your perceptions. If you're still smarting from a wounded heart," he added, as gently as he could, "you may feel less kindly toward Célie's young man, and more cynical about other people's amours, than you otherwise might. Are you sure you aren't merely seeing a villain in every good-looking young man who professes love to a young woman, because you see the girl you were in Célie?"

"So you're going to denounce this woman with nothing more than this mad speculation?"

"I don't denounce anyone. I offer Brasseur a theory of what might have happened. If he finds it plausible, he'll have her taken in for questioning."

"And what if she can give an account of herself for the time of the murders?"

"If so, I imagine she would be released. If the evidence against her is insufficient."

"But there's no other evidence against her, is there?"

"In truth, no," Aristide admitted, "except for the fact that she had known and admired Aubry some years ago."

"That's rubbish! How could you arrest her when you have no evidence but such a stupid idea?" Rosalie sprang to her feet and stormed away.

He caught up with her in a few strides, seized her wrist, and jerked her about so that they were face-to-face once more. "All right, *enough*! What is it you're not telling me? Why don't you tell me why it is that you can be so cocksure about what's true, and what's rubbish?"

"Let me go!"

"First answer me."

"Let me *go*!" she snapped, flailing at him. The other patrons began to turn from their dinners to stare at the commotion. He managed at last to seize both her wrists, and held her in place.

"Why the devil are you so intent on finding Aubry guilty?" he demanded, suddenly enlightened. "What do you have against him? What aren't you admitting? Perhaps that you did know Aubry, before Célie ever told you about her sweetheart?"

She stopped struggling as the merest gleam of alarm flickered in her eyes.

"Don't be ridiculous."

"I think you're lying. What haven't you told me?"

"I don't have to tell you anything."

"What is it between you and Philippe Aubry?" he insisted, loosening his grip on her wrists as she put up no resistance.

"Nothing. Let me alone."

"Not until you start telling me the truth."

Abruptly Rosalie wrenched herself away from him and fled out of the common room to the busy street beyond. By the time he reached the door, cursing at having let himself be deceived by her sudden docility, she was gone.

21

Rosalie was nowhere to be found when Aristide asked for her at the Maison Deluc an hour later. Leaving instructions that he was to be sent for as soon as she returned, he hastened to Rue Traversine to lay his new theory of the affair before Brasseur.

No message arrived for him and at last he returned to Rue des Cordiers at half past eight, in the middle of the dinner hour, determined to corner Rosalie and have his questions answered. A flustered maidservant assured him that Citizeness Clément had not been seen since that morning. He stalked away, fuming, imagining what Brasseur would say to him: perhaps, *Funny how all our witnesses keep disappearing, isn't it?*

4 Frimaire (November 24)

Rosalie had not returned by the time Commissaire Fabien questioned Hélène Villemain two days later at the commissariat of the Fontaine-de-Grenelle section. She seemed calm, though astonished at being summoned by the police for questioning.

"Citizeness, where were you on the afternoon of the tenth of Brumaire?"

"I must have been at home," she replied. "My husband was away in Douai for several days. I don't often go out when he's away from Paris."

"You're not sure? You must have considered where you were at the moment when your friend was murdered."

She let out a soft breath. "Yes, I remember now. I was at home, reading a comic novel. I remember thinking, later, how dreadful it was that I must have been laughing at the moment when poor Célie died."

Aristide gnawed at his lip, watching her, suspecting they had erred once again. Rosalie still had not returned to the Maison Deluc. Where could she be, and what was it she knew? If only, he thought, he could put Philippe Aubry and Rosalie Clément together in a small room—then he would soon have some answers.

"Can your servants confirm this?" the commissaire inquired.

"Well," Hélène faltered, "it was *décadi;* they always have the afternoon and evening off on *décadi* . . . aside from the kitchen maid. Most of them were at the theater. Fanette would have been in the scullery, scouring the pots, but otherwise I think I was alone after my luncheon . . . from three o'clock until perhaps half past ten."

"What about a nursery maid?" Fabien asked. "Wasn't she there with your children?"

"No, both my children are still with wet nurses in the country."

"So no one but your kitchen maid can vouch for your whereabouts on the afternoon and evening of the tenth," Fabien said. "Did this girl ever come out of the scullery that afternoon?"

"I doubt it. I assure you, Commissaire, I didn't do this dreadful thing. Célie and I were like sisters. Why would I have wished her ill?"

"You were in love with one Philippe Aubry some years ago, were you not?"

Hélène laughed. "A girlish infatuation. Scarcely love. I was seventeen. I've not thought about Aubry for years."

"Infatuations have led to murder before this," the commissaire said dryly. "Did you write to Citizen Aubry on the tenth of Brumaire?"

"Certainly not."

"Kindly write down your name and address," said Fabien, pushing paper and inkwell toward her. Puzzled, she did as he requested.

The porter Deschamps inspected her handwriting, brow furrowed. "No," he said at last. "I don't think it's like the letter I saw. This is smaller writing. Maybe," he added, timidly, "if the writing said 'To Citizen Aubry, Cour de Rouen,' just like it did on the letter, I'd remember better?"

"Do as he says," Fabien instructed Hélène. As she took up the pen again, an inspector slipped into the office and murmured a few words in the commissaire's ear.

"What? Well, send her in."

The inspector went out and returned with Rosalie. Aristide stepped forward, surprised, but she ignored him.

"Citizen Commissaire," she said, marching up to his desk, "I have a statement to offer that will resolve some of your questions, I think. My name is Rosalie Clément and it was I who wrote to Citizen Aubry on the tenth of Brumaire."

"You, citizeness?" he echoed her. "What, then, was the subject of this letter?"

"I was Célie Montereau's friend. I merely wrote to him because he and Célie had quarreled the day before. The silly child ran to me and cried in my lap, because they'd had some sharp words about keeping their engagement secret, and I decided to give him a piece of my mind. That's all."

"Why didn't you reveal this to the police straightaway?" he demanded.

"Because—because I was frightened of getting myself mixed up in a case of murder."

Aristide studied Rosalie. Despite her tranquil expression, her hands were clasped tightly about her reticule, the knuckles white.

"I simply told Citizen Aubry that the quarrel had left Célie terribly unhappy. I thought he had behaved unkindly, and I wished him to apologize to her. It was a trifling matter."

"If you would write the words 'To Citizen Aubry, Cour de Rouen, on this paper," Fabien said after a moment's consideration. She did as he asked and he handed both specimens to Deschamps.

The porter peered at the writing in the light from the nearest window, dimming now in the twilight of a winter afternoon. "*This* could be the same, Citizen Commissaire. I remember the writing on the letter was bold and a bit untidy."

Rosalie turned to the commissaire. "It was I. This citizeness had nothing to do with any of this affair."

"According to this dossier, Aubry has never mentioned your name," said Fabien. "Do you claim you are acquainted with him?"

"No. I wrote to him as a stranger."

"He claimed that the woman who wrote to him was a certain prostitute."

Rosalie shrugged. "Not, perhaps, the most tactful of subterfuges," she said, "but evidently he was trying to keep a lady out of this, as a gentleman would do. Why not ask him?"

"Citizen Aubry isn't here," Fabien told her. "He's not responded to the summons to testify."

"I know. He's unaccountably vanished. Don't you think that's highly suspicious?"

"I understand that Aubry was questioned some days ago in regard to this affair, and released," said the commissaire. At last, with a sigh, he adjusted his spectacles, bent to his papers, and added a few notes more. "Citizens, I thank you for your testimony. Citizeness Villemain, I thank you for your cooperation, and I see no reason to inconvenience you further."

"I've never been so glad to be mistaken," Aristide told Hélène after she had shyly thanked Rosalie for coming forward. "If you're not offended by the sight of me, may I help you to a carriage?" He escorted her outside, then returned and glanced about for Rosalie, at last discovering her at the other end of the chamber with Fabien's secretary.

"They want a signed statement from me," Rosalie told him before he could demand where she had been. "I may as well wait here until a copy is ready, rather than come back tomorrow. Are you going to go hunt for Aubry now? And what about that poor woman at Monceau?"

"You know," he told her, "that your own statement, that the letter was innocuous, eliminates any motive for him to have murdered Célie.

And if he didn't murder Célie, then he certainly had no motive to harm Citizeness Beaumontel."

"Who's to say he didn't learn the truth in some way other than a letter?" she retorted. "I've never doubted for a moment that he did it. Perhaps that silly quarrel of theirs set him to sniffing about and asking questions about her. He might have concluded on his own that she had something to hide—"

"Where the devil have you been, Rosalie?" Aristide interrupted her. "I wanted to talk to you."

"I needed to think things out, without you badgering me, so I spent the night at an acquaintance's flat. I didn't want to get mixed up in this—but I didn't want you to make trouble for Citizeness Villemain, either. Are you satisfied now?"

He looked at her for a moment, wondering if she had told him everything, but at last lifted her hand to his lips. "Shall I escort you home?"

"Better you should spend your time finding Aubry, and finding proof of his guilt. I can blunder my way home without any help. Thank you," she added with a faint smile.

Aristide bade her farewell and trudged back to the Right Bank and Rue Traversine. Brasseur was at his desk, frowning at a letter. "This arrived half an hour ago, by the local post. Postmarked this morning, from the Droits-de-l'Homme section. What do *you* make of it?"

It was addressed, in an crude, childish hand, *To the citizen who is investigating the murders at Rue du Hasard*. Its contents were brief:

> *Citizen:*
>   *You have arrested an innocent woman. Citizeness Villemain did not commit this horrible crime. Look farther afield to discover the monster who murdered Célie Montereau.*

"Whoever it's from," Aristide said, "he's a bit tardy."

"Who do you suppose wrote it? A friend of the Villemains?"

He shrugged. "Probably. It's a pity he didn't share any useful information with us, such as who this 'monster' may be."

"I doubt he knows himself. Some crank always thinks the police will make or dismiss a case on his word alone." Brasseur crumpled the letter and threw it on the fire.

5 Frimaire (November 25)

The next day's weather had turned rainy and cold and Aristide had intended to pass the time quietly at home in his shabby armchair, with a generous fire and the newspapers from the past fortnight, but a messenger boy interrupted him early in the morning with a note from Brasseur. Exasperated, he hastily tied his cravat, threw on his coat and hat, and stalked downstairs. By the time he arrived at Rue Traversine, fifteen minutes later, he was chilled and irritable.

"Another anonymous letter's come," Brasseur told him, before he could tartly remind his friend that the weather was filthy and he did not relish being denied his occasional day of leisure. "Perhaps more helpful than the first."

Aristide read the letter. It was in the same looping script, probably the writing of someone who wished to disguise his hand, and equally as brief.

> *Citizen Commissaire:*
> *If you want to find the real murderess of the citizens Montereau and Saint-Ange, you would do well to lay the hand of the law upon one Juliette de Vaudray, who knows more than she is saying.*

"So," Brasseur demanded, echoing Aristide's thoughts, "who the devil is Juliette de Vaudray?"

"And who has betrayed her?"

"Think it's worth pursuing?" Brasseur inquired.

"A name . . . we can't afford to ignore it. But who *is* this woman?"

"Well," said Brasseur, "it sounds as if he thinks we already know her."

"Know?"

"Or at least know of her. Maybe she's hiding behind an assumed name."

Aristide pulled the dossier of the case toward him and sifted through Brasseur's notes. "One of Saint-Ange's other victims, perhaps?"

"No, not one that I know of. Well, if she was Citizeness Beaumontel, then the question's moot. But I doubt this Juliette de Vaudray is Hélène Villemain, or Célie's great-aunt."

"No," Aristide agreed with a faint smile, "I can scarcely see the old lady pulling a pistol out of her pocket."

"What about this other friend of Célie's, Citizeness Clément? She's been keeping a few secrets from us. I'd guess *she* knows more than she's saying."

She knows much, much more than she's saying, Aristide thought, *and damned if I can fathom her game.*

He suddenly recalled that Madame Letellier, Rosalie's stout fellow boarder, had mentioned that Rosalie had changed her name after her husband's execution. A thing natural enough to do, perhaps, if a widow was ashamed of a husband who had been condemned as a common criminal rather than a political victim of the Terror. And many ex-nobles had discreetly dropped the aristocratic "de" from their names when, after the fall of the monarchy in 1792, it had become increasingly more perilous to be thought of as an aristocrat and potential enemy of the Revolution. But he had assumed, he realized, mentally chastising himself—*never assume!*—that Rosalie Clément had once been Rosalie Ferré.

What might it mean if Rosalie Clément had once been Juliette Ferré, née de Vaudray?

"I'm going to the Palais de Justice to follow a hunch," he told Brasseur.

After the usual tedious round of approaching one official after another, three hours later Aristide found himself in a dim, dusty storage chamber at the law courts, an anxious clerk hovering about him as, one by one, he lifted the massive red record books from their shelves.

Revolutionary Tribunal, October-December 1793. Some patriotic registrar had carefully inked 10 VENDÉMIAIRE-11 NIVÔSE, YEAR II OF THE RE-

PUBLIC onto the leather binding, below the offending Christian months. Aristide opened the book and began to skim the pages.

He found Maurice-Étienne Ferré, lawyer, among those condemned on 9 Frimaire, formerly 29 November. "I want to see the dossier of this man," he told the clerk, hoping he might find a footnote mentioning names of the members of Ferré's household.

After a further search through several cabinets, the clerk placed a thick folder before him. The record of Ferré's arrest lay near the top of the pile of papers, together with the transcript of the trial and the signed order of execution.

> *Maurice Ferré, advocate, residing at No. 8, Rue des Capucines, Section de la Place-Vendôme, arrested this 18 August 1793, on suspicion of corresponding with and sending gold out of the country to enemies of the Republic. Seals put upon his domicile and premises searched. Records of correspondence with émigrés discovered by representatives of the Office of the Public Prosecutor in the residence of the said Ferré, with the assistance of Citizeness Juliette Vaudray, wife of the said Ferré.*

Aristide sat back and frowned at the document a moment. The mere fact that Rosalie Clément was Juliette Vaudray proved nothing more than that the anonymous letter-writer knew they were one and the same.

But why would Rosalie have murdered her friend?

Because Juliette Vaudray had, as he had suspected, once known Philippe Aubry?

His gaze strayed over the report once again. *With the assistance of Juliette Vaudray, wife of the said Ferré.*

He leafed past the records of Ferré's arrest to those of his trial, taking notes as he read. It seemed the usual shabby tale of a selfish and grasping man whose financial misdeeds, merely unethical before the Terror, had become worthy of death in 1793. The fatal letters lay before him in the folder: a dozen or more in three different hands, postmarked

Brussels and Cologne, detailed plans to smuggle gold across the frontier to Belgium, Germany, and Holland.

Spouses were forbidden to testify at trial against their partners. But she had done the nearest thing to it: she had guided the authorities to the evidence that had led to Ferré's arrest. In the autumn of 1793, such a denunciation would have been deliberate, calculated murder, a swift and certain death sentence.

He had come searching merely for a name, an identity, the solution to a puzzle, and had found far more than he had wanted to know. He winced, as if she had slapped him.

22

Aristide hired a fiacre to the Place Vendôme and trudged in the rain along Rue des Capucines toward the tree-lined Boulevard. On the north side of the street, the buildings of the former Capucin convent, national property since 1790, had become the Mint—or rather the printing works that had spewed out millions of nearly worthless assignats. A row of comfortable bourgeois apartment houses stretched along the opposite side.

He paused before number eight as a maidservant threw open a pair of shutters at a first-floor window. " 'Morning, citizen," she said, as he tipped his hat to her, and heaved a pail of dirty water into the street. "Watch your boots, there."

"I'm already wet."

She grinned, with a quick grimace at the unrelenting drizzle, and muttered something about nasty December weather. Before she could vanish inside the house again, he inquired if she might have known one Ferré, a former tenant of the house.

She shook her head, uninterested. "No, I was engaged here eight months ago. I don't know any Ferré."

"This citizen was guillotined in the Year Two—three years ago."

"Saints preserve us," she exclaimed, eyes widening with relish. "What did he do?"

"Sent gold abroad to émigrés."

"Serves him right, then. Well, I'm sorry, but I never heard of him. But you might ask upstairs," she added. "Marthe, the cook at the second-floor flat, she's been there for years."

"Do you think you could introduce me?" Aristide asked her, summoning a smile and reaching into his pocket. "It's worth a good deal to me."

He parted with five sous as she let him in through the carriage gate to the courtyard and led him upstairs, crying, "Marthe, got a moment? A gentleman here wants to talk to you."

Aristide stepped into the kitchen, blinking through the haze of steam and wood smoke. The cook turned from her stockpot and peered at him from beneath her mobcap's frills, with the habitual suspicion of the domestic or peasant confronted with authority.

"Citizeness," he began, "I understand you might remember the previous tenant of the first-floor flat, Citizen Ferré?"

"Who are you?" she demanded, brandishing a large wooden spoon as she might have shaken a pike in a bread riot three or four years before. "A police spy?"

He reached into his pocket again. "His name was Ferré?"

"Ferré, that's right," the cook said, still clutching the spoon as she eyed the franc he placed on the table. "But he's long gone. They arrested him back during the troubles, years ago. I heard he ended up looking out the little window." She grimaced and drew her finger across her lean throat. "They took everything, you know, all the furnishings, even his wife's fine gowns, and turned everybody out. 'National property,' they said. Doesn't seem right."

"Do you know what happened to Ferré's wife?"

"Me? No." She returned to the kettle of soup bubbling gently at the opposite side of the hearth. "I don't know where they went except for Angélique, what was the kitchen maid there, because I took her on myself; happened ours had just run off with a soldier and I was shorthanded. Angélique! Come here and answer the gentleman."

A mousy girl turned from silently peeling potatoes and bobbed Aristide a curtsey. "How well did you know Citizen and Citizeness Ferré?" he inquired, reaching into his pocket for the third time and jingling the few remaining coins.

"Oh, I never saw much of them," she admitted reluctantly. "I just worked in the kitchen. I saw her sometimes, but she was talking to the cook, not to me."

"What did she look like? Was she an attractive lady with dark brown hair and dark eyes, about twenty-five years old?"

Angélique nodded. "That could be her."

"What can you tell me about her?"

The girl pursed her lips for a moment, thinking. "I wasn't but thirteen then, and I slept in the kitchen. She was a deal younger than monsieur, I remember that much."

"Did they seem affectionate together?"

"I wouldn't know that. I never saw them together but once or twice. But some said he had a little friend on the side, and so did she."

"That's right," interrupted the cook, softening at the prospect of passing on some juicy rumors. She stirred the soup kettle and plumped herself down on the nearest stool. "Marie-Madeleine, who was housemaid there then, she said her mistress was carrying on with some young fellow under her husband's very nose. That was what the great to-do was all about."

Aristide wheeled about. "What 'great to-do'?"

"Why, Madame Ferré, she used to have guests to dinner every week, mostly gentlemen who were something in the government, and Marie-Madeleine said madame seemed specially taken with one of them. Must have been the talk of the household."

"They were lovers?"

"Well, that Ferré, he was twice her age and a dry stick of a man. You can't hardly blame her for looking somewhere else for amusement, and Marie-Madeleine said the fellow she took up with was pretty enough. . . ."

"What happened there?" Aristide demanded. "Ferré discovered his wife had taken a lover?"

"Oh, yes, citizen!" Angélique said, glancing up from the potatoes. "Gilles, the footman, he told us all about it. Monsieur found her hiding this young man, that she'd been carrying on with for months—ever so handsome, I heard—and the young man was wanted by the government, because it was right after all that ado at the palace, and so monsieur sent for the patrol and had the young man arrested!"

"All that ado at the palace" might mean one of any number of revolutionary upheavals during the past several years. "When did this happen?" Aristide said cautiously. "When they overthrew Robespierre?"

"Oh, no, before that. When they threw the traitor deputies out of the Convention. Spring of 'ninety-three."

"You mean the second of June?"

"That's right, when they threw out the Brissotins like the dirty traitors they were."

"And this young man was wanted—you mean by the Jacobin government? Because he was associated with the Brissotins?"

"Yes, that's what Gilles said. And madame was so upset. Because the young man said something to her just before they took him away: 'The next time, I'll kill you!'"

"'The next time, I'll kill you,'" Aristide repeated. "You're sure?"

"That's what Gilles said. It was so exciting, you can't imagine," the girl added, a rosy flush rising in her pale cheeks. "I mean, I'm sorry for the poor young man, but maybe he wasn't as nice as madame had thought he was. 'You treacherous bitch, the next time I'll kill you.' Those were his very words, at least as Gilles told us."

"So he thought that the lady had betrayed him, not Ferré?"

"I suppose so, citizen. But it was monsieur who had done it, because then madame and monsieur had it out. We could all hear them going at it, shouting at the top of their lungs, but mostly her. She was calling him a spiteful, underhanded worm, and a coward, and a villain, and all kinds of horrible things."

"I don't suppose you would remember this young man's name?" Aristide said.

"No, I never knew it."

"What's all this about?" the cook demanded. "Don't you go hounding Angélique, she's a good girl."

Aristide smiled. "I believe Citizeness Ferré may be my distant cousin," he improvised, "for whom I've been searching for some months now. Her uncle died and left her a small legacy."

"Well!" exclaimed the cook. "That's generous of you, I'm sure. See here, are you wanting to know anything else? Because we've work to do, or the master's dinner will be late. Saints, girl, give me those potatoes and go set the table!"

Aristide lingered for another five minutes but learned little more of importance about Citizeness Ferré, née Juliette Vaudray. At last he took his leave and returned to the Left Bank, thinking hard.

The skies had cleared to a damp pearly gray by the time he reached the Luxembourg Gardens, where a few fashionable strollers promenaded amid the beds of the season's last windblown pansies and primroses, enjoying the mild weather before winter set in. He found an empty bench not far from the gates, where he could keep watch on the passersby, and settled down to wait.

As he had expected and hoped they would, Madame Letellier eventually heaved into view, her niece straggling behind her, like a dinghy dragged behind an ocean-going warship. He rose and doffed his hat.

Madame Letellier paused, beaming as she recognized him. "Monsieur Ravel, I think? And why are you not calling on Madame Clément?" she added with a coy smile and a glance back at her niece. "Laure, say good day to Monsieur Ravel!"

The girl stumbled forward and offered a limp hand. Aristide bent over it with what enthusiasm he could muster and in turn offered her his arm.

"Might I escort you both around the gardens?"

Madame Letellier accepted with alacrity and they rambled about the formal beds, exchanging commonplaces. At last Aristide deposited Laure upon a bench near the central fountain.

"How long have you known Citizeness Clément?" he inquired carelessly.

"She only came to Citizeness Deluc's establishment this summer—" Laure began.

"Madame Clément?" interrupted Madame Letellier. "Her husband's brother-in-law was my second cousin. I knew Monsieur Ferré, her husband, that is, but only to nod to. I thought I recognized her when she first took a room at Madame Deluc's, so finally I asked her if she was Madame Ferré."

"What did she say?" Aristide asked her as she paused for breath.

"She told me yes, she was Ferré's widow, and she'd changed her name, and asked me to keep it quiet. Didn't want to be known as the wife of a criminal, I suppose. Although plenty of people of *very* good family lost their lives in the Terror, God rest them," she added, hastily crossing herself.

"Perhaps she was more concerned about the scandal," he ventured.

"Scandal?"

"The young man who was reputed to have been her lover . . . I understand Ferré betrayed him."

"Oh, yes, I did hear about that!" She turned away from Laure, who was staring morosely into the murky waters of the fountain, and added in a dramatic whisper to him, "They say Ferré must have discovered them in a *compromising position*. He had the boy arrested and locked up!"

"But Aubry was never tried at the Revolutionary Tribunal, was he?" Aristide inquired in the same conspiratorial whisper.

"No, I heard Monsieur Aubry escaped and fled Paris not long afterward. . . ."

She chattered on, eagerly, but Aristide stared into the pool, his chest tight. Finding his suspicions confirmed left him feeling as though someone had kicked him in the stomach.

He had been very nearly right, he thought. But it was not Hélène Villemain who had committed murder for the sake of long-harbored spite, but Rosalie. Rosalie, who, supplanted by a younger, prettier—wealthier?—woman, had murdered her old lover's sweetheart and then done her best to see him condemned for the crime.

Suddenly he remembered words Rosalie herself had once said to him: *Only lovers can turn so violently from love to hatred.* Yes, he thought, she would know.

Rosalie.

At last Madame Letellier slowed, like an automaton whose springs had run down, and Aristide abruptly took his leave of her and her ward and strode off through the trees.

"Brasseur," he said, striding into the office without knocking, "I think you'd better hear what I learned today."

He rapidly summarized what he had discovered about Rosalie at the Palais de Justice, at Rue des Capucines, and from Madame Letellier. "She and Aubry carry on an affair," he said at last, "until her husband catches them together and promptly turns Aubry, who is now a wanted man, over to the patrol. In revenge, Rosalie denounces Ferré when she learns what he's been up to with his friends across the frontier." He paused and took a swift swallow of the wine that Brasseur had pushed toward him.

"But imagine how she must have felt when she learned, probably from Célie Montereau herself, that Aubry now cares nothing for her, that he loves Célie instead."

"And this is the man," Brasseur said, nodding, "for whose sake she'd sent her own husband to the guillotine."

"Brasseur, if you were a woman capable of denouncing your husband in revenge for an injury, might you not also be capable of murdering a rival in love, and of carrying out a pitiless vengeance on the lover who had spurned you?"

When Aristide had concluded, Brasseur fetched Dautry and they sped across to the Left Bank to call upon the commissaire of the Thermes-de-Julien section, who brought an inspector and a pair of soldiers with them to Rue des Cordiers.

"Are you Rosalie Clément?" Commissaire Noël said without preamble as the door to the attic opened and Rosalie peered out. "I order you, in the name of the law, to follow me before the justice of the peace. You are wanted for questioning in connection with the murders of Célie Montereau and Louis Saint-Ange, in the Butte-des-Moulins section, on the tenth of Brumaire last."

"Murders!" Madame Deluc shrieked behind them. They ignored her and crowded into the room. The inspector took up a place beside the open door.

"Murders?" Rosalie echoed her, astonished.

"Stand aside, citizeness," Noël told her. "We must search your lodging."

"How dare you!"

"We're the police; we have every right to search through all your effects for evidence—now that's enough of that!" he added, as suddenly she turned and was through the doorway in a flash, only to run straight into the arms of the guardsman who had been posted at the head of the stairs for just such an eventuality. "You can't get away, so you may as well just wait quietly and not give us any trouble. Now are you going to cooperate, or do we have to put the bracelets on you?"

She had ceased struggling as soon as the guard seized hold of her arms, but glared at the four men in mute fury. The two commissaires set to work, Dautry hovering behind them with notebook and pencil ready. Avoiding Rosalie's gaze, Aristide joined them.

The room was small and modestly furnished. In half an hour they had searched through her belongings, from the chest at the foot of the bed to the hidden crannies of the writing-desk and washstand, to the pages of the three battered books that stood neatly on a shelf beside the bed.

"A few letters from Célie Montereau," Brasseur said, glancing through them. "Women's chatter."

"Célie and I were friends," Rosalie said. "Is that against the law?"

Aristide inspected her wardrobe, but found nothing more unusual than a carmagnole jacket and two gowns of muslin and lawn, one white and one pale rose, summer gowns at least five years old, altered, like her India cotton dress, to something approaching the prevailing neoclassical fashion. He looked further and found a straw bonnet, a pair of dainty kid slippers, and two pairs of darned gloves. The two small drawers at the bottom of the wardrobe brimmed with assorted chemises, fichus, handkerchiefs, and stockings.

"There's nothing to find here," Commissaire Noël grumbled at last, just as Aristide felt the rough texture of paper beneath his fingertips as he searched through the underlinen.

"You think not?" he said. He lifted two chemises away and extracted the creased letter hidden below them, nodding in satisfaction as he saw the handwriting: *To Citizeness Clément, at the Maison Deluc, Rue des Cordiers, Section des Thermes-de-Julien.* He unfolded it.

Citizeness,

I write to you today in order to inform you that I do not intend to see you again. Kindly cease your persistent attempts to reach me or to seduce me with false promises and appeals to old sentiments. What childish affection we once shared is in the past, is over and done with, and best forgotten; why, knowing how easy you find it to foully betray me in all things, should I look upon you now with anything other than horror, contempt, and hatred?

I once believed you the brightest angel in the heavens, until my trust was so cruelly betrayed, until the scales were torn from my eyes and I saw my angel was soiled and corrupt. I do not intend to allow you ever again to betray me. I am marrying a young woman dear to my heart in three months' time and wish only to make a new beginning, praying that your path and mine should never cross again. Perhaps in my dear fiancée's youth and innocence, I shall once more find that pure angel that, long ago, I so mistakenly thought I had found in you.

I remain your obedient servant.

Aubry

"So," Aristide murmured. He stood thinking for a moment, suddenly back in his own room on Rue d'Amboise surrounded by his books, his well-worn old volume of English plays. A verse in one of the plays—"Heaven has no rage, like love to hatred turned"—yes, that was it—"nor Hell a fury, like a woman scorned."

"Brasseur—a letter like this one might drive me to murder, too."

"I've seen that writing before," said Brasseur, taking the letter.

"Certainly you have. It's Philippe Aubry's."

"You have no right to read my private correspondence!" Rosalie cried.

"When it's a question of murder," Aristide said without looking at her, "indeed we do."

"I thought you were my *friend*, Ravel."

"And *I* thought *you* were innocent, Citizeness Clément."

"A nice sort of letter for a gentleman to send to a woman," Brasseur muttered. He refolded the letter and slipped it into his coat. "Citizeness," he told Rosalie, "you'd better come along with us. So what was the idea, then—murder the girl, and let young Aubry be topped for it? Or have you done away with him, too?"

Rosalie clasped her hands in front of her and drew a deep breath without replying.

"Just as you suggested about Hélène Villemain," Brasseur added to Aristide. "The spurned woman and all that. We only had to look a little farther for the right woman. Well done."

He busied himself with taking notes and sending the inspector downstairs to ensure that none of the lodgers left the house, and conferring with Commissaire Noël as they prepared to question witnesses. Aristide nodded mechanically at Brasseur's brisk remarks, too weary and sick at heart to congratulate himself at having found Célie Montereau's killer at last. Without further words, as the commissaires hurried off with Dautry he turned away and plodded down the winding staircase.

6 Frimaire (November 26)

They took her, the next day, to a justice of the peace. Aristide watched her, uneasy at her chilly composure. It was not such a strong case, he knew, built as it was on the evidence of an anonymous denunciation, a few hazy recollections of an illicit love affair, and a single letter. But

Judge Nourissier, he recalled, unlike Judge Geoffroy, had a reputation for severity.

"Citizeness Clément, is it not true your real name is Juliette Vaudray?"

"Yes," she said after an instant's hesitation. "That's my name. I adopted another name after my husband, Maurice Ferré, was guillotined in 1793—the Year Two, I mean—for plotting against the Republic. I was frightened and wanted to dissociate myself from him and his reputation. Is that a crime?"

"It is if you intentionally change your name to evade the law. You are suspected of the murders of Célie Montereau and Louis Saint-Ange, and have been summoned here on the strength of the evidence the police found among your belongings. What have you to say for yourself?"

"This is nonsense. I didn't murder Célie."

"Do you deny you know Philippe Aubry, and were once in love with him?"

She lifted her chin a fraction. "I can scarcely deny it, can I, when you find his correspondence among my belongings. We've known each other for some years."

"In your previous testimony, you claimed you had no personal acquaintance with Citizen Aubry. This has been proven to be a lie by the statements of Henriette Letellier and your own former domestic, Angélique Morin. On the contrary, in 1791 you entered into an adulterous liaison with Citizen Aubry which was only broken off when Aubry was arrested on the seventeenth of June, 1793."

"That's not against the law."

"You claimed you wrote to him on the tenth of Brumaire merely in order to resolve a quarrel between him and the late Célie Montereau. Isn't it true, rather, that in this letter you threatened harm to the girl he loved?"

"Ask Philippe; he'll tell you I said no such thing. If you can find him."

"What, then, do you claim was the substance of your letter?"

"I wrote," she said with a scornful twist of her lips, "to tell him he was a complete swine. No gentleman would write a lady a letter like the one he sent to me, when she had appealed to him for help. I didn't take kindly to being so contemptuously brushed aside."

"Some people might call that a motive for murder," Judge Nourissier said dryly. "You desired revenge for his heartless treatment of you, didn't you?"

"Yes, but—"

"And you were jealous of Aubry's affection for Célie Montereau, were you not?"

"Of course, as any woman would be. But I didn't kill her because of it."

"Where were you on the afternoon and evening of the tenth of Brumaire?"

Rosalie shrugged. "I suppose I was walking in the gardens of the Luxembourg. That's what I do most afternoons."

"Can you furnish any proof of this? Did you meet anyone you knew there? Perhaps other regular visitors, or caretakers, might remember seeing you?"

She shrugged again. "Perhaps. I wouldn't know."

"Citizeness Vaudray, do you own a pistol?"

"Of course not. I didn't kill her!"

"I shall be pleased if you can furnish proof to that effect," said the judge, "but at present, I find sufficient evidence to hold you until you go before a jury of accusation and then, if so ordered, to trial before the Criminal Tribunal of the Département of the Seine. Search the prisoner," he added, beckoning forward a gendarme.

"I'd prefer you didn't touch me," Rosalie snapped, backing away. She swiftly dropped her reticule, gloves, bonnet, and shawl on his desk. "Search that all you like. I've nothing else on my person."

The gendarme glanced at the judge. Aristide stepped forward.

"Citizen Judge, surely women's gowns today leave nothing to the imagination."

Nourissier scowled, looked Rosalie up and down, and nodded. "Very well, then." He gestured to the gendarme. Her little purse contained only the small ordinary items any woman might have carried with her—four hairpins, a few copper coins, a handful of assignats, two keys, a stubby pencil, a clean handkerchief, a civic identity card bearing the name ROSALIE CLÉMENT, and a penknife.

Aristide glanced once again at Rosalie, and for an instant their eyes met before a clerk presented the judge with a transcript of her statement. She took the quill he offered her and signed the statement: *Séraphine-Juliette-Marie Vaudray, widow Ferré, called Rosalie Clément,* a signature at the bottom of each page as the secretary directed her.

23

Aristide went to see her after the jury of accusation had sat. He found his heart was beating a trifle faster as he followed a turnkey up the staircase toward the privileged cells. "How does she behave?"

His companion chuckled. "You'd never think she was in prison. That polite, she is. Like the fine ladies who lodged here in 'ninety-three and 'ninety-four."

The fellow spoke as if he were an innkeeper, Aristide reflected. Perhaps it was all the same to him.

"You shout when you're done," said the turnkey. "I won't be far away." He unlocked the thick, iron-bound door to the cell and stepped aside.

Rosalie was sitting near the fire, wrapped in a blanket against the wintry chill. Aristide doffed his hat as she rose. "Your servant." The polite commonplace slipped out before he realized it. "I had your clothing and necessities sent over," he told her, thankful to busy himself with trivial matters. "I hope they arrived safely?"

Rosalie smiled. "Yes. Thank you for taking the trouble."

He thrust his hands in the pockets of his overcoat and gazed at her for a moment. "Immediately after we took Citizeness Villemain in for questioning, someone sent an unsigned letter to Commissaire Brasseur, accusing one Juliette de Vaudray of murder. Do you know who might have informed against you?"

"I have no idea."

"Do you have an enemy?"

"No, of course not. I'm too unimportant to have either enemies or friends. Why ask these questions," she added, "after you helped them to put me here?"

"Because . . . because, despite your past association with Aubry that you never chose to tell us about, I'd like to think I was mistaken. Because of our friendship. If you know anything at all that might prove your innocence, tell me. There is, after all, little tangible evidence against you, and no eyewitnesses."

"So now you believe I'm innocent?"

"I don't know. But I like you, as you know, and some loose ends about this affair still trouble me, and I would like to believe you're innocent. There's a difference."

She gazed at him, eyebrows rising a fraction, and at last her lips curved in the barest suggestion of a smile.

"I like you, too, Ravel."

"If you didn't do it," Aristide said, "isn't it possible that the person who sent that anonymous letter to Brasseur was the real murderer? An unknown young man was seen there, after all. You've no rejected admirers, have you?"

"Me?" she said with a brief laugh. "I assure you, no one takes any interest in me, once they discover that I can barely pay for my lodging in a rundown boardinghouse." She gestured him to a chair but he shook his head and remained standing. "I didn't kill Célie, and I don't know who could have done it, except for Philippe. And what about this other woman, the one you found dead? You say whoever murdered Célie probably murdered her to silence her. Have you any proof that it wasn't Philippe?"

"There's little the police can do until they find him."

"Yes. Gone without saying a word to his servant, or anyone. Hardly the behavior of an innocent man."

Aristide sighed. "Rosalie . . . until someone identifies him as having been on Rue du Hasard on the evening of the tenth, they haven't enough evidence to arrest him, much less convict him. But if you're innocent after all, and he is guilty, or some other man is guilty, I want to help you."

He took her hand in his, surprised at its warmth in the chilly stone cell. "Listen to me. Before the Revolution, the courts scarcely cared who might be guilty or innocent of a crime, so long as someone who could be a likely suspect was punished for it—the idea was that the punishment would deter others. That's one of the abuses that we reformed straightaway. No one ought to suffer for a crime he didn't commit. But old ways of thinking still persist . . . though the police and the magistrates gain nothing by sending the wrong person to trial, or to the guillotine, it happens. I imagine they'd rather see the wrong person convicted than no one at all; at least it's proof they're doing their job. For God's sake, if you know anything about this matter that you've not mentioned, help me to help you."

Rosalie drew away her hand and sat down again, pulling the blanket back around her shoulders. "I thank you for your kindness—but I don't know anything." She stifled a yawn and glanced at him apologetically. "Truly I'm more afraid of going mad with boredom than of anything else. They won't let me do anything except walk in the courtyard once a day, for an hour. It's enough to make one demand the guillotine immediately. Perhaps you could find me some books?"

"I might," Aristide said. "Meanwhile . . . one of your guards must have a pack of cards."

"Yes, we've played a few hands, but what's the point of playing if I haven't any money worth speaking of?"

"I was thinking of patience."

"What's that?"

"A game that you play alone. You saw me play it once." He rose and shouted down the corridor for a turnkey. Obtaining a greasy old pack of cards, he sat at the table with her. "You start like this," he began, turning over the first card, "and lay them out in four vertical overlapping rows as you please, and the object is to collect all the cards in order, from ace to genius, in four other piles above . . ."

She caught on quickly and soon was eagerly placing the cards in rows and piles with a soft slap-slap of cardboard. Aristide watched as she played out the round, unsuccessfully, then another, and a third, the least successful of all, where the cards lay stubbornly across the table in long columns. She sighed and pushed them together. "This isn't going to come out. Don't you know a game it's possible to win?"

"It will come out, if you play it long enough. You need luck, of course; but it also requires some skill. Keep trying."

"Yes . . . I shall." She gathered up the cards and began again.

20 Frimaire (December 10)

Aristide shouldered his way through the milling, clamorous crowd in the public hall to François, who had secured two places on the last bench but one in the Great Chamber of the Palais de Justice. "Damn stifling crush," François shouted cheerfully above the din of voices as Aristide dropped onto the seat beside him. "Couldn't get any closer. I don't suppose you thought to rent a couple of cushions? These benches are hard."

"Your backside wasn't one of my pressing concerns, I'm afraid." Aristide rubbed his eyes and sighed. "I begin to think this whole affair is a great web of lies, a labyrinth of lies, and that I'm caught in the middle of it. I don't know what to think about Rosalie. Now what am I to do?"

"Keep hunting for the man in the round hat, I suppose," François said. "Maybe Célie really did have another admirer—somebody she wouldn't have given the time of day. A deranged servant or such. Love can make people do funny things, inexplicable things. And thwarted love can turn some people into madmen—or madwomen. People who never had much of a grip on reality, sometimes they spin pretty illusions . . . and when the illusion shatters, they become capable of anything."

Aristide opened his mouth to respond but fell silent as the five judges entered the chamber. They still wore the same costume, robe and black hat with three black plumes and tricolor cockade, as had the judges at the Revolutionary Tribunal.

The clerk of the court read out the Act of Accusation against Séraphine-Juliette-Marie Vaudray, widow Ferré, called Rosalie Clément, who, it was alleged, had of her own free will and with premeditation perpetrated the homicide of Marie-Célie-Josèphe-Élisabeth Montereau and Jean-Louis Saint-Ange, on the evening of the tenth of Brumaire.

"Accused, how do you plead?"

"Not guilty, Citizen President."

Maître Tardieu, her defense counsel, adjusted his robes about stooped shoulders and proceeded with his address to the court, kindly, avuncular, more sorrowful than indignant. He painted a picture of a young widow of irreproachable and quiet habits. How was it possible this young woman could be a murderess?

Aristide studied the accused. She sat demurely on the prisoners' bench, the picture of feminine virtue, dainty in a touch of face powder and rouge and wearing the rose-colored gown he had found in her wardrobe. Something nagged at him, some small hunch that something he had seen, somewhere, sometime, something about Rosalie, was not quite right, was out of place.

President Gohier rang his bell and the testimony of the prosecution's witnesses began. The clerk of the court called Commissaire Brasseur.

"I arrived at the scene of the murders at quarter to nine in the morning on the eleventh of Brumaire. The apartment was in disarray, as though a violent struggle had taken place . . ."

Rosalie stared at her hands, clenched on the rail before her. A tear slid down her cheeks, glistening in the pale sunshine that streamed in through the windows.

Brasseur at last concluded his testimony and retreated to the witnesses' chambers. The porter Grangier was called to the stand and the chamber fell silent. After he had repeated his story, Gohier directed him to look at the accused.

"Look carefully, citizen. Have you ever seen this woman before?"

Grangier drew a deep breath and peered at Rosalie. "I don't think so, Citizen Judge. If she ever came to the house, I don't remember her. She wasn't living there. But she could have been a visitor. I don't keep track of visitors."

"So you have claimed," the president said, pouncing on the porter's statement. "Now, during this crucial afternoon and evening, you stated previously that you were asleep, did you not, and that you woke only when you heard running footsteps on the staircase?"

"Yes."

"So any number of people, both residents and strangers, could have gone in and out of the house during the hour or two while you were asleep, without your noticing them?"

"Yes, if they knew which apartment they wanted."

"And Citizeness Vaudray might have gone to Saint-Ange's apartment, committed these murders, and left the house again, all without your being aware of it?"

"Yes, citizen," Grangier admitted, avoiding the judge's gaze.

Grangier left the witness stand and the president announced a recess for dinner. "The prosecution's case isn't very strong," François muttered.

Aristide nodded. "I know. It's all circumstantial. But if Aubry didn't do it, who else besides Rosalie could have had a motive? And if the man in the round hat did it, who the devil is he?"

"Does she have an alibi?" François continued as they elbowed their way through the excited crowd. "Did she ever claim she was somewhere else that afternoon?"

"Not that I know of. The other lodgers in the boardinghouse all swore that she was rarely absent from meals, and that they would have remembered if she had gone missing on a *décadi*, when everyone turns up because the food is better that day. That puts her at the Maison Deluc by eight o'clock in the evening. She might have been anywhere between dinner and supper, though."

He shared a roast chicken and a dish of beets with François in a nearby tavern and, when they were done, could not remember a word of what they had talked about.

Something small, inconsequential, something he had overlooked . . . something to do with Rosalie, something he had seen on the day the examining magistrate had questioned her.

They returned for the afternoon session, hurrying through the great gilded gates to the courtyard of the Palais de Justice. Abruptly Aristide stopped short, looking up at the gates and their heavy locks.

Locks—no, *keys*. Something about a key. Rosalie's key.

"You go ahead," he told François. "Don't save my seat for me. I've business elsewhere."

He hurried down the steps to the door of the Conciergerie. Presenting his police card to the prison clerk, he asked to be shown the inventory of the items that had been found, upon admission, on the person of the prisoner Juliette Vaudray.

"Nothing out of the ordinary, it seems to me," said the clerk as he fetched his records. "Vaudray, Vaudray . . . here we are, transferred from La Force, admitted on the fourteenth of Frimaire, Juliette Vaudray, widow Ferré, called Rosalie Clément—that the one?"

Aristide nodded.

"A charming young woman, by all accounts." The clerk turned the book about and thrust it toward Aristide. "The turnkeys are quite taken with her. We let her keep most of her personal possessions," he added. "Handkerchiefs, things of that sort."

Aristide glanced over the short list of articles. One civic identity card made out in the name of Rosalie Clément; one penknife; four steel hairpins; money to the sum of two livres six sous in copper coin, and 370 livres in assignats, a paltry sum that might buy the value of four or five livres in gold or silver; two dissimilar latchkeys of ordinary type—

"*Keys*," Aristide said, staring at the inventory. "*Two* keys, unalike. Do *you* carry two latchkeys?"

"No, just one." The clerk closed the book, uninterested. "To my lodgings. The porter opens the street door for us."

"Exactly. So do I. So does nearly everyone who hasn't a household to run. Only bourgeois housewives carry bunches of keys with them. But the rest of us—bachelors, folk who live alone or in small establishments—the porter opens the front door for you, or one of the servants if it's a boardinghouse; or if the porter can't be bothered, the front door remains open all day, then by law is bolted at ten o'clock and you have to ring. Why two keys?"

The clerk shrugged. "How should I know?"

One key for her room at the boardinghouse, Aristide thought, *and one key for . . . what? A trunk or a strongbox? She didn't have one. The front door? Why can't the maid open it? For . . . for the door to Aubry's apartment, even?*

"Citizen, I'll need to borrow those keys for a while."

Neither key fit the lock to Aubry's apartment. Aristide went on to Rue des Cordiers and rang the bell at the Maison Deluc. The middle-aged servant soon answered the door and warily ushered him inside.

"Before I interview the other tenants," he said, after assuring her that the police were not about to invade the house again, "I should like to try a key in this door."

"Who gave you a key to the front door, citizen?"

"Do the tenants not have keys to it?"

"No. The front door is always unlocked during the day, from six in the morning till ten, when it's bolted according to the regulations, and someone's there to let them in until midnight. The guests only have keys to their own rooms."

"So why would a tenant here be carrying two latchkeys with her?"

"I wouldn't know," said the maid. "One would be for her room. Maybe the other is for someone else's. They do that sometimes, exchange spare keys, if they strike up a friendship."

Frowning, Aristide tried the keys in the front door. Neither would turn. Marching up the five flights to Rosalie's room, he tried them again. One of them opened the door to reveal a startled young man hunched over a pile of books at his desk.

"Citizeness Deluc's already rented it out," the maid explained, apologetic. "As soon as the police took away all Citizeness Clément's things and took the seals off . . . there's no money to be had from leaving it empty."

"Heaven forbid," Aristide said. "All right, then. This larger key opens this door. Can your mistress spare you to go round with me to the other rooms?"

The maid led him down through the lower floors of the boarding-house. Several of the tenants were at home and volunteered information, or opinions, about their former fellow boarder. Hadn't been living in the house long, only since the summer; quiet; kept to herself, even at mealtimes; spoke little about herself; seemed to have no family. Occasionally went out by herself in the evening, to the theater she said, but returned before midnight. Never received letters. No one could have *ever* imagined they were living in the same house as a murderess.

The extra key fit none of the locks.

With some relief, Aristide extricated himself from a disagreeable old lady and proceeded to the next tenant, a medical student named Lumière who had just arrived back from the nearby Academy of Surgery.

"What can you tell me about Rosalie Clément?" he asked, for the seventh time, strolling with the young man into the empty dining room where a persistent odor of boiled cabbage seemed to cling to the tatty tablecloth and curtains.

"I thought the police were done asking their questions," Lumière remarked with a saucy grin. "They sending their spies to nose around and finish the job?"

"To ask the questions they neglected to ask," Aristide said, ignoring his impertinence. "What did they ask you?"

"Oh, the usual rubbish. Did I see her on the day of the murders, and did I see her looking guilty or apprehensive afterward, all that. How am I supposed to remember what I saw a month ago?"

"How well did you know her?"

"Not as well as I'd have liked. She was civil, but no more."

"You admired her?"

"Well, she was passably pretty. And she lived alone, without any tiresome chaperons to get in the way. Lonely young widow, easy enough, you'd think. But she already had a lover."

Aristide stared at him for an instant, speechless. Rosalie? A *lover*?

"Are you quite sure?"

"Well, she had a friend in the background, to be sure. She never mentioned anyone, when the talk and the gossip got a bit racy at dinner, so I thought perhaps I had a chance with her. But she never played along. *You* know." He winked and threw himself into the nearest chair.

"How do you know about him? Who is he?"

Lumière grinned. "Don't know. Might have been a woman, for all I know. One late afternoon a couple of months ago I'd no lectures, and nothing else to do, so when I saw her leaving the house, I thought I'd trail after her. If it was only a stroll to the Luxembourg, it was still an opportunity to start a conversation."

"And did she go to the gardens?" Aristide said, disregarding Lumière's leer.

"No, she set off across the river, to a mangy quarter near the Hôtel de Ville. *Not* a very pleasant area for a rendezvous. But she went into a house and didn't come out again. I waited for over an hour, and plenty of other people went in and out, but she didn't. What else would she be doing in a place like that except meeting a lover for a cuddle? So I gave up on the pretty widow and found myself a little shopgirl instead."

He remembered the approximate location of the house, a street or two away from the city hall, with a tavern on the ground floor. Aristide returned to the Right Bank and, after two fruitless inquiries at taverns, found himself at last on Rue du Cocq, in the ancient, crowded, and squalid quarter north of the Place de Grève. At the tavern once known, according to the painted-over carvings above the door, as the Cabaret du Fleur-de-Lys, and now as the Good Patriot, a barmaid pointed him to an unshaven man reading a newspaper in the corner and puffing at a pipe.

"Would you be wanting lodgings upstairs?" the man inquired, swinging his legs from a chair. "Furnished rooms, reasonable rent, pay by the quarter. The name's Barbier. Care for a glass?"

"I might be looking for a simple room," Aristide said, hailing the barmaid. "Nothing too large. For one or two people."

"Just big enough for a bed, eh?" the landlord said with a knowing smirk. "I have a few like those, on the upper floors, cheap. If the lady doesn't mind climbing stairs."

Aristide decided subtlety would gain him little. "I am an authorized agent of the police," he said, showing Barbier his police card, "and I'm tracing one of your lodgers, or one of your lodgers' guests. A woman of twenty-eight, medium height, dark brown hair, brown eyes, modestly dressed, speaks well. She probably arrives here alone to meet a friend. Do you know her?"

"A woman by herself?" The girl brought their glasses of cheap brandy and Barbier tossed down a swallow, smacking his lips. "It's probably Citizeness Clément you want. Good tenant—"

"Clément?" Aristide set down his glass untasted. "Show me her room."

None too pleased at having to climb to the garrets, Barbier led the way up the narrow, rickety staircase that spiraled at the back of the noisome courtyard, to the sounds of squalling babies, hoarse shouting, and the clatter of cooking pots and crockery. At the seventh-floor landing he pointed, puffing, at the second door and pulled out a ring of keys, but Aristide raised a restraining hand.

"Let me try first."

The spare key slid neatly into the lock. Within, the sloping garret ceiling constricted the room until it was scarcely large enough for the battered bedstead, traveling trunk, table, chair, brazier, and washstand that were its only furniture. Prompted by Lumière, a secret love nest had been his own first notion, but he began to doubt it with a glance at the lumpy, narrow bed, little larger than a cot. Two could not have lain on that bed with any comfort, let alone pleasure.

"Is the furniture yours or hers?" he inquired, dropping his hat on the bed.

"The trunk is hers. The rest comes with the room. She said a double bed wasn't necessary and took the cot instead, in exchange for a lower rent."

Aristide's gaze roved to the wall and a row of pegs. Two men's coats hung from them, one a plainly cut redingote in dark moss green, the other a more elegant fawn-colored frock coat in last year's exaggerated cut with oversize collar, still passably stylish. A pair of top boots stood below them, one leaning against the other like a weary comrade.

He turned to Barbier. "You did say a young woman let this room? These are all men's things."

"Oh yes, Citizeness Clément." He described Rosalie and rocked back on his heels, blowing a smoke ring. "Though I did see a well-dressed young fellow once or twice, just going in or out, late at night. I asked her who he was, and she said he was her brother."

"The world's oldest subterfuge," Aristide said dryly.

"He might have been her brother, at that; I didn't get a good look at him, but I'd say he resembled her. She said he rarely came to Paris. But it's not *my* business if she has a friend to stay the night now and then."

A glance beneath the bed revealed nothing but dust and mouse droppings. Aristide ran his fingers through the handful of gossamer black ash in the brazier, soft and frail as cobweb, but found no clue as to Rosalie's purpose.

A shelf beneath the tiny mirror held a box of rice powder, a pot of rouge, a comb, a pair of scissors, a clothes brush, and a small cardboard box full of hairpins and a few frayed ribbons. Nothing else betrayed a woman's presence. At last Aristide threw open the trunk's lid and peered inside.

On top of a stack of neatly folded shirts lay a black low-crowned round hat.

24

So he does exist," Brasseur said. He peered into the chest. About to quit the commissariat for the night, Aristide's urgent message had sent him jouncing irritably across Paris to Rue du Cocq. What Aristide had found had quickly put him in a better humor. "I was beginning to think he was just a myth."

"He *is* a myth," Aristide said.

"Eh?"

"She told her landlord here that he was her brother—"

"Her *brother*," Brasseur scoffed.

"—and he believed her because he saw the resemblance. But at her boardinghouse, no one remembered her ever mentioning any family at all."

Brasseur grunted and lifted out the hat. "Smallish head," he muttered, gazing at it. He clapped it on his own head, where it perched precariously and then slid off as he turned to Aristide. "Wouldn't fit me, or you either. The man, whoever he is, isn't very big. Look at this coat. I doubt you could struggle into it, and you're no Hercules."

"Exactly," Aristide said. "Not even a weedy fellow like me could fit into that coat. It belongs on a small, slight figure, easily the person whom Grangier saw, and who presumably did the murders. Don't you see it yet?"

Brasseur gaped at him for a moment.

"Her *brother*!" he exclaimed with a hoot of exasperated laughter. "Of *course* he resembled her. It was she all along!"

"*She* was 'the man in the round hat.' *She* was the man whom Grangier saw!"

"The devious little . . ." Brasseur said, not without admiration. "You realize what this means, don't you? Though Grangier said he didn't know her . . ."

"He was looking at a pretty, feminine woman wearing powder, rouge, and a pink gown. You know how unreliable most witnesses are; they think they saw one thing when in fact they saw another . . . the president asked him if he recognized a woman. Why should he connect her with the young man he's sure he saw?"

"But if they can bring her before him in *these* clothes, in this coat I should think," Brasseur said, taking up the green redingote again, "and the hat, I'll wager you he'll recognize her."

"Her counsel will raise an unholy fuss."

"That's the public prosecutor's dilemma, not mine. My job is just to find the evidence. Good God, Ravel," he added, "I've been hunting for a woman who wears men's clothing. D'you think she could be the hotel murderess as well?"

Aristide stared at the grimy wall, remembering a conspicuous coat he had seen on a slight, slim figure one evening at the Palais-Égalité.

"The coat's not here," he said at length. "A blue striped coat with overlong tails, such as an *incroyable* would wear. And Rosalie Clément is dark. The person I saw was fair; and your witnesses said the woman at the hotels was fair-haired."

"A wig?"

"See for yourself. There's no wig here, just shirts, cravats, gloves, and such."

Brasseur poked a hand thoughtfully through the tidy pile of linen and at last straightened, dusting off his knees.

"Well, if she's already on trial for murder . . . they can only guillotine her once. And this case is easier to prove than the hotel murder, God knows. We can always pursue it if she's acquitted of this one."

"I daresay more women go about in male disguise, from time to time, than we'd like to think," Aristide said. "It's a man's world, after all; disguise must offer them such freedom. You and I couldn't imagine it."

Brasseur handed Aristide his hat. "You go home and get some sleep; you look worn out."

After Brasseur had departed, leaving a guardsman behind to keep watch outside on the landing, Aristide lingered alone in the tiny room and gazed about him, frowning. It was an ugly possibility, but one he had to confront: though if Rosalie was indeed the hotel murderess, then where were the blond wig and the coat, that ostentatious striped coat calculated to draw attention from a woman's features?

He gazed again into the brazier and took up a flake of ash that trembled in his fingers before disintegrating. You could still see the smooth surface on a bit of burned, curled paper, he thought; this was lacier than paper ash. Cloth?

If she had cut up and burned the telltale wig and coat, then this was what remained of them. Though there would have been many more ashes than a mere handful. He threw open the window and leaned outside, gazing across the tiles that sloped, layer upon layer, at either side. To his right, in the sheltered corner formed by the next dormer projecting from the roof, out of the wind, lay a few wisps and flecks of black that the rain had not yet reached.

21 Frimaire (December 11)

The morning session was slow in starting. At length the president and Faure, the public prosecutor, took their seats and the trial resumed.

"Citizen President," said Faure, "owing to the extraordinary nature of some evidence that has just come to light, the prosecution has an unusual request to make of the court. The police yesterday discovered a secret domicile let by the accused, which contained a number of significant garments. The prosecution requests that the accused be ordered to dress in these garments for identification by a certain witness."

President Gohier frowned. "Have you proof the prisoner let this lodging?"

"The landlord of the house in question has given a signed statement, and is present and ready to testify."

"Call the witness," said the president. Barbier entered and was sworn: Jean-Baptiste Barbier, owner of a furnished lodginghouse on Rue du Cocq, in the Section des Droits-de-l'Homme.

Yes, he recognized a certain person in the chamber, that young lady. She was a lodger of his. She lived in Amiens, or so she said, and only came up to Paris perhaps once a month. Two or three times he had seen a young fellow going to her lodging, or coming out of it, late at night. She claimed he was her brother. All the personal property found in the room was the property of the citizeness, or perhaps of her brother. There were only two keys to the room; Citizeness Clément— Vaudray—had one, and he kept the other himself.

"Citizen Prosecutor," said the president, "having established to the satisfaction of this court that the items in the room in question are the property of the accused, or the property of a man allegedly the brother of the accused, what is the request of the prosecution?"

"That the accused don a certain suit of clothes found in this lodging, presented as evidence, for the purposes of identification," said the public prosecutor, bobbing from his chair. Maître Tardieu leaped to his feet.

"May I remind the prosecutor, and the court, that it is illegal to compel an accused person to undertake any action which may furnish evidence against him."

"So it is," said the president. "Have you no other evidence against the accused, Citizen Faure?"

"There is the evidence of the garments themselves," Faure declared, indignant. "The eyewitness Grangier is sure to identify them. The prosecution merely asks the court to allow these garments to be worn by their owner in order to facilitate—"

"Citizen President!" cried Maître Tardieu.

"If necessary," the public prosecutor continued, doggedly, "the prosecution requests permission to hold the garments against the accused's person, in order to demonstrate that they are of the proper size—"

Rosalie rose to her feet. "I have no objection to the public prosecutor's request."

"Citizeness," Tardieu cried, "I must protest! The prosecution wishes you to incriminate yourself."

"I can't deny that the clothes were found in a room I'd let," she said, smiling, "and Citizen Faure seems determined to have his own way. Citizen President, if I may be allowed somewhere to change my clothes in decent privacy?"

Aristide gnawed at his fingernails. A dull throbbing hammered at his head and he closed his eyes. What could have prompted her to cooperate with the public prosecutor's demands?

A quarter hour passed. Suddenly a murmur rose from the spectators' benches and rippled about the chamber as Rosalie returned.

"Christ!" François hissed beside him.

In male attire she seemed lean and boyish. The suit fit her slender body and long legs faultlessly. Buttoned across her breast and hanging gracefully in a cutaway from her slim hips, the green redingote's long lines concealed her feminine figure. Hat in hand, she strolled into the center of the chamber.

"Death of the devil," François muttered as Aristide pressed cold fingertips against throbbing temples. Rosalie unpinned her hair, shook it loose, and clapped the hat on at a debonair angle. The president rang his bell for silence as the public prosecutor recalled the witness Grangier.

"That's the one!" Grangier exclaimed before the president could address him. "See, I wasn't dreaming. I know his face. *That's* the young fellow I saw on the stairs the day citizen Saint-Ange was killed! The man with the round hat!"

"I object, once again," shouted Maître Tardieu over the clamor that rose at Grangier's words, "to the accused's being compelled to incriminate herself!"

Rosalie doffed the hat, bowed gracefully to Grangier, and sauntered back to the dock. The astonished gendarmes drew back to let her pass.

Gohier informed her that she might withdraw to change her clothes, but she smiled. "That won't be necessary. I'm quite comfortable as I am."

Tardieu darted an anguished glance at her. She ignored him and leaned forward on the rail before her.

"Citizen President, I won't waste any more of the court's time. It's plain the game is up. I am guilty."

Aristide drew in his breath as about him a hissing whisper of many voices grew and crested and died away.

"It was I, not Philippe Aubry or anyone else, who murdered Célie Montereau and Louis Saint-Ange. Nor do I have a brother; the clothes are mine. I am guilty; make an end of this."

The chamber echoed with footsteps as the spectators rose from their benches and pushed forward, craning their necks for a closer glimpse of her. President Gohier angrily rang his bell but the crowd pressed on, unheeding.

"Citizeness," said the president, "tell the court, if you please, how you committed these murders."

"Certainly." She straightened and rested her fingertips on the rail. "I was once in love with Philippe Aubry, some three years ago. Because of a terrible misunderstanding brought about by my late husband, Philippe discarded me, but I never ceased loving him. When I learned he'd returned to Paris, I went to him to remind him that he had once loved me. Not only did he turn me away, but a few days later he sent me a letter, the letter that's already been read here, in which he repulsed me in the most contemptuous terms.

"This past summer Célie Montereau told me she was secretly engaged to be married. On the the ninth of Brumaire, she asked me for advice, and told me that Saint-Ange was extorting money from her because of an indiscretion in her past. In her distress, she also told me her fiancé's name; it was Philippe Aubry. I was furious, though I didn't show it, to learn he might prefer a naïve child like Célie to me.

"I believe I went mad with jealousy then. I couldn't bear any more. The next day, I wrote to Philippe and told him I knew he was in love with Célie, and that he had better look out for her safety. I wanted to hurt him as much as possible. Then I went to the room I'd let on Rue du Cocq and disguised myself in a suit of men's clothing, which I frequently wore for my own protection when I walked alone in the city; and took a small double-barreled pistol that I kept for the same reason, and went to Rue de l'Université and followed Célie when she left her father's house."

"Why did you keep the room on Rue du Cocq?" inquired the president.

"I let it to store my costume, and to have a private place to change my clothes. My landlady," she added with a dry smile, "is narrow-minded and given to prying through her lodgers' effects, and I fear she wouldn't have taken kindly to discovering articles of male attire in my room. She would have assumed, incorrectly of course, that I'd let a man into my room. She would have asked me to leave the boardinghouse; and it was all I could afford, and I was reasonably comfortable there and didn't wish to risk eviction."

"Very well; continue."

"I followed Célie to Rue du Hasard, where she had gone to pay Saint-Ange. I climbed the staircase after her to Saint-Ange's apartment, but she had already gone inside and the door was shut. Then my nerve failed me and I ran downstairs and out of the house. I walked through the neighboring streets for perhaps a quarter of an hour.

"At last my jealousy grew so strong that I returned to the house, climbed the stairs to the landing, and knocked on the door. Saint-Ange let me in. I walked straight inside, saw Célie, and shot her. But Saint-Ange had seen everything. He tried to get away, and pushed some furniture in front of me, but my pistol had two barrels and I shot him, too, to defend myself and silence him."

Aristide glanced up sharply, frowning, remembering a contused wound and the evidence of a pistol aimed coldly and deliberately, from a finger's breadth away, at the center of a man's forehead.

"Then I crept quietly down the staircase and returned to Rue du Cocq. After I changed my clothes again, I went back to the Maison Deluc for supper and I threw my pistol into the river as I crossed the

Pont Nôtre-Dame." She withdrew her hands from the rail and straightened. "That's all. Is that sufficient?"

"But how do we know," the president demanded, "that you're not merely shielding Citizen Aubry, whom you claim to have loved, and who has also been suspected of this crime?"

"Faith, would I choose to shield the man who wrote me that letter?" She laughed sourly. "I know every word of it. 'I wish only that your path and mine should never cross again,'" she recited. "Are those the sort of words to inspire self-sacrificing love in a woman's heart? I assure you I don't do this out of love for Philippe Aubry. But I don't want this process to drag on, and I don't wish to see anybody punished with death for a crime that wasn't his."

"Very well," said the president after a moment's deliberation. "The jury may consider the accused's testimony as it pleases. You realize, citizeness," he continued, "that you are confessing to premeditated murder, a capital crime."

She nodded, once. "I understand perfectly."

The jury was out only half an hour.

They filed back to their benches, casting uneasy glances at the empty prisoners' dock. The accused would not be recalled into court before the jury's verdict was read. Aristide felt his stomach turn over.

"What is the decision of the jury?"

The foreman rose, clutching a sheet of paper.

"Séraphine-Juliette-Marie Vaudray, widow Ferré, called Rosalie Clément, is convicted of having of her own free will, without any necessity of personal defense, and without any provocation received, but with full premeditation, perpetrated the homicide of Marie-Célie-Josèphe-Élisabeth Montereau and Jean-Louis Saint-Ange, on the evening of the tenth of Brumaire, at Rue du Hasard, Section de la Butte-dês-Moulins, in Paris."

When the spectators' excited babble had died down and the president had rung his bell for the last time, the gendarmes returned from the waiting room, Rosalie between them. She had not changed her clothes.

"Séraphine-Juliette-Marie Vaudray, called Rosalie Clément," said Gohier, "you have been found guilty of premeditated murder."

You would think, Aristide brooded, that the world would shift slightly—that the earth would tremble underfoot, perhaps, or all the colors change their tint a little. But nothing remarkable happened that he could discover, except that the crowd let out a little hiss, as if expelling an indrawn breath.

"For the crime of premeditated murder," the president continued, "the Criminal Tribunal of the Département of the Seine condemns Séraphine-Juliette-Marie Vaudray, widow Ferré, called Rosalie Clément, to death. She shall be taken to a place of public execution, clothed in a red shirt, and there be decapitated as the law ordains."

Silence.

Won't she say something, Aristide wondered.

She inclined her head toward the judges. "I thank the court for its patience."

"Mercy!" someone cried. No matter how heinous the crime, some crackpot would always cry it. And others, jaded voyeurs with a taste for blood, would as noisily demand—

"Death!"

"Mercy!"

"Death!"

"The accused reserves the right to appeal her sentence," Maître Tardieu shouted above the growing hubbub.

Condemned prisoners were allowed three days to register an appeal, Aristide knew. He flinched at the shouts assailing his ears. The clamor was intolerable. *Mercy mercy mercy* and *death death death* mingled into a single chaotic roar.

Three days . . . the Terror was two years past and the Criminal Tribunal would cling for dear life to the civilized system of appeal and delay and formalities.

Three days.

25

24 Frimaire (December 14)

It was more difficult to gain access to prisoners under sentence of death, but with Brasseur's help Aristide obtained it and, three days after Rosalie's trial, once again hurried through the chilly corridors.

"How is she?" he asked the turnkey who led him to the condemned cells.

"The citizeness?" The man pushed aside his woolen cap and scratched his head. "Calm. She doesn't seem to mind it a bit."

They had taken her back to the Conciergerie, but not to her old cell. She was lodged on an upper floor in a cell separated from the corridor only by steel bars, the better to keep watch on her. A little midday light gleamed from a window somewhere down the corridor, and the cell had its own small high window with a pot of crimson geraniums some well-wisher had sent her. Aristide was grateful she had been granted the additional light, though he could not suppress a queasy twinge as he saw the cot, table, and chairs set up in the corridor for a twenty-four-hour guard.

The guard sat with palms on thighs, watching her with a phlegmatic stare. "Just ask Gilbert here if you want anything," the turnkey said, elbowing the guard, and disappeared.

Aristide glanced into the cell. Rosalie sat with a shawl and blanket wrapped about her as she ate the last morsels of a mutton chop on a well-laid tray. She had donned her pink gown again. Though part of Aristide's mind rebelled against the idea of a woman dressed as a man, another part of him had found it somehow alluring. In women's clothes Rosalie, though tolerably pretty, was no conventional beauty; in redingote and breeches she had possessed a certain sharp, alien grace.

"Rosalie," he began, "I need to talk to you."

She blew on a spoonful of soup and cautiously tasted it. "By all means. I hope you don't mind if I eat my dinner before it gets cold. In fact, why don't you join me?"

He clutched at one of the bars. "I didn't come here to share your dinner. I've spoken with your defense counsel, with Maître Tardieu."

"Why would you want to do that?"

"He'll speak with you tonight, when your appeal is ready to be signed."

"My appeal?"

"Your appeal for clemency. The public prosecutor exceeded his authority by demanding that you wear those clothes. You must appeal— I'll pay any necessary costs."

"Why?"

"Why what?" Aristide echoed her, bewildered.

"Why should I appeal? I did it. Let's get it over with."

He clutched harder at the cold metal, steadying his hands. "Rosalie . . . you didn't tell the court one word about the murders that I hadn't told you first. Why did you kill Saint-Ange?"

She dimpled. "If you'd just murdered a rival, would you allow a witness to the murder to go free? Saint-Ange, of all people! He would have been demanding hush money from me within five minutes."

"How did it happen?"

"Happen?" She paused, infinitesimally. "Just as I said in court. I shot him as he tried to get away from me."

"How did you shoot him?"

She looked at him as if he had asked an especially stupid question.

"What part of him did I shoot, do you mean? I shot him in the head."
She pointed to the center of her forehead. "Right there."

"Was it so easy, then?"

"It was a lucky shot. I just—shot him."

"How far away were you?"

"I don't know . . . a few paces?"

Rosalie, he said to himself, if you had truly murdered him, you
would have hit him with your pistol, watched him strike his head
against the marble-topped buffet, seen him fall stunned to the floor. You
would have known that you had held that pistol against the center of his
forehead and fired it in icy, vengeful anger, as the exploding powder
scorched and blackened his skin like that of a chicken roasting on a spit.

"Where did you get the pistol?" he added.

"I bought it from a man in a tavern, some time ago." She gazed at
him, her look saying *I challenge you to prove me a liar.*

"And you claim you threw it in the river?"

"Off the Pont Nôtre-Dame, on the way home."

"Where did you learn to fire a pistol?"

"An acquaintance taught me, in 'ninety-three. He said it was dangerous for women to go out alone."

She had an answer for everything, he thought. She was a cool liar, to
be sure—but she had known nothing of the blow to Saint-Ange's temple, and the wound on the back of his head.

"And are you going to claim you murdered Citizeness Beaumontel,
as well?"

"That wasn't part of the indictment," she said with a smile.

"But if someone asked you?"

"She saw me outside the house. It was pure bad luck that she saw
me again when I was visiting the Palais-Égalité in disguise, in the same
coat; she probably wouldn't have recognized me if I'd been wearing a
gown. I couldn't run the risk."

"You strangled her."

"Yes. And dragged her inside the pyramid. I'm quite strong, you
know."

She was simply repeating everything he had told her on the day he had found the corpse. "So you followed her home from the Palais-Égalité? To what address?"

"I don't remember," she said calmly, though he saw her swallow. "Somewhere in the faubourg Saint-Honoré."

Aristide shook his head. "No. You'd remember. You're lying."

"Why do you care, anyway?" Rosalie inquired. "Forget about me. *I* don't care. What should I live for?" She poured herself wine from a small decanter, tasted it, nodded approvingly. Aristide opened his mouth to argue with her but she continued, her voice hard, before he could speak. "Do you think I'm eager for triumphant acquittal in order to go back to life at the Maison Deluc? Please. You and I both know that I have no place and no future. Don't you think I would rather step up to the plank and the blade and be done with it? Go on, go back where you came from; don't waste your time."

Aristide sighed, at a loss how to reason with her. "Are you comfortable, at least?"

"Yes, as well as can be expected."

"I spoke to the warder two days ago," he continued, "and offered to pay what I could for your lodging, to ensure you were in reasonably comfortable quarters, but was told that some anonymous person had already sent money for your expenses. All your expenses."

"Did they?" she exclaimed, staring at him. "Who?"

"Your Henri, perhaps, whoever he may be?"

"Perhaps," she agreed with a ghost of a smile. "Well! So at least I need have no fear about the quality of my meals."

"A caterer is sending them in, I imagine. And they'll bring you the makings of a good fire, and a better bed, with a warm coverlet, if you ask for it."

"That's a mercy." She returned to her dinner and ladled more soup into her soup plate. "There—it's gone cold while we were talking. Gilbert, perhaps you would be an angel and have them set the tureen by the fire for a while?"

Gilbert bore away the tureen and Rosalie pulled the pack of cards Aristide had sent her out of her pocket.

"I do appreciate your thoughtfulness," she said, laying them out on the table. "It's an excellent way to pass the time."

Aristide watched her set the cards down one by one. She had clearly deduced the necessary strategy. "People have confessed before now to crimes they didn't commit," he said at last. "Usually because they wish to shield someone."

She went on with the game, silently, completed it without success, and pushed the cards together. "You don't give up, do you? Are you implying I would sacrifice myself in order to save Philippe, because I still love him?"

Aristide nodded. She eyed him, sardonic pity in her glance.

"I think you must be the kind of contrary person who by nature refuses to believe anything that others accept as fact. I do hate to disappoint you . . . but I'm guilty as sin of those three deaths." She shuffled the cards and started over.

"I don't believe you. The tiny details—they don't add up—"

"Enough!"

Abruptly she sprang to her feet, jarring the table and scattering the cards on the floor. In a few strides she crossed the room to seize the iron bars and stand face-to-face with him, her cheeks flushed.

"Listen to me, Ravel!" No trace of bantering irony remained in her voice. "*I did it.* I murdered her. I'm ready to accept the punishment. For God's sake, stop meddling where you're not wanted. I'm guilty! And I won't thank you for dragging this out, when all I want is for it to be over!"

"I can't accept that," he said. "It's not right."

"Look, Ravel . . . Aristide," she continued, more calmly, "I think you've made it rather clear that you've come to care for me. God knows why, but you have. So if you do care for me, let it be. Just let it be. That's the greatest favor you can do me."

He gazed at her, trying to fathom her. "I've not had an easy life myself," he said at last, "but I never felt myself so utterly without hope that I wished to end it all, to cease wondering what tomorrow might bring me, hoping that it might be better than today. Aren't you curious to know what tomorrow might bring?"

She did not answer him, but glanced at the corridor, where another guard had temporarily replaced Gilbert. After a moment of silence she suddenly turned to Aristide. "They still let me go outside to walk in the courtyard. Come with me, where we'll have a little more privacy, and I'll tell you a story."

The guard preceding them, they went downstairs and out to the women's yard, which once, during the Terror, had been busy with chattering prisoners, eager to wash their clothes in the stone basin kept filled by a ceaseless trickle of clean water. Now the courtyard was silent save for the splashing of the water and the twittering of a few sparrows perched in the branches of a solitary tree in a patch of garden. The sky hung pale pewter gray above them. Rosalie sat on a rough bench near the tree and gestured for Aristide to join her.

"That day by the river," she began, "you told me about somebody." She looked away at the dun-colored walls surrounding them, and the tree that flourished in the center of the courtyard as if defying its imprisonment. "A woman who wore men's clothes, who had murdered a man in a hotel."

Aristide felt his pulse suddenly race but said nothing, waiting for her to continue.

"It happens that—somebody I know, a woman, has endured a great many cruelties, and blames men for her misfortunes. So she decided to murder them in revenge."

A faint breeze, soft and damp with approaching rain, found its way into the courtyard and stirred her loose hair. Aristide thought he saw her shiver and he silently draped his overcoat about her shoulders. "This woman," he ventured, "she might have been partially responsible for another man's death, long before. Her husband's, perhaps."

Rosalie twisted about and met his gaze for an instant. "I see," she said, after a frigid hush. "Well . . . if you know that much, then you also know he was guilty. They would have caught him sooner or later. She only . . . hastened matters along."

Aristide nodded. "What happened then?"

"Then she turned to a friend, a faithful and loving friend, for help. You know the rest, I think."

"And at length he left her, for no apparent reason, although they were passionately in love; and this woman resolved to revenge herself on the entire male sex simply because her lover had spurned her?" Aristide shook his head. "If every slighted woman, or man too, turned to murder, they would depopulate the world. I'm sorry, Rosalie, but I can't condone her motives."

Rosalie rose from the bench and strolled toward one of the round stone tables that stood in the courtyard. "She might have had more reason than that to despise mankind."

"She ought not to blame all men for the vileness of a few."

"You think not?" she said. She turned and leaned against the table, arms folded. "Men are all alike. When—when this woman's lover left her, she was penniless, she didn't know where to turn; she sought out the only man she knew who might help her. She tried to remind him of the love they'd once shared, because they did love each other for a time, and—because he refused to believe that it was her husband and not she who'd been responsible for sending him to prison—he called her a deceitful, treacherous trollop to her face, in front of his friends. At least Henri—at least her other lover had had the elementary decency to refrain from publicly calling her a whore."

Aristide said nothing, though, despite all, he agreed with her. Why had Aubry been so needlessly cruel to her?

"They laughed at her," she continued, "and made coarse remarks, and propositioned her as if she were a low, filthy courtesan. And then he turned to them, in her hearing, and told them her real name and her whole history, every particle of it. She could have killed him right then—she could have killed them all, and then killed herself. And soon afterward she decided to do just that—to kill herself by forcing the law to guillotine her; but she wanted to have her revenge against as many men as she could before they put an end to her."

"And to survive, until she was caught, by living on the profits she might secure from robbing her victims?" Aristide said. "Because she knew no other way to keep herself alive, now that she no longer had a fortune or a name. It was starving in the gutter, or suicide, or murder, wasn't it?"

"The guillotine seemed a much easier death than starvation, or throwing herself in the river. If she was going to die, as she wished, it would be a death with style and celebrity, not a sordid, lonely little suicide in an attic, or in the Seine. Who cares, or notices, if you hang yourself, or fling yourself off a bridge at midnight? But the guillotine—that's different. That has a certain cachet to it, and fame."

"Fame? Or infamy?"

"What's the difference?"

Aristide digested that for a moment, and then spoke again, abandoning their careful fiction.

"You truly wish to be remembered as a criminal who died on the scaffold?"

Rosalie shrugged. "It's better than dying poor and anonymous, with no one who cares a damn whether you live or die."

He shook his head. "I shall never understand you."

"I don't ask you to. All I ask from you, now, is that you don't breathe a word of this conversation, to anyone, ever."

"Why?"

"That's *my* business. But you must see that even if you were clever enough to find proof—which I don't say that you will—proof that I didn't murder Célie . . . you see, don't you, that I still deserve that sentence, that the guillotine is waiting for me, no matter what?"

Aristide looked away. Could I really, he thought, in good conscience let a confessed murderer go free, no matter what my feelings toward him—or her?

"Listen to your conscience," she said, as if reading his thoughts. "You have such a strong instinct for justice. Stay true to yourself and let me be."

Slowly Aristide nodded, without daring to look at her. She had known there was little chance of a happy ending to her story; it was time, he told himself, to shed naïve hopes, and surrender to the implacable truth.

"So," he said after a long silence broken only by the steady trickle of water into the stone basin, "this woman whom you know . . . she resolved to avenge herself upon every man she could, until the law might stop her. She rented a room in a crowded quarter where no one cared who she was, and bought a knife, and some secondhand men's clothes."

"And a fair wig. Men like blondes."

"And one night murdered and robbed a complete stranger."

"Three strangers . . . if you must know." She nodded, with a faint smile, at his look of disbelief. "Three or four weeks between each one. In different parts of Paris. Evidently the police from different sections don't share information as often as they should."

Aristide could well believe it; Brasseur had complained about the decentralization of the police force often enough. "Why did she not simply murder her old lover, the man who had treated her so shabbily?" he said when he had recovered his composure.

"She considered it. But he wouldn't have let her get near him—she couldn't have reached him and hurt him without being immediately arrested for it, and she wanted to do far more damage than that before she was caught."

He could not decide whether it was repugnance or pity he felt. He looked at her, remembering all she had told him of her brief unhappy life, and found he could comprehend her motives: comprehend, though not condone.

"She could have killed just that one man," he said softly, "who probably deserved it, in order to be put to death as she desired. Even an unsuccessful attempt on his life would have brought her to that. But instead of hastening her own death, she found she would rather live a little longer, in order to keep on killing, in order to feed her desire for revenge. Don't you find that an interesting paradox?"

She glanced at him, frowned, and quickly looked away again, without speaking.

"What of the strangers she murdered, and intended to murder?" Aristide added. "They had never done her any wrong."

"They had wronged every woman on earth, by being men who just wanted to satisfy their appetites with a miserable woman who was nothing more to them than a piece of flesh, and walk away. Don't you think that debases all women? Do you imagine women would sell themselves as they do if there weren't a ready market of men eager for them, and willing to pay? They deserve it."

"I think you're still blaming the entire race for the misdeeds of a few."

"Why should I care? I just want to die now and find peace or oblivion, it doesn't matter which—and I hope the guillotine will be as quick as they say it is."

"There must be something for which you would want to live."

"What do you think would inspire me to live? Love? You must be joking."

"For God's sake, other things in this world are worth seeking besides *love*!"

"Tell me what. Children, mother-love? I can't have children. The doctor told me that when I was fifteen, when I had that stillborn baby, at the hands of an ignorant midwife, and caught a fever from it, that the fever must have hurt me somehow inside. It did something to me that meant I could never have any more babies."

Some women would consider it a great blessing never to have children, Aristide thought, but said nothing.

"And do you think, after all I've endured, that I would consider I was doing a child a favor by bringing it into this world?" Rosalie shook her head. "Let's see . . . what else is worth living for? Doing good works? I did that; I was a nun, and then they closed the convents and threw me out. The chance of amassing some money, of a comfortable life? I doubt it. How does a woman like me earn a living that will buy her some comfort and a few modest pleasures, except by selling herself? And that I will not, *cannot* do. Do you know of any other way a penniless, half-educated woman of 'good family,' who knows no useful trades, can make her way in the world?"

She met his eyes, challenging him. He could think of nothing to say to her in the face of that stark truth and at last bent his head beneath her relentless gaze.

"I can see my future quite clearly," Rosalie added quietly, "as a pathetic, useless creature living on and on, always moving to smaller, shabbier rooms as my income shrinks; and I don't want that future. I'd rather go fast and without pain, and knowing they'll say I was still young and pretty and vital when they cut my head off."

"You need not have been a courtesan to find a good man who would have supported you," Aristide said, moving closer to her. "There's always honorable marriage. Surely some decent man—"

"You fool, don't you *understand*?" she cried. "I want nothing to do with men. What difference is there between marriage and selling myself on the street corner? I've been humiliated enough, and I'll have no more of it!"

"That's what you really can't bear, isn't it?" he retorted. "The loss of your pride. My God, woman, most of the population of this world has suffered far more than you ever have. Have you ever labored until you were too weary to stand? Or seen your loved ones die of hunger or smallpox or plague? No. You've been humiliated in front of your 'good society,' and discarded by your lovers. Too bad! Let me tell you, you self-centered spoiled brat, there are far worse things in this world than that!"

She crimsoned and slapped him across the face.

"You don't know what it's *like*! How could you know what it is to be discarded by one after the other, to be rebuffed even by someone you loved desperately, someone who you believed was the love of your life!"

Aristide cupped a cold palm against his smarting cheek and said nothing as she raged on.

"All because of something you'd never asked to happen. Did I deserve to be raped and ruined when I was fifteen years old? How would *you* care, by no fault of your own, to be bitterly humiliated in front of everyone you ever knew? You can't *possibly* know what it's like!"

"Can't I?" snapped Aristide.

"How on earth could you? You're a *man*!"

"I know *exactly* what it is like," he shouted, smacking his hands down on the stone table, "because when I was a boy my father murdered my mother!"

He paused, breathing hard. At length he leaned forward, head bowed.

"There; now you know."

After a long seething moment he dared to raise his head again. She was staring at him, pale, lips trembling.

"I—forgive me . . . I—I didn't guess—"

"Do you think I can ever say my father's name with anything but shame? Whatever humiliation you've endured, it cannot have been worse than the ignominy society visits upon the family of an executed felon."

"What . . . what happened?" she whispered.

"My mother had taken a lover. Father was often away, and I suppose she was lonely. He discovered their affair, and shot them both, and then tried to kill himself, but they arrested him, and executed him. Did you ever see a man broken, before the Revolution?"

Rosalie shook her head.

"They bind you to a wheel or a wooden cross, and then they take an iron bar and they smash you over and over again with it, your limbs, your ribs, your vitals, until all your bones are broken and your flesh is battered to a pulp and you die slowly, in agony, while the crowd jeers. Then they burn the body, so that you're even denied burial in consecrated ground. That's what they did to my father. I heard later that he took four hours to die."

Aristide paused and met Rosalie's mute gaze. "But at least his agony ended then," he continued, his voice even. "My sister and I—my mother's brother took charge of us, and it made his life no easier. By mere association with a felon who had perished on the scaffold, we all had to bear his infamy. We all had to endure the stares and whispers, and the insults, from every dirty street brat who recognized us, and every smirking servant who refused to work for us, and every schoolboy who called me filthy names, and every smug, squeamish family that sent us no invitations when my sister grew old enough to marry. Now do you think I can never understand what *you* have endured?"

He glanced up at the sky as a few cold droplets spattered his hand, and snatched up his hat. "It's going to rain. You had better go inside. Good-bye, Rosalie; I won't trouble you again."

"Please . . . aren't you coming back?"

"I can't imagine you would want me to."

"Please," she said. She touched his arm. "Please don't leave me."

Aristide halted. At last he sighed and turned back to her.

"How could I?"

26

The rain spattered down suddenly, in a heavy shower, and they fled inside and returned silently to Rosalie's cell. Faure, the public prosecutor, was waiting in the passage with Maître Tardieu and a clerk. Rosalie slowed, glancing from one to another.

"I think I know why you're here, citizens."

"Citizeness," Maître Tardieu said, "you must be brave."

"The . . . your sentence will be carried out tomorrow at four o'clock," said Faure. He looked uncommonly somber, Aristide thought. "The executor of criminal judgments will take charge of you at three. Do you wish the services of a priest?"

"Thank you, no," Rosalie said. "But I do have one trifling request. Is it absolutely necessary that I wear that ugly red smock?"

"It's part of the sentence for murderers."

"Surely the most inconsequential part of it, Citizen Prosecutor," Aristide said quietly.

Rosalie smiled. "Call it vanity if you will, but I'd like to go looking well, not draped in a shapeless rag."

"I'll convey your request to the president of the tribunal," Faure said with a small half smile.

Tardieu stepped forward but Rosalie shook her head. "I won't need your services any more. Thank you; you've been most conscientious. All of you."

When they had retreated down the corridor, she dropped easily into a chair and stared out the window into the empty, twilit sky. "Tomorrow at four . . . finally . . . do you suppose the blade will be cold?"

"I don't know," Aristide said.

"In winter it must be cold."

He crossed the cell to stand beside her, a hand on her shoulder. "You ought not to dwell on it."

"It's been mild, citizeness," Gilbert assured her. Imagination, Aristide reflected, was not one of his strengths. "Not too cold. Fine weather for the time of year, they've been saying."

She laughed. "So it is—a fine climate for dying!"

25 Frimaire (December 15)

He woke early, before the slow winter dawn, but he stayed in bed a long while, nursing a headache and gazing at the dark shape of the wooden crucifix on the opposite wall. Clotilde, stubbornly indifferent to the prevailing anti-Christian sentiment and heedful of her lodgers' souls, had hung one in every room she let, and he had left it hanging for the past three years to indulge her.

He studied the crucified Christ, limbs distorted in agony. Public death was kinder now; you were spared at least the hideous intimacy of betraying your torment to the staring mob.

She will die today.

The thought of it roiled his stomach and he closed his eyes. One moment she would be warm, living, breathing, the next—

Strange how the guillotine's swift dispatch left no lingering moment for dying between the last instant of hot pulsing life and the first of stone-still, mute death.

He tasted the sourness of bile in his mouth and contemplated burying his face in the pillows, sending word to them all that he was ill, a sudden fever. Easy to tell them a quick lie, so easy to lie and escape. She had seen through his armor; she would understand.

A firewood seller began to shout his wares below in the street, a water carrier soon joining him, the strident voices piercing his throbbing head. He pressed a palm against his queasy stomach. Yes, he decided, he would simply refuse to leave his bed today.

If you shrink from this, said a small cold voice within him, *you will never find your self-respect again.*

He swallowed down the sickness and struggled upward, wincing as he swung his feet to the cold floor. He pulled on his clothes and boots so as not to shock the servant girl when she arrived with his hot water, and stood at the window, staring at the roof opposite and the empty sky above. It was a pretty sunrise, rose and gold. He turned from the window as the last golden-pink streaks faded into clouds and quotidian wintry blue, and the girl came scurrying from below with the steaming jug.

I must look my best for her, he thought. She would be piqued if he attended her looking less than his best.

A cadaverous face, eyes gleaming within dark hollows, stared back at him from the mirror as he washed. As he tied his cravat, knotting it crisp and precise above the high collar of his black satin waistcoat, his fingertips brushed across rough stubble on his cheek and he reminded himself to visit a barber for a proper shave before he set out on the business of the day.

Three o'clock.

He arrived at her cell just after nine o'clock. She was still wearing her nightgown and peignoir.

"I thought they couldn't come for me so early," she said with a brief smile. "You look very smart. You'll outshine me if I'm not careful. By the way," she added, "what do you think happened last evening, after you'd left?"

"I couldn't say."

"I finally made the patience come out. Twice." She touched the cards, sitting in a tidy stack in the center of the table. "It worked itself out beautifully, at last."

A guard brought her breakfast tray. Rosalie gestured to the second chair as she sat down. "Won't you join me? We have plenty of time. Gilbert—a cup for Citizen Ravel, if you please."

"No," Aristide said, raising a hand. "Thank you, no."

"No appetite? You do look a little green." She poured herself coffee and hot milk. "I hope you don't mind if I take my breakfast, though. I'm famished." She buttered a roll and began to eat.

"Well," she said when she had done. "I must wash, and dress. If you leave now, will they let you return?"

"Certainly."

"Then humor me, and come back in an hour. I'd like your company."

"As you wish."

He left the Conciergerie and paced the length of the quays, breathing in the weedy, watery smell of the river as it gently lapped at the wharves and the tethered boats. The struggling sun had vanished beneath a thick blanket of cloud as pale as river ice. He wandered past the Tuileries and stood staring down at the gardens, at the topiary hedges whose damp bitter scent rose to him on the breeze.

With a shudder he remembered the corpse-smell, heavy and sickly in the cramped chamber of the pyramid. Poor Sidonie Beaumontel, condemned to death as surely as Rosalie for what she had chanced to see. But if the slight figure with whom she had collided had not been Rosalie, who had it been? Had Aubry murdered her after all—or had he been silenced, too?

He found, to his unease, that the notion of Aubry lying dead in some out-of-the-way spot did not trouble him in the least. Though Aubry might not be a murderer, beyond all doubt a contemptible soul lurked behind the face of an angel.

And then he turned to them, in her hearing, she had said, *and told them all her name and her whole history.*

He glowered at the muddy, desolate garden, wondering how any man could treat a woman so cruelly, and then wondered suddenly: How had Aubry known Rosalie's whole history?

Surely she would not have told him herself. A shameful past that had sent her fleeing to a convent was not something one revealed to a young man of rigid morals and lofty principles.

Or had Aubry known more than Rosalie was saying?

He slunk into Brasseur's office, avoiding Dautry's sidelong gaze.

"I didn't expect to see you today," Brasseur said. "I'm sorry. I know you've become . . . attached . . ."

Aristide pulled off his overcoat and hat and dropped them on a bench and flung himself in the nearest chair, ignoring the hat as it slid off his crumpled coat with a soft thump. "I can't seem to sort it out . . . *why* . . ."

"Crime of passion, plain as plain. Here," Brasseur added, "best pick up your hat before you tread on it. Good hats aren't so easy to come by."

"What?" Aristide said, startled.

"I said, good hats—"

"The *hat*," he whispered, a restless hand hovering at his lips. "Not so easy to come by. . . ."

"Eh?"

"The hat, Brasseur, the *hat*!"

"Don't just keep saying 'the hat'! What about the hat?"

"Brasseur—from the first, the porter said a young man ran upstairs, ran out again, and then returned twenty minutes later. As soon as we began to learn who the actors were in this drama, we supposed the young man had been Philippe Aubry. But Grangier said Aubry wasn't the young man he'd seen."

Brasseur nodded. "And you then discovered that the 'young man' had been Juliette Vaudray dressed in men's clothes, and Grangier identified her in court, and she confessed. What about it?"

"Rosalie claimed she went upstairs, lost her nerve, retreated, and then returned to do the murders. It's all quite plausible. But we all overlooked one thing. The hat."

"What *about* the hat?" Brasseur repeated.

"It all hinges on the hat. She might have run upstairs wearing a hat, then left, and somehow lost her hat in the next quarter hour—people do lose hats. The wind blows them into the muck, or under carriage wheels, or they're stolen. But this young man—"

"Juliette Vaudray."

"This *person* whom Grangier saw, he—she—first came *without* a hat, then returned *with* a hat. Where's your file?" He snatched up the dossier Brasseur pushed toward him and feverishly sifted through its contents. "Here: Grangier's statement." He pulled the papers from the folder. " 'He wasn't wearing his hat when I saw him run out; he must have been carrying it under his arm.' Carrying it—or perhaps he didn't have a hat at all when he first arrived, and Grangier merely assumed he'd had one because he saw one the second time. Witnesses *will* make assumptions with nothing to base them on, and think they're telling perfect truth. Now how, and why, do you suddenly acquire a hat within a quarter hour, especially when you have far weightier matters on your mind than your clothes?"

"Are you suggesting," Brasseur said slowly, "that Grangier actually saw two different people?"

"Precisely." Aristide smacked the folder closed and dropped it on the desk. "Look: Grangier hears hurried footsteps running up the stairs. Ten minutes later a hatless, dark-haired young man in a dark coat, whom he sees only for a second or two and from the back, rushes *down* the stairs and out the door. Then twenty or thirty minutes later a dark young man in a dark coat *and a hat* returns, a fellow of the same general height and build, still in a terrible hurry. Grangier naturally assumes it's the same young man returning; wouldn't you? This time Grangier sees his face for an instant, enough to get the impression that it's a young man whom he doesn't know. But if Grangier never saw his face the first time, what's to prevent the first, hatless man from being an entirely different person from the one who ran in wearing a round hat?"

Brasseur frowned. "But his clothes?"

"It was early evening and Grangier hadn't yet lit the lamp in the passage," Aristide said, stabbing a finger at the porter's statement. "In

the twilight, one dark redingote is much like another, if you're not paying attention and you've had a few glasses of brandy. Black breeches,
top boots. Everyone wears them. It's possible. What if the man whom
Grangier saw first, the man *whose face he never saw*, did the murders, and
Rosalie was only following him?"

"But he could be anybody," said Brasseur glumly.

"Yes. He could be *anybody*."

"You mean—"

"Of course. It's obvious. Aubry. It always *was* obvious. This case
ought to have been perfectly simple. Except that I was led astray by
Rosalie, we all were . . . and by my own doubts and fears of arresting the
wrong person. . . ."

"But the Vaudray woman is going to be executed for it! If she's innocent, then it has to be stopped—"

"She's not innocent," Aristide said, feeling his throat grow tight as if
he would choke upon the words.

"You just said—"

"Do you remember what you asked me the other night, when I
found the room on Rue du Cocq, and her men's clothes?"

Brasseur stared at him for an instant before murmuring "Ah," with a
slow shake of his head. "So why confess to the murders she didn't commit, and say nothing about the ones she did?"

"I'm damned if I can see." Aristide began to pace from end to end
of the small office. "She can't possibly be shielding Aubry out of love
for him. Would *you* shield someone who'd treated you like dirt? Who'd
threatened to kill you?"

Abruptly he paused, staring at the wall. "The servant girl from
Ferré's house . . ." He seized the dossier again and found his notes.
"She told me that as her mistress's young man was arrested in June of
'ninety-three, he'd said 'You treacherous bitch, the next time I'll kill
you.' The *next* time. Brasseur—doesn't that sound as if she had betrayed him—or he thought she'd betrayed him—more than once? That
their liaison, when Rosalie was married to Maurice Ferré, wasn't the
first time they'd had a love affair?"

Brasseur nodded thoughtfully. "You mean . . ." He paused, frowning, and searched through the dossier. "Saints above, we missed it—look at the letter Aubry wrote her." He thrust the copy of the letter at Aristide. "He tells her, right there, 'why, knowing how easy you find it to foully betray me in all things, should I look upon you now,' and so on. 'How easy you find it'! That's a man who's been burned twice, I'd say. It's plain as day: they'd already had an affair that had ended badly, and then they must have met again, later, and patched up their differences."

"And then—then Ferré informs on Aubry, and Aubry immediately concludes that it's Rosalie who has betrayed him, because he already knows she deceived him once, played him false. I wonder . . ."

"What?"

"Never mind; I'd have to confirm it first. But any love he once felt for Rosalie has now curdled into hatred, just the way people tend to hate most those whom they once loved, if the love goes sour. And so he takes his petty revenge by treating her contemptibly when she appeals to him for help. . . ."

"But you're saying," said Brasseur, "that Juliette Vaudray didn't take her own revenge by murdering Célie Montereau?"

"No—she was there in Saint-Ange's apartment all right, and saw the bodies, but she didn't do the murders. She made a few mistakes when she told me how she'd killed Saint-Ange. Killing Célie wasn't part of her revenge upon Aubry. . . ."

Brasseur suddenly snapped his fingers. "The letter! To Aubry! She admitted herself to writing it! If Aubry was the murderer after all, then it's perfectly likely that that letter did tell him about Celié's secrets."

"Yes," Aristide said. "Yes, of course." He stopped short, thinking furiously. "Revenge . . . my God, yes . . . it's possible . . . it all fits. . . ."

"What is it?"

"A—a sort of revenge I'd never have imagined."

Aristide rushed out of the commissariat and hailed the first cab he saw heading toward the river. "Rue de l'Université. Hurry!"

Citizen Montereau was not at home, the maître d'hôtel protested. Citizen Montereau and the young master had retreated to the country for at least a month. If the citizen would like to leave his card, and return another time—

"What about Madame Laroque?" Aristide demanded. "Surely she's at home. I am an agent of the police, and I must speak to madame."

Cowed, the maître d'hôtel gestured a lackey toward the staircase. Aristide followed him to the old lady's chambers, as the clocks chimed noon, and brushed past the protesting maid.

Madame de Laroque was dozing in her chair, frail chest gently rising and falling beneath her cashmere shawl, the black-and-white cat asleep in her lap. Wrinkled eyelids fluttered open as he repeated her name. "Eh? Who's that?"

"Ravel, madame. We spoke together some weeks ago, after Célie's death."

"Oh yes," said the old lady, blinking and fixing him with a dour glare. "Have you found the monster who murdered her?"

"I'm close to doing so, madame. But I need your help." He crossed the parlor to the wall where the portrait hung. "This portrait, madame—you told me it was of your great-nephew, Marsillac de Saint-Roch. Who was killed in a duel some ten years ago?"

"That's correct."

"The young man who killed him was one Philippe Aubry."

She nodded. "Yes. He stayed at my little château once, with his aunt, before it all happened. An agreeable boy, I must admit, from a good family; though none of them had two sous to call their own."

Aristide drew a deep breath. "Aubry challenged Marsillac because of a woman, didn't he?"

"If you could call her a woman. She was a chit of a thing, fifteen years old, a little nitwit straight out of the convent."

"And Marsillac—"

"Had seduced her, of course. She was going to be married to a marquis, an excellent match, and Marsillac seduced her two months before the wedding. But it seemed Aubry and the girl had had an understanding."

"You mean a love affair."

"Well, an affair of the heart, certainly. Aubry was a straitlaced little prig, for all his impetuosity: the sort who announces that he sleeps alone by choice. He declared afterward that he'd fought Marsillac not as a rival, because he wouldn't have any woman who'd surrendered so easily to a scoundrel, but to avenge the girl's honor, because Marsillac had ruined her. I imagine it was really his own pride he was avenging, though." She paused and Aristide gestured to her to go on.

"That was when the truth came out, publicly, about what Marsillac had been doing with her—in my own house, I may add!—and the girl immediately took the veil. It was the only thing she could do, after such a disgrace. So I daresay Aubry's illusions about her were rudely shattered."

Sometimes they spin pretty illusions, François had said, using nearly the same words, *and when the illusion shatters, they become capable of anything.*

"Madame, what was the name of the girl—the girl whom Marsillac debauched?"

"Vaudray," she said, with a soft sigh. "Juliette de Vaudray."

You treacherous bitch, the next time I'll kill you.

She had known him since they were almost children, known his character intimately. Aubry had killed a man already, because of what he had seen as her weakness; she had known he was capable of killing, and from a duel incited in brokenhearted rage it was only a step to half-crazed, passionate murder . . . but her own rancor and misery had blinded her, for a fatal instant, to the consequences of her own spite.

Madame de Laroque sighed, breaking into Aristide's thoughts. "A charming boy, as I said. But prone to fly into a passion when provoked. Though it's all forgotten now." The cat woke and yawned, gaping a wide pink mouth. "People forget so fast," the old lady added, absently scratching the cat's head. "Imagine what I thought when I came to live here with Honoré and Josèphe, and saw young Aubry sitting cool as you please in Honoré's study! Of course Honoré dismissed him when I—"

She straightened and pushed the cat from her lap as one hand gripped the arm of her chair. "Young man, are you about to tell me that Philippe Aubry was the man with whom Célie was in love?"

"Did Monsieur Montereau not tell you?"

"Bah, Honoré never tells me anything. He thinks I'm too old and frail. But yes . . . yes, it's the likeliest thing in the world. Young Aubry was the sort of high-minded ninny she'd have adored . . . and I daresay he was ready to fall in love with another pretty, innocent young creature who wouldn't disappoint him this time." She peered up at him, her old eyes bright. "Was it the same sorry tale, then? Was Célie not as pure as she seemed?"

Aristide shook his head. "I fear not."

"And so he learned of it, and killed the man who had defiled her . . . and this time killed her, too?"

As simple as that, he thought, ten minutes later, as he hurried back to the courtyard and the waiting fiacre.

And the bitter, unhappy woman who once had been Juliette de Vaudray, who discovered too late what she had done—she had known Aubry, known his guilt, known his character; and when it had become apparent that, through her own actions, Aubry would escape the nets of justice, she had chosen to punish him in her own unique fashion. A punishment that was, for her, all at once revenge, atonement, and deliverance.

Aristide glanced at his watch. It was nearly two o'clock.

27

An empty cart waited in the courtyard of the Palais de Justice, the single horse standing patiently, flicking away flies with its tail. Sanson's assistant Desmorets leaned against the cart, arms folded, head lowered, staring at his feet. Aristide hurried past him to the door at the bottom of the steps.

He encountered Sanson near the prison clerk's office. The executioner turned at the sound of his footsteps.

"Good day," Aristide said, wincing at the banality of the words as soon as they had left his lips. Sanson nodded. Like Aristide, he wore only black, save for his cravat. Aristide could not help thinking it suited him, though he looked taut and wretched; or perhaps "haunted" was a better word. It was rumored that executioners found it especially distressing to put a woman to death.

"They tell me you've been visiting her," Sanson said, his voice hoarse, scarcely above a whisper. "Are you going to see her?"

"I've already been; I'm returning."

"How is she?"

"Very calm, the last I saw." He met Sanson's eyes for the first time and was startled at the torment he saw in the young man's pale face, in the bluish shadows beneath his eyes that spoke of disquiet and sleepless nights.

"Sanson . . . this woman—I've often spoken with her. She's not afraid. She's sick of life; I can't say I understand her despair, but I do know that she *wants* death, that she welcomes it."

"Should that cheer me?" he said. "Make the job easier?"

"No, of course not. Forgive me." Aristide stole another glance at his watch. Half an hour; all he needed, he thought.

"You're late," Rosalie said dryly as Aristide entered her cell. "I was beginning to think you'd lost your nerve again."

She had rouged her cheeks and lips, and smudged a little lampblack about her eyes until they shone large, dark, and lustrous. Her long hair fell about her shoulders. She was wearing shirt and breeches and gleaming riding boots, with unbuttoned waistcoat and collar hanging open.

Aristide stared at her a moment. "Forgive me, but do you intend to wear those clothes? To exhibit yourself in male costume?"

"The great advantage of being condemned to death," she said calmly, "is that you're free to do anything you wish. What more can they do to me?"

"They'll call you brazen, a whore, a lesbian. Are you sure you want that?"

"I should like to die in the clothes in which I had my revenge."

Aristide turned. "Gilbert, do you think we might have a half hour alone together, in privacy?"

"I'll be at the end of the corridor," Gilbert said, and stumped away. "My hearing's not so good, you know."

"Rosalie . . ." Aristide began, when Gilbert had vanished into the gloom.

"Thank you for returning."

"I talked to Madame de Laroque just now," he said after a moment's silence. "She told me all about you—or enough to allow me to reason out the rest."

She cast him a quick sharp glance.

"It was you whom René Marsillac de Saint-Roch ruined, and whom Aubry loved; for whose honor he fought Marsillac and killed him in 1785, and ruined his own career and future, at least until the Revolution unexpectedly provided him with new prospects. Madame de Laroque told me that once Aubry had fled the country, he declared, in a letter he sent to Marsillac's family, and yours, and all the news journals that would print it, that he had killed Marsillac for your sake but that you had proved to be a corrupt, wanton, deceitful whore, and that he wouldn't have you for all the wealth of the Indies." He paused. An ugly crimson blush crept into Rosalie's cheeks.

"I don't suppose it made any difference to Aubry," Aristide added, "that you hadn't been a willing victim of seduction, that Marsillac had raped you as surely as if he'd held a pistol to your head. To somebody like Aubry, a woman should have died rather than give up her 'honor.' " He thrust cold hands in his pockets and paced the length of the cell, turning to face Rosalie once more.

"You disguised yourself in coat and breeches and murdered Célie because you were bitterly jealous of her, and Saint-Ange died because he was a witness to your crime."

"Yes."

"No," Aristide said.

"That's the truth!"

"No, it's not."

"The porter recognized me."

"Yes; he identified you as the young man he saw rushing up the stairs toward Saint-Ange's apartment. He was right, of course. But the young man came twice; let's not forget that." He gestured to a chair. "Why don't you sit down? This may take a little while."

She did not sit down, but leaned against the back of the chair, her eyes never leaving him as he paced back and forth.

"It was such a simple affair, really," he said. "A simple, obvious crime of passion, a trail easy to follow. A matter of people behaving exactly as anyone might have predicted they would. It should have been resolved within the fortnight. Until you muddied the trail." He paused, waiting for her to insist once again that she had committed the crime herself, but she said nothing.

"Aubry sent you that letter," he continued. "Because he hated you for, as he thought, betraying him not once but twice. First with Marsillac—breaking his heart and making a fool of him by becoming Marsillac's whore—no matter that Marsillac had terrorized rather than seduced you into submitting—and ruining his future by driving him into fighting that rash duel."

Rosalie nodded. "To Philippe, nothing was ever *his* fault."

"And then you betrayed him, or so he decided, by giving him up to the authorities in 'ninety-three, this time putting his very life in danger. But why did you keep his letter? If a former lover had sent such a letter to me, I'd have burned it, praying that the flames would scorch his vitals to cinders."

"To remind myself how much I despised him," she said with the faintest of smiles.

Aristide nodded. "Yes, I suppose you might. Then, I think, not so long afterward, Célie asked you for help. She didn't dare ask anyone who might have revealed her secret to her father. She confessed to you that she was in trouble, that Saint-Ange was extorting money from her, and why, and where she went to pay him. And she told you, whether intentionally or inadvertently I don't know, that Aubry was her secret fiancé. I don't suppose she had the faintest idea who you were, or that you and Aubry shared a past.

"Now you possessed Célie's secret, that she had lost her virtue years before to a seducer, and what was more, had had a child by him and—with her mother's connivance—had successfully deceived the world as to the child's true identity."

Rosalie drew a quick breath. "How—"

"I've known *that* for some time. One only had to look at Saint-Ange to see the resemblance."

"She was terrified it would come out . . . the scandal would have ruined her whole family."

"You knew Célie's secret now," he continued, "and all you could think of was the satisfaction it would bring you to fling it in Aubry's face. In that heartless letter, he laid extraordinary stress upon the innocence and virtue of the girl he intended to marry. How better to hurt him than to tell him he was a colossal fool, that his precious, perfect Célie had been deceived and traduced just as you had been, was no more a virgin than you had been? So on the tenth of Brumaire, you wrote to him—anonymously, I suppose—and told him the truth about Célie, and that Saint-Ange was the man who had had her and who was extorting money from her to keep her secret safe—what better proof than that? 'Go to Saint-Ange, on Rue du Hasard, and ask him about it yourself,' you probably said. And then you found an errand boy in the street and sent the letter off to Aubry, enjoying your revenge.

"But I don't think you savored it for long. It must have occurred to you rather quickly, once the first flush of triumph had faded, that Aubry was not one to closet himself away and brood over the world's villainy. You remembered that the moment he learned Marsillac had had you, he flew off in a blind rage to challenge him. And suddenly you feared what he might do. But it would never do to go and warn Célie against him, for then it might all come out again, the sordid old tale, who you were, and what you had just done. Better to try to prevent Aubry from doing anything rash. You sent another street boy to his house to intercept him, but he had already left."

He paused for breath. She watched him, expressionless.

"There was only one place where he could be. He'd gone to confront Saint-Ange, of course, and offer him challenge, just as he had confronted Marsillac. You decided to follow him, in disguise, and stop him, or warn Saint-Ange, whatever was necessary. You hurried to Rue du Cocq and threw on one of the men's suits you kept hidden there, and a hat to shadow your face. Then you sped to Rue du Hasard and ran into the house, past the porter, up the stairs to Saint-Ange's apartment, but they were already dead.

"I expect Aubry went merely to threaten Saint-Ange and challenge him to a duel; but by great ill luck Célie herself was there, paying Saint-Ange, and in his rage and misery Aubry simply snapped. He was carrying a loaded pistol, and in his delirium of fury he killed her. Perhaps he almost imagined that he was killing you, whom he believed to be the source of all his past misery and hardship, rather than Célie. Then—well, shooting Saint-Ange was no more than disposing of a bit of filth. And twenty minutes later, you arrived, and found you were too late."

Aristide paused and gazed at Rosalie. She said nothing.

"It all made sense," he added quietly, "as soon as I wondered if the young man whom the porter saw had, in fact, been two different people. The light was failing, and he'd had some brandy, and Aubry is not much taller than you are. Two slim, dark-haired young men wearing dark coats look much alike if you only get a glimpse of them, and you're not paying them much attention."

"You have no proof that I was not the one who killed them."

"No. Except for your own nature."

"My nature?" she echoed him with a wry smile.

"You hate men for how they've used you—but you couldn't have murdered Célie. She'd been a victim, as you once were, of a callous libertine. You must have seen yourself in her as soon as she confided in you. You might have been bitterly resentful of her, but you could never have made her your victim. After all," he added, "you began to throw suspicion on yourself as soon as we detained Hélène Villemain, whom you didn't even know, but who was as innocent as any newborn kitten. You couldn't bear the thought of a blameless woman being wrongly accused of Célie's murder, and took steps to ensure her release. You sent those rather amateurish anonymous letters to Commissaire Brasseur yourself. They were sent from the district post office in the same section as Rue du Cocq."

"And if Philippe were guilty and not I, why would I allow myself to be executed for his crime?"

Aristide paused for an instant. "Of course I wondered about that. At first I supposed that if you wanted to see Aubry suffer as much as he had made you suffer, years ago, with his moral arrogance and his self-conscious rectitude and his intolerance and priggishness, you would be delighted to see him condemned and executed for what he had done. And you did keep trying to steer my suspicions toward him, because you knew perfectly well he was guilty. You did a masterful job of it—not giving me too much information, not enough to draw attention to yourself, just enough to set us on the trail.

"But as I grew to know Aubry a little, you see, it occurred to me that because of those very qualities, that lofty rectitude of his, he might torment and punish himself far more cruelly than any court ever could. The guilt of having murdered the girl he loved, and the hideous chagrin of discovering his precious moral integrity was a sham . . . I think it might be worse for him to live with that than to die for it."

Rosalie nodded. "You've seen through him quite well."

"And the one thing worse even than that would be to see someone else, some innocent person, suffer for his crime, and yet to lack the courage to come forward and confess. Because he's a physical coward, you know. Rushing out and fighting a duel in the heat of passion is one thing; facing the scaffold is quite another. His terror of death, and of the shame of public execution, is so great that I believe he would let you die in his stead, thinking that you're sacrificing yourself for love of him, and then suffer the torments of Hell for the rest of his life because of it. And that," Aristide concluded, "that is exactly what you want."

She looked up at him calmly.

"You may believe that if you wish."

"I believe it because I know that you were already indifferent to your own life before this whole business began. And I believe it because I can think of no other plausible reason why you would confess to murdering Célie, and yet forbid me to reveal that you were the hotel murderess; why you would destroy all the evidence at Rue du Cocq except that which would condemn you for Célie's murder. Because for your revenge to be absolute, Aubry must believe you are a lily-white innocent under the law, guiltless of any crime."

Rosalie smiled.

"This is all very interesting . . . but if it had happened that way, why would I not have simply declared to the police, or to a judge, straightaway, 'I told Philippe Aubry the ugly truth about Célie and Saint-Ange, which would have enraged him, made him angry enough to kill'?"

"For two reasons I can imagine . . . One, because even your testimony might not have convinced a judge and jury. You didn't actually see him commit the murders. No one saw him, and the porter would always be ready to swear that it was not Aubry he'd seen. All the evidence was circumstantial; and most judges are being more cautious since Lesurques was executed. Even with the truth laid bare, there might not have been enough evidence to convict Aubry. He might still have escaped unpunished."

"And the second reason?"

Aristide ceased his pacing and dropped into the nearest chair, head bent and hands clenched between his knees.

"You couldn't bear to confess the truth, to confess your part in it," he said, staring down at the floor. "You couldn't bear that everyone would know *your* actions had driven him to murdering Célie, and then Sidonie Beaumontel. If you'd told the truth, every particle of it, from writing that letter to the moment you found them dead, you couldn't have borne that shame, knowing what Célie's family would have thought of you, what everyone would have thought of you. I think . . . I think you'd rather die to absolve yourself of their deaths, though you never touched them, than live a lifetime—or even a week—with the guilt."

"Do you think that's so very compelling a motive?" Rosalie said.

"Oh, yes." He glanced up at her for a moment and swiftly looked away again. "I know exactly what sort of torment is devouring you. Because *I* live with that guilt, and know how bitter it is."

"I don't understand."

"You see . . . my mother died, and my father became a murderer, and died on the scaffold, because of me."

"You!"

"I was only nine. It was childish chatter. I had no idea what it implied, that Monsieur Godeau had been visiting frequently while my father was away, and that once I'd seen him in the house, half dressed, early in the morning. So I babbled it all out to my father when he came home from one of his journeys. He deduced the rest, and lay in wait for them, and then he killed them. But it was I who killed them, really, and him, too. . . ."

He thrust the chair aside and returned to his pacing, still not daring to meet her gaze. "I've never told that to a soul. I've lived alone with that guilt for almost thirty years. You try to reason your way out of blame, to convince yourself that you acted innocently, that it might have come about no matter what, that murder was someone else's choice, not yours; but you can never free yourself of that burden. I live every day haunted by the terror that someone, somehow, will learn it was *my* fault. And I think you must believe yourself as guilty of Célie's death, and Citizeness Beaumontel's death, as I believe myself guilty of the death of my parents."

Rosalie stared at him. At last she sat down in the chair he had pushed aside, with a long sigh.

"Are you now going to tell all this to the prosecutor and the president?"

"No."

"Thank you."

"I think it was Montaigne who wrote, 'Some defeats are more triumphant than victories.' Why should I deny you what you wish?"

"You're right," she whispered. "If I'd never unleashed my spite and told Philippe what I knew about her, he would never have done what he did, and that other woman would still be alive, too . . . I'm as guilty of Célie's death as if I'd pulled the trigger myself. I would have killed myself right there in Saint-Ange's apartment, I was so sick with shame . . . or given myself up for the hotel murders and let them guillotine me . . . if only I hadn't wanted, more than anything else, to see Philippe punished for what he did. But instead he managed to evade justice, so I had to do it, somehow . . ."

He turned to her, in time to see the first tears glimmering in her eyes. She squeezed her eyelids shut, to no avail. A great painful sob escaped from her and she pressed the back of her hand against her mouth.

He touched her shoulder. "Weep if you want—there's no one to hear you, not even Gilbert."

She stumbled toward him and clutched unseeing at his shoulders, her slender body shuddering with sobs.

"I thought revenge would bring me happiness—I wanted to make them all as wretched as they'd made me, I wanted to ruin them and take away their lives as they had ruined me and taken away the life I should have had. And I thought that when I tasted revenge, I'd be happy at last, because I'd won. But I'm not—I was happy for a moment, and then it meant nothing; then I was empty, and purposeless, like a broken pitcher, and there is nothing any more in this world that I want, and nothing I can feel but a black cloud that surrounds me and chokes me. . . . Oh God, I want to die and find peace, and even an hour is too far off. . . ."

She buried her face in the folds of his coat. He held her tightly, saying nothing, smoothing her hair. Gradually her sobs abated and for a long while she huddled against his shoulder. He felt her body's warmth through his shirt, and the beating of her heart.

Doors opened and closed a long way off, the creaking and thudding growing louder. Rosalie stepped away from him and sat at her small table to repair the ravages her tears had made to her powder and rouge. Calm once more, she rose and pulled on her coat, brushing away the last specks of dust before the mirror.

Footsteps sounded, steady, light, approaching. Aristide looked at his watch. Quarter to three: they were early.

For a moment all was silent but for the muffled sound of voices, and then the footsteps again in the corridor. The lock clicked and the door creaked open. Rosalie turned from the mirror.

Sanson had come alone, without clerk or priest or assistant trailing him. He doffed his hat.

"Forgive me."

Brasseur claimed he had sometimes seen condemned criminals, hardened men who had preserved their *sang-froid* all through trial and prison, collapse at their first sight of the executioner. But Rosalie had not collapsed; she had not even paled, but stood staring at him, the color rising in her cheeks.

"Forgive you?" To Aristide's astonishment, she gave Sanson a smile of pure joy. "I knew you would come, at last."

He seemed to wince.

"You don't understand."

"Understand what?"

"It's my duty to come here today," he told her softly, "my curse that

I must come here for you." He reached out as if he would touch her cheek, her hair, but swiftly drew back his hand. "Haven't you guessed, even now?"

"Guessed?" she echoed him, staring at him, somber and pale in his black coat and spotless white cravat.

All at once Aristide understood, understood everything: Rosalie's prince, her strong handsome lover, was her executioner.

28

Rosalie drew a sharp breath and stepped back a single pace. Five hundred years of tradition and prejudice were not so easily unlearned in an instant.

"Henri?" she said, puzzled, her voice high and soft like a child's.

"Forgive me," he repeated. "How could I tell you what manner of man I was?"

"Who is 'Longval,' then?" Aristide said in the frigid silence.

"It's an old family name," said Sanson, without turning to him. "Sanson de Longval. All of us have used it, at times."

A chill silence hung among them, like a winter fog on an empty road. Aristide imagined he might have heard her heart thudding.

"Tell me one thing," Rosalie whispered. "Tell me you love me."

Sanson bent his head to hers, with a sigh of immense weariness and perfect despair. "Juliette . . . I do love you, I confess it."

"Don't lie to me to spare my feelings. I want the truth."

"On my honor."

Aristide saw tears on Sanson's cheek. He looked away, wishing desperately to be anywhere but in that close stone chamber with a man and a woman who had forgotten his existence.

"I—I feared you would thrust me away in disgust if you knew

whose son I was," said Sanson. "My father, my family, we've been outcasts all our lives. How could I ask you to share that? I knew I wasn't worthy of someone like you. I was so terrified of losing you that at last— when I had to take my father's place—I pushed you away rather than see you shrink from me in horror."

"Oh, Henri," she sighed. "You know we're twin souls, you and I. How could you think I would do that?"

"Do you imagine it's not happened before?"

The stillness seemed to howl in Aristide's ears until she spoke again, in a gentle whisper.

"Dearest, I'm not afraid. Do what you have to do."

"How can I be the author of your death—"

"No. *I* am the author of my death. You wouldn't be here if I'd not chosen to do what I did. *Ego te absolvo.* You are merely . . . a solicitous friend, a guiding hand."

Silence ruled for a moment, for the length of a kiss.

"Juliette . . . I must cut your hair."

So this is the moment, Aristide realized, or the penultimate moment— for in a cell there was always tomorrow, always another day of waiting, but your hours were numbered when at last they stripped you and bound you; then you knew, to the depth of your being, that you were on your way to the knife.

He slipped away, through the open door, and fled down the corridor and out of the prison.

He did not look at the waiting cart but strode forward through the May Courtyard, head down, toward the side gate. Shrill voices babbled in his ears, voices of the idlers who had gathered to catch a glimpse of the condemned. Hands reached for him, pawing at him. He shook them off, dizzy, as the world trembled and blurred around him. He had eaten nothing all that day, he remembered.

He stopped, squeezed his eyes shut for a moment to regain his equilibrium, and went on, to collide an instant later with Philippe Aubry.

They stared at each other, speechless. Pointing and gibbering, the crowd surged past them. Aubry was white and gaunt as death, his coat streaked with dust, the thick dark hair hanging limply about his haggard face.

"Couldn't you stay away?" Aristide said at last. He shouldered the young man aside and pushed his way toward the gate through the relentless babble of the crowd. A voice rose nearer him but he paid it no attention until someone plucked at his sleeve.

"*Ravel!*"

At last he fathomed the sound of his own name and he paused.

"It's true?" Aubry demanded. "Tell me! They're really . . . going to do it?"

"You mean, cut her head off?" Aristide said. "Yes. Of course they are."

"What the devil is your game?"

"My game?"

"You know as well as I do that"—he lowered his voice to a furious whisper—"that she never did it. It—it was I who killed them. You must know that by now."

"And then you were too much the coward to admit to it."

Aubry flinched and Aristide continued, pitiless. "Damn you. If you'd turned yourself in like a man of honor—if you'd confessed to an unpremeditated crime of passion—thrown yourself on the mercy of the court—they might have been lenient with you! But instead you killed another innocent—you strangled the Beaumontel woman—a cold-blooded, calculated murder for the sake of preserving your miserable skin. After all your talk of virtue and integrity. A fine example, Aubry!"

"How dare you let her sacrifice herself to save me!"

Aristide laughed suddenly, a harsh lacerating sound that hurt his chest and grated in his ears, and seized the young man's wrist. "How dare I? You little worm, do you still have the colossal conceit to believe she's sacrificing her own life for you?"

He turned, dragging Aubry behind him from the courtyard to the street beyond, toward the Pont-au-Change, the bridge to the Right Bank.

"I—I don't understand. . . ." Aubry gasped, trying to pull away from his grip.

"Go live on your precious virtue now, and think over and over again, until the day you die, how you murdered the woman you adored, and then didn't even have the nerve to accept the penalty."

Aubry stopped suddenly and jerked him backward, lips quivering, eyes burning.

"I've looked death in the face more often than once."

"But never as a certainty," Aristide said, pulling him inexorably along once more. "You've never waited in a cell, like your Brissotin friends, like *my* friend, and known, without a shadow of a doubt, that you will die in a day, or an hour, in the middle of a public square, with strangers gawking at you. And the thought of that, the thought of watching your death—such a public death—creep nearer, and nearer, terrifies you beyond measure, doesn't it?" He paused at the end of the bridge. "Your precious integrity has escaped you in the end, and you know you'd be dragged off to the Grève weeping and begging for mercy."

Aubry twisted away but Aristide seized him again and drew the miniature pistol he kept concealed beneath his coat. "All right, that's enough," he said, sliding the pistol into a pocket, near to hand. "You're coming with me. And if you try to get away, I will empty this pistol into your guts, where it will hurt you very badly indeed before it kills you in a few days' time. Or perhaps I'll aim it toward your balls—if you have any, which I'm beginning to doubt."

"They'll take *you* up for assault and murder!"

"Come to think of it, I have little to lose."

"Where are you *taking* me?" Aubry hissed, breathing hard but offering no more resistance.

"The Grève—where do you think?"

"I beg you—stop this charade."

"Why should I?"

"Why are you doing this?"

"Because I care enough about her to grant her what she most wants!"

They had reached the end of the bridge. He thrust Aubry forward, along the quay. The sound of the procession rose not far behind them.

The Place de Grève. The waiting crowd. The guillotine. Aristide shouldered himself and his unwilling companion toward the low barrier that surrounded the scaffold, growling "Make way!" when they did not yield before a black suit.

"Now," he told Aubry when they had reached the forefront of the crowd, with a clear view of the guillotine, "you are going to stand here and watch." Aubry closed his eyes and he seized the young man by both arms and turned him toward the scaffold.

"*Watch*, damn you!"

She was standing, head high, cropped hair dancing about her face in the brisk breeze. The public prosecutor had acceded to her request; she was not wearing the red shirt.

Sanson stood beside her in the cart, one hand gripping the rail, his other arm about her shoulders. From time to time she turned to him and they spoke together. It was a pity, Aristide found himself thinking, that the journey was so short.

The cart rolled to a stop. He might have reached out across the paling and touched it. "Don't let me go," he thought he heard her say, as someone lowered the cart's tailboard and Sanson stepped forward.

She saw them as Sanson was handing her down from the cart. Her gaze darted from Aristide to Aubry and back again. She gave Aristide a fleeting half smile and deliberately turned her head away, and Aristide knew she had put them out of her mind, had forgotten Aubry, forgotten her revenge, forgotten everything but the touch of her lover's hand on her bound wrists.

Aubry ceased struggling with him and stood petrified, his face the color of the overcast sky.

Ten steep steps to the platform. Sanson guided her to the top, his hand always touching hers, though his handsome face was rigid as carved bone. As his assistants reached for her she balked for an instant, long enough to turn and rise on tiptoe and brush her lips across his cheek.

The assistants took hold of her, leading her to the upright plank, buckling the straps, though Sanson kept a hand resting lightly on her shoulder. Sanson stepped away and the plank tipped forward beneath the blade.

"Oh, God," Aubry whispered.

Aristide had almost forgotten his presence. He tightened his hold, turning him pitilessly toward the guillotine.

A click, a scrape, a dull thud, the three sounds coming so fast upon each other that they were scarcely distinguishable. The crowd applauded.

No one raised the severed head for the spectators to see; that disagreeable, centuries-old custom had ceased with the Terror.

Aubry bent double and retched. His own stomach sour with nausea, Aristide turned away and closed his eyes. When at length he looked about him, the spectators were beginning to drift away and a boy was sponging down the guillotine. The two assistants loaded a long, covered wicker basket into the back of the cart.

Aubry lurched to his feet and Aristide seized hold of him again before he could escape.

"You have no right to hold me!"

"I'll think of a reason."

Sanson spoke briefly to the driver and with a gesture sent the cart on its way. Turning, he exchanged a swift silent glance with Aristide before crossing the straw-littered cobbles to him.

"Ravel."

His gaze flicked to Aubry, who shrank back. He looked the young man up and down for a moment with a hard, impassive stare. "Who's he?"

"Someone who should have been guillotined today," said Aristide.

"That's interesting," Sanson said, "because last month I was out riding in the afternoon, at Monceau, and I passed a woman struggling with a man in the lilac grove near the follies. I supposed it was lovers' horseplay and thought nothing more of it until I heard about that woman who'd been found murdered in the gardens. I told the police what I'd seen, and described the man . . ."

"Did you," Aristide whispered.

"I look forward to seeing you once again," Sanson added, to Aubry. "Right here."

Aubry wrenched his arms from Aristide's grip and dodged away amid the thinning crowd. Aristide plunged after him but realized in a moment that he had lost him and halted, dizzy, gasping for breath.

"Never mind," said Sanson, striding up behind him. "He can't run forever."

Aristide returned to the wineshop under the shadow of the Châtelet later that evening, after the winter twilight had faded into rain and dark. Wordlessly he joined Sanson at his secluded corner table and they sat staring at the wine stains in the battered wood. The candle beside them gently sputtered.

"Is justice served?" Sanson said a long while later.

"Yes."

"No regrets, no remorse?"

"Only for Célie Montereau and Sidonie Beaumontel."

"Not a thought for the other one? The murdered man?"

"No more than you have, when you drop your blade on a felon's neck."

Sanson nodded. "She paid with her head for what she did, while I'm paid a salary for what I do; but she and I are not so different, are we?"

"You are a servant of the law, like me."

"Don't tell me the ends are not the same. We're both killers, she and I, whether we like it or not. I'm not so new to this trade. I assisted my father for years, even after I'd joined the Guard to escape it."

He paused, brooding, still avoiding Aristide's eyes.

"How many during the Terror?" he continued. "How many innocent people did I help to execute while serving the law? She often said we were twin souls . . . it was truer than we knew."

26 Frimaire (December 16)

The message arrived at Rue Traversine the next morning.

Aristide trudged into Brasseur's office, shut the door behind him, and leaned against it without speaking. Brasseur set his quill down and began to straighten his papers. Outside the window, the fine rain fell silently, glistening on the stones below. "So," Brasseur said at last, "were you right? It was all about revenge?"

"Revenge . . . and love; love gone sour."

"All the sweetness of love," Brasseur murmured, "is steeped in bitter gall and deadly venom."

Aristide glanced at him. "Racine?"

"No, it's from a long poem written a couple of hundred years ago. Not well known." He fell silent for a moment as he reread a letter at the top of his heap of papers. "This arrived fifteen minutes ago from the Conciergerie," he added, handing it over.

Aristide read it through twice and returned it to Brasseur. "I'll come by later," he said, pulling the door open.

"They brought him in early today," the prison clerk at the Conciergerie told him. "Went off the Pont-Neuf at about two in the morning. Somebody saw him and raised the alarm, and they managed to pull him out half drowned. Then they found the letter on the parapet." He handed Aristide a folded sheet of paper. "What should we do with him?"

The note was brief, only a few sentences:

> *To the Commissaire of the Section de la Butte-des-Moulins.*
> *I do not wish to live. I loved Célie and it was I who killed her.*
> *Juliette de Vaudray did not commit the crimes attributed to her. I,*
> *and I alone, am guilty of the deaths of Célie Montereau and Cit-*
> *izen Saint-Ange and Citizeness Beaumontel. May God forgive*
> *me. I regret, with all my heart, everything that has come to pass.*
> *Tell Citizen Ravel that he was right.*
>
> *Aubry*
> *This 24 Frimaire, Year V.*

The prison clerk eyed him mournfully. "Do you want to see him? It would help if you could provide us with a preliminary identification.

His identity card was spoiled in the water. . . ."

Aristide nodded. Once again he followed a turnkey through the ill-lit corridors to the door of a cell. The turnkey drew back the spy hole's shutter with a bang.

The young man jerked about and for an instant Aristide glimpsed a pallid, haggard countenance before the prisoner buried his head in his hands once more, trembling. His hair hung in lank tangles as it had dried from the waters of the Seine.

"Do you know him?" the clerk began, behind him.

"That's Philippe Aubry."

"Does this letter make sense to you? Should we be taking it seriously, or should he be sent to Charenton, to the lunatic asylum? He claims he committed the murders at Rue du Hasard, and surely—"

"Keep him safe," Aristide said. "And send word to the police at Monceau that you have him." He slid the shutter back into place. "Keep him safe for Sanson," he repeated as he marched away, without looking back, through the cold stone corridors once more to the courtyard, where the rain had ceased and a feeble sun was struggling through the cloud of the winter morning.

HISTORICAL NOTE

This is a work of fiction, although inspired by some actual people and events. Aristide Ravel is entirely fictional; Rosalie Clément is based loosely on a young woman executed for multiple murders in 1808; Henri Sanson was a real person.

The memoirs of the stylish thief, murderer, poet, gutter philosopher, and folk hero of 1830s Paris, Pierre-François Lacenaire (1800?–1836), suggested aspects of Rosalie's character. Lacenaire claimed he had committed murder because he was at war with the society that had rejected him, and had chosen to commit "suicide by guillotine" in forcing the state to execute him. He tells us in his memoirs that he knew he was destined for "the widow" since the moment when his father pointed at the scaffold and brusquely told him "That's where you'll end up if you don't mend your ways!"

The little-known history of an attractive and spirited, though undoubtedly sociopathic, young Parisienne named Manette Bouhourt suggested the bizarre details of Rosalie's homicidal career. Manette, who called herself Auguste and dressed in men's clothing to attract unsuspecting, random victims, was guillotined in Paris on May 16, 1808, for the murder of two men and a woman. The *Journal de Paris* described her as "an unheard-of example of the coldest calculation in crime and of unbridled audacity in the most tender youth . . . [she] defended herself with as much coolness as energy, and pleaded her cause in a manner that astonished the judges, the jury, and the public."

Manette claimed to have murdered "eighteen or twenty" men during trysts at hotels, bludgeoning them to death with a hammer while they slept, in revenge upon the male sex for having been heartlessly seduced and abandoned as a young girl. She chose to go to her execution wearing her male costume. Invariably charming and coquettish, her final words on the scaffold were "Don't you think it's a pity to cut off such a pretty head?"

Henri Sanson (1767–1840) was the son of Charles-Henri Sanson, executioner of Paris, who executed nearly all the leading figures of the French Revolution. Described in 1793 by a contemporary English witness as "a very handsome, smart young man," Henri accepted a commission in the National Guard that year, perhaps hoping that the upheaval in society would allow him to avoid inheriting his ancestors' profession. He attained the rank of captain of artillery before transferring to the company of gendarmerie detailed to maintain order at the law courts. Eventually submitting to the inevitable, he succeeded to the position of "executor of criminal judgments" upon his father's retirement in August 1795. His person, his character, and the principal events in his life are more or less drawn from historical fact. The relationship between Henri and Rosalie is, however, entirely an invention of the author's imagination.

The case of the Lyons Mail robbery was sensational in its day and became a folk legend in nineteenth-century France, owing to persistent questions of mistaken identity. It has never been conclusively determined whether Joseph Lesurques was among the highwaymen who robbed the mail van and brutally murdered the courier and postilion on April 27, 1796.

Though Lesurques claimed to be a respectable landowner and had never been suspected of any crime, several eyewitnesses identified him as one of the gang upon seeing him, by chance, in the corridors of the Palais de Justice. Other witnesses insisted that Lesurques strongly resembled one Dubosq, an elusive career criminal who was probably the mastermind behind the robbery. Four years later Dubosq was captured, tried, and executed for complicity in the affair, but he refused to confess or to clear Lesurques's name.

The question remained in the public gaze until the mid-nineteenth century, as Lesurques's widow and children petitioned successive governments for reexamination of the case and a posthumous pardon. The affair has not, even now, disappeared from the public imagination in France; in the 1980s the French stage saw a new dramatization of the case, which invited the audience to be the jury and vote on the fate of Joseph Lesurques.

SELECT BIBLIOGRAPHY

Christophe, Robert. *Les Sanson: Bourreaux de Père en Fils Pendant Deux Siècles*. Paris: Librairie Arthème Fayard, 1960.

Cobb, Richard. *Death in Paris, 1795–1801*. Oxford: Oxford University Press, 1978.

Emsley, Clive. *Policing and Its Context, 1750–1870*. London: Macmillan, 1983.

——. "Policing the Streets of Early Nineteenth-Century Paris," *French History* 1, no. 2 (1987): 257–82. Oxford: Oxford University Press, 1987.

Heppenstall, Rayner. *French Crime in the Romantic Age*. London: Hamish Hamilton, 1970.

Hillairet, Jacques. *Connaissance de Vieux Paris*. Paris: Éditions Payot et Rivages, 1993.

Irving, H. B. *Studies of French Criminals of the 19th Century*. London: William Heinemann, 1901.

Lacenaire, Pierre-François; Monique Lebailly, editor. *Mémoires*. Paris: Éditions de l'Instant, 1988.

Levy, Barbara. *Legacy of Death*. Englewood Cliffs, N.J.: Prentice-Hall, 1973.

Minnigerode, Meade. *The Magnificent Comedy: Some Aspects of Public and*

Private Life in Paris, from the Fall of Robespierre to the Coming of Bonaparte. New York: Farrar and Rinehart, 1931.

Oman, Sir Charles. *The Lyons Mail.* London: Methuen, 1945.

Restif de la Bretonne, Nicolas-Edme. *Les Nuits de Paris or The Nocturnal Spectator.* Translated by Linda Asher and Ellen Fertig. New York: Random House, 1964.

Robiquet, Maurice. *Daily Life in the French Revolution.* Translated by James Kirkup. New York: Macmillan, 1964.

Stead, Philip John. *The Police of Paris.* London: Staples Press, 1957.

———. *Vidocq: A Biography.* New York: Roy Publishers, n.d.

Williams, Alan. *The Police of Paris, 1718–1789.* Baton Rouge: Louisiana State University Press, 1979.

Wills, Antoinette. *Crime and Punishment in Revolutionary Paris.* Westport, Conn.: Greenwood Press, 1981.